To M
self-pr
marketin

I will work in my own way, according to the light that is in me.
— Letter from Lydia Maria Child to Ellis Gray Loring in 1843

Chapter One

Sacramento, California
December 27, 1858

"It is not fair!"

Cora Fielding's cry rang with the full-throated indignation for which her mother had long excoriated her as being unladylike.

Her twin brother Carl's triumphant smirk only infuriated her further. She ignored him and crossed the room to where her father sat reading the newspaper, her freckled face red as a tomato, her fists clenched in disappointment.

"I am twice the student as Carl! I have memorized every medical book in the house despite having to spend hours each day attending to my position as tutor to the Isaacs children. When I am able to be present at the clinic, I anticipate what treatments you will prescribe before you speak a word to the patient. Why am I not as qualified to study medicine as any man?"

Richard Fielding sighed, his craggy face a mask of pity and frustration. "My dear child, you know very well you would be free to follow your heart's desire in a world of my own choosing. Indeed, I believe one day young women such as you will have that freedom. God knows, you are amply qualified, as you rightly say. But we live in the present age, and despite the prodigious efforts of Professor Rowell..." For emphasis, he lifted the day's edition of the *Sacramento Daily Union* from which he had just been reading aloud. "...the faculty has decided that people of your gender will not be admitted to the new school. And there is damn all any of us can do to change that fact."

His use of profanity, normally so rare, affirmed for Cora as nothing else could the passion with which he held his convictions. It did little to quell her outrage.

Carl sniffed with smug superiority, saying, "Father is, as always, being kind. But everyone knows the female gender is not in the least suited for the rigors of medicine. Not to mention its necessary assault on a lady's sensibilities over issues of physical delicacy."

"Horse feathers! I am not the one who fainted dead away at the sight of butcher Harper's nearly-severed hand dangling from his wrist by a mere tendon or two."

His cheeks, even more freckled than her own, flamed. "Why must you always throw that one weakness up to me? You know I was tired and ill when it happened."

"A few sniffles do not constitute an illness sufficient to cause such a humiliating debacle. You simply did not have the stomach for it!"

"Perhaps you should look to your own deficiencies before faulting others. Why do you suppose Herbert Roskam has stopped calling on you? You with your haughty airs and sharp tongue could not attract a proper gentleman if your life depended on it!"

"He stopped calling because I sent him packing. Who would want such a fool as that?"

"Please, children, do not bicker," said their mother, her tone shimmering with weary forbearance. "We are but one day past Christmas, and I refuse to allow this unpleasantness to ruin the lingering spirit of that holy day."

Cora felt an immediate stab of remorse. Maude Fielding sat bundled in a blanket in a rocking chair pulled close by the hearth, her diminished frame and pale complexion reflecting the close call she had recently had with pneumonia. They were lucky to have her still with them, and for Cora to have caused her such distress was inexcusable. She shot her brother one last angry glare and retreated to the stuffed chintz chair where she had been sitting when her father roiled her day with his dream-shattering announcement.

How excited she had been to learn some months before that Dr. Elias Samuel Cooper had pulled together a Board of Trustees and Faculty of Medicine in order to establish the first medical school on the West Coast. Dr. Cooper was not a figure without controversy, having inserted himself with bold arrogance into the medical community soon after his arrival from the East in 1855. His widely advertised series of anatomical and surgical lectures and demonstrations had earned him a reputation for self-aggrandizement. This plus an infamous malpractice lawsuit had greatly diminished his reputation among local physicians. However, his success with the proposed school could not be denied, and many were enthralled with the prospect of students being able to pursue their medical studies here rather than traveling far to the east.

Richard Fielding had greeted this news with special satisfaction, for he had two prospective students in his own household. It had long been expected that his only son Carl would succeed him in medicine; Cora's similar aspiration had come as a surprise, dismissed at first, but given greater gravitas as her interest burgeoned during the years since their journey west when she was but a girl of sixteen.

For her part, Cora had prided herself on the perseverance that finally convinced her father of the seriousness of her ambitions, prompting him to serve as preceptor to her as well as to Carl so both could complete the required two years of study before they would be allowed admittance to a school of medicine. She had rested her hopes on the fact that the new faculty had not yet decided whether or not enrollment would be coeducational. One of the professors in particular, a Dr. Isaac Rowell, had been vocal in his belief that the school should be open to aspirants of both genders. However, his point of view had not held the day, as was just now verified in the *Union's* account of the school's third faculty meeting held six days before. Carl would be going off to pursue his studies in a few months' time while she stayed home in her dreary tutoring position, a fact all the more galling for her deep-seated belief that were he given a choice, her brother would not enter medicine at all.

Long before the family embarked on their difficult overland trek from Indiana in 1854, Carl's obsession with wood carving had born witness to the fact that he had a true artist's gift when it came to creating figures of lifelike proportion. That skill would surely give him entry into any number of trades. Instead, he would bow to their father's wishes and become a physician whose lack of passion would assure a career of but mediocre dimension.

She sighed, her mood contrary to the room's cozy ambiance. Their father had built the house with its attached medical office shortly after their arrival in Sacramento. The city had just been declared the capital of California and was still shedding its infancy, crude planks and adobe and canvas being slowly replaced by sawn lumber and brick and mortar. In the years since, the house had taken on an aura of settled permanency with its white-painted exterior, green shutters, and yard graced by young oak and apple trees and flowering camellia plants. Likewise, the gradual acquisition of furniture and fixtures had transformed the interior so that it now reflected the professional stature of its master.

At this time of year, the parlor in which the family was now gathered took on a special aura of cheery hominess. The fire crackled around a freshly-laid log, candlelight brightened the rainy winter day, and the pine tree standing in the far corner, decorated with popcorn chains, colored ribbons, and little candles with burnt wicks, still gave off a fresh tangy odor. Having co-opted this charming custom from their father's German patients, they had gone to the surrounding hills to cut it just days before. It had been a true sight to see on Christmas morning when they lit the candles and stood around it to sing carols in honor of the day. This afternoon, however, the season no longer held any charm for Cora. Her inner person seethed with resentment even as she pondered the long path that had led her to this moment.

She had felt the scourge of her gender from earliest childhood, all the more poignant for the freedom her twin brother enjoyed simply by virtue of being male. While he was outdoors with his friends playing stickball or hunting for frogs in a nearby stream, she was kept indoors at their mother's knee learning how to crochet, knit, sew, and any other skill deemed suitable for a young lady. While her brother went off to her uncle's school for boys in nearby New Harmony, Indiana, she learned her ABC's from books whose drawings depicted the importance of the female's role in the home. She perfected her penmanship and writing skills and practiced on the pianoforte, all with the purpose of one day employing her feminine wiles to attract an advantageous husband. True, she had been allowed to enroll for two years, along with Carl, in The Sacramento Academy and Female Institute where her uncle taught on first arriving in Sacramento. However, the curriculum for the twins had been vastly different, again reflecting the cultural bias as to which subjects were suitable for girls and which for boys, the former being much less demanding than the latter.

In the face of this seemingly impenetrable wall of expectation, she had rebelled in whatever manner she could. She had developed the habit of speaking her mind in a bold, direct fashion, eschewing the demure feminine reserve she had been taught. She had read her father's discarded newspapers and listened intently to any discussion among his male friends and colleagues in order to form her own independent opinions about matters of governance and politics. She read the writings of Elizabeth Cady Stanton as well as Harriet Beecher Stowe's popular novel *Uncle Tom's Cabin,* which led her to become a champion of the oppressed, whether of her fellow females and their status as second-class citizens or the Negro race and its hateful misuse by supposedly enlightened society

Her father had always looked upon her defiant views with forbearance, even admiration as they reflected much of his own thinking. Thus, when she persisted in her highest form of mutiny, her insatiable desire to become a physician, he was not only sympathetic but secretly delighted. Her mother, however, was more perplexed than judgmental. Nor had she given up hope for a more conventional path for her daughter, as evidenced by her ill-concealed pleasure when Carl's friend Herbert Roskam began calling on Cora.

He was a nice enough fellow, she thought as she brought his soft round countenance before her mind's eye. And his intent to succeed his father in the grocer's business assured him of an income sufficient to support a wife and family. His expectation of said wife's traditional role, however, had doomed his effort every bit as much as his lack of physical appeal. Cora had the same carnal appetite as any other young woman of twenty years, and she hoped one day to find a man who would trigger those feelings while at the same time valuing her for her independence and quest for self-determination. Alas, she feared her brother was right in his assessment that capturing such a man's fancy was highly unlikely. Her slight five-foot frame, flame-red hair, and freckled countenance hardly personified the day's standard of female pulchritude. Add in her willful, bombastic personality, and even she had to admit that her chances of romantic success were scant at best.

She pushed the thought from her mind. The only thing that mattered now was devising a way to achieve her tattered but still passionate dream. There had to be a way.

Chapter Two

San Francisco, California
Saturday, January 29, 1859

Before even opening her eyes, Cora's senses reminded her she was no longer at home. There, her mornings started with the sounds of a waking household and the tantalizing odors of coffee and baking bread. Now her nose detected only the faint essence of salt brine. She heard no sleepy grousing from the bed where her little sister Lilly slept. Instead, her ears met the dead silence of an empty chamber overlaid with a distant cacophony of shouts, curses and braying animals. She felt a gentle rocking motion foreign to one who lived on the land. The paddle wheels no longer splashed, the warning bell and scream of escaping steam no longer pierced her ears, but she soon oriented herself to the dim cabin she had occupied on the *SS Antelope* since boarding the previous afternoon.

It had been a crisp, sunny winter day when she stood on Sacramento's Embarcadero and bade her family goodbye. She felt a twinge of guilt over having deceived them. She had told them she was going to San Francisco to accept a position in a milliner's shop, an opportunity secured for her by her Aunt Lizzie, who was a friend of the shop's owner. She had also been invited to live in the Collins household for as long as she wished. This portion of the conspiracy was true. As she had known she would, her aunt had responded to Cora's early January letter by offering immediate and long-term sanctuary. She had also joined in the subterfuge by suggesting a position of employment with a friend who might or might not be real.

Her family had met the plan with skepticism, especially from Carl, who knew her as only one twin can know the other.

"I find it exceedingly strange," he had said, "that you would make such a drastic change so soon after learning you would not be going to San Francisco as a medical student. Indeed, you floated the idea of boarding with the Collinses months ago as you theorized about your possible enrollment in the proposed school. Why would you wish to go there now, knowing that you will never be a medical student?"

"Because that very fact makes it impossible for me to stay here as if nothing has happened. And now Lizzie—" She caught herself. Her aunt had been a friend long before she married Uncle Jonathan, and Cora frequently forgot, out of habit, to use the familial title she now deserved. "—Aunt Lizzie has found me a new position, so there is no reason why I should not accept it and be thankful."

"What of the position you already have?"

"I warned the Isaacs family that I might be leaving their employ months ago. Is it so difficult to understand why I need a change of scene?"

"No. But I would think you would be eager to put as much distance as possible between yourself and the site of your recent disappointment."

"What do you know of the sentiments surrounding disappointment?" she snapped. "You who is able to do whatever you wish by simple reason of your gender!"

He clucked his tongue. "When will you understand that bitter rejoinders such as that are what makes you so disagreeable to my fellow males? God did not intend for women to take up the same pursuits as men. You are fortunate to have the role of wife and mother in your future. Providing you can squelch your tendency to make statements that drive away anyone who would otherwise find you pleasing."

"I would not wish to please the type of man you describe, so your judgment means nothing to me."

A shrug. "Well, if you think you are going to fulfill your strange passion for medicine by shadowing me and my fellow students in San Francisco, you are sadly mistaken."

"Why would I wish to do that? I already know more about medicine than you will ever learn."

She had stalked off before he could respond, and they had barely spoken since. Now, a new chapter of her life was about to begin, and she refused to soil the moment with reminders of her brother and his smug superiority.

She sat up, forgetting to duck and thus striking her head on the cabin ceiling. She had taken the upper bunk out of deference to her rather elderly cabinmate, who had apparently already risen, dressed and left for breakfast. Cora hopped down and looked out through the small window onto the boat's guards, curious about the sort of day that awaited her. She saw only an impenetrable curtain of swirling gray fog. She turned and reached for her clothes, only to hear a light knocking on the interior door that led to the saloon.

She put on her wrapper and opened it to the ladies' chambermaid, a light-skinned, middle-aged Negro woman who had the responsibility of looking after the female passengers. She gave a little curtsy and said,

"There's a gentleman at the gangway askin' after you. Says you's expectin' him."

Cora saw that the saloon beyond was empty. She leaned out and looked forward. A few people still lingered at the breakfast tables, but it appeared that most of the passengers had already debarked.

"What time is it, please?" she asked.

"Gone ten past nine, ma'am."

"Oh. Oh, my. Please tell the gentleman I shall be along directly. And thank you for bringing the message."

"Yes'm." Another curtsy, and she was gone.

Cora fumbled for the bodice of her dress and looked at the delicate little watch pinned there, a gift from her parents two years before on her eighteenth birthday. She held it up in the dim light and confirmed that it was, indeed, nearly nine-fifteen. She had slept poorly, not achieving deep sleep until well after the boat docked sometime around midnight. As a consequence, she had overslept. She had been told her uncle would pick her up at nine o'clock, which would give her plenty of time to dress and have breakfast in the forward saloon. Instead, she had kept him waiting.

She dressed quickly and coiled and pinned her nighttime braid into a bun at the back of her head. She put on her cloak, gathered up her overnight satchel, and stepped through the outer door onto the guards, following them around the stern to the gangplank.

Her uncle was an indistinct wraith through the fog on the dock below. She stepped onto the slippery boards and proceeded down with special care lest she lose her footing and end up in the brackish water that sloshed between the boat and the dock's edge.

Jonathan stepped forward to meet her. He was a tall man whose long arms and legs gave him a somewhat gangly appearance. The excessive damp had plastered a shock of light-brown hair to his forehead and rendered his spectacles all but opaque. Despite having stood in these inclement circumstances for she knew not how long, he wore a welcoming smile that dimpled his cheeks and softened his chiseled, sharp-featured face. He doffed his hat and kissed her cheek in greeting.

She hugged him and said, "I do so apologize for keeping you, Uncle."

In a deep, warm voice, "No need. It being Saturday, I have the entire morning at leisure. And how better to spend it than in fetching my dear niece home? If you will show me which trunk is yours..."

The stack of luggage that had been offloaded much earlier was now diminished from what it had no doubt once been. Cora easily spotted her own dome-top trunk. Jonathan picked it up by its leather handles, took a moment to steady his balance, and staggered forward.

Fearful that he might injure himself with such a heavy load, she said, "Should we not ask one of the porters for help with that?"

"I do not...hire...someone...to do...what I am...perfectly...capable of...doing myself."

Cora scolded herself for not having arranged ahead of time for someone to deal with her trunk. She should have realized a teacher with a growing family had no spare resources for the type of help a physician such as her father might engage without thinking. She bit her tongue and scurried along beside him.

Fortunately, they had not far to go. Jonathan's dapple-gray horse Shadow, whom Cora remembered making the long trek with them five years before, was hitched to a buckboard buggy in front of a fishmonger's stall on the opposite side of the wharf. He heaved the trunk into the vehicle's bed and helped her onto the front seat, taking his place beside her and turning the horse toward the wharf's end.

People and conveyances passed to and fro, appearing as indistinct shadows through the thick blanket of fog. The heavy air dulled the sounds of the busy wharf but not the pungent odor of rotting seaweed, ripe fish and animal offal. She could tell there were many shops and stalls and storeships lining the long wharf, but their purposes remained hidden behind the impenetrable murk.

They reached the street beyond and continued forward along a plank road that she would later learn was Pacific Street. A short distance later they came to Front Street and turned south. Buildings loomed through the haze on either side, many several stories high and built of brick or granite. In the distance to the south and east, she could see the shadowy bulk of the many hills for which San Francisco was known. They shared the road with other buggies, carriages, and individual horsemen as well as delivery drays, carts and wagons carrying everything from water, bread, meat, milk and vegetables to parcels and supplies.

Uncle Jonathan made polite inquiries about Cora's family, not alluding to her purpose for being there but leaving that subject to be pursued later when they arrived at the family home. He entertained her with lively stories about the San Francisco area's colorful history, from its early beginnings as a possession of first Spain then Mexico through its settlement as Yerba Buena by American pioneers. Then came the Mexican-American War and independence, the Gold Rush of 1849, and finally the admission of California as a state within the Union. Her uncle was a scholar who loved acquiring any and all knowledge, whether of present-day affairs or of the writings of the philosophers of old. In what seemed the twinkling of an eye, they had arrived at Market Street, which angled southeast and was even more congested than Front Street.

The farther they went, the more the fog thinned, and Cora was able to identify the small white St. Patrick's Church beside a fine brick building housing the Catholic Orphan Asylum. Shortly thereafter, they turned south on Third Street to Harrison Street, then east to the short, dead-end Elizabeth Street, a name Cora found fitting in that it mimicked the given name of her dear friend and aunt, Lizzie.

The house before which they stopped was large and rambling, clothed in white clapboard with black shutters at its windows and a wide deep front porch. Jonathan explained that they were leasing it from a wealthy industrialist who had built a much grander Greek-Revival house near the summit of Rincon Hill, which rose one hundred feet to the immediate west. The gentleman had taken a proprietary interest in Jonathan when he first arrived the year before to teach at the newly-reorganized San Francisco High School.

Recognizing Jonathan's intellectual and teaching skills, he had encouraged him to organize private classes to further the classical education of the children of the city's elite, thus providing an additional income that allowed the Collins family to live in comfort and thrive.

Cora's feet had barely touched the ground when she saw her Aunt Lizzie flying down the front path toward her. She was still beautiful, her rich auburn hair framing lively green eyes and a creamy complexion, but there was no doubt she had put on weight even since Cora had last seen her the previous year. She recalled their first meeting five years before aboard the steamboat *Princess* on their journey up the Missouri River. Then Lizzie had been a haughty southern belle intent on keeping her beauty and former rank as shields against the disaster her life had become. Now she was a content, loving wife to a man who adored her, caring not a whit about the aging process that had already begun within her body.

They embraced. Then Lizzie held her at arm's length to survey her. In the soft drawl she had never quite been able to eradicate, "As lovely as ever, my dear Cora. You look the picture of health, tiny though you still are."

Ever disappointed that her short stature and slight build failed to match her carefully-constructed tough, no-nonsense interior, Cora pulled a wry face and said, "I suppose I must give up on my ambition to become a formidable Amazon. I am, after all, now twenty."

A delighted laugh. "What you lack in stature you more than surpass in fortitude, dear girl. As this incredible journey proves. Now come into the house. Missy and the other children are most anxious to see you."

They walked arm in arm to the narrow steps leading to the porch while Jonathan tended to Shadow and the buggy. Inside, Lizzie took Cora's cloak and hung it on a hook in the hallway. What seemed like a horde of children but was in fact only three with an infant crawling behind swarmed out from the parlor.

Ten-year-old Missy vaulted into Cora's arms. She was tall for her age, blonde with the delicate features of her mother, Jonathan's first wife Sarah. Right behind her came Caleb, four, and Eleanor, three, both tugging at Cora's skirts for attention. Caleb, who had barely survived the long westward pilgrimage after the death of his mother from childbed fever, was now a sturdy youngster who resembled his father to a great degree. Eleanor had come along barely ten months after Lizzie and Jonathan married. She was a pretty child with curly brown hair and her mother's green eyes. Chubby little Isaiah was too young at six months for her to assess which parent he favored, but he certainly had his mother's gritty tenacity as he scooted as fast as he could in order not to be left behind even though he had never met his Cousin Cora and had no notion of what the fuss was all about.

Cora laughed and picked him up to carry him with the others into the family parlor. Having determined that her niece had missed breakfast, Lizzie disappeared into the kitchen while Missy and the others regaled Cora with exuberant childish chatter. Jonathan lugged her trunk into the entry hall and up the stairway, returning just as Lizzie came in with a tray bearing slices of fresh bread, a bowl of home-canned cherries, and a steaming mug of coffee. After Cora had eaten, Lizzie shooed the children to their playroom, and Jonathan excused himself to prepare for the afternoon session of his private classes.

Cora watched her aunt throw another log on the flagging fire, thinking as she often had about the difficult adjustment a person of her privileged background would need to make in order to run a growing household without the benefit of hired help. Yet she had never heard Lizzie complain, even during the hard-scrabble months of their cross-country odyssey. Indeed, she seemed perennially cheerful, often expressing her gratitude for the life she had found here in California with Jonathan.

At last Lizzie settled into a chair opposite Cora and said, "Now, then, tell me about this scheme of yours. I could glean nothing from your recent enigmatic letter. Only that you wished to start afresh in San Francisco and needed an invitation to live with us while you pursued some phantom employment, the details of which could be invented in any manner I chose as long as it was presented as legitimate in my answering letter."

Cora said, "I know how perplexing it must have been, and I apologize for my inability to be forthright. However, secrecy was of the utmost necessity. Even though I knew my parents would not pry into my private correspondence, I had no such assurance where my brother was concerned."

"My curiosity grows hotter by the moment. It is obvious there is more to this than a change of living arrangements, delighted though we are to have you."

With clasped hands and an earnest face, "You are right. I do have an ulterior goal, and you are my one and only hope of achieving it."

"Well, then, you had best tell me how I can help. After all—" Her eyes twinkled. "—this is not the first time you and I have conspired together to achieve an objective." She referred to her own bid for freedom at a time when she was in thrall to a corrupt, deceitful man, a bid that was planned and executed with Cora's invaluable help. She went on, "I have much to thank you for, dear Cora. If I can repay you in some small way, I am most happy to do so. So tell me, what are you planning?"

Chapter Three

Monday, January 31, 1859

Cora and Lizzie stepped down from the omnibus at the northeast corner of Portsmouth Square. Until the day before, Cora had never seen, much less ridden on such a conveyance, a horse-drawn, elongated coach seating more than a dozen people. Now she had enjoyed this new experience twice in as many days.

To celebrate her arrival and show her a bit of their city, the Collinses had taken her on a Sunday-afternoon outing to the Mission Dolores, a religious and farming community established many years before in order to educate and convert the native Indian population but now a popular resort getaway for the city's populace. They had boarded an omnibus on Folsom Street, a fine plank road a mere block and a half from their house. Beyond the close-in residential areas, they had passed between low sand hills and through the intervening valleys, each bringing its own interesting sights: lovely gardens and nurseries, a large sugar refinery with black smoke billowing from its chimney, several noxious-smelling hog ranches. Before long, they crossed the bridge over Mission Creek and continued on the new San Bruno Turnpike to the green, fertile valley where the mission lay nestled among the surrounding hills. Lizzie had packed a picnic lunch, and after they ate, the children frolicked in the fresh air of an unusually warm sunny day while Jonathan entertained the ladies with stories of the mission's history.

On this day, however, frivolity played no part in their excursion. Lizzie had hired a neighbor's teenaged daughter to watch the children while she took Cora to meet someone who might be able to help in her quest. Cora had tried to pay the girl's fee, but Lizzie had been adamant.

"We are not poor, Cora. Frugal, perhaps, but we always have resources to help the people we love. Which, of course, includes you."

And so, they stepped around the others who had disembarked the omnibus and turned back along the plaza's northern side.

Cora was impressed more than ever by the unusual size of this city, marveling at the horse and vehicular traffic on Washington Street as well as the size and number of buildings that lined the square, nearly all of brick or concrete construction and several stories high. There were hotels, stores, offices, the city hall, the post office, and a few remaining gambling halls. The square itself was a lovely verdant park enclosed by decorative iron railings with a lamppost at each corner. Even on a weekday, the place was being well used: people lounging, children playing, hawkers selling their wares from makeshift stalls.

They turned onto Kearny Street and proceeded one block north to Jackson Street, then veered west to a large boxy brick building five stories tall with a sign atop that read *International.* They entered the hotel's ornate lobby and proceeded past the dining room to the central staircase with its gilded iron railing. They climbed to the third floor and turned right along a gaslit corridor with rooms on either side. They followed the numbering on the doors around the corner and along another corridor until they came to the one marked 348. Lizzie raised her gloved hand and knocked.

A rustling came from within. Then the door opened to reveal a fashionably dressed black woman. She wore a mauve silk day dress with a wide, bell-shaped skirt, black piping down the bodice and at the hem, and lace at the neckline and sleeve cuffs. She was no taller than Cora with the same wispy frame. Her hair was coiffed in the latest style, her nut-brown face blemish-free with elliptical brown eyes, prominent cheekbones and a small rounded nose.

Her mouth with its charming Cupid's-bow upper lip lifted in a smile. Lizzie stepped forward and enclosed her in an embrace, saying,

"My dear Rachel." She pulled back and reached out to Cora. "I am most eager to present my niece, Miss Fielding, who has come from Sacramento to live with us. Cora, this is the famed Black Nightingale and my dearest friend, Miss Rachel Barnes."

Cora already knew who this remarkable woman was. As a teenager, she had thrilled to Lizzie's stories of their time in Quincy, California when Rachel, a golden-voiced slave who had been freed upon her master's death, was re-captured and nearly returned to bondage. Lizzie's testimony alone had saved her, thus freeing Rachel to pursue a much-acclaimed career. Cora, who believed with a burning passion that slavery was an evil affront to mankind and must be resisted at every turn, could not suppress a shiver of awe as Rachel reached out to take her gloved hand, saying,

"I am most pleased to meet you, Miss Fielding. Lizzie has spoken of you so often I feel as if I already know you."

"And I you," said Cora. "My family and I have heard of your travails in Quincy in such detail that we might have been there ourselves. Thus, let us dispense with formalities. Please call me Cora."

"Then I shall be Rachel to you. Please come in."

The room was not large but airy with high ceilings and a long window that overlooked Kearny Street. It contained a bed, an armoire and chest of drawers, and a small table by the window equipped with three chairs. A tea set with cups and saucers and a plate of pastries beckoned them over.

Lizzie and Cora removed their bonnets, gloves and cloaks and sat down while Rachel poured out the tea. After she had offered cream and sugar and the pastries, she sat back and said,

"Now tell me. How may I be of service?"

Cora took a deep breath and said, "I wish to transform myself into a man."

The singer's eyes widened in surprise.

Cora continued, "Since you are in the theater, if as a musical artist rather than a dramatic actor, Lizzie and I hoped you would have some ideas how I might accomplish this. The fact that you are in town to perform for the next few weeks seemed too propitious to ignore."

"I am certainly happy to advise you. But this? A rather difficult proposition, especially given your stature, which, as you may have noticed, is similar to mine. In the pursuit of my profession, I am often required to costume myself as someone other than myself, but never so drastic a change. May I ask why you wish to do this?"

"It is my dearest ambition to become a physician like my father. I have studied medicine on my own by reading his many clinical tomes. Then when he became a preceptor to my twin brother two years ago, he allowed me to study alongside him. I have learned all I can up to this point, but I will never be allowed to practice medicine unless I graduate from a medical college. A brand new school is opening here in San Francisco in a few months, and my brother has applied and been accepted as a student. I, however, am not allowed to apply because I am a female. Therefore, the only way I can continue my education is to disguise myself as a man."

Rachel considered. Then gave a slow nod. "I understand. When I was a slave, I was denied the freedom to pursue my own destiny due to the unfair customs and dictates of society. I overcame those strictures with determination and the help of your aunt. Thus, I can only encourage you to fight in the manner you have suggested. But how is it to be done?"

She picked up her cup and sipped, concentration furrowing her brow. Cora and Lizzie drank their own tea and ate their pastries. Some moments later, Rachel said,

"It seems to me the biggest obstacle is the one to which I have already alluded. Your diminutive height will be impossible to disguise. However, even though few gentlemen are as short as you, some youths fail to reach full stature and physical maturity until they are well into their twenties. So we must present you as such a person, which would also explain your smooth facial skin. Beyond that, we must create diversions that will draw attention away from those traits and allay any suspicion that you are not who you claim to be."

Cora was mesmerized by the fact that this famous singer thought her charade had a chance of success. She had conceived of it out of anger and bitterness and a nearly unstoppable urge to prove to the world that she could not be defeated. However, if she were honest with herself, even as she schemed and planned, doubts had plagued her during every unguarded moment. Now they disappeared like fog before the morning sun, and a wellspring of confidence surged through her with such force she nearly swooned.

"Diversions," Lizzie repeated. "Such as...?"

Rachel pushed away from the table and said, "Come. I shall show you."

They all three donned their outerwear and left the hotel. They walked toward Montgomery Street, turned south for one block and rounded onto Washington, where they came to the Maguire's Opera House. It was a three-story concrete structure, its two upper stories fronted by iron grillwork and tall double windows. A row of six large glass globes hung in front of the arched entrance with a higher row of lamps in front of the second-story grillwork, and Cora could imagine how beautiful it would be of an evening with those bright lights beckoning theatergoers to the show. A free-standing easel advertised the performances of Rachel Barnes, the Black Nightingale, singing assorted arias from the operas of Giuseppe Verdi.

Rachel walked up to a narrow side door and knocked. Nothing. She knocked louder and longer. Eventually the door opened, and a wizened little man with a shock of unruly white hair and a broom in one hand peered out. His shaggy eyebrows shot up.

"Miss Barnes. I thought your rehearsal was later this afternoon."

"It is, Mr. Wedley. I have some costume issues and wish to see what the wardrobe department has to offer."

"Of course. But..." His eyes shifted to Cora and Lizzie.

"These are my advisers in the matter. May we come in?"

He hesitated only a moment before swinging the door wide and admitting them into the theater's lobby. Light from the glass entry doors revealed plush red wall coverings, a carpet of the same color, and a large, multi-tiered crystal chandelier, now unlit.

"Wait here," said Mr. Wedley.

He turned and disappeared through a nearby closed door. He returned moments later carrying a lit oil lantern, which he offered to Rachel.

"Lights're on in there..." He jerked his head toward the bank of doors leading to the building's interior. "...'cause I'm sweepin', but you folks'll need this down in the hole."

The hole? Cora could not suppress a small shudder as she and Lizzie followed Rachel into the theater's main auditorium.

A glowing chandelier, even larger and more elaborate than the one in the lobby, revealed an expansive hall that must have seated hundreds. Two balcony tiers rose on either side, no doubt seating hundreds more. Ahead, the stage rose behind a substantial orchestra pit. The curtain was down, its face painted to depict a scene from Venice, Italy with the city's domes and towers and palaces forming a backdrop for the barques and gondolas of a canal.

They made their way around the folding chairs Mr. Wedley had pushed asunder in order to clean the parquet floor. They climbed a short flight of steps to the stage and followed Rachel through a side door into the backstage area. The lantern cast unearthly shadows into the empty stage to their right, the ropes and rigging forming grotesque shapes high above. They took a dark narrow stairway down into the building's bowels, the sound of scurrying feet preceding the lantern's circle of light. Cora shrugged deeper into her cloak and put the images the sounds evoked out of her mind.

At the bottom, they turned into a murky corridor that gave off an unpleasant musty odor. Rachel stopped near the corridor's end and opened a door marked *Wardrobe*. She stepped in first, the lantern held high before her, and Cora caught sight of a rat's tail disappearing into the gloom. Rachel hung the lantern on a hook on the wall, its light revealing several long racks whose hooks held various items of clothing. Other accessories were piled on roughhewn tables or in storage boxes.

Rachel turned to Cora with a smile. "Now, let us see what we can find for you."

Chapter Four

February 7, 1859
  R. Beverly Cole, M.D., Dean
  Medical Department
  University of the Pacific
  Mission Street
  San Francisco, California
  Dear Sir,
  I wish to apply for enrollment in the Medical Department of the University of the Pacific. I am twenty years old and the son of a Methodist minister, now deceased. I studied medicine for two years under the preceptorship of Dr. Edward Butler of Stockton, California, completing my studies in December of last year on the event of Dr. Butler's accidental death.

  Since this untimely tragedy prevented Dr. Butler from writing to verify my course of study, his widow has graciously agreed to attest to the success of my years with her husband and to recommend on his behalf that I be admitted to the Medical Department. One of my father's parishioners has also agreed to write a testament as to my moral character.

  You may expect these letters in the near future. Meanwhile, I eagerly await your decision on my application. You may forward such to me at my place of boarding, 110 Elizabeth Street, San Francisco, California.

  Yours very respectfully,
  Cornelius Sanderson, II

∞∞∞

February 10, 1859
Dear Dr. Cole,

My late husband, Dr. Edward Butler, spoke highly of his student, Mr. Cornelius Sanderson, in regard to both his dedication to his studies and his ability to apply what he learned in a clinical setting. In addition, Mr. Sanderson's pleasant manner with the patients was noteworthy. Dr. Butler encouraged him to continue his education with an eye to earning an M.D. degree. I highly recommend him for acceptance into your school, as I know my husband would also have done.

With highest regards,
Mrs. Mary Jane Butler
Lately of Stockton, California

∞∞∞

February 11, 1859
To: Dr. Beverly Cole
My dear Sir,

I write to recommend to you a young man of my acquaintance, Mr. Cornelius Sanderson, II, who wishes to pursue the profession of medicine. I knew Mr. Sanderson for a period of some years when his father, the Reverend Cornelius Sanderson, was pastor to the congregation of which I was a member. I found him to be a person of exemplary character and the highest moral virtues. You need have no hesitancy in granting him access to the noble profession of medicine.

I am humbly yours,
Mrs. Otto Ferris
Quincy, California

∞∞∞

Cora broke the letter's seal with trembling hands and read:
February 24, 1959
Mr. Cornelius Sanderson, II
110 Elizabeth Street
San Francisco, California
Dear Sir,

I am pleased to inform you that your enrollment application dated 7 February of this year has met with a favorable determination by the Medical Department of the University of the Pacific.

I request that you present yourself at my office, 137 Montgomery Street, at ten o'clock a.m. on Monday, March 7 for a personal interview. At that time, you will be required to post your five-dollar matriculation fee as well as the thirty-dollar fee for each professor's first-session course of lectures.

Yours truly,

R. Beverly Cole, M.D., Dean

Professor of Obstetrics, the Diseases of

Women and Children, and Physiology

Medical Department

University of the Pacific

"Well?" said Lizzie.

Cora huffed out a sigh of relief. A wide smile spread across her face.

"I am in!"

Lizzie caught her by the hands and pulled her into an embrace, proving that she was as invested in the outcome of this venture as was Cora. Gratitude flooded her heart. She might have been the one to supply the passion and determination, but she could not have achieved success were it not for the help of both Lizzie and Rachel Barnes.

The three women had met again two days after their excursion to Maguire's Opera House to compose and write the necessary letters. They decided that each of them would write one of the letters so the contents would appear in three different hands. The fictitious Cornelius Sanderson's medical-school application would need to be written in a hand that suggested masculinity. After some experimentation, they decided Cora was the most successful in coarsening her penmanship. Thus, they assigned that letter to her.

The other two would use feminine aliases, making it unnecessary to disguise their writing.

It had been Rachel's idea to use Dr. Butler as the fictional preceptor. His accidental demise had been much in the newspapers while she was performing in Stockton. He had been traveling to a remote rancho to treat a patient when something spooked his horse, resulting in a wild ride over rough terrain. Dr. Butler was thrown from the buggy and died in an instant from a broken neck. Rachel also remembered that his childless widow had made known her plans to return to her family in Boston. As a result, there would be no one with whom to check the veracity of a letter purporting to come from her.

Cora had felt a slight twinge of guilt over using such a tragic circumstance to further her ambition. On the other hand, she could see no harm resulting from the subterfuge. She even posited that the good doctor would surely not object to the use of his name in the furtherance of his profession.

The parishioner, Mrs. Ferris, had been a complete fabrication. Placing her in faraway Quincy, site of Lizzie's final adventure five years before, gave a reasonable certainty that Dr. Cole would not bother to check the veracity of her recommendation. It was certainly no more a risk than the impersonation Cora was about to attempt.

Now it appeared that the ruse had worked. With the first step taken, she allowed herself to contemplate what came next.

She told Lizzie, "It will all be for naught, of course, if I am not able to take on the believable persona of a man. How accomplished an actress do you suppose I will be?"

"You are a determined one, of that I am certain. You remind me of myself when I sought a way to get to California despite my being penniless and friendless. I was unwilling to give up, and it turned out well for me. As I know it will for you."

A frisson of doubt shuddered through Cora. "But I must fool not only my professors but my own brother, who will be a member of the same class. We have not been particularly close in recent years, but we are twins and as such share an invisible bond that has shown itself in strange ways since we were children. Will he recognize me no matter how effective my disguise?"

"There is no way to know until you try, my dear. Once first impressions are past, I doubt he will give it another thought."

"I hope you are right."

Cora took the letter upstairs to the room her aunt had made available to her and slipped it into her rosewood writing box. The beginnings of her costume lay on top of her closed trunk. It occurred to her that if she were successful, she would be wearing these items nearly every day for the next two years. Not only that, if she were able to graduate with the degree of M.D. and establish herself in a clinical practice, she would need to perpetuate the fraud for the remainder of her life. There would be no courtship, marriage, or children in her future. Was she prepared to make that sacrifice?

She had often scorned the traditional role into which women were forced by society. Did that mean she did not yearn for love and companionship and someone to share her life someday? Her body was healthy and imbued with the same urges and instincts possessed by all people, male and female alike. She had always assumed that someday she would meet someone who appreciated her for who she was. Someone who would treat her as an equal partner. If she were forced to establish a male identity in order to practice her profession, she would never have that opportunity.

Resigned melancholy swept over her. Life was chock full of choices. She had made hers. Now she must accept the consequences without complaint.

She squared her shoulders and turned her thoughts to the preparations that still remained.

Chapter Five

March 7, 1859

Cora stepped into the black worsted trousers, tucked in the white shirt, and buttoned the fly opening, blushing as she remembered the true use of such a device. She had worn the pants in the privacy of her room numerous times, striding to and fro in an attempt to mimic and imprint on her mind the gait of a gentleman. Now there was no more time for practice. Her public debut as a man was at hand.

She and Aunt Lizzie had visited the home of Mrs. Samuel Willey, wife of the pastor of the Howard Street Presbyterian Church where the Collinses now worshiped, in order to join with other church ladies in organizing the piles of clothing that had been donated for the benefit of the San Francisco Protestant Orphan Asylum. Cora's conscience had pricked her as she professed concern for the poor orphans while surreptitiously searching for garments she might use for her disguise. In the end, she had salved her guilt by making a donation to the cause from her carefully-guarded cash reserves.

The clothes she was now donning had been meant for a youth and required only minor alteration in order to fit her small frame. She slipped on the plaid double-breasted vest and buttoned it, checking in the mirror to make sure the binding she had wound around her small bosom was adequate in hiding her feminine figure. Satisfied, she reached for the long silk tie, which she placed around the stand-up shirt collar and tied in a half bow.

Next she turned to the enhancements she had obtained in the costume department of Maguire's Opera House. She opened the small jar of lampblack-and-oil paste, dipped a fresh quill pen into it, and proceeded to draw a set of thick black eyebrows over her own tawny ones. She dipped a fingertip into the gooey substance and rubbed it lightly over her eyelashes. Next she pulled a black curly wig over her hair, which she had already pinned as close to her head as possible, and tucked any loose strands of her own flaming locks out of sight.

The final touches were a large pair of oval tortoiseshell spectacles and a long black frock coat that had lapels of a fashionable width and a soft velvet collar. She stood back from the mirror for a critical look. And grinned. Not even her own mother would recognize her, of that she was certain.

She heard a light knock on the door.

"Who is it?"

"Lizzie."

"Come in."

Her aunt poked her head into the room and burst out laughing. "Oh, Cora. It is perfect. You will fool them all!"

"I hope so. But Carl..."

"Do not even think it. You must remain confident. If you do, no one will doubt you. Not even your brother."

"I want to see!" came a high-pitched voice from behind Lizzie. Ten-year-old Missy.

They had made no secret of Cora's plans within the family, explaining to the younger children that it was a game that would be spoiled if anyone talked about it outside the house. It was Cora's greatest blessing that they supported her to a person. Lizzie stepped aside and allowed her daughter to enter.

The child's eyes grew round. "Oh," she breathed.

Cora deepened her voice as she had practiced. "Good morning, Miss Collins." She strode forward, took Missy's hand in her own, and bowed over it. "Cornelius Sanderson at your service."

Missy looked from Cora to her mother, then back again. "It is...amazing!"

Cora reached out and stroked her soft cheek. "What better endorsement could I wish for? Now if you ladies will excuse me, I must be away."

She picked up the pile of banknotes she had retrieved earlier from her trunk and stuffed them into her trouser pocket: five dollars for her matriculation fee and one hundred eighty for the six professors who would be lecturing that session. She thought about how long it had taken her to save enough money to make this adventure possible juxtaposed against how quickly her resources had now been depleted. She would need to supplement what remained by finding employment between her first and second course of lectures. This task would be easier, of course, now that she had established her male identity. It was one of the outrageous truths of their culture that gentlemen had many more opportunities for gainful employment than did ladies. Rail against it as she would, it was a fact for which there was no current remedy, and she took a perverse satisfaction in knowing she could benefit from it without her male counterparts having the slightest clue she was very much a female beneath it all.

Taking heart from the thought, she settled a tall silk hat on her head, smoothed on a pair of gloves, and took up her walking stick, all of which she had obtained from Maguire's wardrobe department. It was time for the play to begin.

She walked into the hall and downstairs, encountering three-year-old Eleanor, or Ely as they called her. The little girl giggled and said, "You look silly, Cousin Cora."

Cora bent down, her finger to her lips. "Remember. This is our secret."

Ely mimicked the gesture, her own finger pressed hard against her own lips. "Like Christmas presents. If we tell, it will spoil the surprise."

"Exactly. Now run along to your mother."

She watched the child scamper off then went out through the front door.

She walked the short distance to Third Street and stood on the corner to wait for the omnibus. Within minutes she saw it coming up from the South Park terminus. She climbed up and handed the driver her ten-cent fare.

There were only a few passengers, but more boarded at each stop as they proceeded up Third Street, turned on Folsom around the base of Rincon Hill to Second Street, and then up toward the busier sections of town. By the time they reached Market Street, the seats were full, and it took some pointed looks from her fellow passengers before she remembered she was now a gentleman and must surrender her seat to the female rider who hovered nearby. She stood and gave a little bow, taking the lady's hand and easing her into the seat. She took hold of one of the hanging hand straps, glancing about to see whether her performance had elicited any suspicious glances. Not a one. Her confidence soared.

The omnibus jogged onto Market Street, then around into Montgomery Street. She stepped up to the door a block later. The driver pulled the horses to a stop so she could alight.

Halfway up the west side of the street, she came to Little's Drug Store on the first floor of a three-story concrete building. The sign on the doorway bore the number one thirty-seven. Below it the words: R. Beverly Cole, M.D. She pushed through the door, a small bell announcing her arrival.

The room was of average width but rather short in depth. Glass-fronted shelving lined both walls, displaying a dizzying array of bottles, vials, jars and tins of various sizes. To the right, a white-coated druggist stood behind a counter on which might be seen mortar and pestle sets, knives, cutting boards, various instruments of measurement, and other items the use of which she could only guess. She approached him and asked for the offices of Dr. Cole.

He gestured toward a rear door. She entered and found herself in a small anteroom where a matronly lady and a mother and her infant sat waiting. A young man no older than she worked behind a small desk. She approached and said,

"I am Mr. Sanderson. I have an appointment with Dr. Cole for ten o'clock this morning."

He pursed his lips with a pointed glance at a pendulum clock that hung on the wall. She was ten minutes early. He waved her into an empty chair and returned to whatever paperwork he was preparing.

Ten minutes later, a door at the back of the room opened and a young woman who was very much with child came out followed by a handsome, impeccably dressed man with dark wavy hair, dark eyes and a pale complexion whom she assumed to be Dr. Cole. Cora gathered herself to rise, thinking he would call her for their appointment, but his eyes slid past her and alighted on the mother and infant.

He bowed and said, "Mrs. Wilton."

Annoyed, Cora settled back to wait. In the interim, she reviewed what she knew about R. Beverly Cole.

In addition to being the new school's dean, he was also to be Professor of Obstetrics and Diseases of Women and Children and Physiology. He had been the subject of a minor scandal the year before when he read a committee chair report to the California State Medical Society that decried the general lack of chastity among the current crop of California's ladies. The resultant outrage prompted the Society to conduct an inquiry, the result of which was to exonerate Dr. Cole while admitting that his language had been loose and improper. Cora thought this result was neither fair to California womanhood nor nearly harsh enough toward the perpetrator. She took it as an introduction to the degree to which men of a particular profession would go to whitewash one of their own. Nevertheless, this man held such power over her both as dean and as a future professor that she swallowed her disgust and prepared to be as obsequious as the next student.

The mother and infant emerged from the office some twenty minutes later, but again Dr. Cole bypassed Cora and called the older lady into his office. Thus it was going on eleven o'clock before he finally approached her with outstretched hand, which she squeezed with the vigor she imagined would come from a man, and invited her inside.

The room was longer than wide, two windows on the back side giving onto an alleyway. At one end there was an oak rolltop desk and swivel chair. A long narrow table of the same wood stood along the wall between the windows, its salient features being a number of nondescript bottles, a set of scales, a mortar and pestle, and a white-bleached human skull. An examining table occupied the other end, two iron clawlike appendages standing upright at the near end above a footrest. A small cabinet nearby had a stethoscope lying on its top.

Dr. Cole pulled a straight-back chair over beside his desk and bade Cora to sit. He took the swivel chair and turned to face her.

"Free at last," he said, waving his hand in the general direction of the door into the anteroom. "That last one. Seven pregnancies, and she wonders why she suffers from prolapsis. If the ladies would learn to curb their passions, many of the ailments about which they come whining to me would not trouble them." He reached for a humidor, took out a cigar, and offered one to Cora. She felt her face color as she declined. After lighting it, he said, "Might do you some good, young man. You look to have, shall we say, some less than manly tendencies. How old are you again?"

Remembering to lower her voice, "Twenty, sir."

He studied her. "Hm-m. Yes, well, I suppose you will mature eventually. Are you attracted to the opposite gender, Mr. Sanderson?"

More blushing. "Oh, indeed, sir. They are not much attracted to me at present, but I assure you my time will come. My late father was slow in attaining full manhood. In the end, though never particularly tall, he was fully, uh, functional. I am apparently cast in a similar mold."

"Meanwhile, I cannot help but wonder whether your lack of sexual maturity acts as a particular motivator for your entry into medicine." A lascivious grin. "Compensating by means of a profession where you will be allowed, without condemnation, to have a good look at what they keep hidden beneath all those skirts and petticoats."

Although sickened by his disrespectful words and attitude, she composed her face into what she hoped was a conspiratorial leer and said, "I admit the thought has crossed my mind, sir."

A loud guffaw. "As it would for any red-blooded gentleman. Now then, tell me about yourself. Your father was a man of the cloth, I believe?"

"Yes, sir."

She launched into her prepared remarks concerning a family made up out of whole cloth: a father whose Methodist parish was in Quincy, the governmental seat of Plumas County, and a mother who had died when he, their first child, was born. She went on to describe her preceptorship with the unfortunate Dr. Butler, transposing the details of her work under her father onto this Stockton physician.

He puffed on his cigar and nodded. "Your passion for medicine is evident from the manner in which you speak, although I believe you will find the reality somewhat more prosaic, even boring in actual practice. Nonetheless, if Mrs. Butler's letter is to be believed, her late husband thought you a worthy student, and we are pleased to welcome you as such. Since the upcoming session is the school's first, we are determined to set high standards from the very beginning. We shall require regular attendance at the lectures and associated clinics and diligent study habits. That is not to say, however, that we expect our students to live as monks."

With a lewd gleam in his eyes, "You, in particular, would be well advised to use those balls of yours for more than scratching. There is plenty of snatch to be had out there, but someone of your obvious inexperience must be mindful of avoiding the clap. That said, your stature as a successful physician will depend to a great deal on your credibility as a fully masculine specimen. I recommend that you put your mind—and prick—to the task forthwith."

His vulgarity came as a shock to Cora and brought a flush of color to her cheeks. She had always supposed that men talk rough among themselves when ladies are not present, but this crass disrespect for the most basic of human functions left her speechless. Fortunately, he did not seem to expect a reply. He leaned forward and pointed his cigar in her direction.

"Enough of that. You are prepared with your matriculation and first-session fees?"

She nodded and dug into her trouser pockets for the notes she had placed there before leaving home. She handed them over and watched him count them out. Satisfied, he picked up a small stack of items from beside his right elbow. He handed it across to her, saying,

"These are your tickets for admission to the various lectures for the coming session. You may present them at the beginning lectures, but your professors will soon come to know you as a paid student."

She glanced at the top ticket, a document printed on heavy cream-colored stock paper with *University of the Pacific Medical*

Department centered in two lines across the top. Beneath it was written *Session of 1859* and below that *Admit Mr. Cornelius Sanderson*, the latter printed in by hand, *to Lectures on the Principles and Practice of Surgery*. At the bottom came the signature of E. S. Cooper, Professor of Anatomy and Surgery.

A shiver of awe cascaded over Cora. She was truly about to embark on her life's dream, the proof of which she now held in her hand. She vowed then and there to be the most attentive, the most industrious student in the class, proving that women were every bit as capable and intelligent as men. It would be her own private triumph, of course, since no one must ever know her true gender. But it would be sweet nonetheless.

She rose to thank him and remembered to reach across the desk and offer her hand as any gentleman would do. The adventure was about to begin.

Chapter Six

April 14, 1859

Cora exited the lecture hall along with the other participants, being careful as always to guard her anonymity by avoiding the eyes of her fellows. It was the middle of April and the halfway point of the free preliminary lecture courses required of each professor during the month prior to the official opening of the 1859 session. She had already learned that thirteen other students were enrolled in the session. Whether or not they were taking advantage of these extra lectures she could not tell, the audience being so diverse she could not distinguish fellow students from practicing doctors eager to hear the latest thought on a particular subject or regular folk simply interested in health issues, including a number of ladies. Her brother, at least, had not been in attendance, a fact that did not surprise her—when had he ever stirred himself beyond what was strictly required?—but one that brought her much relief. She knew the day would come when she must face him and test the authenticity of her disguise. The longer that moment was delayed, the better for her equanimity.

She descended the stairs from the third-floor hall, settled her tall hat on her head, and went out onto Mission Street. It was a beautiful warm day with a few high-flying clouds. She had been pleased to learn that the school, which was housed in the upper stories of the Pacific Clinical Infirmary owned by founder Dr. Elias Samuel Cooper, was located some four-and-a-half blocks from the Collins home. This close proximity allowed her to walk when the weather was fine or access the nearby omnibus when it was not.

Today was exceptional, and she set out with a spring in her step, making sure her strides were long and loping in the manner of a man.

She was becoming accustomed to the physical freedom her new identity allowed. No more tight bodices or heavy skirts to impede her movement. It occurred to her to wonder whether prevailing fashion had been devised specifically to slow the female gender and reinforce the perception of inferiority promulgated by a male-dominated culture. How had womankind allowed itself to be cast in such a role?

She shook the thought off and turned her mind to the subject matter of that day's lecture: the latest developments in the science of anesthesia. As a child, she had heard the screams of patients who required some sort of surgical procedure. Now those excruciating but necessary experiences could be pain free thanks to the blessings of modern science. What other miracles would be uncovered in her lifetime? She could only thrill at the thought that as a physician, she would be at the heart of the innovations of the future. What more noble pursuit than that could there be?

She came to the house and climbed the porch steps, aware of how tired she was. All she could think of was shedding her disguise with its heavy fabric, putting on her cotton wrapper, and lying down for a quick nap before supper. She opened the front door and walked into the entry hallway.

The first thing she noticed was that the parlor door was closed—itself an oddity, there being no secrets in this happy, rambunctious family. Then from behind the door she heard Missy cry,

"There she is!" followed by Lizzie with,

"Missy, no!!"

Too late. Missy threw the door open and came barreling toward her, saying, "Cousin Cora, you will never guess who is here."

Even before the child uttered his name, she saw him framed tall and slim in the doorway. He was attired in casual elegance, his hair, a shade darker than Cora's, combed from a center part, a thin moustache decorating his upper lip. His expression slid from expectation to puzzlement—and finally to incredulity.

"What in God's name are you doing? Have you taken leave of your senses?"

∞∞∞

Carl stared at his sister, for it was indeed she despite her attempt to present herself otherwise. He watched her face blanch, then color, attesting to the fact that she was as stunned by his presence as he was by hers. Then, true to her damnable conceit, she squared her shoulders and came toward him.

"Truth be told, I have *found* my senses at last. I have already interviewed with Dr. Cole and been accepted into the school. Which is certain proof that a prejudice against skirts and petticoats is the only obstacle between me and my chosen profession. And if I must pretend to be male in order to achieve my goal, then that is what I shall do."

"Over my dead body! This is an outrage, and one I shall quickly put to rights."

Her chin quivered, and tears sprang to her eyes. "Why do you care? How does my acceptance as a student in any way threaten your own? Do you hate me so much that you would spoil my chances, chances I have made for myself through great diligence and foresight?"

Her accusation took him aback. Did he indeed hate his twin? It was true they had been in constant competition ever since Cora came up with the ridiculous notion of herself becoming a doctor. Then when her superiority became clear as they worked side by side with their father, resentment had poisoned his brotherly feelings. But were those feelings so tainted that he would expose her subterfuge merely as a means of punishment for his prior humiliations?

"Please, you two," said Aunt Lizzie, who was standing in the doorway, "come into the parlor and discuss this in a rational manner before either one of you says something catastrophic for our family."

Carl was grateful for the interruption. He needed to get a hold on his thoughts so he could proceed with clarity.

"I am willing," he said. "But I refuse to speak to Cora dressed as she is."

"Oh, Carl, do not be—" Aunt Lizzie began, but Cora cut in with,

"Never mind, Aunt. I prefer to change before this battle is joined."

She spun on her heel and made for the staircase. Relieved to have still more time to compose himself, he followed Aunt Lizzie into the parlor, where the smaller children were engaged in various activities. His aunt turned to Missy, who was trailing behind, and said,

"Please take the children upstairs and keep them occupied until we are finished here."

The girl's expression spoke plainly of curiosity overlaid with disappointment at not being allowed to stay, but she hesitated only a moment before shooing her siblings from the room and up the stairs.

They took their seats and waited in silence for Cora's return, the awkwardness between them palpable. A new thought hit Carl like a thunderbolt: the Collinses themselves were complicit in Cora's deception. How could they not be? She was living in their house. Aunt Lizzie had supposedly found her a position with a milliner friend, an obvious lie whose purpose could only have been to deceive the Fielding parents into allowing their daughter to come to San Francisco. Most damning of all, Aunt Lizzie had attempted to stop Missy from flying into the front hall when Cora returned, knowing rightly that the child's actions would give the secret away.

Yes, their betrayal was nearly as egregious as Cora's.

It was in this frame of mind that he greeted Uncle Jonathan when he returned home a short time later following his day of teaching. The older man shook his hand, his initial pleasure quickly followed by awareness that all was not as it should be.

"Why the dour faces? And where are the children?"

"Upstairs," Aunt Lizzie answered. "As is Cora. She came home from her lecture to find Carl here for an unexpected visit. She has gone up to change and will be down momentarily so we can see what is to be done."

"There is no doubt what must be done," said Carl, his voice tight with indignation. "She must stop this charade at once." Then to his uncle, "Surely you can see it is doomed to failure. She cannot pass herself off as one of us for any length of time. It is beyond absurd."

Uncle Jonathan sat down on the sofa beside his wife and said, "But my dear nephew, she has already done so. Not only has she completed the admission process, but she has been attending lectures for over two weeks with no one being any the wiser."

"Lectures you have not even bothered to attend," said Cora from the doorway.

She came in dressed in a gingham day dress, her red hair flaming. She sat and fixed him with a belligerent stare.

"I have only just arrived in the city," he countered. "I have been busy finding a place to live and making..." He waved his hand in the air. "...arrangements."

His excuses sounded lame even to his own ears. In truth, he could have come early enough to take advantage of the free lecture series, but he had had no desire to do so. Medicine was his chosen profession, but he did not hold the same passion for it as did she. There would be plenty of time to learn what he needed to learn. No need to bore himself with the redundancy certain to be found in these watered-down lectures intended for anyone in the community who desired to attend.

"I, however," Cora said, "have attended every one. And have aroused not a hint of suspicion. There is no reason to believe I cannot carry on as I have been for as long as I choose."

"How you deceive yourself! It is one thing to be part of an anonymous crowd in a lecture hall. Quite another to be one of only a dozen or so students who will have the undivided attention of their professors. You would be unmasked before the first class was over."

"It has been my experience," said Uncle Jonathan in a maddeningly mild tone, "that people see what they expect to see. The thought of a woman disguising herself as a man would never occur to the average gentleman. I believe Cora stands a very good chance of continuing on undetected."

It was true the disguise was a good one. Would he have seen through it had he met up with her in the classroom, not expecting any such deception? Impossible to say, although he would not admit that here.

"Such odds do not persuade me, Uncle," he said. "If she were exposed, the result would be humiliation and expulsion not only for her, but for me as well. You must know I cannot risk that. Will *not* risk it."

He spoke with an adamancy that finally seemed to put a chink in their resistance. They might not like it, but they could see that the only way for him to protect his own standing was to expose her. By doing so, he might ruffle a few feathers and create some momentary dissension within the family, but in the end, they would come to understand that the entire foundation of society's concept of womanhood was at risk here. And Cora would one day thank him for saving her from herself. She would accept her rightful place as a wife and mother and realize the great rewards such positions brought to a lady. To attempt upending what God had ordained from the beginning of time was folly. As well as blasphemy.

Satisfied that he had convinced them, he was about to stand and take his leave when Aunt Lizzie said, "Haste always carries the possibility for disaster, Carl. Before you take any action, I beg you to ask your father to come and advise us on this matter. It is the least you can do to maintain the harmony of our family."

He frowned. "Do you honestly believe Father would agree to this nonsense of Cora's?"

"I have no idea what he would think. But I strongly urge you to give him the chance to be part of the discussion. It is his ultimate right as yours and Cora's father. Not to mention that he is the one financing your future."

Carl took pause at her words. It was true that his father had agreed to bankroll his medical education as well as to supply him with a monthly stipend for his expenses. He did not know how Cora had acquired the funds to enroll in the school, but he was quite certain they had not come from their father. Would he not be as horrified by his daughter's actions as was Carl? Thus, the wisest course would be to wait for that certain reinforcement before exposing his sister's duplicity.

"Very well. I shall send a telegram this very afternoon. Until he responds, I shall say nothing about this to Dr. Cole."

He could see from their expressions that he had made the right choice. If he had acted summarily, he would not only have alienated these, his closest relatives, but also possibly his father, who had an inordinate tenderness for Cora. By waiting to receive his parent's full support, he would strengthen the bond between them and put Cora in her proper place at last.

He rose and smiled around at them, avoiding Cora's wounded, angry eyes as best he could. "Then I shall take my leave. I shall notify you of Father's response as soon as it arrives."

Chapter Seven

The next four days were some of the most miserable of Cora's life. No matter the pitfalls of ordinary life, including the hardships of their overland travel from Indiana five years before, she had always maintained an optimistic view of her future. Now she felt adrift as she never had before.

A flurry of telegrams had brought news that her father would be on the steamboat docking in San Francisco on the morning of Saturday, April Twenty-third. In the interim, she had attended no more lectures and kept to her room except for meals. The Collins family was sympathetic toward her plight, but they could offer no reasonable assurance that her father would agree to her continuing on her current course. Indeed, she knew that he would not. He might believe her supremely capable of becoming a doctor, but at his core, he was a traditionalist who would not condone an outright fraud on the medical community.

No, her dream was dead.

She did not go with Uncle Jonathan to meet the steamboat but waited with Aunt Lizzie in the parlor. Carl had not returned to the house since that fateful afternoon, but he was in the buggy with the other two when they arrived home. No surprise to Cora. He would certainly want to be present to witness her humiliation in front of their father. She did her best to swallow her bitterness as she rose to meet them.

Richard Fielding opened his arms to embrace her. She had expected his face to be grim, even accusatory. Instead, he smiled with a happy satisfaction she could not fathom. Even Carl did not wear his expected look of triumph. Indeed, he seemed more subdued than she had seen him for many a year.

Richard greeted Aunt Lizzie. Then they all sat down, anticipation humming in the air. He said to Cora,

"Well, my dear, you have managed to surprise even your old father, who thought he had seen all the exploits of which your creative little brain could conceive. But this—beyond even my imagination."

Aunt Lizzie cut in with, "That is because most men lack the imagination to think beyond their own ingrained prejudices. Cora would have made a fine doctor. At least as fine as any man."

An amused smile. "I agree with you. That is why I am pleased to announce that she will have the opportunity to prove that very point."

Cora's gasp punctured the stunned silence. "Wha—What do you mean?"

To the room in general, "I have often expounded on the fact that women will soon be an integral part of my profession. The female rights movement may not draw much attention in California as of yet, but I have discovered it has many devotees in the East, where the first woman received her medical degree exactly ten years ago. Others have followed, thanks to two colleges dedicated to the medical education of women: the New England Female Medical College in Boston and the Female Medical College of Pennsylvania in Philadelphia." To Cora alone, "It is to this latter school that I have made inquiry on your behalf."

Still not daring to believe it, "And?"

"It seems that you fulfill all of the requirements to enroll."

Nearly delirious with joy, she barely heard the others pepper her father with questions.

"How did this come about?"

"Why was this not explored long ago?"

"What about her acceptance here and the money she has already expended?"

Finally, from Carl, "Why would any school accept her after she successfully defrauded the University of the Pacific?"

Richard held up his hand for silence. "I understand your skepticism. Allow me to explain."

"First," said Aunt Lizzie, "I believe some coffee is in order. We could all use a little tonic as we digest this news."

She returned shortly with a tray and cups of steaming liquid. After dispersing them and offering cream and sugar, she took her place and said, "Please continue, Richard."

He took a fortifying sip and set the cup back on its saucer. "I very recently became aware of these two schools thanks to a medical bulletin to which I subscribe. An acquaintance from my own school days practices in Philadelphia, a Dr. Manfred Faraday. After a succession of telegrams over the past days, I now know what is possible where Cora is concerned. The Female Medical College begins its 1859-1860 session on October 19th, which gives Cora a little over six months to travel to Pennsylvania, get settled, and enroll in the session. All easily accomplished in that amount of time."

Uncle Jonathan frowned. "Indeed. But surely you would not send her to the other side of the continent without suitable escort."

"Yes," Carl echoed. "She could not possibly travel so far alone."

"Of course not," said his father. Then in smooth, affable tones, "You will accompany her on your way to your new school."

His eyes bulged. "*What?*"

"The University of Pennsylvania's Medical School is also in Philadelphia. Their session begins on November 7, just two and a half weeks after Cora's first lectures. The timing could not be more suitable."

Carl sprang to his feet and glared at his father. "How dare you meddle with my life in this manner! I do not want to go to Philadelphia. I am duly enrolled right here in California, and that is where I intend to stay!"

Richard's demeanor remained calm despite the tension quivering in the air. When he spoke, however, his words came out like flint against stone.

"Must I remind you that it is I who am financing your medical education? I do so gladly, but I also have your sister's future to consider. Her desires hold equal weight to yours. If there is a way to serve both, then that is the direction we shall take. Now stop laying down ultimatums you have no power to enforce, sit down, and hear me out."

They held their collective breath until Carl backed away and sat down.

"I realize I have surprised—even shocked you," said his father. "But the superiority of this option cannot be denied. Not only does it give Cora an opportunity to pursue her own career, but it allows you to attend the finest and most renowned institution in the nation."

"But you yourself have expressed delight over there being this new school right here in California" said Carl, his expression making it clear he was not yet ready to yield. "You said it was a great step forward for our state and one we should support."

"That has been and still is my sentiment, even though I am sorely disappointed by the board's decision not to allow women to enroll. That aside, the school is as yet untried, whereas Pennsylvania's has been established for the better part of this decade and has earned acclaim after acclaim as to its excellence. You should be excited to have this chance, my boy."

"Excited? I am embarrassed. And humiliated by my sister's outrageous behavior. Not only does there seem to be no consequence for the fraud she has committed, but it seems she is to be rewarded for it!"

"I am mindful that her zeal has carried her into murky waters. I do not condone it. But I also admire her passion for medicine, a passion which I do not perceive in you. Nonetheless, she will be held accountable. She and I will go before Dean Cole, and she will expose herself and apologize for deceiving him. I expect the interview will be most unpleasant and very likely let out to the newspapers and the entire City of San Francisco. I should think you would be glad of an opportunity to escape the scandal and start afresh in Philadelphia."

"What of the money I have already put down for the current lecture series?"

"I shall appeal for it to be returned, of course."

"What about Cora? I assume she somehow managed to pay the required lecture fees as well. Where did those funds come from?"

"From my own hard work," Cora retorted, speaking for the first time since her father had broken his amazing news. "I have saved every penny possible, foregoing any pleasures my salary might have afforded me in order to attain a goal I cherish."

"A selfish goal that cares not for the consequences it brings to others! Now it seems I must postpone my own education in order to further yours. Have you no shame?"

Cora softened her voice and pleaded with her eyes. "Carl, I never meant to harm you. I merely hoped that we both might prosper in our chosen profession. I regret the pain you feel on my behalf, and I apologize for it. I pledge to you that I will honor you to my dying breath if you agree to accompany me to Philadelphia. My heart's desire is for us both to attain success, and I shall do all in my power to make certain the future is as bright for you as I hope it will be for me."

His mouth twitched, but it was apparent her words had neutralized much of his anger.

"Then we are agreed," said their father. "Cora and I shall visit Dean Cole tomorrow and put things right with him and the school." To Carl, "You may accompany us if you wish. You will need to tender your withdrawal from the current session. However, I am willing to act on your behalf if it will make things easier for you."

A lingering scowl. "I doubt I would be in a civil frame of mind to do it. I accept your offer to take care of this for me."

"Very well. When the unpleasantness is past, we shall have much to plan concerning both your futures. Jonathan, if I might impose on your hospitality, may we have a glass of spirits to toast this new beginning for my children?"

His words seemed to break the tension in the room. Jonathan rose to collect the required glasses and bottle of brandy while Lizzie went to invite the children into the room. Cora watched it all through a haze of joy. She did not relish visiting Dr. Cole to admit how badly she had deceived him, but the embarrassment would pass as soon as she left his presence. It was a small price to pay for the chance to see her dreams come true at last.

Chapter Eight

September 20, 1859
10:00 p.m.

Cora stood on the dock and looked up at the *SS Orizaba*, her heart stuttering with excitement and uncertainty. Excitement because she was about to embark on a dream-affirming journey; uncertainty because she was leaving everything she had known and relying on her as-yet-untested belief that she could conquer any circumstance.

It had been an emotional two days, beginning with the family farewells on the Sacramento Embarcadero the afternoon before. Her mother had already lost one daughter to marriage and exile to Louisiana where her new husband owned a cotton plantation. Now Cora was leaving along with her twin brother for the East Coast and careers that might never bring them back to California. Fifteen-year-old Lilly remained, but for how long? Cora could see the anguish of separation in her mother's tear-brimmed eyes, and it resonated as only a daughter could feel it. For her part, Lilly's pretense of sadness was overlaid with a barely-concealed glee that she now ruled the roost as the only remaining child at home. Only her father exuded genuine pleasure that his two offspring were embarking on a journey that would bring them success and fulfillment in their future lives.

The five months since Cora had been found out had been the strangest of her life, as if she were suspended in a dream where neither past nor future existed—only a present that stretched before her to infinity. She had managed to hold her head high during the confrontation with Dr. Cole over her deception. His shock and anger were expected, but she had refused to bow before them. She believed in her heart that the school had invited her subterfuge, and she had told him straight out that he could no doubt expect the same tactic to be employed by other women who wished to access the profession that males had unilaterally usurped as their own. Fortunately for her, her father had smoothed the dean's injured pride and been successful in attaining a full refund of the fees she had put down, as well as his own on Carl's behalf.

Their father had insisted that both Cora and Carl return to Sacramento and resume their preceptorships while he arranged for their enrollment in their respective schools. Those weeks had been exhilarating for Cora because she had not been required to split her time between the clinic and her former tutoring position. Overlying this happiness was a niggling awareness of her transience. She was home, but she was more guest than kin. A traveler taking refuge rather than a daughter residing in her rightful place. As for Carl, he had seemed to accept the situation with a commendable grace. She, however, could sense his seething resentment beneath the surface, and she had done everything in her power to curb her tart tongue and be as deferential as her nature would allow. She hoped and prayed that their unique bond would triumph in the end and leave them as friends and professional allies.

The days had passed, and then the time had come for them to depart. The Collins family met their steamer in San Francisco and hosted them for the following two days, a period permeated by a subtle awkwardness as Aunt Lizzie and Uncle Jonathan did everything in their power to suppress, for Carl's sake, their delight over Cora's triumph. Nonetheless, their warmth and love were there in abundance, as always. Then came the final goodbyes, the one to her aunt and dear friend Lizzie nearly as difficult as the one to her parents in Sacramento. The two women had been through much together, from their first meeting on that steamboat to St. Joseph, Missouri five years before to their nearly-successful attempt to install

Cora as a medical student in San Francisco. That bond would remain with them no matter where life took Cora, and she was more grateful than she could ever express.

Now she pulled her cloak tight around her and accepted Carl's arm up the gangplank of the *Orizaba*. She was a three-decked, wooden-sided vessel with side paddle wheels and two masts to complement her exhaust stacks. The night was cool and damp, the great ship appearing surreal through swirling tendrils of fog. The gaslight marking their path was barely adequate to show them the way along the plank and up into the brightly-lit grand salon, which took Cora's breath away for its luxurious appearance. Gilded mirrors hung on mahogany panels crowned with gothic arches of pure enameled white and separated by pilasters enameled to imitate dark-veined marble. Rosewood furniture upholstered in gold and purple damask sat among variegated Italian marble tables. The glass skylights overhead were dark at the moment, but Cora could imagine how the room's beauty would be enhanced with the sunny blue skies of California shining down during the day.

An officious-looking man wearing a porter's uniform examined their tickets and led them through the salon, which bustled with organized chaos as crewmen distributed luggage among the first-class staterooms and passengers sought their assigned quarters. He stopped midway along the salon and opened a door into what was to be Cora's stateroom. She thanked him and bade her brother goodnight. Carl gave her cheek a dutiful kiss and turned to follow the porter aft toward the second salon where his stateroom was located.

Cora had been trying to assess her brother's mood all evening. He had said little, but she knew he was as excited as she. Since he was a little boy, his ears had always given away any high emotion he was experiencing, turning them a bright red impossible to miss. Tonight they were as aflame as she had ever seen them, although his outward demeanor had been bland and seemingly aloof. Their conversation had been respectful if limited, and she had sensed no underlying current of ill will toward herself.

She entered to find the cabin empty except for two trunks, her own containing enough clothes and accessories for the journey, and another that she assumed belonged to her cabinmate, whoever she might be. The lady had already retired, as attested by the white-damask curtain pulled across the left-hand berth. The ship was not scheduled to cast away until midnight or later depending on the arrival of high tide. Cora would have liked to experience the drama of departure, but she was tired and decided to mimic her cabinmate and retire. She retrieved her nightdress from her trunk, put it on, and poured water from the pitcher closest to her bunk into its companion basin. Within moments she was climbing into her own bunk, pulling the curtains fast, and settling herself for sleep.

∞∞∞∞

Carl entered the thirty-five-foot-long gentlemen's social hall and peered through the smoky haze to find a gaming table where he might try his hand. His gaze had just fallen on a faro bank in one corner when he heard a hale and hearty call over the general din,

"Fielding! Is it really you?"

He recognized the tall, stocky, black-haired young man coming toward him as Randolph Carter, the son of a New Jersey iron industrialist whom he had met back in April on his first night in San Francisco. He had been taking full advantage of his freedom from his parents' watchful eyes by making the rounds of the city's Portsmouth Square gambling saloons. A novice gambler, he was losing badly when Carter approached him with a tip or two. It was the beginning of a two-week friendship during which the men had stalked the underbelly of San Francisco together. Cora's treachery and their father's insistence that they return with him to Sacramento had cut the good times short, and Carl had not even had a chance to say goodbye to his new friend.

Now they met and clasped hands, Carter saying, "What the devil are you doing here? Thought you would be deep into your boring medical studies by now."

"Alas, it is a long story," said Carl. "But what of you? Last time we met, you gave no indication you planned to leave San Francisco."

"My days of youthful dalliance have, unfortunately, come to an end. My father has fallen into ill health and has summoned me to come and begin learning the family business. But you—I am most intrigued. First, a drink. On me. Then you must tell all."

They obtained and downed their whiskey, then went up into the fresh air of the deck to smoke and converse in an atmosphere more conducive to private confession. By the time Carl had unburdened all that had happened, Carter was aghast with indignation.

"The little hussy! Got herself up as a man, you say? Shameful!"

Despite his displeasure with his sister, Carl did not like to hear her characterized in such terms. He said, "It was a desperate act, to be sure. Done out of an overabundance of ambition, which I admit is not the most feminine of attributes. But I assure you she is a respectable lady in every other respect."

"Such brazen behavior hardly seems ladylike to me. Most gentlemen require a sweet, pliant disposition in the female gender rather than one that seeks to transplant her nature onto their very own. I certainly would never be drawn to such a creature were she the most beautiful, alluring being on earth."

"Sadly, those are not terms I would attach to my sister. She is attractive enough in an elfin sort of way, but I fully acknowledge that she is more opinionated and obstinate than is desired by most of our peers. From her perspective, however, these are traits of value rather than hindrance. I have never understood where she came by such notions. Our mother is the most traditional of women and has never encouraged Cora's aspirations. Our father, however, has always been enchanted by her rebelliousness of thought. I lay the present circumstances squarely at his feet."

"That's as may be, but the question is, what are you going to do about it?"

"Do?" He shrugged. "Continue on the course that has been set for me. It would have been grand to be part of the first class of physicians to come out of the West Coast's first school. But the University of Pennsylvania's is the most reputable school in the nation. I will graduate with the highest credentials possible, which will insure a profitable future."

"And your sister?"

Another shrug. "We will share a medical degree, but there her advantage ends. I cannot imagine who would choose to have his most intimate parts exposed to a female, much less to take advice from such a person. I expect her practice will be limited to females and their troubles. It is not a field I wish to pursue, in any case."

"So you believe women should be allowed to muscle their way into a profession that has been wholly the provenance of men?"

"Of course not. But I appear to have no say in the matter."

"Why not? Do you not feel it your duty to stop her from achieving her goal?"

If Carl were honest with himself, he would admit to having entertained such thoughts. In the end, his love, strained though it was, for the person with whom he had shared their mother's womb had prevailed. Even so, the thought that she and he would emerge in two years' time with the same title of M.D. was not an easy one. She had always challenged him in matters of the mind, and he knew she would do so once again in a profession which, again if he were honest, was not a calling for him but the fulfillment of an obligation to their father. His only consolation was that they would be in different schools, would reside in different accommodations, and would not need to interact except on the most superficial level.

Finally he said, "It is a matter of family. The die is cast, and I am making the most of it. But now I have an itch to play a round or two of faro. What do you say?"

Carter regarded him for a long moment, shook his head in bafflement, then said, "Your call, my friend. On to the hustings it is."

Before heading below, they paused to watch the stevedores loosen the thick ropes holding the ship fast to the pier. The journey was about to begin.

Chapter Nine

October 4, 1859
Panama City, Panama

Cora took Carl's arm and stepped onto the ship's gangway. It was a fresh dewy morning, the rising sun beating back the gray of dawn and casting a brilliant halo around the mountain peaks that comprised the Isthmus of Panama's interior. All was cool and lush and green, although the heavy atmosphere portended a drastic reversal as the tropical day unfolded.

The first week of the voyage had passed pleasantly enough. Cora's cabinmate had turned out to be a lady by the name of Emmeline Norton, whose lined face and silvering dark hair placed her somewhere on the underside of fifty. She was rather tall for a lady, towering over Cora by at least half a foot, but her frail form and reliance on a cane due to debilitating rheumatism reduced what might otherwise have been a formidable appearance. Cora took to her immediately on introduction and looked forward to many days of pleasant conversation. Indeed, their discourse over the early hours of the first morning had revealed they had much in common. Not only were they destined for the same city of Philadelphia, Mrs. Norton being a recent widow who was traveling to live with her older brother, a minister of the Methodist Episcopal Church, but both had immigrated to California, Mrs. Norton in 1850 from Iowa, Cora in 1854 from Indiana. Finding such a high degree of comity, they had soon decided to dispense with formalities and address one another by their Christian names.

By noontime, however, the ceaseless rolling of the ship had incapacitated Emmeline and sent her to her bunk, from which she

seldom rose for the remainder of the voyage to Panama. Left on
her own, Cora had spent her time in the main salon either reading
and visiting with whomever was there or up on the deck taking in
the fresh sea breezes. However, by the eighth day when they docked
in Acapulco to take on coal and supplies, the air had turned hot
and oppressive, causing unremitting misery for all. When clouds
appeared on the horizon on the sixth day, there had been great hope
for a storm to provide relief, but it had not come, and the sun had
remained relentless throughout.

She had seen little of Carl but enough to realize he had taken
up with a large, handsome man some five years their elder. Curious,
especially because he seemed to be deliberately avoiding her, she put
herself in their way and forced an introduction. The gentleman, a Mr.
Randolph Carter, had made all the polite utterances expected under
such circumstances, but his dark eyes had regarded her with what she
could only identify as contempt. Puzzled at first, she soon realized
there could be but one reason for his apparent enmity: Carl must
have unburdened himself as to Cora's behavior in San Francisco.
Such a bias would be impossible to overcome, and she had resigned
herself to keeping clear of them.

Even at a distance, however, she could see her brother's
appearance gradually deteriorate. Dark pouches undergirded his
eyes, his skin had a sallow cast, and his clothing lacked his usual
fastidious care. Eager to discover the source of these changes, she had
followed the two men at a discreet distance from the supper table to
the social hall, where she saw them take their places at a gaming table.

She had never known her brother to engage in that nefarious
pastime. Indeed, she wondered what funds he was using to indulge
himself now. Their father had given each of them an allowance
designed to cover their reasonable expenses going forward. She was
certain he had not allowed any room for frivolous pursuits. Indeed,
she would have found it immoral for either of them to take

advantage of his loving generosity by squandering one unnecessary penny. She had tried to raise the issue with Carl on one of the few occasions when they found themselves alone, but he had told her to mind her own affairs before brushing past her.

Now they had reached Panama, the end of the first portion of their journey, and he was fulfilling his duty by escorting her off the ship and down the docking wharf. The city lay a short distance to the north, its cathedral towers, high tiled roofs, and dilapidated fortifications rising above the treetops while nearer at hand, the long metallic roofs of the Panama Railroad Company's administrative buildings peeked out from a grove of cocoa trees.

The passengers' luggage had been offloaded during breakfast and subsequently transferred to the train that would spirit them across the isthmus to the ship awaiting them on the Atlantic side. Cora had never traveled by train and was eager for that new experience. She was also looking forward to getting away from the whining mosquitoes that had begun to swarm about her head oblivious to her efforts to bat them away.

The passenger terminal was a tall, rectangular, wood-sided building with a convex metallic roof. Freight and luggage entered it through a wide arch accessed by a ramp while passengers climbed to the canopied platform where the train sat waiting, its coal-stoked firebox already belching smoke skyward through the funnel-shaped stack. Twin iron tracks emerged from beneath its front fender and curved inland and out of sight.

Carl assisted Cora into one of the cars, where they found the seat next to Emmeline Norton vacant. It was the first chance Cora had had to introduce her friend to Carl. She did so, and he bowed in polite acknowledgment but made no effort to engage in conversation, soon turning to walk away, no doubt in search of his friend Mr. Carter. Even though the windows were open at the top, the stagnant air inside the car was most unpleasant, the temperature rising by the moment as more people came aboard. Emmeline took a fan from her handbag and waved it with enough vigor that the woefully inadequate breeze reached Cora but did little to dry the perspiration that was beginning to bathe her body. Too enervated to even talk, they sat in companionable silence, allowing Cora time to concentrate on the clinical question of how much heat a human body could sustain before shutting down. She very much hoped not to discover the answer for herself.

It seemed an eternity before all the passengers had settled themselves and the conductor signaled the engineer that all was ready for departure. The train's lusty steam whistle sounded, and they began rolling forward. Billows of smoke and steam drifted past the window as they picked up speed through tree-dotted, undulating countryside. With air now circulating through the open windows, the two women felt enough relief to comment on the view outside. Primitive huts dotted the landscape amidst cultivated fields where brown, half-naked natives toiled. The fertile land formed a skirt around the base of a high, bald-headed mountain that seemed to rise straight out of the sea.

Soon the train crossed a bridge over a muddy riverbed. Beyond it stretched an area of alternating swamp and rolling savannah. They passed the first of the twelve station houses situated along the track in four-mile intervals. These were fine, two-story residences with double piazzas and a pretty garden enclosed by white-picket fencing. Each housed a track master whose job it was to supervise a crew of ten native laborers in keeping the track and its surrounding embankment free of new growth. Later, Cora was to witness one such crew wielding their machetes against a tangle of encroaching vegetation, and she marveled that they could perform such strenuous work in the blazing sun.

Two more iron bridges later, they began to climb, leaving the swamps and heavily-forested lowlands behind. The train labored

across ravines and along the slopes of the mountains that make up
the interior of the isthmus. Then came a beautiful undulating valley
known as *Paraiso*, the native name for paradise. On the far side, they
began rising again through thick forests where exotic trees Cora had
never before seen formed a black wall into which it was impossible
to see.

The higher they climbed, the starker the vistas outside the
window became. Lofty mountains rose on every side with irregular
ridges forming the upper boundaries of the tumbling Rio Grande
River far below. The track crossed steep rocky spurs and deep ravines,
its path often cutting through the earth to form high embankments
on one side or the other. Cora was forced to look away, even to hide
her face in her hands when a particularly treacherous stretch of road
found the track clinging to the mountain's rock face with nothing
but air seeming to support it.

Less than a mile later, they entered a level depression that had
been cut from the mountain's top, the clay walls rising high on either
side. The train slowed and came to a stop at the little native village of
Celubra. They had reached the summit of the forty-seven-mile road.

The train's conductor passed through the car announcing there
would be a short stop before the train continued its long descent to
the Atlantic Ocean. Cora rose with a groan of relief and stretched
her body to and fro to relieve the aches of long inaction. She offered
a hand to Emmeline, who thanked her and rose slowly to her feet.
They joined the cue waiting to climb down.

A thatched hut sat beside the track but there was no formal
platform onto which they might alight. Instead, a short stepstool was
in place with a smiling native standing alongside to assist the ladies.
Emmeline made the descent with some difficulty then waved Cora
on.

"You go take your exercise, my dear," she said. "I am content
simply to stand here for a time."

"May I bring you something? A drink?"

"No, thank you. I have been told the porters will be passing out water in a short time. You go along. I shall be fine right here."

Cora raised her parasol against the vicious equatorial sun and took her bearings. On the far side of the tracks from the station, a cluster of buildings were strung along rising ground some sixty or seventy feet beyond the roadbed. Closer at hand, various street vendors were hawking their wares from oranges to grog. Cora approached one of them. She was trying to retrieve a coin from her handbag while juggling to keep her parasol in place, the thought of a juicy orange raising a flood of saliva, when she felt a hand on her arm. Expecting it to be Carl, she was shocked to look up into the amused brown eyes of Randolph Carter.

"Miss Fielding," he said. "I fear you and I have gotten off to a bad start."

"More like no start at all, Mr. Carter," she retorted. "I see no reason to rectify that now."

"Ah, so. My fault entirely, I admit."

She heard a measure of humility in his voice, but she was quite certain she could not trust it. Before she could reply, he continued with,

"I do so enjoy the company of your brother, and he speaks most highly of you. It seems a pity and a waste not to extend the same friendship to you."

"I have no interest in gaming, Mr. Carter, so I do not see that we have much in common on which to base any sort of friendship. Where is my brother at present?"

"I left him snoring away in the car. I am certain he would wish me to see to your needs in his absence."

"I have no needs, sir. Now if you will excuse me, I should like to purchase an orange."

He moved his hand from behind his back, an orange globe resting in his palm. "Then allow me to offer you this one. As a peace offering of sorts."

She hesitated, the warmth in his voice diffusing some of her pique.

"Come now, Miss Fielding. Surely you can accept such a small gift." He dug his fingernails into the orange and began to strip the peel away. "And while you eat it, I would be pleased to tell you the story of this place and its beginnings."

Intrigued, she allowed him to place the peeled fruit in her hand. She separated one of the sections, put it in her mouth and bit down, nearly swooning with pleasure as the sweet juice exploded onto her parched tissues.

"Now, then, to my story. Come with me. I have something to show you."

"Come where? The train will leave shortly."

"I have it on good authority that it will not leave for at least a half hour. We have plenty of time to explore this little piece of history."

He offered his arm. She stared at it for a moment, then took it and allowed him to guide her up the rough terrain toward the village.

"You might be interested to know that as little as four and a half years ago, only the most hearty of souls undertook this journey across the isthmus. Train tracks had been laid from the Atlantic terminus of Aspinwall to this point only. Anyone desiring to cross from the Pacific side or to continue on after arriving here from the Atlantic was required to make a ten-mile journey by mule. You can imagine what that must have been like given the incredibly rough terrain we have already seen. Add in drenching rains, the broiling sun, and danger from the packs of marauders who frequently attacked and robbed the hapless travelers, and you can see it was not a journey for the faint of heart."

They had reached the forlorn and dilapidated row of huts that formed the town's main street, but Cora saw nothing of note that would justify this extra exertion in the relentless sun of midday.

"Very interesting," she said, "but what was it you wanted to show me?"

He continued forward, saying, "First you must know that in those days, this little village was a thriving place of commerce with numerous hotels and eateries where travelers could pause before or after that difficult ride. The premier hotel was owned, oddly enough, by a Negro by the name of Joe Prince. His place is but a wreck today—" He stopped and gestured toward a pile of ruins with one tilting wall still standing. "—but there is an interesting artifact left to commemorate its passing."

He led her beyond it to a large tropical tree rising some five feet then splitting into two main trunks. Wedged into the crotch thus formed was a large, crude wooden sign with uneven letters of varying size painted in black, the first line of which read: *THIS WAY Gentlemen, FOR Warm Meals.* The line below read: *I AM Going TO Old JOE PRINCE'S.*

Cora thought it a sad testament to the ambition of a black man who could have looked for prosperity nowhere else in the world but in this godforsaken place. She was turning away and saying, "We had best—" when a hand clapped across her mouth, cutting her off. A strong arm wrapped itself around her waist and lifted her off the ground.

"Now then, missy," his voice grated in her ear, "we shall see how well your high and mighty independence fares without your daddy here to fix things for you. Perhaps you will learn that a lady's place is beside her man, keeping his house and raising his children, not mucking about in a profession meant for those of superior intellect and temperament."

Cora's instinct for survival kicked in even as her mind struggled to comprehend what was happening. She wrenched her body to and fro. Clawed at his confining hands. Kicked her heels back at his legs. Gnawed against his palm in an effort to catch a bit of flesh on which to bite. None of it prevailed against his overwhelming size and power. He carried her into the encroaching forest as easily as if she had been a sack of potatoes.

Shortly, they came to an abandoned hut that still stood for the most part intact. He took her inside and set her down, his bulk blocking the entrance. The moment his hand left her mouth, she whirled around and let out a piercing scream.

A satisfied smirk. "No use, hussy. No one can hear you."

"Why?" she cried. "Did Carl put you up to this?"

"My idea entirely, darlin'. If a man does not make a stand for his own gender, he is not much of a man. But I mean you no permanent harm. I simply mean to delay you until the train leaves. From there on in, it will be up to you. My personal suggestion would be for you to take the next train back to Panama and return to your parents until some poor fool decides to marry you against his better interests."

Infuriated beyond all reason, she charged forward and plowed into him. It took him by surprise, enough so that she was able to slip past him and make for the door of the hut. She was just beginning to taste freedom when something struck the back of her head, causing a massive explosion of pain. She felt her knees buckle, and her body hit the forest floor. As darkness overtook her, she had but a moment to vow that not even this would defeat her.

Chapter Ten

Carl walked up and down the exterior of the train, eyes searching the diminishing crowds for his friend Carter. He had fallen asleep shortly after they left Panama, the prior night's revelry having left him with an overwhelming drowsiness impossible to resist. On waking to an empty car and stifling heat, he had stumbled outside and found the nearest vendor from which he could purchase a measure of grog. Now people were heading back to their places prior to departure, but Randolph Carter was nowhere to be found.

He was near the train's puffing engine when he heard a faint call and looked up the incline to see Carter coming toward him. When he arrived, he clapped Carl on the shoulder and said,

"Miss me, old pal? Just taking in the sights."

"Mm-m. Not much to see, seems to me."

"A bit of history is all, but it looks as if I cut it rather close. Everyone else seems to have boarded."

Indeed, the boarding area was now deserted. They hurried along toward their car, the last one of the train. As they passed the windows of the car before theirs, they heard a frantic rapping. Carl looked up to see the lady who had shared Cora's cabin knocking on the glass and gesturing to the empty seat beside her."

"Ignore the old biddy," said Carter. "The conductor wants us to board."

Carl saw that the conductor was indeed motioning for them to get onto the train. As an added incentive, the train's whistle sounded. He looked back at the lady behind the window glass. Her gesticulations seemed more urgent and distressed than ever.

"Cora," said Carl. "She does not appear to be in her seat."

"Probably just took a different one. Nothing to worry about."

Carl was not convinced. He ran toward the conductor, who already had one foot on the first car's platform. He skidded to a stop and shouted,

"We must wait! My sister appears to be missing from the train."

"Ignore my friend here," said Carter. "He tends to be overwrought at times. I am sure the lady is aboard but in a different seat."

Carl gave him a puzzled look. "Overwrought? Why would you say such a thing?" Then to the conductor, "Please delay our departure until I am certain my sister is safely on the train."

The conductor looked up at the engineer, who was leaning out from his perch and taking in the conversation. The engineer shrugged and said, "A few minutes will do no harm."

The conductor, a slight man with a dark complexion similar to that of the other natives on the isthmus, turned back to Carl and said, "Where did you last see her?"

"She was seated with the lady who shared her cabin on the voyage down. The lady, Mrs. Norton, flagged us down and seemed quite distressed over my sister's absence."

"Take me to her."

They walked back down the train. When they arrived at the car in question, Emmeline Norton was standing on the platform and leaning heavily on her cane. "Miss Fielding never returned from her jaunt," she said. "I am most concerned for her welfare."

Carl exchanged a look with the conductor, who asked, "What jaunt, ma'am?"

"He is the one you should ask," she said, pointing at Randolph Carter. "I saw him give her an orange, after which she took his arm and they went up toward the village."

All eyes focused on Carter. He gave a guilty smile and said, "Yes, I did escort Miss Fielding on a little field trip. She was most eager to hear about the history of Celubra, which I had learned for myself on my trip out two years ago. There is a most interesting artifact from the days before the railroad went clear through. A sign left by one of the hoteliers who thrived in those days. She wanted to see it."

"And you left her up there?" cried Carl. "Why would you do such a thing?"

"Calm down, my friend. We went as far as the sign. Then she excused herself for some unexplained reason. No doubt a delicate feminine question such as no lady wishes to discuss with a gentleman. When she did not return, I assumed she had made her own way back."

"Well, she obviously did not. We must search for her. Show us the way!"

Carter shrugged. "As I said before, she has no doubt taken another seat somewhere on the train. But if you insist on this wild-goose chase, follow me."

He led Carl and the conductor up the incline to the village and along to the ruined Joe Prince hotel. Carter waved his arm at the surrounding area. "Here is where she left me."

Carl's heart was thudding with prescient dread. Something was not at all right about this situation. Relations between him and his sister might have been strained of late, but she was as close to him in physiology as any two people could be, and his innate love for her could not countenance the notion that she had come to harm.

He cupped his hands around his mouth and yelled, "Cora! Where are you?"

Meanwhile, the conductor bent down to retrieve something from the ground. He held it out for Carl to see. A partially eaten orange.

He sent his friend a fierce, penetrating look.

"Carter?"

An elaborate shrug. "Beats me, Fielding. I do not remember her throwing the orange away. Perhaps it was fermented and she did not care for it."

His mind now mired in panic, Carl plunged forward into the tangled undergrowth, calling Cora's name as he ran. He had gone but a short distance when he heard a faint reply. He stopped a moment to listen and get his bearings. When the sound came again, he charged hell-bent in that direction.

∞∞∞

The sound of her name roused Cora from her extreme lethargy. She remembered hearing the train whistle blow, and she knew it meant she must get up. But her head ached with such ferocity that she could not lift it, and in the end, she had decided to rest a moment before even trying. Now she knew that Carl was out there searching for her. Her sweet, wonderful brother had not abandoned her. With a surge of love in her heart, she called,

"Here!"

It came out as little more than a squeak. She cleared her throat, gathered all of her reserves, and called out again, "Here I am!"

This time the sound must have carried because she soon heard someone crashing through the forest in her direction. Relieved, she decided she could go back to sleep for a bit until he arrived. She closed her eyes and was soon insensible again.

The next thing she knew, Carl was kneeling beside her and cradling her in his arms. Tears streamed down his face as he stroked her cheek and murmured, "Thank God, Cora. Can you hear me?"

Despite his supporting her head against his chest, it felt as if it would explode at any moment. She tried to look up at him, but the light stabbed into her eyes like the blade of a knife. She closed them again and tried to nod, sending shards of pain throughout her head.

"We must get her back to the train," came another voice, one tinged with a native accent. "We cannot delay much longer."

Carl said, "First I must make certain she can be moved. Cora, can you tell me what happened? Do you have pain anywhere?"

Another feeble nod. "Head," she managed to say.

His fingers gently probed her scalp, finally coming to rest on a large lump on the back.

"Yes, it is a huge contusion. Did you fall?"

This time her head wagged side to side. "Mr. Carter. Hit me. To keep me off the train."

∞∞∞

Carl's thoughts went wild. Randolph Carter lured her here to harm her? What possible motive would he have for doing that?

Then he remembered some of their conversations, especially those revolving around Cora's outrageous ploy to get into the Medical School of the Pacific. Carter had excoriated him for not taking a stronger stand. For not making sure Cora's ambition was foiled. For not standing up against this encroachment on manhood. In the end, Carl had demurred by pleading the bonds of family. Disappointed by this lack of action, Carter had apparently taken it upon himself to avenge his gender.

On some level, Carl understood the other man's motivation. But to kidnap Cora and knock her insensate in order to achieve his goal? It was disgraceful, not to mention criminal, and Carter must face justice for it. He looked about him, but the man was nowhere to be seen.

"Where did he go?" he asked the conductor, who was hovering nearby and wringing his hands with anxiety over the delay this was causing the train.

"The other fellow? He must have returned to the train. Which is what we must do. We are already well behind schedule."

Carl reasoned that there was but one way down the mountain, and Carter was as dependent on it as were they. There would be opportunity later to turn him in to the authorities, but for now, he had his own and his sister's welfare to consider. He lifted her in his arms, and they slowly made their way back through the village and down to the train.

Cora moaned in agony with every step, causing a shiver of worry to prickle his skin. He had seen patients come into his father's surgery with head injuries. The more severe they were, the more dire the consequences, and he hoped the blow to Cora's head was not so harmful as to cause permanent damage to her prodigious intellect. He comforted himself, however, with the knowledge that most patients recovered fully after a period of pain and confusion. He could but pray she would be among those.

∞∞∞∞

Cora would remember the remainder of the trip down to the Atlantic only in terms of sensation. Carl had carried her back to Emmeline, who had moved close to the window so Cora could lay with her head and shoulders reclining in the older lady's lap. The other passengers had crowded around, their questions and murmurings rolling like thunder through her brain. Carl's pleas for calm and silence had soon stilled them. He had taken the seat directly across the aisle from them, the knowledge of his hovering protection coming as a balm to the continuous ache in her head.

Once the train was underway again, the rocking motion added a new layer of discomfort—a roiling of her stomach that required her to purge. Thankfully, Emmeline was prepared with a cotton shawl to contain the resultant mess. Nonetheless, the dear lady's soothings and "never-you-minds" could do nothing to remove the pungent odor that permeated the car despite all the windows being open. Cora could only suffer her embarrassment in private and be grateful that once the voyage was over, she would never see these people again.

She heard the others exclaim over various wonders passing outside the train, including a bridge of uncommon length over the

River Chagres, but her entire being was focused on simply surviving for the next hours. At last it was over, and the train rolled to a stop. It took all her fortitude to sit upright and endure the subsequent pounding in her head. Carl appeared at her side and scooped her up into his arms. She made a feeble protest, mortified to be carried off the train like a child, but she knew deep within that she would have been incapable of proceeding on her own.

The train's Atlantic terminus was the town of Aspinwall, which was located on what had once been an island. A causeway had been built connecting it to the mainland so that the train could now cross over the intervening water and down the center of Front Street. This roadway was bordered on one side by the town's buildings of commerce, while the waters of the bay lapped close at hand on the other. Numerous ships' masts towered above a series of wharves a short distance away.

Once again Carl leaned down to pick her up, but this time she insisted on walking with his strong arm to assist her. They made their way across to the wharves at a snail's pace, their slow progress fitting well with Emmeline's limitations of mobility.

The *SS North Star* lay waiting for them. She was a two-masted, wooden-hulled side wheeler that had once been the private yacht on which Cornelius Vanderbilt and his family toured Europe. Cora cared little for this bit of history, her only goal that of attaining her bunk so she could find relief from her pain in sleep.

Chapter Eleven

Each day of the following week saw gradual improvement in Cora's symptoms. Even Emmeline grew somewhat accustomed to the toss and roll of the sea, and they were able to spend many delightful hours getting better acquainted with one another's history.

Cora already knew that Emmeline had immigrated to California from Iowa. What she did not know was the hideous nature of that journey, for her first husband and two sons had succumbed to cholera along the way. Arriving in California alone and with limited resources, she had hired on as a cook for a hotelman's boarders, where she met her second husband, Hiram Norton. Hiram had come out during the gold rush fever of 1848 and had accumulated a modest fortune before an injured foot incapacitated him. The wound festered until the limb required amputation, a surgery that put an end to his mining days. The knowledge he had gained, however, served him well when coupled with a keen aptitude for business. He started a company that outfitted miners and met with immediate success.

After he and Emmeline married, the two worked together to expand the business into a flourishing mercantile company. Their one sadness was their failure to conceive a child. Nonetheless, they kept busy with the store and had a satisfying life until Emmeline's gradual physical decline required her to curtail her own involvement. When Hiram died unexpectedly, she had had no heart to continue the business and had sold out. Her brother had urged her to come east and live with him and his family, and she had decided it was her best course of action.

For her part, Cora shared her own story and received a surprising degree of support. Someone such as Emmeline, who had surmounted her many difficulties by relying on herself alone, could well understand a young woman's yearning for her own place in the world. With a twinkle in her eye, she had said,

"I confess to having wished for the tender touch of a lady doctor more than one time in my life. So rest assured, I shall be your first patient, supposing God wills that I survive until your education is complete."

Whereupon Cora had wrapped her in a warm embrace while making a silent vow to learn as much as she could about her friend's condition and any new treatments medicine might have to offer.

With the return of health, Cora began to ask questions about the fate of her attacker. Although Carl remained as solicitous as before, she sensed an evasiveness that she attributed to guilt. He had, after all, vented his pique over Cora's ambitions to a person whose temperament was easily inflamed. A person who had little regard for the female gender to begin with and was primed and waiting for an excuse to act beyond reason. Carl promised he had done everything he could to alert those in authority of the man's crime, but the scoundrel had apparently vanished into the forests of Panama. He maintained that he would make inquiries when they reached their destination, but Cora suspected he would rather forget the entire incident. She herself was not opposed to such a stance. They would never encounter the young man again, and if his disposition inclined him to violence, then he would offend again and eventually be caught in the snares of justice.

A week to the day from their Panama departure saw them steaming into New York City's harbor. Cora stood at the rail in cloak and bonnet and was amazed by the sprawling city before her. She had thought San Francisco the epitome of urban sophistication, but it paled before the breadth and depth of this metropolis. The closer they came, the more she marveled at the height and number of buildings surrounding the waterfront, which in itself was vast and teeming with activity. Despite the early hour, they disembarked into a world of cacophony and seeming chaos. Carts and drays of every size and description navigated amidst vast stacks of barrels and crates. Men shouted and cursed, animals neighed and brayed, ships' horns blasted. It was a dirty and foul-smelling place, and Cora could not wait to escape it.

Fortunately, it was but a short walk to the ferry terminal where they would board a steamer to cross Raratan Bay to the New Jersey port of South Amboy. From there they would take the rails again, this time aboard the Camden and Amboy Railroad to Camden, a short ferry ride across the Delaware River from Philadelphia.

As they approached their journey's end, Cora found herself plagued by a maelstrom of conflicting emotions. Foremost, of course, was excitement at finally completing the first step in her quest to become a physician. Her joy was tempered, however, by unease over the unknown.

Some arrangements had already been made. Both she and Carl had been accepted into their respective schools with final enrollment to be completed after they arrived in the city. Each school had recommended lodging facilities, and rooms had been secured beginning on the first of October. Beyond those certainties, she could not help anxious feelings over a new life in an unfamiliar city far away from all she had known. Would she be able to secure the part-time employment she had vowed to find? Their father had provided each of them with a monthly allowance, but she knew his generosity would require a measure of sacrifice for the remainder of the family, and she was determined to find some way of easing his burden. School would begin in eight days. Would she be up to its rigors? Would she fit in with her fellow students, who no doubt came from an urban background vastly different from hers? Or would she be a lonely outcast?

She did her best to put these troubling thoughts out of her mind, resorting even to prayer. Religion had never occupied a particularly important role in her life. She had attended church with her family, but she had never thought much about how Providence might or might not affect her daily life. She knew there were certain ideals and beliefs that rose from deep within her soul, but she had never thought much about whence they came. The notion of a God-inspired mission had never occurred to her. Now she wondered whether her own innate skills would be enough. Or might she need a little divine help in overcoming the likely obstacles that lay ahead?

She was aided by her growing friendship with Emmeline, whose side she rarely left during their final transit. The older lady had sent a telegram to her brother from the New York ferry terminal advising him of her imminent arrival. She had not seen him since he left home to pursue his liturgical studies when she was but a child of ten. Thus, her anxiety over coming to live with a virtual stranger seemed to be nearly as intense as Cora's own. They comforted one another with the assurance that regardless of their future challenges, each knew she would have at least one friend in the City of Brotherly Love.

The train arrived in Camden at a few minutes past five o'clock. As was her habit, Cora assisted Emmeline to her feet and took a firm, protective hold on her arm. Carl offered his arm on the other side, and the three disembarked from the car. They passed through the depot and emerged at the base of a wharf that extended into the Delaware River.

The late-afternoon air was crisp and carried a faint hint of autumn, reminding Cora of her days in Indiana before the family migrated to California. The sun sat on the horizon of a cloudless sky. A light breeze played with the smoke drifting from the single stack of an odd-looking vessel docked at the wharf ahead. It sat low in the water, its boxlike iron superstructure a dull gray. There seemed to be but two decks, the top one supporting only a pilot house on each end and a smokestack. A wide aperture yawned in the middle of the lower deck, and it was there that their fellow train passengers were streaming. Off to the side, a line of carriages and wagons awaited their turn to board. A sign above the opening gave the boat's name as the *Dido*.

They joined the queue, wondering among themselves how the vessel could possibly stay afloat with such a heavy superstructure. A portly gentleman in line behind them offered,

"Do not be deceived. She looks cumbersome, but she is the speediest, most powerful boat on the river. You should see her cut through great slabs of river ice as if they were made of *papier-mache*. She never misses a run even in the deepest of winter."

Passenger cabins on either side offered benches for repose. Cora and Carl settled Emmeline onto one of them and went forward to look out a round porthole as the boat got underway. The Delaware was a tidal waterway and thus offered a ride somewhat less smooth than would have been found on more landlocked rivers. They steamed straight for two islands that occupied the middle of the river. As they drew closer, they saw that a canal separated the two land masses, and the boat glided easily between them. Ahead they could see the wharves, spires, and smokestacks of the City of Philadelphia. Within fifteen minutes, they had pulled up alongside another wharf, and the docking procedures began.

They joined the line and disembarked at the end of a busy street that gradually ascended into the city. It was lined on either side by substantial brick buildings of varying heights. Similar buildings stretched to either side along the riverfront. One such, a wide, four-story structure marked overhead as Bloodgood's Hotel, seemed to be the destination of many of their fellow passengers.

The trio followed along and entered the hotel's parlor, which seemed to function as a waiting room for the ferry and its sister railroad. Some of the debarking passengers were already being greeted by those awaiting them, but Emmeline's anxious eyes roamed in vain for a familiar face. Cora had determined to stay with her until she could be passed along to her family, and she was beginning to wonder what she would do if no one came to collect her when a young gentleman in business attire approached, hat in hand, and inquired,

"Aunt Emmeline Norton?"

With obvious relief, Emmeline smiled at him and said, "You must be my nephew, Peter."

"Indeed I am. And most pleased to finally meet you, dear lady."

He took her hands in his and leaned in to kiss her cheek. He was but a few inches taller than Emmeline with a mass of curly black hair. Cora would have thought him handsome were it not for his pronounced facial features: thick straight eyebrows over deep-set brown eyes, strong high forehead, prominent cheekbones, a long straight nose, a square jawline. Each characteristic competed with the others for prominence, failing to mesh into a whole pleasing to the eye. There was only sincerity, however, when Emmeline directed his attention to Cora and Carl by saying,

"Before I say another word, I must introduce my benefactors, Miss Cora and Mr. Carl Fielding, who have been my constant companions and protectors. They have made what would have been a most tedious journey more than tolerable." To Cora and Carl, "This is my brother's son, Mr. Peter Ware."

He bowed to Cora and shook Carl's hand. "On my family's behalf, I am most grateful to you both. What brings you to our fair city all the way from California?"

Emmeline said, "You will hardly believe it, but both of these young people have come to attend medical college. Their father is a physician in Sacramento, and they both desire to follow in his path."

"Indeed?" His intense gaze passed from Carl to Cora, taking on a glint of some emotion she could not read. "I was not aware that Philadelphia boasted a coeducational medical school."

Carl's mouth twisted in distaste. "Nor does it. I am admitted to the esteemed University of Pennsylvania's Medical School, while my sister will attend the Female Medical College. The two do not equate in any significant manner, I assure you."

"Both grant the same degree," snapped Cora.

"As I have said many times, dear sister, there the similarity ends. I cannot think the public will hold the same regard—"

"I do not agree, Mr. Fielding," Emmeline interrupted in a rare display of ill manners. "We ladies have long wished for a healer of our own gender to assist us with our unique complaints, which are generally ignored or made light of by the men in your chosen profession."

Her outburst clearly caught Carl by surprise. His cheeks colored and he stammered, "Well, I...I mean no offense, but..." His voice trailed off.

"And I am certain none is taken," said Mr. Ware. Turning to his aunt, "I must collect your luggage. Father and Mother and Annabelle are eager to greet you, and I am loath to keep them waiting any longer than necessary.

"Thank you, Peter, but we must surely offer transportation to the Fieldings as well. It is the least we can do to thank them for their great care over the past weeks."

"Not at all necessary, Mrs. Norton," said Carl. "Mr. Ware has surely come unprepared to manage the three of us. We shall engage a cab to take us to our lodgings as has been our plan from the beginning."

"Nonsense," said Mr. Ware. "My father's carriage is quite adequate for two extra passengers. It is small repayment for the care you showed to my aunt on her journey." He gestured toward the exit. "Shall we attend to the luggage?"

When they were alone, Cora said, "I wish you had not imposed on your nephew. It causes me much embarrassment."

"The embarrassment is mine. He should have made the offer himself. I can only attribute his lack of manners to his obvious fascination with you."

"Me?" Cora could not hide her amazement. "Why on earth should I cause any such feeling in your nephew?"

A sly wink. "If you cannot puzzle that out for yourself, you must not be as bright as I thought you were."

Cora gave a small shake of her head and a rueful smile but made no reply. As they waited, she mused on her friend's strange turn of mind. She acknowledged having noticed Mr. Ware's rather charged demeanor, but she hardly thought it had anything to do with her. Emmeline was meeting her nephew for the first time this day, and she could not possibly know his character or moods well enough to make any prediction as to his thought processes. Nonetheless, the possibility that she had been especially noticed by such a gentleman sent a frisson of pleasure through her body. At the same time, she acknowledged that she would no doubt never see him again. Which was probably just as well.

Chapter Twelve

Philadelphia, Pennsylvania
October 11, 1859

Fifty-four North Seventh Street turned out to be a tall narrow red-brick building with a bay window opposite the front door, three plain windows on each of its upper three stories, and a double dormer at the very top. It had front steps and windowsills of white marble, a slanting cellar door that protruded onto the brick sidewalk, and a look of past grandeur now somewhat the worse for its present use as a boardinghouse. It shared the street with another residence to the north, separated from it by a narrow passageway, and several commercial buildings to the south, among them a saddlery, a confectionary, and a bootmaker. Gas streetlights glowed against the growing dusk.

Mr. Ware pulled the carriage horse to a stop, this being the first stop on the route he had planned for seeing them all to their respective destinations. He went around to the rear platform to unloose Cora's trunk while she said her goodbyes to Carl and Emmeline. She had no compunction in bidding farewell to her brother. Their relationship had healed somewhat following the attack in Panama, but the underlying tensions remained, and she was glad their paths would now diverge.

Parting from Emmeline was a different matter, accompanied as it was by a surprising knot in her throat. They had known each other but a few weeks, but even that short tenure still marked Emmeline as her only friend in this vast city, and she felt a strong sadness at their parting.

Perhaps sharing a similar reluctance, Emmeline pulled her into an embrace and said, "I shall not think of this as a final goodbye, my dear. I have so enjoyed your company and am most grateful for all you and your brother have done for me. Dare I hope you will keep me informed of your progress as you pursue your studies?"

Comforted, Cora vowed to do so.

Mr. Ware had placed Cora's trunk on the sidewalk and come around to offer her his hand in stepping down. He escorted her up the three steps to the door then returned for the trunk. By the time he returned, Cora's turn of the bell handle had resulted in the door being opened by a stout, matronly woman wearing a simple gray dress beneath a copious white apron.

She peered out, her squinting eyes suggesting she needed spectacles but was too vain to wear them.

"May I be helpin' you?" she asked in a thick Irish brogue.

"I am Miss Fielding," Cora answered. "I believe my father engaged lodgings for me at this address."

She smiled, revealing teeth either missing or blackened with decay. "Sure and begorra he did, lass. I am Mrs. Gallagher. Please to come in."

She stepped back to widen the doorway, and Cora entered, followed by Mr. Ware carrying her trunk. Mrs. Gallagher waved him away and said, "Ach, and you needn't mind that. My Seamus will see to it."

He hesitated, then set it down and turned to Cora, saying, "Then I shall bid you good evening. Again, thank you for caring for my aunt. We did not realize she was so debilitated when my father suggested she make this arduous journey alone."

"The pleasure was mine, I assure you. She is a delightful lady, as I am sure you will soon discover."

He bowed and retreated, leaving Cora with the realization that he had bidden her good evening, not goodbye. It was a small thing, but it left her with a pleasant tingle she was quick to dismiss.

"Now, then," said Mrs. Gallagher, "we'll be about gettin' you settled 'n all."

She bustled toward the back reaches of the house, giving Cora a moment to assess her surroundings. She was in a long hallway, gloomy despite the lone gas fixture that burned in a sconce on the wall. It was surprisingly warm in the house given the chilly air outside, telling her they had some form of central heating, a novel idea to a Californian. To the right, pocket doors had been slid back to reveal a parlor from which she heard the low murmur of conversation. A hint of cooking odor lingered in the air, causing her gastric juices to flow. It was well past suppertime, but she had not eaten since lunch and felt ravenous.

Mrs. Gallagher returned carrying a kerosene lamp. She was followed by a male version of herself—round bewhiskered face beneath graying hair, thick compact body. He was barely an inch taller than she and had the considerable girth, flushed face and bloodshot eyes of a heavy drinker.

She gestured to him and said by way of introduction, "Mr. Gallagher." Then for his benefit, "Miss Fielding. Another one about bein' a student doctor."

He grunted and gave a little bow, after which his wife said, "Sure and would ya ever shift that trunk to the lass's room?"

"Not a bother, luv." He bent to heave the trunk onto his shoulders.

"Along this way, then," said Mrs. Gallagher as she started toward the stairway that rose into the gloom up ahead.

They reached the second story, but instead of turning along the hallway, Mrs. Gallagher continued upward, her husband laboring behind them with the trunk. They continued on to the third floor, then up to the fourth, the air growing colder with each level. Still they did not stop but proceeded to the end of this much shorter hallway, where a second, more utilitarian staircase emerged from below. Opposite it, a steep, narrow staircase disappeared upward. Cora found herself worrying about Mr. Gallagher, whose breathing was increasingly tortuous, but his wife seemed not in the least alarmed. She put her hand on a crude railing and plodded upward, her own huffing and puffing audible.

They finally reached the uppermost limits of the house. A narrow passageway led forward, its ceiling low, its walls presumably barricading off the attics. Two doors presented themselves at the front of the house. Mrs. Gallagher opened the one to the left and led the way in.

Cora's spirits had been plummeting with each of the house's successive stories as she wondered what sort of place she was expected to occupy for the next two years. By the time she had entered the room and was able to look around, however, much of her trepidation fled. The space was small but compact, the ceiling sloping from a peak along the centerline to an outer wall some four feet high, leaving plenty of room to stand and move about. A dormer window on the front wall would let in the daylight. The furnishings were simple but adequate: a narrow iron bedstead beneath the window with its head against the long wall, a low chest of drawers beside it with an oval mirror mounted above, a small table at the foot of the bed and to the left of the window along with a sturdy chair, a shelf on the low outer wall, presumably to accommodate her books, and in the corner behind the door, a small cast-iron stove with its accompanying basket of kindling and scuttle of coal. With winter coming, this latter was a welcome sight.

Mrs. Gallagher placed her lantern on the table, lifted the one that was already there and lit it. She turned and said, "Now, the rules. This place is meant to be respectable, so. Ye young ones'd want to be in house at a decent hour. Ye'll be seein' any gentleman visitors in the parlor only. Meals're at eight, two and seven bells, so. If ye're late, ye'll go hungry. Same for one as t'other. Tonight, though, seein's how ye got here past time, I'll be sendin' Katie up with a tray. Ye be havin' any questions?"

Cora shook her head and thanked them. When she was alone, she took off her bonnet and cloak and hung them on one of the wooden pegs positioned on the wall beside the doorway. She stood a moment listening to the silence. Here she was at the end of her quest. She should feel exhilarated. Instead, she felt oddly flat. And out of place. She found herself wishing Emmeline had come in with her, a notion made completely ridiculous and impractical given the poor lady's debility of movement. Still, the presence of another human being would have eased her sense of isolation. The next best thing, she decided, would be to surround herself with her own things. She unlocked her trunk and began to unpack.

When deciding what to bring, she had favored her beloved books over clothing. Thus, she had but four dresses to hang on the pegs provided: three for everyday and one for special occasions. Her undergarments, nightclothes and shawls went into the bureau drawers. She laid her toiletry articles on top of the chest of drawers beside the basin and pitcher already there. The books—a volume of Emily Dickinson's poetry, two Dickens novels, Harriet Beecher Stowe's *Uncle Tom's Cabin*, and a collection of short stories by Nathaniel Hawthorne—went on the shelf provided, leaving the trunk empty.

What to do with it? She supposed she could ask Mr. Gallagher to move it to the attics. Then her eye fell on the small space between the head of the bed and the chest of drawers. She pushed the chest to the side until there was enough room to accommodate the width of the trunk. She slid it into place, pleased with the idea that it would hold the lantern and whichever book she might be reading while she lay in bed before sleep.

A knock came at the door. Expecting it to be the maid with the promised supper tray, she opened it without inquiry. The young woman facing her was certainly not a maid. She wore a pale green day dress with lace about the neck and down the bodice. She was taller than Cora, making her of average height, with glossy brown hair done up in the latest fashion, a heart-shaped face, and hazel eyes that shone with good will. She smiled and extended her hand.

"Hello. Allow me to introduce myself. Gwendolyn Pickering from Illinois. We are to be classmates."

Cora grasped her hand as if it were a lifeline, delight chasing away her former malaise. "I am so happy to meet you, Miss Pickering! I am Cora Fielding from California."

"Oh, my. And I thought I had traveled a long distance. Welcome to Philadelphia. And please call me Gwen."

"Happily. And I must be Cora to you. Please come in."

She pulled the chair out from the table and waved the newcomer into it. She sat on the end of the bed nearest her guest and said, "How long have you been in Philadelphia?"

"A little more than two weeks. I was the last before you, which might explain why we two are stuck up here in the rafters. Now that you are here, I believe our class is complete."

Cora felt a shiver of destiny. *Our class.* Those two words marked the end of her long nightmare of exclusion and the beginning of the future. She was actually a student of medicine with the prospect of earning the same degree her father and every other physician held. And she would share her journey with this young woman. She was no longer alone.

She could barely keep the excitement from her voice as she said, "Have you met the others? Are they living here as well?"

"Three are. The rest are either staying in another boardinghouse, with relatives, or they live in Philadelphia."

"How many are we to be?"

"Eleven altogether. Ten of us are in our first year. And we come from all over the nation. It is rather remarkable. Wisconsin, Ohio, Washington D.C., New York. Pennsylvania, of course. And you and I from California and Illinois."

"Have you seen the school?"

"I have. The day after I arrived. And so will you when you meet with the dean to finalize your enrollment."

There was another knock on the door. Cora rose to answer it, saying, "That will be my supper. Mrs. Gallagher said she would send up a tray since I arrived so late."

"My, my, you are the privileged one. She is a lioness about promptness to meals. If we are not there, we go hungry."

"So she told me. I shan't expect anything of the like in the future."

She opened the door to admit a young girl wearing a brown dress beneath a not-overly-white apron. She was thin enough to remind Cora of a starving cat her family had once rescued. Her black hair escaped her cap in curly tendrils, and her greenish eyes were the largest Cora had ever seen on such a small person. Her red, chapped hands held a wooden tray on which was a plate bearing a thick pork sandwich.

She dipped in a curtsy and said with an Irish accent not as thick as her mistress's, "Katie Dugan at your service, ma'am. Where'd you like the tray?"

Cora stood aside and gestured toward the table. On seeing Gwen, the girl curtsied again and said, "Miss Pickering," before setting her burden down.

Cora said, "Thank you, Katie. I am Miss Fielding."

Another curtsy. "Yes'm. Anything else I can do for you?"

"No. You are very kind to have bought the tray."

She blushed and backed out of the room.

"A dear girl, that one," said Gwen. "You would not think her capable of the hard work she does, but she is stronger than she appears."

"Is she the only servant?"

"Yes. Except for old Seamus. The two of them hop to Fiona's tune and no mistake."

"It seems to be a very large house. How many boarders are there?"

"You are the twenty-first, I believe."

"All ladies?"

"No. We have several young men as well as a newly married couple. I gather that all-female boardinghouses are looked on with some suspicion as possible houses of ill repute. And if there is one thing our Fiona prizes, it is the reputation of this place."

"So I gathered."

She took the plate with its sandwich to the bed, sat, and began to eat. Between bites, they exchanged information about their lives, and Gwen offered brief descriptions of the other three classmates who lived in the house. Cora hung on every word, but with her stomach satisfied, she found herself nearly overwhelmed with drowsiness. By the time she had stifled her third yawn, Gwen laughed and said,

"Enough of my prattle. You must be exhausted after your long day of travel. I shall bid you goodnight."

Cora saw her out, her heart warming with the knowledge that she had a new friend.

∞∞∞∞

Carl flopped down on the bed, hands behind his head, eyes fixed on the large water stain in the corner of the ceiling. He was glad to be rid of his obligations to Cora and hoped to see as little of her as possible from now on. She was on her pathway and he on his. So why did he feel so discontented? He knew he had less passion for medicine than his sister, but necessity required that he have a trade that would support him and a future family. He had accepted long ago that his one joy, wood sculpting, provided no path to the income or prestige expected of a well-educated, middle-class gentleman. That plus his father's not-so-subtle nudging had convinced him that becoming a physician was the best course for him to follow. So why could he not reconcile himself to medical school and the intellectual effort that would be required of him?

Instead, the thought bored him beyond measure. How was he to muster the will and determination to succeed when he could not care less how well he performed?

A thrum of drowsiness made his eyes grow heavy. He had talked the boardinghouse keeper, a sour-faced, morbidly-obese woman named Mrs. Hillman, into a bowl of leftover mutton stew. With his belly sated and the long day's journey over, he was about to nod off when he heard an indistinct babble of voices rising from below. He soon made out rowdy male banter interspersed with uproarious laughter. His room was opposite the stairway on the third and top floor. The commotion rose to his level then retreated toward the front of the house. Intrigued, he rose, opened his door, and looked out. Light sparked from the open door of the end room, and the clamor was, if anything, louder. Ever loath to miss out on a good time, he walked down the hall and looked into the room.

Two young men sat on the bed, one with his back to the wall, the other askew on the other end. A third held a bottle of whiskey, which he was in the process of raising to his lips. They saw him and fell silent for a moment before the one with the bottle, a tall lanky man with curly yellow hair and a hawk-like face, jabbed it in his direction and said in a honeyed southern drawl,

"Who do we have here?"

"Carl Fielding," he answered. "Here from California to attend medical school."

This information elicited a suspicious scowl. "Franklin or Penn?"

Carl shook his head, not understanding.

"Your school? Franklin Medical or University of Pennsylvania?"

"Oh. The University."

Apparently it was the right answer, because the fellow's face broke into a wide grin and he waved his arm in invitation. "In that case, come on in and have a drink. Rufus Mills here. These two reprobates are Herman Dietrich..." He indicated the small man with light hair already thinning on top who sat at the end of the bed. "...and Joseph Robinson," pointing to the brawny, dark-haired man with his back to the wall.

Carl gave each a nod and entered the room. Rufus handed him the bottle, and he tipped it up for a welcome swallow. It burned as it went down, but the resultant warmth rose almost immediately. He wiped his mouth on his sleeve and handed it back, saying,

"Are you men medical students as well?"

"Damn right. Herm and I are first year. Joey over there is the old hand in his second year." He passed the bottle off to his friends. Then he hooked his foot around the leg of the room's only straight-back chair, pulled it out and waved Carl into it. "Some Franklin men are down on the second floor, but we keep to our own."

The big man, Joseph, gave an emphatic nod and let loose with a loud belch. "Drink with our own, too." His slurred words made it clear that the bottle being passed around was not the first of the evening.

A high-pitched giggle from the balding one. Then, "Fuck with our own, too. Damn fine strumpet, that Sally. My balls are still quivering."

Rufus gave him an indulgent nod. "Herm over there is just getting acquainted with the finer things in life. What about you, Fielding? You like to let the inner man loose from time to time?"

Carl knew the vulgarity of the last few minutes was the liquor talking. He normally preferred to keep his discourse on a more socially acceptable plane, but he also appreciated the camaraderie that gentlemen enjoy when they find themselves at a safe distance from the gentler sex.

"Absolutely," he said as he accepted another round of the bottle.

"Then stick with us. We go to the Bluebell Tavern most nights, and you are welcome to join us. Do you like cards?"

Carl grinned. "I have been known to play a few hands."

"That settles it. Welcome to our merry little band of miscreants."

Chapter Thirteen

After notifying the school that she had arrived in Philadelphia, Cora was given an appointment with Dean Edwin Fussell, M.D. for Friday, October 14 at 10:00 a.m. She donned her cloak and bonnet and stepped out onto Seventh Street, pausing a moment to appreciate the bright sunny day and draw the fresh fall air into her lungs. She tucked her gold-embossed black leather folio, a parting gift from her parents, under her arm and set out to the north.

She knew it would be to her advantage that her boardinghouse was within a block of the school, something she would especially appreciate as autumn progressed into winter. Within half a block, she came to Arch Street. She waited for a horse-drawn streetcar to pass along its inlaid tracks, then crossed over and turned east. She passed a line of shops before coming to a dark narrow passageway that separated two of the buildings. She turned into it, emerging some yards later into a small but sunny courtyard.

At its rear, she saw a three-story red-brick building with a high central dormer set into a shingled roof. The front facade was symmetrical with three windows on each of the top two stories and one on either side of a handsome central entrance. By contrast, an extension protruding from the right-hand aspect had a slanting roof and irregular construction. Cora set her course for the wide marble stairs that rose between two stately lamp posts. A brass plaque announced that the Female Medical College of Pennsylvania lay within.

The dark-paneled interior was warm and still. A corridor lay ahead with a stairway on the left. She peeked into the rooms on either side. One appeared to be a lecture room. Three tiers of risers faced a sizable table behind which stood a large chalkboard, its black face now blank. The other room seemed to be the school's museum. Numerous colorful charts and posters depicting human anatomy hung on the walls, while tables displaying an abundance of specimen jars and *papier-mache* models took up nearly every foot of floor space. A glass materia medica cabinet occupied the full length of the back wall. Exhibited within were a collection of the substances used as medicinal agents as well as an extensive series of colored drawings illustrative of medical botany.

She was curious as to what might lie in the rooms to the rear, but she pulled her attention back to the purpose for her visit and approached the stairway. A sign on the wall read *Dean's Office* and pointed upward.

She found Dean Fussell sitting behind his desk in a front corner office that was light and airy due to the windows on either wall. He was a man of average build with a head of longish wavy hair, a full beard, and bushy eyebrows. His countenance was formidable in repose but warm and welcoming as he rose to greet her.

He came around the desk and took her hand in his. "Cora Fielding. Here at last."

"I understand from Miss Pickering that I am the last to arrive."

"Thee is. And we are most delighted to have thee here."

Cora tried to squelch any facial reaction to his odd turns of phrase. She had been forewarned that many of the professors and students at the school espoused the Quaker religion, their speech being somewhat different from that to which she was accustomed.

He waved her into a chair facing the desk and took his own seat again. "How was thy journey? Uneventful, I pray."

"Arduous but pleasant for the most part," she replied, thinking to herself: except for the part where I was nearly killed.

"And how does thee find thy lodgings?"

"Highly satisfactory. I thank you for the recommendation as I would have been lost without it."

"It is our pleasure to make certain our students are safe and secure as they pursue their studies. Which brings me to the business at hand."

He began with an eloquent summary of the five months ahead, his obvious enthusiasm for his role as teacher coming in stark contrast to the terse, often vulgar discourse to which she had been subjected by Dr. Cole in California. He spoke of the everyday lectures she would hear on the subjects of chemistry and toxicology, anatomy and histology, materia medica and general therapeutics, physiology and hygiene, principles and practice of medicine, principles and practice of surgery, and obstetrics and the diseases of women and children. Beyond the lectures, she would enjoy hands-on practical experience in every aspect of medicine. She would study physiological specimens under a microscope. She would take part in dissections, both inanimate on the school's *papier-mache* mannequin and on actual deceased bodies. She would receive instruction in pharmacy and observe the actual treatment of patients in the biweekly clinical demonstrations, most of which would take place in the school's clinic but on occasion in a patient's home, especially in obstetric cases. In short, she would, if diligent, emerge from her first year of study well on her way to becoming a physician.

He moved on to more practical matters. She paid her lecture fees, which at ten dollars each were a third what they had been in California, and received her tickets for each course, these on paper of a light-blue hue. In addition, she paid a demonstrator fee of five dollars. He gave her a list of acceptable textbooks and directions as to where she might purchase them. Finally, he produced the leather-bound matriculation book and opened it to a page that already contained information on the other ten students who would make up their class.

He said, "If thee will be so kind..." and turned it around to face her, offering a steel pen and pot of ink for her use.

There were columns across both pages with "Tenth Session" written atop the left-hand page and "Commencing Oct. 19th 1859" on the right. The first column, entitled Matriculants, already contained ten names, the last one being Gwendolyn Pickering. Cora wrote her name on the line below and moved on to the next column, entitled Post Office. She wrote Sacramento there and again in the next column which asked for County. She wrote California in the State column and quickly scanned upward to see that, as Gwen had already told her, her fellow students hailed from a remarkable variety of states.

The first column on the facing page asked Course Year and had already been marked "1st," as had all the lines above except for one, which read "2nd." This notation was opposite the name Frances Davis, and she assumed this was the single student Gwen had mentioned who would complete her degree that year. The next column was blank and she left it so as it asked whether the student had completed courses elsewhere. The one next to it was headed Preceptor, and she was proud to write *R. J. Fielding, M.D.*, her heart swelling with gratitude over his loving persistence in finding her this place to complete her studies. The column after that already contained the number eleven, indicating she was the eleventh student to enroll. The final column headed "No of Tickets – Remarks" had also been filled in with the word All. She gave a sigh of satisfaction and handed the book and pen back to Dean Fussell.

"Excellent," he said, rising to take her hand. "My correspondence with thy father was filled with high praise for thy love of medicine and determination to become a physician. We are most pleased to welcome thee to the Female Medical College of Pennsylvania."

Cora felt light as air as she made her way downstairs, into the courtyard, and along the narrow passageway to Arch Street. Following Dean Fussell's directions, she turned east, passing the Arch

Street Theater with its colonnaded entrance and sculptures perched high above on its pediment. She continued on, marveling at the many shops and the hustle and bustle of a large city. She crossed Sixth Street, paved with cobblestone like the other streets she had seen, and continued another block past a cemetery to Fifth Street, where she turned south. Another large cemetery occupied nearly the entire eastern half of the block. Beyond it were several more brick buildings, after which came a narrow street named Commerce. She turned east until she came to the even narrower Paradise Alley. Just beyond it lay a mammoth, seven-story building whose lofty sign read: *J.B. Lippincott & Co. Publishers and Booksellers.*

She entered a dark-paneled lobby and saw the doorway to the retail bookstore. She inhaled the distinctive odor of leather, cloth, ink and glue that never failed to excite her as to the endless possibilities of the written word. She approached the counter and waited for a small, lean man of middle age to emerge from the rear. She returned his greeting and handed him the printed list of books given her by Dean Fussell.

Each of the seven lecturers had indicated two or three acceptable textbooks for the student to purchase. After considerable deliberation, Cora chose *Lectures and the Theory and Practice of Physic* by William Stokes and John Bell, *A Manual of Elementary Chemistry* by George Fownes, *The Physiological Anatomy and Physiology of Man* by R. B. Todd and W. Bowman, *Quain's Elements of Anatomy* by Jones Quain and E. A. Sharpey, *A Theoretical and Practical Treatise of Midwifery, Including the Diseases of Pregnancy and Parturition* by Pierre Cazeaux, *The Principles and Practices of Modern Surgery* by Robert Druitt, and *General Therapeutics and Materia Medica Vol 1* by Robley Dunglison. After paying and receiving her change, the clerk bound the books into two bundles with strong twine and wished her good day.

The books were heavy, and she was tempted to spend ten cents on the streetcar. In the end, she decided the expense was an extravagance in which she did not need to indulge and set out again on foot. By the time she arrived back at her boardinghouse, it was but a few minutes before two, and she was in danger of missing her dinner.

She climbed to her room and met Gwen just coming out of hers.

"There you are," said her new friend. A sly grin. "And just in time. Our good keeper lives for the opportunity to catch one of us 'young ones' in a failing."

The dinner bell sounded before she had even finished speaking, and Cora said, "Then this is one circumstance in which I am happy to disappoint."

Gwen eyed her packages. "I see you have been to Lippincott's. I will be interested to see what you have chosen. After dinner, of course."

"Just let me drop these, and we can go down together."

She entered her room and laid the bundles on the floor beside the low shelf where the books she had brought from home already resided. She noticed a letter addressed to her lying on the tabletop. Curious but aware that the impatient Mrs. Gallagher was awaiting their arrival at the table, she picked it up and stuffed it in her pocket before hurrying with Gwen to the stairway.

Her growing friendship with Gwen was one of the greatest surprises of the past three days. She had experienced few close connections with people of her own sex, and most of those had been with those who were older than she. Now, for the first time, she was enjoying the easy back and forth of two young ladies of similar ambition and goals. Gwen was warm, funny, unassuming—all attributes she admired and wished she herself possessed. Given that neither had much to do in these days before their classes began, they had spent much of their time exploring their immediate environs.

They had visited Independence Square, marveling at the flanking parklands and stately approach to the magnificent red-brick State House with its distinctive bell and clock tower. They viewed the carefully-preserved room where the Declaration of Independence was signed and climbed the tower to avail themselves of the spectacular views of the city and its surrounds. They strolled through Washington and Franklin Squares, where the trees were in their autumn glory. Graceful gravel paths, artfully-placed shrubs, splashing fountains and an abundance of wildlife charmed them into sitting and whiling away the time until the chilly air drove them on. They ventured along the streets of commerce, especially intrigued by the covered arcade down the center of Market Street where myriad stalls sold a variety of goods. They gazed at the displays in the windows of the white-marble retail stores along Chestnut Street where the rich purchased their jewelry and designer hats, clothes and furs. All the while they had learned more about each other and enjoyed a camaraderie that brought pleasure to both.

Now they descended to the fourth floor and took the back staircase to the third floor. The top level of a three-story addition extended to their right. Two washrooms, one for each gender, lay down this hallway. Each contained several screened-off tubs where one might take a bath. It was a novelty to live in a place where running water came through wooden pipes originating at the Fairmount Water Works. Even more astounding was the fact that one of the pipes ran alongside the brick hot-air flue that rose from the cellar furnace, producing automatic warm water. Cora had not yet taken advantage of this amenity, but she looked forward to doing so soon.

They continued down and turned into the dining room, which occupied the second level of the addition where food was brought up from the kitchen below for each meal. The majority of the boarders were already seated at the long table, steaming bowls of potatoes and vegetables and platters of meat and bread at the ready. Cora and Gwen took their seats under the stern glare of Mrs. Gallagher, who sat at the head of the table while her husband took his place at the foot. It was obvious whose iron fist ruled this household.

The keeper made a show of folding her hands and bowing her head before intoning a too-lengthy prayer. After she had finished, a few stragglers tiptoed in, doing their best not to draw attention to themselves. While they seated themselves and the food began its circuit around the table, Cora took the letter from her pocket, broke the seal, and held it in her lap to read:

My dear Cora,

I pray you are acclimating to life in Philadelphia and feeling well settled in your new lodgings. I am pleased to report that my brother and his household have been every bit as welcoming and gracious to me as I had hoped. I feel reassured that my final years will be as happy as possible without my beloved Hiram by my side.

I wish to express once again my gratitude for the companionship and assistance you offered me on the journey from California. My brother echoes my feelings and wishes to meet you and your brother in person to thank you. At the same time, I am eager to extend my acquaintance with a young lady whose companionship I enjoyed to a degree I have seldom before experienced.

Will you give us the pleasure of your company for dinner this coming Sunday afternoon at two o'clock p.m.? If you are unable to accommodate us, please send word by return post. Otherwise, my nephew Peter will call for you at a quarter before the hour.

Your friend,

Emmeline Norton

Cora felt a flush of delight bloom on her cheeks, whether at the prospect of seeing her friend again or of being escorted there by Mr. Peter Ware she could not say.

Gwen nudged her, her eyes moving from Cora's face to the letter, then back again. "What is it? You look as if a gold nugget the size of New York just dropped in your lap."

Cora's blush deepened. "It is nothing. Just an invitation."

"Mm-m. If you think that will satisfy me, you can think again." She waggled her eyebrows and continued in a fake French accent, "Madame Gwendolyn *will* know all, or she will call down the curse of the disobliging upon you."

Cora laughed. "All right. But later."

She glanced up and saw Mrs. Gallagher's frown. Sobering, she reached for the bowl of green beans being passed to her by the gentleman to her left, helped herself, and passed it on.

Chapter Fourteen

Cora glanced at her watch, an act she had been performing every few minutes from the moment she entered the boardinghouse parlor over half an hour before. The stubborn large hand had finally moved to the position of one forty-one. He should arrive any moment now.

The parlor was a large, high-ceilinged room where autumn sunshine streamed through the front bay window. A fire burned in the fireplace, and the various chairs, settees and divans were occupied by boarders waiting for the two o'clock dinner bell. Cora was beginning to know their names and found them to be a diverse but friendly lot, although she and Gwen had quite naturally gravitated toward their fellow students, who were seated even now in proximity.

Mary Reynolds, a stocky farm girl from Wisconsin, was telling a story about a recalcitrant cow, her round pink face alive with humor. Blonde, blue-eyed Jane Payne, who was from Ohio, was watching her with the little frown of concentration that seemed to appear whenever someone engaged her attention. Gwen wore her usual sweet smile in anticipation of the story's ending. Only Frances Davis remained unmoved. She was a tall, slender woman from New York who had a long, thin, serious face and an attitude of superiority that raised Cora's hackles.

As for Cora herself, she was smiling and pretending to listen, but her mind was on Peter Ware, whose arrival she awaited with some impatience.

She had seen him that very morning, although he had not seen her in return. She had gone with Gwen to nearby St. John's Lutheran Church for Sunday services. Her friend was from a small Illinois river town where the German influence was strong and the teachings of Martin Luther sacrosanct. She never missed a Sunday's worship service unless she was physically unable to attend, and Cora had accepted her invitation out of curiosity.

The church was a federal-style red-brick building enclosed by a wrought-iron fence attached to twin stone pillars. There were intricate stained-glass windows above and to either side of the handsome front portal. The interior was like no other church Cora had ever visited. The elevated pulpit, communion table and reading desk were in the center of the long east wall faced by rows and rows of pews that looked to accommodate over a thousand people. An ornate crown-like sounding board hovered above the pulpit. A chain rose from its peak to the top of the chancel arch, where hung a large gilded sculpture of an eagle poised for flight, its talons clutching a gold orb.

Cora found herself enjoying the service, which leaned heavily on Luther's message of grace through faith rather than works. Afterward, as they were exiting, she saw Mr. Ware through an opening in the crowd. She thought at first to push her way through to him but decided in the end it would be unseemly. Better to see what transpired when he called for her that afternoon.

Now she looked through the bay window and saw a light buggy pull up in front of the house. Peter Ware secured the reins, stepped down to the street, and came toward the house. The bell rang within moments.

It seemed to take Mrs. Gallagher forever to come from the quarters she shared with her husband at the rear of the house and answer the bell. Moments later, the keeper came in and whispered into Cora's ear as if she were telling a great secret, "Gentleman'd be askin' for ya."

Cora feigned nonchalance, but Gwen flashed her a glance and a wink. Try as she might, she had been unable to keep a tone of indifference as she told her friend about the invitation, and Gwen had immediately picked up on her interest in the intriguing Mr. Ware. Cora ignored her now and carried her cloak and bonnet out into the entry hall.

He took her hand and bowed over it. "I am delighted to see you again, Miss Fielding."

She murmured something inane, feeling her color rise under his frank gaze. His strong features were every bit as noteworthy as they had been the first time she had seen him, but she did not find them off-putting. Quite the opposite.

He helped her with her cloak and settled his hat on his head while she put on her bonnet and gloves. He tucked her hand in the crook of his arm and said, "Shall we?"

He handed her up into the buggy, which was a much smaller conveyance than the carriage in which she and the others had ridden from the ferry. He climbed up beside her, took up the reins, and flicked the handsome chestnut horse forward. They continued along Seventh Street to Market then turned east.

"I trust you had a pleasant morning," he said.

Cora had hoped she would have a chance to bring up his presence at church that morning without her having to admit she had seen him. She could hardly believe he had given her the opening with his first utterance.

"Indeed." she said. "My friend and I went to Sunday services at St. John's Lutheran Church."

He turned to her, eyebrows on the fly. "Is that so? I was there myself."

Feigned amazement. "I had no idea. I would have expected you to worship at your father's church."

"An understandable assumption. But as it happens, he and I have differing opinions on matters of religion. That aside, the building where I live and conduct business is on Race Street but two doors east of St. John's. So it is a convenience."

In keeping with her forthright style despite its being perhaps bolder than was seemly, she said, "What is your business, if I may ask?"

"I am an attorney, Miss Fielding. You may or may not regard that as a respectable profession, but my family, alas, believes I have joined forces with the devil himself."

She glanced at him, unsure whether or not he was being serious. The gleam in his eye and twitch of his lips gave her the answer.

"Well, sir, I have had little experience with lawyers. Certainly none that would lead me to form any such negative opinion."

Grinning now, "That comes as a great relief to me. And may you never have reason to change your mind."

They had turned south onto Sixth Street and were now passing along the western edge of Independence Square. He gestured and said,

"Have you had an opportunity to visit our State House?"

"My friend Miss Pickering and I came two days ago. It is most impressive."

"Hm-m. I had thought I might have the privilege of showing it to you."

The comment stunned her into momentary silence. He had wanted to escort her to see one of the city's landmarks? At last she managed, "How kind of you."

"Well, no matter. There is much of interest to see in Philadelphia. I must give it some thought."

Cora could think of nothing more to say, so she turned her head to watch Washington Square pass by on their right, vowing that if he asked her whether she had been there as well, she would feign ignorance. However, he said no more as they continued on.

They were leaving the central business district with its retail stores, hotels, theaters and assembly halls. A number of frame buildings now supplanted the almost universal brick and stone of the central city. The faces of the pedestrians were of a darker hue, their clothing less grand. Just past Lombard Street, they passed a large boxlike brick-and-stone building enclosed by a wrought-iron fence where a sizable gathering of Negoes milled about. They were all dressed in their Sunday best, and she assumed the place was a house of worship.

As if knowing her thoughts, Mr. Ware said, "That is the Mother Bethel African-American Methodist Episcopal Church. The first of its kind in the nation, although it now has many sister churches. In fact, its origin is an interesting story, especially to me, a practitioner of the law."

Encouraging him, "I always enjoy a good story."

"Then allow me to elaborate. The church's founder, a man by the name of Richard Allen, was a slave in the last century who was converted to Christianity by an itinerant Methodist preacher. He eventually purchased his freedom and followed the preaching circuit for some years before settling in Philadelphia. He preached at and became a member of St. George's Methodist Church, which has its own claim to history as the first church of that denomination in the country. Allen was so successful that the free black portion of the congregation swelled, causing consternation among the white members. The attendant acrimony and distrust resulted in an edict forcing the black worshipers to sit at the rear of the church rather than among their fellow white Christians. Allen and his supporters refused to accept such a state of affairs. They walked out and never returned."

"As well they should!" Cora exclaimed.

Her outburst seemed to amuse him. He continued, "The next part is where my particular interest lies. Allen and his fellow Methodists decided they needed to form their own congregation. To that end, Allen purchased the piece of property we just passed. Meanwhile, the leaders of St. George's were threatening the splinter group with expulsion from Methodism while at the same time trying to lure them back into the fold. The two entities made a peace of sorts, but St. George's was intent on controlling what was now Mother Bethel A.M.E. Church. At the time of incorporation, one of the St. George elders had tricked Allen into signing over the land so that it would revert to the Methodist conference rather than to the members of Bethel were the congregation ever to disband. The struggle for control continued for nearly twenty years, culminating when the elders at St. George's decided to put the property up for auction, in essence selling the very ground from beneath the church. Allen had no other choice but to buy back his own church."

Cora sucked in a gasp. "That is outrageous."

"Yes. As was the asking price. Over ten thousand dollars. But that is not all. St. George's was still unwilling to give up control, insisting their ministers had a right to preach at Bethel any time they wished. When Bethel refused, St. George's took their claim to court. The court ruled against them, in effect affirming that Bethel was finally free to determine its own destiny."

Cora would later wonder how he came to be so knowledgeable about an obscure black church, but for the moment, she was so mesmerized by its plight that she did not realize he had pulled the buggy to a halt and they had arrived at their destination.

They were in front of a sizable three-story red-brick residence. Mr. Ware came around to help her down. St. Paul's Methodist Episcopal Church sat next door behind a wide fenced lawn graced with numerous maturing trees. Its front path was deserted, the worship service long over. Mr. Ware offered her his arm, and they proceeded to the residence's white-marble entrance. They were shown in by a maid who took their outerwear and escorted them to the parlor.

Cora took quick note of the room's occupants, her gaze finally falling on Emmeline Norton. Her friend rose, reached for her cane, and came forward with her free arm outstretched to embrace Cora. When they drew apart, Emmeline spoke to the room at large, saying,

"This is my dear girl, Miss Cora Fielding. Cora, may I present my brother, Reverend Matthew Ware, his wife Gertrude, and their daughter Annabelle?"

Cora approached each to offer her acknowledgment. The reverend appeared to be in his mid-fifties and was tall and lean like his sister. His once-dark hair was now more white than brown. He had a high forehead, piercing blue eyes, a long gaunt face, and a full beard. His wife Gertrude appeared to be much younger than he. No more than late thirties, in Cora's estimation, which made sense when she remembered Emmeline telling her that Peter's mother died when he was but ten years old. This second wife had a soft, full figure and a fleshy face that still retained a hint of its former beauty, a beauty now evident on the face of her daughter Annabelle. The girl, who looked to be seventeen or eighteen, wore her shiny ebony hair pulled back with ringlets spilling down her back. Her maroon taffeta dress had a bell-shaped skirt circled with fringe-trimmed tiers, the bell sleeves decorated with similar tiers, and was the perfect foil to her pale creamy complexion.

When the amenities were complete, Cora joined Emmeline on a deep-blue settee while Peter Ware sat in a high-backed chair to one side of the fireplace, where an inviting fire now crackled, and his father took the opposite one.

The minister turned to her and said, "I trust my son conducted his escort duties to your satisfaction."

"It was a most pleasant journey, I assure you," she said. "The day was fine, and I was delighted to see a portion of the city as yet unknown to me. Mr. Ware's entertaining disquisition on the history of Mother Bethel Church of your own denomination made the time fly by."

Stone silence fell over the room. She saw distaste etched on the reverend's face and realized, to her horror, that she had made a gross error. But what was its nature? And how could she correct it?

The sound of the front doorbell broke into the awkward moment.

"That must be your dear brother," chirped Emmeline, her tone an obvious attempt to brighten the mood. "I was beginning to wonder whether my written directions were clear enough."

"I am sure they were most adequate," said Cora, herself desperate to repair the damage she had unwittingly wrought. "He has a remarkable sense of direction. From my earliest memory, I cannot think of a single instance in which he lost his way."

She felt Peter Ware's amused gaze. *What a stupid, insipid thing to say*, she told herself. If anything, her embarrassment deepened. Fortunately, the maid was escorting Carl into the room, and the focus thankfully shifted.

Chapter Fifteen

The moment he entered the room, Carl's eyes gravitated toward the beautiful young woman who sat near the window. He had accepted Emmeline's invitation out of obligation with no particular expectation of enjoying himself. Now he waited with a frisson of pleasure for Emmeline's introductions to come around to the girl. Finally she gestured and said,

"And this is my niece, Miss Annabelle Ware," allowing him to approach and take her hand with a bow.

"It is my great delight to meet you, Miss Ware," he said in his warmest tone.

She raised violet eyes to his, her demure smile sweet and appealing. "Thank you, Mr. Fielding. We have all been captivated by my aunt's tale of your protection during her arduous journey. As well as your tender treatment of your sister following her shocking assault."

He felt Cora's cool gaze, reminding him that the entire ugly incident had been due to him and his vitriol against her ambitions. He tried to wipe any sign of guilt from his expression and said, "I assure you, it was no more than any brother would do."

Annabelle turned to Cora, saying, "I cannot imagine how distressing such an attack must have been for you. That you were not seriously injured is a sure sign that our Lord was watching over you that day. I trust the miscreant is facing the justice he deserves."

Still watching Carl, Cora said, "I fear not. He disappeared and was not seen again. Of course, my brother has pledged to track him down." To Carl, "Have your efforts produced any results as of yet?"

Carl could have kicked her. She knew very well the chance of ever finding Randolph Carter was next to none. He had long since decided the effort was not only futile but held no interest for him. Cora's health was as good as ever, and that was an end to it. At the same time, he knew the episode had given his sister a stick with which to poke him now and again, and he supposed he did not blame her. He had, after all, been morally responsible for what she had gone through.

"Alas, no," he said. "He was traveling to New Jersey, if memory serves, so I doubt he will ever show his face in Philadelphia. However, I expect his violent tendencies will out him in the end, whether as a result of this incident or another yet to happen."

Miss Ware gave him a beguiling smile, saying, "He should consider himself lucky if he manages to live out his life without encountering a strong, righteous brother who would surely deliver revenge should their paths ever cross again."

"Do my ears deceive me?" Peter Ware injected. "Is my sweet innocent sister advocating brutality?"

The lady's cheeks took on an appealing pink tinge. "I think only of the Biblical admonition to exact an eye for an eye."

Her father cleared his throat and said, "I believe we are getting far afield from our Savior's teachings concerning the treatment of our enemies. Perhaps Mr. Fielding would care to tell us about his upcoming course of study. Medicine, I believe?"

Carl disliked the manner in which the old goat and his son had twisted an exchange of polite conversation into something requiring mild rebuke. Nonetheless, he knew the quickest way to ease the lady's discomfort was to change the subject. He launched into a banal description of the medical training on which he was about to embark. Beneath it all, he thrilled with the good fortune that had transformed a tedious journey with all of its difficulties into an invitation that allowed him to meet an enchanting being such as Annabelle Ware. His gaze returned to her as often as he judged seemly, her willowy frame, pale flawless skin, pert little nose, and sensuous mouth rendering him nearly giddy with admiration.

He could not help comparing her to Eve, the sultry, bodacious hussy with whom he had been spending his time over the past evenings. He had met her the first night he accompanied his new friends to the Blue Bell Tavern, a noisy, energetic, smoke-filled place where girls in scant attire circulated among the customers. His companions were already known there, and a swarm of girls immediately gathered around them. The men had their favorites, however. Little balding Herm snaked his arm around a large-bosomed floozy half a head taller than himself and pulled her down into a deep kiss. Sally, Carl assumed, the tart of whom Herm had spoken the night they met.

Beefy Joey grinned at a small but plain girl of no more than fifteen years and scooped her up as if she were a doll. "Hey, Peachy. Give Daddy a big smooch!" He proceeded to open his mouth wide and thrust a thick tongue into her mouth.

Two hoydens were tugging at Rufus, one on each arm. One was tall and dark, the other short and stout, her bosoms fairly bursting out of her low-cut bodice. Had it been up to Carl, he would have chosen the tall one, whose bearing was quite genteel despite the pock marks on her cheeks. The Southerner, however, pushed her away and grabbed a breast of the other, drawling, "Hello, darlin'. Buy you a drink?"

The other girls had drifted away, and Carl's three friends turned toward the bar with their prizes, leaving him alone and embarrassed. He was unused to this sort of crude flirtation, having always acquired sexual companionship by negotiating the terms on a business basis, and he had no idea what to do next. Then Rufus took pity. He swiveled back and said to his companion, "What about our buddy there? Looks all sad and lonely."

The chubby girl giggled and said, "The red-headed one? Got just the gal for him. She's new."

She disappeared into the crowd, emerging moments later with a girl whose hair was also red but of a brighter shade than Carl's. She was not as curvy as some of the others, but she made up for it by the way she moved, chest thrust forward, behind wiggling, head held high. She had a broad forehead, large brown eyes almost black in the tavern's lantern glow, a cute button nose surrounded by freckles, and a wide, full-lipped mouth that was smiling in a come-hither manner.

"This here's Eve," said Rufus's girl. "Like the lady in the Bible, she knows all about forbidden fruit. I 'spect if you give her a nice hard apple, she'd be happy to take a lick or two."

With that, she cackled and returned to Rufus and their journey to the bar. The girl Eve hooked her arm in Carl's and led him in the same direction, laughing up at him and saying, "So what do I call you, big guy?" With a teasing leer, "Want to be Adam to my Eve?"

He knew his face was flaming over the outrageous comments that had been bandied about. At the same time, he felt a familiar, pleasant stirring in his nether regions.

He said, "That did not turn out so well for him, did it? My name is Carl."

"You gonna be a doctor like your mates?"

"That is the plan."

"Well, then, I got lots of ailments we could explore. Later and in private. For now, how about that drink?"

From the bar, they had all moved to the gaming tables, where Carl and his friends proceeded to lose more than they won. The girls kept bringing them drinks while nursing their own so that they remained gay but sober. Carl's head told him this was exactly why the tavern hired them, but he was enjoying himself too much to care. Afterward, they all went out onto Arch Street and staggered the short distance west to Nonnaters Court, a cul-de-sac with residences of various sizes and level of upkeep on each side. The girls led them to one of the smaller buildings, Number 5. They had more drinks in the parlor then went upstairs to enjoy private time with their respective partners.

It had been the most amazing experience of Carl's life. Eve went all shy and innocent, pretending to be reluctant as he disrobed her, her lips pouting, her eyes downcast in modesty. She shielded her eyes with her hands as he took off his own clothes, gasping in fake modesty when she finally looked at him and his aroused member. She allowed him to take her hand, lead her to the bed, and push her back onto the cushions. She suffered his caresses with mock reluctance, lying still as a statue but not preventing him from the most intimate of explorations. Then suddenly she became a she-lion, taking charge and overwhelming him with the most debauched acts one could imagine. When he left her an hour later, his last two dollars on her bureau, he felt more sated than he ever had and could think of nothing except seeing her again.

The next morning, he had been sane enough, despite his roaring headache, to realize Eve's behavior was but an elaborate, calculated game designed to entrap him. But he did not care. Her combination of debauchery and innocence was addictive, and he had returned each night since, unable to stop himself.

Now he was in the presence of someone who was the polar opposite of Eve and her ilk. A person of great esteem, respect, even awe. A true lady who could take her place as a man's most prized partner in life. Who could make a refined home for him and bear his children. And it had been his good fortune to be introduced to her.

He had barely begun imagining himself wooing her when uneasiness pierced him. As a parson's daughter, Annabelle was much in the public eye. Surely a beauty such as she was being attended by scores of gentlemen. But had some lucky fellow already claimed her hand? He vowed to task Cora with finding the answer. His sister's friendship with Emmeline Norton was such that it would be most natural for her to make inquiries. But would she do so given their distant relationship as of late?

He supposed he had some wooing to do in that direction as well.

∞∞∞

Cora had been watching her brother with some amusement. Despite their recent semi-estrangement, she could read his mind as if it were laid out before her. From the moment he walked in, he had been fairly drooling over Miss Annabelle Ware, his ears a telltale crimson. As for the young lady, her eyes were darting his way more often than would be expected, and her complexion's pink tinge and the nascent smile on her lips signaled that she was enjoying his attention.

Carl sensed her scrutiny and looked her way, his soulful, pleading expression telling her all she needed to know. He wanted to pursue young Annabelle and would welcome her help in doing so. She nearly laughed out loud at his transparency. At the same time, she vowed to do what she could. She held no animus toward her brother. His opposition had not prevented her from pursuing her goals, and she wished only happiness for him. If his lack of enthusiasm for his life calling could be mitigated by finding love, then she would do all in her power to help him achieve success.

The Wares' maid came in to announce dinner, and they made their way to the dining room, a well-appointed room where the mahogany table had been laid for six. After a rather long blessing, the food appeared in order: clam soup, roast duck, peas, potato bread, and a dessert of cheesecake. As they ate, the conversation turned to family matters. Cora learned that Peter had two older brothers by the reverend's first wife, one a preacher like his father stationed in Baltimore, Maryland, the other an accountant who worked at a bank in New York City. The current Mrs. Ware had lost two babies, one before Annabelle's birth, the other afterward. She was from a distinguished Philadelphia family whose wealth had come from textiles, no surprise in that her speech and mannerisms implied a cultured upbringing.

Carl and Cora answered questions about their own family. There was great interest in their arduous pilgrimage from Indiana to California. Although both were in their teens at the time, they still remembered enough stories of peril and conquest to keep the company entertained until the meal was complete and they retired to take their coffee in the parlor.

They had barely been served when the front doorbell chimed. Moments later the maid came in and said to Reverend Ware,

"Mr. and Mrs. Charles Taylor and Miss Taylor beg to know whether they may be received."

The reverend beamed and said, "Why, most certainly." Then, as she retreated to escort the visitors in, "These are two of our most devout and generous parishioners along with their beautiful daughter. Our two families often while away a Sunday afternoon together." A sly smile. "I expect Peter will be especially pleased to greet them."

Cora had only a moment to assess Peter Ware's expression, which did not seem to be particularly gladdened by this news. If anything, his countenance was devoid of all emotion whatsoever. But perhaps her own inclinations were coloring her perception because the moment the three newcomers entered the room, he rose with a gracious smile and approached the young lady, who was introduced as Miss Mary Lee Taylor.

Cora would not have named her a beauty. Her hair was a dirty blonde color, her body straight as a stick, and her face too square with small eyes, a large nose, and practically no chin at all. Nonetheless, her delight at Peter's greeting was obvious. She hooked her arm in his and allowed him to escort her to a sofa, where he helped her down and sat beside her.

Cora struggled to contain her shock. It had not occurred to her that Mr. Ware might have a ladylove, but her eyes could not deceive her. These two were special friends at the least and lovers at the most. His gaze was not particularly amorous, in her estimation, but the young lady's feelings were plain to see.

Meanwhile, she accepted the greetings of the two parents, the father large and beer-bellied with a bushy beard and the same small eyes as his daughter, the mother stick thin and gaunt faced. They both spoke with a decided southern drawl, and it was no surprise when the conversation soon turned to the trials of the South and the distant rumblings of war over the issue of slavery. If Cora expected Reverend Ware to espouse the Christian principles of love and equality for all men, she was to be disappointed. In fact, his disdain for the Negro race could not have been more apparent, which explained why he had received her comments about Mother Bethel Church with such a sour visage.

The following hour was greatly to her distaste, and she was relieved when Mr. Ware suggested it was time for them to take their departure. Carl rose at the same time, and they said their goodbyes. Outside, Mr. Ware offered to drive Carl home, but he refused, saying, "I relish taking some exercise after such a heavy meal. I shall walk up to Tenth Street and take the streetcar home."

He reached to embrace Cora in farewell, giving her the opportunity to whisper in his ear, "You may count on me. I shall call on Emmeline soon and make inquiries."

He pulled back with a surprised expression that soon morphed into fondness. "Your studies begin before mine, Sister, but do not allow them to keep you a stranger."

He tipped his hat and strode off to the west.

Chapter Sixteen

Peter Ware took Cora's hand and helped her into the buggy. She thanked him and settled back, avoiding his eyes. He took up the reins, disengaged the brake, and clucked the horse forward toward Sixth Street.

She was at a loss, her mind still grappling with the revelation that Mr. Ware's heart was taken by another. She faulted herself for giving any credence to Emmeline's suggestion that he was somehow fascinated by her. To compound things, she had allowed his comments about showing her the sights of Philadelphia to feed that erroneous notion. Now she saw that he had spoken only out of kindness to one who was new to the city and had few other acquaintances.

Her discomfort increased with each moment of silence that passed. Never one to shy away from an unpleasant duty, she decided it was her responsibility to clear the air since she was the one whose fancy had led her astray.

"Miss Taylor seems a most affable young lady," she said in a bright tone. "Is it possible wedding bells are in your near future, Mr. Ware?"

He turned to her with a look of pure astonishment. "Wedding bells?"

Her cheeks flamed. Could she have been any clumsier if she had spent hours planning this conversation?

Struggling to redeem herself, "Well, uh, perhaps things have not progressed quite to that extent. I do apologize for my... It is just..."

She fell silent, her misery so deep she wished the earth would open up and swallow her whole. How could she have been so rude as to broach such a personal subject with a man she barely knew? She allowed the crisp air to carry her stuttering comments away, embarrassment morphing into irritation. Why should she care what he thought of her?

"Despite Miss Taylor's charms," she said in her trademark aggressive manner, "I do not much care for the slaveholding sympathies of her parents. Your father seems to be of the same mind. I must say, I was surprised to hear such sentiments expressed by a man of the cloth."

He did not rise to her bait, his voice remaining calm and reasonable. "I agree. It is one of the areas over which my father and I part ways."

"Yet you said nothing to refute their vile ideology."

"Which, had I done so, would have been pointless. I do not require my father to bless my views, nor does he mine. For the sake of family harmony, we do not discuss such things."

More cross than ever, "And what of Miss Taylor? Does she agree with her parents' point of view?"

"I have no idea. I have never asked her, nor has she volunteered her opinion. But I assume she has assimilated the culture in which she was bred. She and her parents but recently relocated here from the State of Virginia where slavery is an integral part of the economy. The thought of eradicating it brings terror to the heart of every landowner there."

"Well...well...it is wrong for one human being to own another."

"I could not agree more."

Frustrated, Cora gave it up. A righteous argument might have helped dissipate her self-disgust, but the man would simply not engage with her. She huffed into silence and said nothing more until the buggy pulled up in front of her boardinghouse.

"Now then," he said, "about that job."

It was Cora's turn to drop her jaw in surprise.

"I believe you mentioned your intent to obtain part-time employment in order to ease the financial burden on your father having two offspring in medical school."

She barely remembered her casual reference while taking her turn at telling her hosts about her upcoming studies. What she did remember, however, was Carl's amazed reaction to her statement. No surprise, of course. Her brother had never been particularly energetic when it came to making his own way in the world. The possibility that their parents might suffer undue financial strain because of him would never cross his mind. Nor would it occur to him that he might help by earning his own money in his spare time.

"Yes, I would like to find something," she answered, "but I have had no opportunity to pursue the matter as of yet."

"Then perhaps I can be of help. How would you like to work for me?"

"For you?"

"Yes. Nothing strenuous, of course. But my law practice engenders a great deal of paperwork. Court filings, letters, trial preparation, billing statements. If you were to see the current state of my office, you would agree I am woefully inadequate at keeping up with the minutia of running a business. I could use your help, say, on weekends or in the evenings. Whenever your schedule permitted."

"I—I do not know what to say."

"If I recall, your classes are to begin this coming Wednesday. If you were to come to my office tomorrow morning, we could go over the particulars. If you liked what you heard, you could begin at once. That day and a full day the next would give you a good start toward organizing the chaos of which I spoke. Then you could give me whatever hours are possible after your courses begin. What do you say?"

Work for a man about whom hours before she had entertained more romantic musings? Which in and of itself had been the source of much self-chastisement? She had never been one to swoon and dream about the opposite gender; that she had allowed herself such facile imaginings was a source of deep embarrassment. Perhaps she could purge her self-castigation by accepting his offer of a purely business relationship. And it would solve her problem of finding employment.

"All right," she said. "I believe you said your office is two doors east of the Lutheran Church."

"Yes. 507 Race Street."

"Then I shall arrive by nine o'clock tomorrow."

She gathered her skirts and stepped down from the buggy, not waiting for him to perform the gentlemanly task of helping her. If they were to be business associates, she was determined to set the proper tone from the beginning.

She turned to thank him and caught his dancing eyes and twitching mouth. He said, "Goodbye then, Miss Fielding."

He was laughing at her. Irritation caused her to swallow the conventional farewell she had intended. Instead, she gave him a curt nod, turned her back, and continued on alone to her front door.

∞∞∞∞

507 Race Street was, like so many others in the city, a narrow, three-story red-brick building flush with the sidewalk. A bronze plaque mounted opposite the brass doorbell read Peter J. Ware, Esq., Attorney-at-Law. She twisted the doorbell and waited.

A tall, skeletal young man with black hair askew and a pronounced moustache peered out at her.

"Miss Fielding?" he asked.

At her nod, he stepped aside, saying, "Mr. Ware is expecting you."

She found herself in a long dark hallway. Stairs rose to the left, no doubt leading to Mr. Ware's living quarters. The doorway to the right had an opaque glass inset on which Mr. Ware's name had again been etched in gold. The young man opened the door and waved her inside.

The small anteroom was furnished with an eye to comfort, having several stuffed chairs and a small sofa, all upholstered in dark-green velvet, arranged around a low round table. Gaslight came from a wall sconce, but the lamps on two small tables were unlit, leaving the room rather dim despite the front window. A second doorway on the back wall stood open. The moment Cora stepped inside, she saw that Mr. Ware's description of clerical disarray had not been exaggerated.

He sat in front of a large desk. Mounted at its back was a tall cupboard containing many drawers, shelves and cubbyholes, all crammed with documents. The desk itself was stacked near to collapse with books and papers, many of which had spilled onto the floor. A straight-back chair and a long auxiliary table on the wall opposite the desk were similarly burdened. A second smaller desk sat beneath a window on the back of the building. A bookcase jammed with heavy legal tomes completed the room's furnishings.

Peter Ware rose to greet her. He gestured to the man who had shown her in and said, "Please make the acquaintance of my harried scrivener, Mr. Reginald Herrick. I believe he is as delighted as I to welcome you to our merry little band since it is his work that will most benefit from your ministrations."

Cora dipped her head and exchanged greetings with the scrivener.

Mr. Ware continued, "Please sit down," even as his eyes searched in vain for a place where she might comply. At last he removed the detritus from the straight-back chair, pulled it over beside his desk, and gestured her into it. "I hope you will not be discouraged by the seeming disorder you see around you. It is not nearly as daunting as it appears at first blush. It needs only the attention of someone whose legal duties do not make constant demands otherwise."

"I confess I do not see how I can be of help. I know nothing of legal matters or of the requirements and procedures for storing—" She waved her arm about the room. "—all of this."

"You need no such technical knowledge. Only the patience to sort and categorize. Let me explain how we function here. I, of course, deal with all matters that concern the law. I meet with and advise clients, do any required research, draft all correspondence and legal documents, and go to trial in the event that is necessary. Reginald here makes fair copies of everything I produce so we have a lasting record of our dealings with each client. There has been such a rush of work of late that he barely has time to keep up with those tasks, much less to organize them for retrieval."

The scrivener gave an affirmative grunt from the small desk to which he had returned, his steel-point pen already scratching in a large leather-bound book.

The lawyer continued, "He is just now copying a letter into our current copybook. He will then record it and its location in the book's index so I can access the letter anytime I desire. The remaining documents you see about the office require a different method of storage. Once a copy has been made, it is placed by client name in a document storage box such as those."

He gestured toward a tall stack of black tin boxes.

"I shall show you how to fold and annotate each document, then how to find any other documents relating to that particular client so everything can be placed together in a tin. Perhaps you will think of a more efficient process than the one we are using now. If so, I would be delighted to consider it."

Cora swept her eyes over the considerable piles of documents. He divined her skepticism and went on, "Please do not be intimidated by what you see. I assure you that many of these documents relate to the same client. It is merely a matter of sorting them into their respective piles for storage in a tin. If you will agree to start on a trial basis, I promise to make myself available concerning any questions or uncertainties that may arise. I am prepared to compensate you fifteen cents per hour, beginning from the moment you arrived this morning. Wages are given out on the last day of the month. So what do you say? Are you willing to accept my offer?"

Cora took a moment to consider. His offered wage seemed quite generous to her. And he seemed most willing to provide time for her to learn his system. He had already told her she could make her own schedule depending on her classes. What better opportunity would she find?

"All right, Mr. Ware. I accept on the basis of the next two days being a trial period. If you find me wanting, or if I am unable to fulfill your expectations, we shall not be bound beyond the end of the workday tomorrow."

"Excellent! And one last thing. We work closely together here and find it more convenient to dispense with formalities. We shall be Peter and Reginald to you, and if you have no objection, we shall address you as Cora. In the office setting only, I might add. Would you find that to be disrespectful given our short acquaintance?"

She smiled. "Not at all. Peter, Reginald and Cora it shall be."

"Then allow me to take your cloak and clear a place on the table yonder where you can work."

Cora was amazed to find that his description of her job was quite accurate and not nearly as taxing as she had feared. In fact, she could see significant progress within the first few hours. She also decided to take it upon herself to answer the door when any visitors or clients came. It was in this function on her second morning that she opened the door to a well-dressed black man who identified himself as Mr. William Still. He had a medium-brown complexion, short-cropped hair parted on the side, and a handsome face with intelligent brown eyes that projected a depth of feeling she had seldom seen in the eyes of anyone else, black or white.

The moment he stepped inside, Peter Ware came rushing out of the office and shook his hand, saying "William! What brings you here this fine morning?"

"A rather urgent matter that cannot wait for our normal meeting."

"Then do come in. First, allow me to introduce the newest member of my staff, Miss Cora Fielding, who is to begin classes at the Female Medical College within days. She has consented to help us out here during her free time."

Mr. Still bowed and gave Cora a cordial smile. "Then I wish her success with both her studies and her task here."

Cora returned his smile and said, "Thank you, Mr. Still."

"Very good, then," said Peter. "Come on through."

He invited his guest to sit in the anteroom while he lit a nearby lamp, giving the room a cozy glow. Cora turned toward the back office, assuming the conversation to be private.

Peter said, "One moment, Cora." He crossed the room and closed the door between this room and the office where Reginald was still scratching away. Then to Mr. Still, "I have known Miss Fielding but a short time, but I have perceived in her a heart sympathetic to our cause. Would you object to her presence for our discussion?"

The gentleman cocked his head, eyes narrowed. "You understand this requires the highest secrecy?"

Cora was embarrassed by Peter's impulsive suggestion. She said, "You have no reason to trust me, Mr. Still, although I do assure you I am no tattletale. That said, I shall excuse myself so you may be assured of utter privacy."

Again she turned away only to have Peter stop her with, "Do you recall our little tiff over my father's guests and their sympathies toward slavery this past Sunday?"

She paused in mid-step.

He continued, "You castigated me rather severely for not refuting their ideology. There was a reason behind my silence, and now that we are colleagues, I wish to explain myself. Indeed, I doubt you will work for me long without my position becoming clear, so we may as well deal with the matter now.

"The truth is I am not merely empathetic toward the abolitionist movement. I am dedicated to assist it in any way possible. Mr. Still is an officer of the Philadelphia Anti-Slavery Society, the members of which are committed to the activities of the Underground Railroad, an organization whose sole purpose is helping any escaped slave achieve freedom from bondage. I am privileged to aid him in his cause. If Mr. Still is agreeable, I would prefer that you stay."

Cora stood poised to flee or stay, her eyes locked on Mr. Still's as she awaited his word. He smiled and gestured toward a place on the sofa, saying, "Please stay, Miss Fielding. Mr. Ware's good opinion of you is enough for me."

When she was settled, he reached into his coat pocket and withdrew an envelope, which he handed to Peter, saying, "This was brought to our office this morning by a clerk from the Philadelphia Public Ledger." For Cora's benefit, he explained, "One of our city's newspapers. Their lobby offers the convenience of two postboxes, one for correspondence directed to the paper and another dedicated to the U.S. Postal Service. The sender of this letter apparently placed it in the wrong box, for it was surely not intended for eyes other than the recipient, a Mr. George F. Alberti."

Cora heard Peter's sudden intake of breath. "That blackguard!" To Cora, "Alberti is a professional slave catcher who makes his living seizing people for the purpose of sending them into slavery, whether they are in fact escaped slaves or just poor souls who happen to come to his attention. Once he was even convicted of kidnaping a free-born child and giving him to a person in Maryland who claimed to be his owner. Alberti was fined and sentenced to ten years in prison, but a new governor pardoned him the following year. After his release, he went back to his vile profession forthwith. He and others like him are the bane of our cause."

He opened the envelope, muttering, "What is the fellow up to now?"

He pulled out the letter, scanned it then read aloud, "*My dear sir, I am a lady from Maryland who wishes to engage you to retrieve a slave who was spirited away from me by the Underground Railroad some while ago. I am told he has been seen in Philadelphia. If you will call on me at my boarding house at your earliest convenience, I should like to settle the necessary particulars so my property may be restored to me. I remain sincerely yours, Mrs. Wilson.*"

He folded the letter, returned it to its envelope, and read the return address in the upper left-hand corner. "The lady apparently resides at 708 Arch Street. I believe that is across from the Ashland House hotel."

"Indeed," said Mr. Still. "It occurs to me we might nip this little conspiracy in the bud were someone to undertake impersonating Alberti."

Peter grinned. "My thought precisely. Being from Maryland, said Mrs. Wilson cannot know any details of his person. Nor can she know that her letter has gone astray. If we are able to pry out the particulars she speaks of, we have every chance of snatching the poor fellow out of harm's way before she discovers her error. Shall I undertake this little subterfuge myself?"

An answering grin. "That was my hope." He rose and extended his hand. "Let me know what you discover. Then I shall take the matter in hand."

After he had left, Cora observed an almost boyish delight in Peter over his agreed-upon task. This was a side of him she had not seen. Heretofore, he had presented a rather dry, even impersonal exterior that gave little hint of the feelings beneath it. Now she saw an enthusiastic willingness to plunge into action on behalf of some unfortunate soul who was in danger of being returned into slavery. Not to mention his stated commitment to a noble cause above and beyond his exercise of the law. It seemed he was a more complex individual than she had thought, and her admiration for him grew.

They returned to the inner office, and he took his seat at his desk without further comment. Cora continued with her chores, curiosity as to how he intended to proceed nearly driving her mad.

She left at ten minutes before two to walk the four-and-a-half blocks to her boardinghouse for dinner. When she came back, he was gone. She continued with her duties, her ears stretched for any sounds of his return, but he remained absent for the remainder of the day.

As closing time drew near, her thoughts about these strange events were eclipsed by the growing realization that her classes were to begin the following day. As intrigued as she might be by the plight of those fleeing bondage and the good people helping them, she had come to the city for one purpose only: to become a physician with all the opportunities that profession offered for aiding mankind in its totality. And that purpose was about to be enjoined.

The clock finally closed on six o'clock. She donned her cloak and bonnet, bade Reginald goodnight, and let herself out, her skin tingling with anticipation as she made her way home through the gloaming.

Chapter Seventeen

October 19, 1859

Cora and her fellow students set out for the college at fifteen minutes before nine. A mutual sense of solemnity tinged with apprehension kept their conversation to a minimum. Only the indomitable Frances seemed impervious to emotion, striding along with haughty confidence etched on her severe face. Several more days' acquaintance had not improved Cora's opinion of her classmate. Fortunately, the other three were most congenial and promised to be good friends as they all moved on with their education.

The hall in which the introductory lecture was to take place was not overly spacious. Three tiers of benches occupied the open walls facing the doorway. The space adjacent to the door was taken by a mounted chalkboard on which a chart of days, times and classes had been drawn. A podium and a large rectangular table sat before it.

The students were surprised to find a group of some twenty or twenty-five ladies already assembled in the room. As they took their seats, Gwen whispered to Cora,

"I believe the lectures are open to anyone in the general public who pays the ticket price. Apparently there are many ladies who are interested in knowing more about their health and bodies even though they do not aspire to become doctors."

"Then I applaud them. Too long we females have surrendered our personal well-being into the hands of gentlemen who may not have our best interests at heart. It is time we took control of our own affairs. But why stop there? Women are every bit as capable as men, and in many areas more so. Why should we not have an equal say in the issues that affect us all?"

Gwen nudged her with a teasing smile. "Well said, my friend. If medicine does not work out for you, you could always hire on as a lecturer for the suffragettes."

Cora grinned back. "One should always provide oneself with a viable backup plan, and you have just given me mine. And a brilliant one it is since my convictions would aid me well in such a role."

Gwen chuckled but said no more, heeding the hush that had fallen over the room when a small woman dressed in black came in. She was no taller than Cora, possibly even shorter, and had a fragile appearance, refined features, and dark hair centrally parted and shot through with silver. Cora judged her to be in her middle forties at the least. She walked to the podium, stepped up onto a stool that had been placed behind it, and smiled at her audience.

"Good morning, ladies," she said. "My name is Ann Preston, Professor of Physiology and Hygiene here at the college. It is my privilege to welcome the students of the Class of 1859/1860 as well as all other interested parties. I am especially pleased to offer this Introductory Lecture of the Tenth Annual Session of the Female Medical College of Pennsylvania. Before I begin, I would ask that the students remain after the lecture is concluded in order to go over their class schedule and receive answers to any questions they may have about the upcoming term."

She paused, her calm dark eyes raking the audience, then said, "Very well, let us begin."

She laid her notes on the podium and read, "Ladies, as I meet you today and on behalf of the faculty of this institution welcome you to the course of study before you, it seems a fitting occasion to scan briefly the position and prospects of the cause in which we are engaged. While to a large portion of thinking and observing men, the medical education of women appears to be the natural result of the progress of society, there are others who still regard it as some abnormal social phenomenon; some abrupt and fantastic freak of unbridled liberty, unfitted to stand the test of time and experience."

Cora was mesmerized by what followed, beginning with a broad review of societal and educational progress that had resulted in the onward movement of women into the study and practice of medicine. Dr. Preston went on to affirm the legitimacy of these aspirations as well as the difficulty of attaining acceptance, especially given the unrelenting opposition of the medical men of Pennsylvania. In counterpoint, she applauded recent inroads as well as the success of the college's graduates as they went out to practice medicine.

Next she gave an overview of the students' current course of study and the advances in modern science that had led to the recognition that chemical and physical forces act within the body precisely as under similar circumstances they would act without it. Not one original property of matter is ever lost. Not a physical or chemical law is ever suspended for an instant. In fact, the main duty of science is to connect all disparate facts into a single order of physical laws.

"Everywhere," she said, "facts once considered as unrelated and detached are becoming arranged into connected groups illustrating some common plan, and science is discovering, one by one, the links of that grand chain of relationships which illustrates the divine unity of the plan of creation and the simplicity and sublime unchangeableness of its laws."

The words resonated within Cora like the strains of beautiful music. The students' ultimate goal went far beyond learning how to relieve the suffering of mankind. They were called to understand the very nature of creation. What greater mission could any human undertake than this?

Dr. Preston went on to discuss the various advances that had been made in procedures, treatments and surgery, all of which were resulting in greater survival and quality of life for patients. Most interesting of all, she opined that the greatest advances of all had been made in hygienic medicine, which had taken its true place as a regular branch of therapeutics so that prevention was more and more regarded as greater than cure.

Her final exhortations were ones of encouragement for the strenuous road ahead and the blessings that would eventually accrue, concluding with,

"Ladies, with you I am thankful today that it is our privilege to engage in a work so satisfying and so beneficent. As you pursue those studies which disclose order amid apparent confusion, stability in the midst of mutation, and law in every department of nature, may your own hearts be attuned to such according harmony that you will realize the presence of God to be the heavenly law of the soul! May you indeed gain the highest end of all study and all effort—that of enriching and ennobling the spiritual nature and bringing out more clearly the Divine Image there."

The spectators rose to their feet as one, their clapping hands attesting to their heartfelt appreciation for what they had heard. As the commotion subsided, those who were mere visitors gathered their belongings and made their way to the door, where Ann Preston stood greeting each one who passed through. When students alone remained, she returned to the podium.

"You will have already noticed the board behind me where the class schedule you will be following for the next five months is written. If you have not already done so, I suggest you copy it into your notebooks. Classes are one hour in length beginning at ten o'clock Monday through Saturday, at which time you will hear lectures in surgery and obstetrics as indicated. Eleven o'clock lectures will be in the subjects of obstetrics and the practice of medicine. At twelve o'clock, you will hear lectures in physiology except for Wednesday and Saturday, which will be clinic days. There you will observe actual patients, hear their history and complaints, and follow along with their treatment. The one o'clock hour will be devoted to lectures in materia medica except for clinics on Wednesday and Saturday. Classes will adjourn at two o'clock for dinner and resume two hours later on every day except for Saturday, the afternoon of which you will have to yourselves. The four o'clock lectures will focus exclusively on anatomy, including dissection of cadavers, and the five o'clock hour will be devoted to chemistry with the exception of Wednesday, which will offer another lecture on anatomical recapitulations.

"You will find it to your great advantage to take detailed notes during the lectures. Many students have familiarized themselves with Sir Isaac Pitman's system of shorthand, which they then transcribe into proper form in the evenings. It is from making and reviewing these notes that you will come to absorb what we are teaching. At the same time, you will be creating a body of material for your future reference.

"I assume you have all purchased your required textbooks, which are valuable resources as you study each discipline. In addition, you will have the opportunity to study the clinic book with its detail as to the individual treatment of patients as well as to make notes for your own records. And with that, I will open the floor to any questions you may have."

A timid hand went up. Cora saw it was her new friend Mary from Wisconsin.

Dr. Preston nodded and said, "Your name, please?"

"Mary Reynolds, ma'am."

"Thank you, Mary, but I must tell you there are no 'ma'ams' or 'sirs' in this institution. Merely students and teachers. We are all equal under the eyes of the Almighty, none more important that the other. Now, your question?"

"Well..." She hesitated, still trying to absorb what had just been said. Then, "...uh, I was wondering. The landlady who keeps the boardinghouse where some of us reside is very particular about mealtimes. She rings our dinner bell precisely at two o'clock. If we are in class until two, how will we obtain our dinner?"

Cora heard Frances mutter from close behind, "She would be the one to worry about her dinner. The cow."

Dr. Preston merely nodded. "The indomitable Fiona Gallagher. Do not be concerned. She knows she must accommodate our schedule or lose our recommendation as a place for our students to board. You will find your dinner waiting for you when you arrive home. If not, please bring the matter to my attention." Then to the room at large, "Other questions?"

None being forthcoming, she said, "Very well. You will have ten minutes to stand and stretch, perhaps take a drink of water, before your first lecture by Professor of Obstetrics Edwin Fussell begins."

∞∞∞

The last class of the day ended at six o'clock. Cora walked back to the boardinghouse with her fellow students, physically exhausted but glowing with inner energy. The day had been the most exciting of her life. She had heard lectures in anatomy, the practice of medicine, and obstetrics, this latter given by the dean himself. In addition, a variety of cases had been presented during the two clinic hours. She had found the professors to be not only knowledgeable but also enthusiastic in conveying their subject matter to the students. She had soaked it up with unabashed delight.

Now the day's classes might be over, but the study day was just beginning. She planned to use the nearly three-quarters of an hour that remained before the evening meal to advantage. She was thankful that she had mastered the essentials of shorthand years before while taking patient notes for her father. Even so, she faced several hours of meticulous transcription into the permanent tablets she had purchased for each class, and she was eager to get started.

She had no sooner stepped inside the front door, however, when Katie the maid came up to her, curtsied and said, "A fella's here to see ya, Miss Fielding. Says he's yer brother."

She went into the parlor and saw Carl sitting beside the fire. He rose to greet her, his appearance causing her instant dismay. He was normally meticulous in his dress, but tonight his clothing was disheveled. His face had an unhealthy gray tinge, causing his freckles to stand out more than ever, and the skin beneath his eyes was puffy and dark.

She stretched up to present her cheek for his kiss, saying, "You look as if you are ill. Why are you not home in bed?"

He waved the question away. "I am quite well. Perhaps I have indulged in a bit too much nightlife of late, but my friends and I have but two weeks before we must submit to our own prison of learning. We are making the best of it while we may. Now, come. Sit with me and tell me about your first day of classes."

Cora was touched that he had remembered the occasion and had come to share her excitement. However, she had barely begun to tell him of the day's events when he cut in with,

"You said you would call on your friend, Mrs. Norton. Have you had an opportunity to do so?"

Somewhat taken aback, she said, "Not yet. I saw her but three days ago."

"Yes, I know. It is just..."

A faint pink had crept into his sunken cheeks, and it took her no more than a few seconds to surmise the true reason for his visit. And it had nothing to do with her first day of classes.

She smiled. "Miss Ware. You are smitten."

"Well, I... Yes, I am much taken with the delightful lady. But I cannot see my way to approach her or her father until I am certain she is not taken by another."

"But surely there is no hurry. We shall be in the city for many months. Years, as it happens. You will be in no position to offer her any permanent favor for some time yet."

"All of that is true. But I feel compelled to make my intentions clear as soon as possible. I am able to think of little else since we met."

His apparent obsession puzzled Cora. He was a handsome young man and had always drawn the eyes of any young ladies of their acquaintance, but she had never known him to single one out for particular ardor. Why now? Perhaps it was a way of compensating for the unfamiliarity of his surroundings. A need to be anchored to another human being besides his twin. Whatever the motivation, she found it impossible to resist his pleading eyes.

"Very well. I will discover what I can as soon as I can. The problem is my lack of free time now that classes have begun. We are even to be engaged on Saturdays until the dinner hour."

"Perhaps you could invite her to tea. Say on this coming Saturday afternoon."

"My landlady is not the sort to provide tea for her tenants' guests. But I suppose I could call on Emmeline at home."

"That option has its own problems. What if Miss Ware and her mother were there and decided to join you? You could hardly make your inquiries in their presence. No, the only way to insure privacy is for the two of you to meet in a neutral setting. And to that end, I have the perfect solution."

He hitched forward, his eyes bright, almost feverish. "In exploring the immediate environs of my boardinghouse, I came upon a ladies' saloon and confectionery by the name of Parkinson's. Perhaps you could invite her there for tea."

He had thought of every contingency from the heated perspective of a lover, but certain cold realities remained.

"Does it not occur to you that it might be difficult, if not impossible for Emmeline to manage such an excursion on her own? That aside, I have another obligation on Saturday afternoon."

In a dismissive tone, "Surely nothing so important it cannot be postponed."

"To the contrary. I have secured employment with Mr. Peter Ware as an assistant of sorts in his law office. I have committed to working on Saturday afternoons unless my studies become too burdensome for me to comply."

He gave a little snort of frustration. "Not that again! Why do you insist on the need to work? Our father was most particular in assuring us he is able to support us during our schooling."

"Perhaps, but I do not expect him to provide for extraneous expenses beyond those connected to my education. Nor should you. You spoke of your nightlife. Is it right for him to subsidize such frivolity while he and Mama and Lily do without for our sakes?"

"I seriously doubt our family is in want," he scoffed, his voice strong even as his eyes slid away from hers. "As usual, your flare for the dramatic drives you to gross exaggeration. Nonetheless, I assure you that I fully intend to live within what Father provides. Now about Saturday afternoon. Surely you could leave this job of yours early enough to meet Mrs. Norton for a fashionable tea around five o'clock."

Cora felt her resistance crumbling. She admitted to herself that she would enjoy seeing her friend without the distracting presence of others. And she could hardly advocate for Carl if the lady in question and her mother were present.

"All right, I am willing to propose such a meeting. However, as I suggested earlier, I am not certain she would feel able to undertake it on her own."

"Please try, Cora."

She found herself unable to resist his soulful plea. "Very well. I shall write to her this evening."

Chapter Eighteen

Cora arrived at Peter Ware's law office a little past two-forty-five on the following Saturday afternoon. He answered her ring himself and led her into the inner room. She was surprised to find Reginald's desk unoccupied.

In answer to her query, he said, "He works only until two o'clock on Saturdays. Which will allow you to assist me with certain matters of which I prefer him not to be privy. I have such a matter for you now."

Intrigued, Cora removed her cloak and bonnet and hung them on the wall hooks provided. She turned to see he had placed a document onto the scrivener's desk.

"You may recall my adventure of last Wednesday on behalf of Mr. Still."

Cora did indeed recall it and had been hoping he would tell her how he had fared.

He continued, "I have made a record of my visit to the redoubtable Mrs. Wilson, but before sending it along to the Anti-Slavery Office, I need a true copy for my records here."

"And you do not trust Reginald with it?"

"Some months ago, sensitive information made its way into the wrong hands. As a result, the well-being of a passenger on the Underground Railroad was greatly compromised. I have no proof Reginald was the source. Even if he were, he might not have acted with intent. Nonetheless, I decided it was best for me to transcribe my own documents henceforth. Now that you are here, you can relieve me of that burden if you are agreeable."

"Of course. And I am flattered by your confidence. Which you also expressed when Mr. Still was here. But I cannot help wondering why you feel as you do. After all, you barely know me."

His eyes held hers, a half smile lifting his lips. "I know enough, Cora. If my instincts about you are wrong, then they are unreliable on other matters as well, making me a danger to the cause I serve. Now, will you sit here at Reginald's desk and begin?"

She did as he asked, dipping her head to hide the flush of pleasure his affirmation brought to her cheeks. She began to copy the document, which proved to be an amazing chronicle written in the style of a fictional story:

Mr. Ware arrived at 708 Arch Street, rang the bell, and inquired of the servant, "Is Miss Wilson from Maryland stopping at this residence?"

"She is," replied the servant.

"I wish to see her," said Mr. Ware.

The servant ushered him into the parlor. Shortly thereafter, a tall, fine-looking, well-dressed lady entered. Mr. Ware bowed and said,

"I have come in the stead of Mr. George F. Alberti, to whom you addressed a note this morning. Circumstances beyond Mr. Alberti's control prevented him from coming, so I am here to look after your interests in this matter. Now I wish you to understand at the outset that whatever transpires between us must be kept strictly confidential. Our negotiations must by no means be allowed to leak out. If they do, the darned (excuse me) abolitionists might ruin me, and we should not be able to succeed in capturing your slave for you. I am very particular on this point."

"You are perfectly right, sir, in your plan to conduct our business in this manner, for I do not want my name mixed up with it in any way."

"Very well, madam. I think we understand each other quite well. Now, please give me the name of the fugitive, his age, size, and color, and where he may be found. Also, how long he has been away and the witness who can be relied on to identify him after he is arrested."

Miss Wilson carefully communicated these important particulars while Mr. Ware penciled down every word. At the close of the interview, he assured her the matter would be attended to immediately and gave his opinion that there would be no difficulty in securing the fugitive for her.

Within minutes of concluding this interview, Mr. Ware was at the Anti-Slavery Office with all of Miss Wilson's secrets. A messenger was sent forthwith to the fugitive's place of employment, where he was found. Greatly frightened, he dropped all and followed the messenger, who led him to safety.

In the meanwhile, Mr. Ware prepared a document printed as a large poster, about three feet square and displayed in large letters, for the enlightenment and warning of all:

TO WHOM IT MAY CONCERN:

Beware of Slave-Catchers

Miss Wilson of Georgetown Cross Roads, Kent County, Maryland is now in the city in pursuit of her alleged slave man, Butler. J.M. Cummings and John Wilson of the same place are understood to be here on a similar errand. This is to caution Butler and his friends to be on their guard. Let them keep clear of the above-named individuals. Also, let them have an eye on all persons known to be friends of Dr. High of Georgetown Cross roads and Mr. D.B. Cummings, who is not of Georgetown Cross roads.

It is requested that all parties to whom a copy of this may be sent will post it in a public place and that the friends of freedom and humanity will have the facts herein contained openly read in their respective churches.

This document attracted much attention and comment, which facts were quickly conveyed to Miss Wilson at her boardinghouse. It is understood that at first, she was greatly shocked to find her name in every mouth. She then took her baggage without delay and started for

"My Maryland," ending this episode in a most propitious manner for all friends of freedom.

Cora finished the transcription and handed it to Peter. He removed a small key from his waistcoat, opened a locked document box, and laid the document on top.

He saw her curious expression and said, "These all relate to my activities on behalf of the Anti-Slavery Society. Perhaps you would like to look through them sometime."

With wide-eyed eagerness, "I would indeed. However, I must get on with my organizing duties since I must leave in another hour or so. I am meeting your aunt for tea at Parkinson's saloon for ladies."

"Are you indeed? Parkinson's is a most fashionable, delightful place. They are renowned for their flavored ice cream. I urge you to indulge."

"I doubt my budget would accommodate such an expense."

"Ah, yes. Miss Fielding the struggling student. Very well. I shall take you there myself one day. Perhaps when the weather turns warm next spring."

There it was again, a hint of some additional level to their relationship. Blushing and confused, she turned away and took up a stack of documents to be sorted and stored.

∞∞∞

Parkinson's Restaurant and Café was in an imposing three-story brick mansion set back from the sidewalk on the north side of Chestnut Street between Tenth and Eleventh Streets. An intricate wrought-iron fence enclosed grassy areas on either side of the entrance, which was reached by white marble steps. A marquee announced the establishment's name in bold block letters, while magnificent arched windows soared above. The one-story ladies' saloon and confectionery sat along its east wall and had its own grand entrance graced by carved masonry and Grecian-style stone columns.

Cora entered and was immediately awestruck by the sumptuous interior with its great arched windows, beautiful frescoes, and rich velvet hangings and furnishings. At first she did not see Emmeline among the ladies and occasional gentleman who stood about in conversation or took their leisure at the tables. She craned her neck this way and that until she saw an upraised hand waving from a table beneath the middle window. As she approached, her friend struggled to her feet and reached out her arms in greeting.

A silver tea service with delicate cups and saucers and a plate of pastries already sat on the table. Cora was embarrassed that she had suggested such a grandiose place for their meeting. She could not even imagine the expense of the fare already placed before them.

"I am late, I fear," she said as she sat down.

"Not at all, my dear," said Emmeline. "I came early in order to find an agreeable setting for our little *tete-a-tete*."

"How did you manage to get here on your own?"

A mischievous smile. "I am not so incapable as you seem to judge me. I simply hired my brother's yard man to bring me in the carriage."

"But the expense..." She waved her hand over the table's delicacies. "...and this..."

"How else is a well-to-do widow to spend her inheritance besides enjoying the company of a dear friend? Now tell me, how are you getting on now that your courses have begun?"

Cora's excitement and satisfaction poured forth in a torrent of words. Emmeline beamed at her, every bit as happy as Cora herself that she was now launched on her longed-for future.

"It is, and will be, a challenge," Cora concluded, "if only from the standpoint of time. Between attending classes, transcribing my notes, studying my textbooks, and putting in as many hours as possible at my position, the days fly by much more quickly than I would like."

Lifted eyebrows. "Your position?"

"Yes. Your nephew has given me part-time employment in his law office."

"Has he indeed?"

"My role is a small clerical one, but I find the subject matter most interesting. He has a large heart for helping people. Especially those who are most disadvantaged."

"I am happy to hear it. We see little of him, and from what I have overheard of my brother and sister-in-law's conversations, it is not hard to understand why. Oh, the boy is as respectful of his parents as a son should be, but the three do not mix well. I gather they disagree on everything from politics to religion. My brother is beyond understanding how he could have raised a person of such contrary attitudes."

Cora had always been grateful to have parents who encouraged her independent thinking. They had often been surprised by her rebellion against the attitudes of the society at large, but they had never condemned her nor expected her to change.

She said, "But tell me about you. We had no opportunity for private conversation last Sunday, and I am eager to know whether you find your new arrangement to be congenial."

A deep sigh. "They are kind and welcoming, and I am most grateful for no longer being on my own. But our years apart have taken us in opposite directions. My sojourn in California has left me with more liberal attitudes toward most of the things my brother holds dear. For instance, he is quite ardent over the issue of slavery, which I find abhorrent. Thus far I have been able to hold my tongue, but it may get more difficult with time. We shall see."

Cora was tempted to mention her own interest in the abolitionist movement and her delight that Peter Ware held the same beliefs, but she restrained herself. Peter had confided his involvement with the Anti-Slavery Society under the belief that she would keep close counsel on the matter. To discuss it in even a general way might result in inadvertent information slipping out. It was time to move on to her main purpose for their meeting.

"You have said nothing of your niece, Miss Annabelle. Is she a more compatible companion than her parents?"

"Well, she is certainly a sweet girl. Perhaps a little empty-headed for my taste, but quite solicitous toward me."

"I must confess to having an added motive for seeing you today. Perhaps you noticed how taken my brother Carl was with Miss Ware. He has tasked me with discovering whether she has a beau, and if not, whether you think she might be open to his interest in her."

"Well, well. Like many old ladies, I do fancy the role of matchmaker. In fact, I am able to share with you that the family's reaction to your brother was most favorable. Annabelle in particular had quite a lot to say about his appearance and his prospects. I understand she does entertain suitors from time to time, most of them out of my brother's congregation, but I do not believe any of them are serious contenders for her hand. I would say that she, and her father, would welcome any words Carl might have to say."

Cora was happy for her brother and eager to share this news with him. As she made her way home after saying goodbye to Emmeline, she thought about how and when she might tell him. As it happened, there was no need, because as she was turning onto Seventh Street from Ebert, she saw him sitting on the front steps of her boardinghouse.

He rose to meet her on the sidewalk, saying, "Well?"

She laughed. "You truly are besotted. But you can rest assured. Miss Ware has no serious suitor at the moment, and according to Emmeline, she found you quite pleasing last Sunday. I would say you are free to pursue her."

She had seldom seen such joy on her brother's face. "That is excellent news. Thank you, Cora. You are a gem."

He kissed her cheek and went away whistling with a carefree stride. Cora looked after him, hoping she had done the right thing.

Chapter Nineteen

Carl wakened to a heavy thumping on the door to his room. He groaned and fumbled for the gold watch his parents had given him for his eighteenth birthday. It read nine o'clock. The pounding continued, and he heard a faint shout, "What in damnation...?" telling him his fellow students did not appreciate the racket. He stumbled to the door and pulled it open. Franny, the stout, plain girl who cleaned the rooms, stood outside, her face rigid with determination.

"You said nine, sir."

He rubbed his face and nodded. "Yes, thank you, Franny."

She curtsied and hurried away. He closed the door and groaned again, palms pressed against his pounding temples. He had known it would be difficult to get up, which was why he had paid the girl a dime to make sure he was out of bed with enough time to dress properly. He would miss breakfast, but he doubted he could keep food down anyway.

He had gone to the Blue Bell the night before resolved to have a few drinks, play a few hands of cards, and go home. Instead, like a helpless lamb to the slaughter, he had gambled away all the money in his pockets, drunk himself into a near stupor, and partaken of Eve's wiles and delights. Not even his fascination with Annabelle Ware could keep him from indulging in the debauchery of the past weeks.

He had mixed feelings about his new friends. On the one hand, they knew how to have a good time, and their companionship had made these days of waiting a time of pure hedonism. On the other, he knew that he was flirting with disgrace by following their example. He told himself his excesses were just a reaction to the first true freedom he had ever experienced. Deep down, he knew he was fooling no one but himself. He was under the spell of a compelling, primordial urge he had not known existed, and if he did not take control of it, the consequences could be catastrophic.

The greatest danger was financial. If his father were to find out about his activities, he knew the registered letters containing funds for his expenses would stop coming. Even if that did not happen, the stipends would disappear in short order if he continued to spend as he had during the previous week and a half. Then he would be forced to either ask his father for more or find some other way to augment his resources.

His sour thoughts turned to Cora. She had taken it upon herself to find employment even though she had no real need. Contrasting her righteous decision with his profligate spending put him in the poorest light possible. If Miss Ware's father were to find out, Carl would have no hope of courting her.

All of which only strengthened his resolve to change.

A glance at his watch told him time was short. He pulled on his trousers and made a trip to the privy out back. He poured cold water into the washbasin and splashed his face and neck before shaving. He put on his best shirt, waistcoat, cravat and coat, took up his gloves and settled his hat on his head.

On his way downstairs, he met Rufus Mills returning from the privy. His friend looked as haggard and drawn as Carl felt, although his final glance in the mirror had reassured him his outward appearance was quite respectable.

"Whoa, there, Red," said Mills, using the nickname with which he had christened Carl early on. "Where the devil are you going dressed like that?"

"To church, you degenerate. Where else on a Sunday morning?"

"Church! Since when did you get religion?"

Grinning, "Since I met a certain Miss Annabelle Ware, whose father is a Methodist preacher."

A low whistle. "Is she that delicious?"

"Absolutely."

"This I have to see. Hold on and—"

"Not on your life! This is one discovery I am not inclined to share."

He tipped his hat and continued down the stairs.

It was cold and cloudy outside with a smell of rain in the air. He thought about returning for his umbrella, but a glance at his watch told him he could not take the time. He picked up his pace, praying the rain would hold off long enough for him to reach his destination. Afterward, he cared not what happened as he would either have been successful in his quest or his hopes would have been dashed. Whichever prevailed, drenched or dry, his mood would already have been dictated.

He walked to the corner of Tenth and Market and waited for the streetcar, which came within just a few minutes. He got off eleven blocks later at Catherine Street. The skies had spit rain a few times during the journey, but for now it was dry. He hurried east the four and a half blocks to St. Paul's Methodist Episcopal Church. A steady stream of people was heading up the long walkway and into the church. Among them he recognized the Taylor family: the portly old man whose belly strained against his waistcoat, his scarecrow-like wife, and their ferret-faced daughter. What Peter Ware saw in her was beyond understanding.

He kept well back and arrived beneath the church portico just as the rain began in earnest. He had a plan, and that plan did not include seeing Miss Ware—or anyone else he might know— just yet. A stairway rose to the right just inside the narthex. He took it and emerged onto a balcony that stretched the width of the church. There were a few other worshipers seated there, but most had remained downstairs. He took a seat in the front row and searched the boxes below for any sign of her. Finding none, he began to worry that for some reason she would not be attending today. It was, after all, but five minutes until the service was to begin.

An anxious few minutes later, he saw her mother appear walking down the middle aisle. Annabelle was close behind. The attire of both women was grand by any standard. They were taking their time, nodding this way and that to the congregants on either side of the aisle. For a fleeting moment, he recognized the ostentation of their entrance, which was designed to draw as much attention to themselves as possible. Then he focused on the young lady's regal bearing—the slim straight back, the glossy black ringlets cascading from beneath her bonnet—and nearly swooned with admiration. When they turned into their box at the very front of the church, he caught a glimpse of her profile with its small straight nose and ripe lips, lips he felt a keen desire to kiss.

His daydreams carried him through the service, which he found to be exceedingly boring. The subject of the reverend's sermon was the need to be content with the circumstances of one's life and the moral obligation to do one's best at every task, whether in a position of servitude or of power. He thought the message was aimed at anyone who might hold views sympathetic to the abolitionist movement, but he could not be sure. Nor did he care. He had no interest in politics. The Reverend Ware could espouse overthrowing the government itself for all it mattered to him. As Annabelle's father, he was simply the gateway to Carl's deepest wishes.

He was unsure why he had developed such strong feelings for the girl after but one meeting. He suspected it had to do with the stark contrast between her and Eve, for whom certain feelings had also evolved. There was the purely carnal side of things, of course, but beyond that, he found Eve's sometimes childlike qualities endearing. They would lie in bed and talk much longer than he was sure her trade encouraged. She told him about her sad upbringing in the Blockley Almshouse, first in the indigent section when the family was destitute and had nowhere else to turn, then in the orphan asylum after her father died and her mother moved to the insane asylum for women. In light of these facts, Carl understood why she had taken up her current profession. How else could a poorly-educated girl with neither family nor friends make enough money to survive on her own? He felt wretched about it, especially when she insisted on knowing every detail of his own story, which resounded with privilege and respectability. He had to use the full force of his willpower to rein in his instinctive desire to promise her deliverance into a comfortable life with him.

It was an impossible situation, of course, and the sooner he set his heart on someone who could actually be his wife, the better. It was nothing short of miraculous that such a person had been put in his way so soon.

The final hymn was sung and people began to depart, taking an infuriatingly long time as they hailed one another and stood about in desultory conversational groups. At last the nave was clear and he was the only person remaining in the balcony. He descended and stood behind the last parishioners waiting to greet Reverend Ware. When they had moved on, he stepped forward, bowed, and offered his hand.

"Carl Fielding, Reverend," he said. "My sister and I had the privilege of taking a delicious dinner with you and your family last Sunday."

The minister accepted Carl's hand, his keen eyes sweeping him from head to foot. "Of course. I am delighted to see you here at worship. I was not aware you are a follower of Wesley."

"But I have been such from earliest childhood. You may recall my sister and I speaking of our journey to California when we were young. We did so in the company of our good friends the Reverend Walter Jamison and his family. We were members of his church for many years."

He did not mention that he himself had given up going to church as soon as he reached maturity, much to his mother's disgust.

"Well, then, we are pleased to welcome you among us."

His tone had a finality to it, but Carl was not ready for the conversation to end.

He felt his color rise and his ears tingle as he said, "Thank you, but I wondered whether I might have a private word with you."

Raised eyebrows. "Certainly. Is it a matter of faith?"

"Uh, no. It concerns your daughter."

"My—" His eyes widened with understanding. "I see. Perhaps you would care to join me in my study at the manse next door. We can be more comfortable there." He turned to the church warden, who stood a respectful distance behind them in the shadows of the narthex. "You may lock up, George."

The man snatched off his cap and bowed. "Very good, Reverend. God's blessings on your day."

He handed the churchman a large umbrella, which he raised and held so it sheltered both him and Carl as they walked out into the rainy morning. When they entered the house, the maid rushed forward to relieve them of the umbrella and their hats and gloves. Carl followed the reverend past the open doorway to the parlor, where he saw Annabelle sitting by the fire with her sewing. She looked up and met his eyes, her expression changing from astonishment to pleased curiosity. He flashed a quick smile and continued on.

Reverend Ware's study was behind the parlor and bore all the accouterments one might expect of a religious scholar. Rows of heavy tomes on wall-to-ceiling bookcases, a large Bible laid out on a pedestal lectern, a brass cross on the wall behind his massive desk. He invited Carl to sit in a chair facing the desk and took his place behind it.

"Now then," he said, "how may I help you?"

Again Carl felt his face flush. He clenched his fists for courage and said, "Even though I have had the pleasure of your daughter's company on only one occasion, I was struck not only by her beauty but by her remarkable depth of character and charm. Based on that experience, I am ardent in my wish to know her further. Therefore, I am hopeful of obtaining your permission to call on her."

"I see." He steepled his hands beneath his chin and sharpened his gaze. "And the intent of such contact would be?"

"Purely honorable, I assure you. I merely ask for the opportunity for us to spend time together. Should she develop the same level of feelings toward me as I already have for her, my ultimate goal would be a lasting union blessed by you and by God."

"Well." A long pause. "Have you spoken to her about this?"

"No, sir. Should you agree to my request, I would certainly ask her whether or not she would welcome my advances. I have no desire to impose myself on a lady who does not find me agreeable in such a context."

He nodded. "A most upright plan. I confess that your approach pleases me. My daughter is dear to my heart, and I would never commit her to a man whom she found unworthy."

"I would expect nothing less. As you know, I am just beginning my education in medicine, after which I must establish myself in practice. I would not be in a position to ask for her hand for at least three or four years to come. But I am a patient man. Knowing she returned my feelings would carry me for as long as was necessary."

He regarded Carl with pursed lips for some moments. Then, "Medicine is a most respectable profession, one that would allow you to support a wife and family in comfort. Given all that has been said, I am comfortable in agreeing to your request." He stood and came around the desk to shake Carl's hand. "Now if you will wait here, I shall send her in to you. The issue might as well be resolved forthwith."

Carl stood waiting, his heart hammering in his chest, sweat pouring down his sides. Would she agree?

She came in, her violet eyes cast down in maidenly modesty. She said, "You wish to see me, Mr. Fielding?"

He crossed over and took her hands in his. "I do, indeed. Has your father apprized you of my purpose in coming today?"

"Only in the most general terms."

"Then, please." He released one hand and lifted her chin with a forefinger. "I would like to see your beautiful eyes as I make my plea."

She gazed up at him with an expression he interpreted as both shy and hopeful.

"My very dear Miss Ware, although we barely know one another, I am already captivated by your beauty and what I perceive to be a most noble character. As you know, I am just entering my chosen profession and will be unable to think of the future until I am established in the world a number of years hence. However, it is my dearest wish in the meantime to call upon you with the goal of establishing myself as your most ardent suitor. Your father has given his permission for me to do so. Now all I need is affirmation from you that you would not find such advances repugnant."

Her sweet smile told him her answer before she had uttered a sound. "I am open to your request, Mr. Fielding. You may call on me as you wish."

He raised her hands to his lips and gave each a gentle kiss. "You have made me the happiest man alive. May I call on you tomorrow afternoon? Perhaps the weather will have improved and we can take a stroll."

"I shall look forward to it, Mr. Fielding."

Chapter Twenty

The days shortened as autumn bled into winter. Cora was so busy, so challenged, so uplifted she barely noticed. She found her studies exciting, expanding on what she had learned from her father's old textbooks and her observations at his clinic. If pressed to identify her favorite subjects, she would have mentioned physiology, which presented the latest scientific research to explain how the human body functions. Another favorite would have been anatomy, which included her academic classes as well as the visual and tactile explorations of cadaver dissection. Truth be told, however, everything she learned—surgical procedures, the mysteries of the female reproductive system, pharmacology, chemistry, the practical applications found in the bi-weekly clinics—stimulated her enough that her chronic lack of sleep failed to weigh her down.

In addition to her studies, she found great stimulation in her Saturday afternoon hours at Peter Ware's law office. She became familiar with various legal terms such as testamentary, litigation, plaintiff and defendant, partition, turpitude, and writ. An odd form of the latter, writ of *habeas corpus*, was of particular interest. Literally translated as "produce the body," it was used to challenge the legality of holding a fugitive slave against his or her will. In addition, she read Peter's clandestine documents concerning his Underground Railroad activities. He always took the time to answer her questions, leading her to a working knowledge of current law concerning slavery.

She learned about Pennsylvania's 1847 Personal Liberty Law, which provided sanctions for purchasing or removing free blacks with the intention of reducing them to slaves. It prohibited state officials from accepting jurisdiction over cases arising under the federal Fugitive Slave Act of 1793, and it provided penalties for claimants seizing slaves in a violent, tumultuous, and unreasonable manner. Most important of all, it repealed the privilege of slave holders traveling through the state with their human property. In effect, it freed any slave brought by his or her owner into the state the moment they set foot on Pennsylvania soil.

Within three years, however, this law and others like it had been superseded by the federal Fugitive Slave Act of 1850. This law provided for the seizure of blacks without any due process whatsoever, thus placing even free blacks at risk of capture based on nothing more substantial than an accusation. Cora was glad to hear that this odious law was generally ignored within Pennsylvania except by a few hard-nosed judges whom the abolitionists learned to avoid in any court proceeding. Perhaps compassion and justice were not dead despite the obscene pall she believed slavery cast on her beloved country.

Her growing zeal for the abolitionist cause gave her much in common with Peter, and their resulting comity was a source of great satisfaction. At the same time, she had difficulty separating their deeper friendship from her undeniable attraction to him as a man. Beyond the magnetic physical pull she felt in his presence, she had always envisioned herself falling in love with someone who valued her for her intellect and her determination to make her own mark in the world. Peter certainly seemed to be such a man. Yet she knew he would never be hers. He and Miss Mary Lee Taylor might not have a formal commitment, a fact Peter had already made clear, but the evidence that they were attached was too clear to be denied.

It was, she admitted, a strange connection in that the young lady's zeal was plain for all to see but Peter's was less apparent. Even given his general cool though affable demeanor, it seemed to her that he would exhibit at least some fervor toward someone with whom he seemed to spend so much time. A case in point had occurred on a recent Sunday morning.

Cora had fallen into the habit of attending St. John's Lutheran Church with Gwen, and they often saw Peter there. He always made a point of greeting them and exchanging pleasantries, prompting Gwen to tease Cora with the fiction that he was sweet on her. Then came the morning they saw him there with Miss Taylor. Even though the sight pierced Cora's heart, she was determined to disabuse Gwen of any notion that he thought of her in any regard other than as an employee and friend. She dragged her friend in their direction.

Peter tipped his hat and said, "Good morning, ladies." Then to his companion, "You no doubt remember meeting Miss Fielding at my father's house."

Mary Lee cast none-too-friendly eyes on Cora, curtsied and said, "Miss Fielding."

Her gaze turned to Gwen as Peter said, "And this is her classmate, Miss Pickering, whom I had the pleasure of meeting several weeks ago. Miss Pickering, allow me to introduce Miss Mary Lee Taylor, a family friend of many years."

Gwen smiled and extended a gloved hand, ignoring the sour look that had descended on Miss Taylor's face over Peter's rather bland introduction. She obviously would have preferred to be placed in some other category than "old family friend."

Cora said, "I am surprised to see you here, Miss Taylor. I understood your family to worship at St. Paul's with Reverend Ware as your pastor."

"Well, of course he is my pastor. However, Mr. Ware has spoken so highly of this place I decided to try it for myself." A little upward, ingratiating glance at Peter. "He has been gracious enough to escort me."

"As he surely would," Cora commented in a wry tone no doubt lost on the young lady.

A few inane comments later, they said their goodbyes and started for home. Cora could not help a triumphant glance at her friend, to which Gwen responded,

"I saw no particular regard in your Mr. Ware's face as he looked at her. If that is the most ardor he can muster toward someone he is supposedly courting, then I think you are well rid of him."

"I never had him, Gwen. For some perhaps unfathomable reason, he is attracted to her, and that is an end to it."

Her certainty was reinforced on the Saturday afternoon before Thanksgiving when Miss Taylor appeared at Peter's law office door. Cora answered the bell as she was wont to do when she was working there.

It would have been difficult to tell which of them was the more surprised.

"Miss Fielding!" the guest exclaimed. "I did not expect to see you here."

"Then Mr. Ware must not have told you he has employed me to work for him a few hours every week."

"Indeed he has not! Well, my goodness, this is extraordinary."

"Not really. I am in need of part-time employment, and he is in need of some clerical help. The arrangement has been beneficial to us both." Then, because Peter had made no mention of an engagement with her, "Is he expecting you this afternoon?"

She pulled herself up, her face a dismissive mask. "No, but I am certain he will welcome my message, which I deliver on behalf of my parents."

"Then please come in."

Cora was accustomed to leaving visitors in the vestibule while she informed Peter of their arrival, but Mary Lee followed her into the inner office, stepped around her and said,

"There you are, Mr. Ware. I hope you will forgive this interruption, but I was in the neighborhood and decided to come in person. I have an invitation to convey."

Peter stood up from his desk, saying, "You are always welcome here, Miss Taylor. Would you care to sit down?"

"No, no, I do not wish to disturb your important work. I merely carry my parents' wish that you join us for Thanksgiving dinner on this coming Thursday. Your father, mother, aunt and sister will be there as well as Miss Fielding's brother. He and your sister have been much together of late, and I gather that Cupid's arrows have found both their hearts."

Peter's quick glance in Cora's direction telegraphed his embarrassment that the invitation had been offered in her presence but did not include her as well. For her part, Cora would not have accepted even if asked. The thought of watching Miss Taylor flaunt her connection to Peter for an entire afternoon held no appeal whatsoever. On the other hand, she was happy for Carl and could say quite sincerely,

"I am delighted to hear that my brother will have such a pleasant way in which to spend the holiday. I shall be otherwise occupied myself and had worried that he might feel abandoned by his only family in the city."

She, of course, had no such plans, but she wanted to signal to Peter that he was free to accept the invitation without any slight attending to her. As he did so, she turned her back on them and returned to her chair, where she had been organizing the past week's documents and storing them where they belonged. She did her best to block out their parting words and did not so much as raise her eyes when Peter returned from seeing his visitor out.

The incident remained with her afterward, leaving an unwelcome pall of dejection. She believed that a person's happiness depended on a proper balance between success and failure.

Disappointment could be borne without undue grief as long as other aspects of one's life offered fulfillment. In her case, she had finally met a man with whom she could envision a future, but she now knew he was unavailable to her. That realization might have been crushing had she not been assured of attaining her overarching goal of becoming a physician.

For Carl, it would be the opposite. He might not be as ardent as Cora in his pursuit of medicine, but romantic success would give him ample reason for joy and contentment. She could only hope he understood this blessing and would take care not to make foolish mistakes that might put it all at risk.

∞∞∞

Thanksgiving Day dawned cold and gray, the low heavy clouds spitting snow. Carl welcomed the bracing air, feeling it sweep away the last vestiges of corruption from the prior night. He and his friends had curtailed their merriment somewhat over the past two-and-a-half weeks after their medical classes began. With Wednesday being the eve of a holiday, however, they had caroused at the Bluebell and ended up, as usual, drunk and broke. He gave himself credit for not having lain with Eve, although in order not to embarrass her, he had paid the usual fee and used their time together to indulge in quiet conversation. It had cost him not to relieve his physical urges, and he had felt none the better for it this morning, but his conscience was clear as he prepared his heart to be in his love's sweet presence.

He considered it a great honor that he had been invited to share the holiday with her family and their close friends, the Taylors. It also suggested he was already being regarded as a member of the family. All he had to do now was continue to present an acceptable demeanor and take care to treat her in such a way that she would have no doubts about him and his love.

He boarded the horse-drawn railway car at the corner of Tenth and Market and rode it west across the Schuylkill River into the much more sparsely populated area known as West Philadelphia. He continued to the end of the line on Forty-First Street and walked south toward the place known as Hamilton Village. The difference between his current surroundings and those of the city could not have been starker. The streets were wide and tree-lined with wooden sidewalks. Any business establishments were tidy and well-situated among stately private homes. Even the less affluent houses had front porches and fenced-in green space on all sides. He vowed that one day when he was a practicing physician he would own one of these fine homes where he and Annabelle could raise their family in serenity and wholesome respectability.

The Taylor house sat at the south end of a block containing five large houses that appeared similar in color, exterior form and window placement but differed in several significant architectural details. As he walked past, he noticed that two were cleverly-disguised twins with separate entrances for each side. The Taylor house, however, was clearly a single-family dwelling, two and a half stories high with a wide front porch and side bay window. He saw the Ware family carriage parked before the central walkway with Peter Ware's buggy right behind it. His heart began to thud with anticipation.

A plump, middle-aged woman in a gray uniform opened the door to his ring.

He introduced himself and said. "I believe I am expected."

"Yes, sir. Come in while I announce you."

He handed her his hat, umbrella and overcoat, which she hung on the walnut coat tree provided. Then she disappeared into a room to the left, only to return and beckon him forward.

They were already assembled, and he realized with some embarrassment that he was late. He greeted each in turn, noting with satisfaction the gleam in Miss Ware's eyes as he bowed over her hand. He took the vacant place beside her, leaving as little space between them as he dared, and entered into the ongoing exchange of small talk until dinner was announced some few minutes later.

Reverend Ware was invited to offer a prayer of thanksgiving, which was rather long and an apparent extension of the sermon he had delivered that morning. A traditional Thanksgiving meal of turkey and ham, stuffing and potatoes, both mashed and sweet, cranberries and coleslaw, oysters and stewed prunes, and, of course, various fruit pies for dessert arrived via two additional servants. The table conversation flowed easily. Carl answered several polite questions about his courses, but he was more interested in listening to see what he could learn about the others.

The Taylors, it seemed, had relocated to Philadelphia from Virginia but a few months before. Mr. Taylor was engaged in the printing business and owned an establishment on the corner of Fourth and Chestnut Streets. His daughter Mary Lee offered glowing compliments concerning the various pamphlets, treatises and advertisements produced therein, her eyes seldom leaving the face of poor Peter Ware, who suffered her batting eyes and flirtatious manner with commendable aplomb. Why he would court the silly girl was beyond Carl's understanding, but who could fathom the whims of a man of such new acquaintance?

When an obscene amount of food had been ingested, Charles Taylor invited the gentlemen to join him in his study for cigars while the ladies enjoyed their coffee.

Miss Taylor giggled and said, "Hurry back. I have directed Lucy to set up the table for us four young people to play a game of euchre." Then, as Carl and the other men rose from the table, "Oh, and Mr. Ware, be sure to ask Father to show you his latest pamphlet on the Scriptural basis of slavery as written by your esteemed father. It is ever so erudite. And the new posters as well, which are masterpieces in and of themselves."

Carl dismissed the foolish girl's insipid prattle and followed his host out of the dining room.

Chapter Twenty-One

Cora's Thanksgiving was a somewhat joyless holiday. Mrs. Gallagher had provided a more substantial dinner than usual with several concessions to tradition, including a delicious cranberry tart. Cora and her fellow students had huddled in the parlor for some post-dinner conversation, but all had soon retired to their rooms to take advantage of a free day to study. Cora was reading her assignment on parturition, her lantern having been lit some time before against the failing late-afternoon light, when she heard a knock on her door.

Katie bobbed a curtsy and said, "Gentleman to see ya, Miss Fielding."

Pleased at the interruption, Cora said, "I shall be down directly."

She felt certain it was Carl come to tell her about his day, but even a visit from her brother offered a diversion from her studies.

She was astonished to enter the parlor and find Peter Ware standing by the bay window. He came to her with a warm smile, saying, "I have come to wish you a Happy Thanksgiving and invite you to take some fresh air with me."

Her startled expression caused him to add, "Unless you are otherwise engaged?"

"Why...why, no, I am simply studying and would welcome a break."

"Then shall we?"

"Allow me to fetch my outerwear. I shan't be long."

"Excellent."

She hurried upstairs and gathered her cloak, gloves and bonnet. She paused to check her reflection in the mirror, dismayed by the heightened color in her cheeks that gave away too much of her inner turmoil. She could do nothing about it, however. She tucked a few stray fiery locks behind her ear and turned to the door.

Peter offered his arm as they descended to the sidewalk. Light snow had fallen intermittently throughout the day, but the temperature, although wintery enough, was such that little evidence of it remained. He guided her north along Seventh Street, saying,

"I trust you had a pleasant holiday. Had it been my choice, I would have included you in Miss Taylor's dinner invitation."

"There would have been no reason for her to do so. I have no connection to her family. You, however..." She let the sentence die away with a small shrug.

"Nonetheless, it was rude of her to handle the invitation in the way she did. As for myself, I can report the afternoon to have been most rewarding."

Cora was glad he could not see her blanch, then color. Why was he here if his afternoon with his ladylove had been so fulfilling?

As if reading her mind, "And I was eager to share it with you, which is why I have come."

"Surely your affairs of the heart are not my business, Mr. Ware. I hardly think—"

"Affairs of the heart? You are quite mistaken, my dear Cora. I have no such feelings for Miss Taylor. I simply use her infatuation with me to further my own interests. Perhaps you will find that despicable. But I think you will forgive me my tactics when you hear what I have discovered today."

Confusion battled with disbelief as Cora tried to absorb what he had just said. Had she been so completely wrong in her assessment of his situation? She waited for him to continue.

They had covered two-and-a-half blocks and were crossing Race Street to Franklin Square, a tree-studded open space that was now barren of the greenery with which it was surely adorned in balmier months. A narrow gap in the ironwork fence gave access to pathways that meandered in an intricate geometric pattern toward the central marble fountain, now winter silent.

After some minutes, Peter went on, "In order for you to understand, I must first give you some background information. Charles Taylor was born and raised on a tobacco plantation in eastern Virginia. His older brother inherited the family farm, which left Charles in search of his own profession. He bought into a printing business in Fredericksburg and was successful enough that he was able to sell it at a nice profit last year. In deciding where to relocate, he relied on his firm belief in the system of slavery and his abhorrence of those who attempt to impede it, which led him to choose Philadelphia as his new home.

"Our fair city is known to runaway slaves as one of the most attractive destinations because it is the closest major metropolis to be found in a free state. We also have a long tradition of abolitionist sentiment and activity. Since this is where the runaways are most likely to come, Mr. Taylor concluded that a printer who specializes in pro-slavery propaganda and has close ties to a number of slave catchers could make a tidy sum as a middleman. He advertises for runaways and passes along any resultant information to the bounty hunters for a percent of their reward. His reputation has spread to all the northernmost areas of the South, and his business here thrives."

"What a contemptible man!" said Cora. "Profiting from the destruction of those poor souls' hopes and dreams. I should find myself hard put to be civil to him should our paths ever cross again."

"That is one possible response to this unfortunate situation. I have chosen another. I have made it a point to ingratiate myself to this family so that I might discover the particulars of any fugitives they are seeking and disrupt their plans. In conjunction with Mr. Still's organization, of course."

"You are a spy!"

"If you will. So far, we have been able to warn dozens of fugitives to hide themselves until they are able to move on to Canada or wherever they choose to go. We have not lost a single one back into slavery."

"As in the incident you had me transcribe several weeks ago. The matter of Miss Wilson from Maryland."

"Indeed."

"And how does Miss Taylor fit into this scheme?"

A shrug. "Merely as another tool. She holds a vastly elevated opinion of her father and cannot help herself from gushing on about his activities. She loves to show off his advertisements, oblivious to the use to which I put this information." He looked down at her with a wry smile. "So how do you judge me? Have I played with the lady's affections in a totally dishonorable manner?"

"Some might say so. As for me, I applaud the result despite the questionable means. Who could fault you for helping the enslaved to gain the freedom all Americans are promised in our constitution?"

"Many, I fear. Nonetheless, I am not surprised to find that you are not among them. Which validates the faith I have put in you. And brings me to the details of this afternoon. We dined, as you know, at the Taylor residence. Afterward, Mr. Taylor invited the gentlemen into his study for cigars. There were a number of fliers and advertisements lying about, and I made it a point to memorize the details therein. After leaving, I went directly to Mr. Still's home to pass the information along, and I trust his people are taking action even as we speak. I doubt the hunters will find any of their prey by the time tomorrow morning comes."

She flashed a delighted smile. "That knowledge brings me great pleasure! I do thank you for taking the time and effort to share it with me."

"It was my pleasure to do so. I have few friends outside the movement, and the burden of knowledge I carry around in my heart is often nearly overwhelming. I am most fortunate to have you in my life, my dear Cora."

There it was again, a second use of the salutation *my dear Cora*. She wanted to think it connoted a growing warmth of feeling toward her, yet his demeanor otherwise was nothing more than that of a close friend. Nonetheless, she was heartened to have learned that her fears about him and Miss Taylor were baseless, and with that she would have to be content.

As the days went by, Cora's heart and mind were filled with the noble work Peter Ware and his compatriots were doing. That it would be so quickly compromised did not even enter her head.

She was working as usual on a rainy Saturday, the tenth of December, when the bell rang and she opened the door to Emmeline Norton. The two women had met at Parkinson's several more times but always according to prior arrangement. Finding her friend at the law office door leaning heavily on her cane was astonishing.

"Emmeline!" Then, surprise yielding to concern, "Do come in out of the weather."

The older lady collapsed her umbrella and maneuvered inside. "I have news for my nephew. Is he here?"

"I am indeed, Aunt," said Peter as he came out into the hallway. He kissed her cheek. "I am most delighted to see you."

"I fear you will not be so pleased when you hear what I have to report."

Noting her grave manner, "So ominous as that? Please, come into the sitting room."

Assuming it was a family matter, Cora said, "I shall excuse myself so you may talk in private."

"No, no," said Emmeline. "I think you should hear this since you are also involved in Peter's abolitionist activities."

The comment startled Cora. She had been very careful not to mention Peter's involvement with the Anti-Slavery Society out of deference to his desire for total secrecy. She had certainly made her own views on the matter clear in her conversations with her friend, but she had never betrayed Peter's trust. Now she looked at him in dismay lest he think otherwise of her. However, Emmeline was quick to clear the air by saying,

"Oh, I know you have never breathed a word to me about this. But it has been easy for me to infer certain things from our conversations as well as from observing and listening to my dear nephew. What I learned today simply proved my suspicions."

"Then please tell me," said Peter, gesturing that Cora should sit and hear what his aunt had to say.

"You will recall your father's odious friend, Mr. Taylor. He came to the house this morning in a rage. He accuses you of being an abolitionist agent who has taken advantage of his friendship to extract information and pass it along to members of the Anti-Slavery Office."

Peter shrugged. "I do not deny it. What gave me away?"

"Apparently various advertisements were passed around among the gentlemen on Thanksgiving Day. Subsequent attempts to find the fugitives were unsuccessful despite having good intelligence as to their whereabouts, and Mr. Taylor became convinced someone there had betrayed him. Since this had been happening frequently of late, he pressed his daughter Mary Lee about her relationship with you, and she tearfully admitted to having been free to share the contents of prior advertisements with you. He had you followed, and you were seen visiting the Anti-Slavery Office and having sidewalk conversations with some of their associates."

"It is a pity, but I knew it could not go on indefinitely."

"He has forbidden his daughter from seeing you, I am sorry to say since you seem to have formed an attachment to her."

"Do not be sorry on that account, Aunt. My association with Miss Taylor was purely for the sake of gaining information, and I would rather have her father put an end to it than be required to disappoint her at some time in the future."

"In that case, it is certainly best. However, other relationships are at risk because of this. Your father was livid on learning of your activities, which he judges to be disloyal to your family. He declared you henceforth unwelcome in his home."

Cora gave a little gasp of dismay. The thought of being banished from one's family was devastating.

"But your dear stepmother intervened," Emmeline went on. "She rose in righteous indignation and declared that if he took such a stance, she herself would leave and never set foot there again. She was passionate about the bonds of family being sacrosanct. And with Christmas but a few weeks away, she vowed she would not participate in any celebration whatsoever unless both of the Ware children were by her side."

"I am astounded. How did Father take it?"

"He backed down. You will be expected for Christmas dinner along with Carl and Cora, whose invitations will be forthcoming. But my concern is for your important work. Will this damage your cause?"

"Not at all. I shall continue as I have been doing for the past few years, assisting with legal matters and making myself available for any work for which I am deemed competent."

"I am happy to hear it. But I am curious as to how you became involved in these activities in the first place. You certainly did not come by your sentiments from your father."

"No. I had a legal mentor who counseled me and set me on the right path, an attorney by the name of William S. Pierce. He was a great friend to the victims of slavery. In fact, he was one of the lawyers who participated in the famous Jane Johnson case."

Reading their lost expressions, he added, "It is a case of which you would be unaware since you lived far from here in 1855 when it was the talk of the Northeast. Jane was the slave of a certain Colonel John Wheeler of North Carolina who had just been posted as the United States Minister to Nicaragua. He arrived in the city in transit to New York City where he was to sail for South America, bringing Jane and her two sons with him. Although he knew the dangers of bringing her to a free state, he was confident he could keep a close eye on her and prevent any attempt she might make to leave him. She, however, had a mighty yearning for freedom. She made her desires known to some free blacks, who quickly notified the Anti-Slavery Office. Mr. Still and an associate found her aboard the Camden Ferry moments before it was to sail across the Delaware into New Jersey. The odious Colonel Wheeler sat alongside her but she nonetheless bravely declared her wishes to be free. Several freedmen who were ship's porters restrained the colonel while Mr. Still and his companion removed her and her sons and whisked them into hiding. Mr. Still, his associate, and the free blacks who had aided them faced various legal proceedings as a result of their intervention, but all except two of the freedmen were eventually acquitted. The two who were convicted spent but a week in jail for their efforts. So the incident ended well, thanks in large part to my mentor Mr. Pierce and his fellow lawyer, Mr. Birney."

Emmeline clasped her hands before her breast. "That is the most uplifting story I have ever heard. Bless you, Peter, for helping to continue this great cause. You may be certain that if I hear anything more that should be brought to the attention of your Mr. Still, I shall do so without hesitation."

"Even if it were to jeopardize your position in my father's house?"

"Of course. How could I remain there if it meant compromising my conscience?"

He rose and went to her, drawing her up into an embrace. "How privileged I am to know you at last, dear Aunt. You are a true giant of rectitude."

She blushed. "Nonsense. Any true Christian would do the same. Now I really must let you get on with your work."

She reached for her umbrella, kissed Cora goodbye and hobbled to the door.

Chapter Twenty-Two

Carl read the letter again, his face flaming with shame even though he was shut in his room where no one could witness his embarrassment.

My dear son,

This is one of the most difficult letters I have ever had the misfortune to write. I am, as you may guess, responding to your latest plea for additional funds.

I confess to being baffled by your inability to live on the monthly stipend I agreed to provide. I attributed your earlier requests to the natural expenses that might occur during the major resettling you have undergone. However, you are now well started in your studies, and I can only conclude that this new request indicates an extravagance of living I cannot continue to finance. The enclosed banknote is the last such supplement you can expect to receive.

I am not a wealthy man, as you surely know, but our Lord has blessed me with adequate income for our family to live in comfort while still providing for your and Cora's higher education. Your younger sister Lily will be requiring the same assistance within a few years, and I must begin making provision for that eventuality.

I hope I will not offend you by noting that your sister Cora manages quite well on her stipend. She even tells me she is supplementing her income with part-time employment. I suggest you either curtail your excesses or follow her example and find private means of supporting them.

With love from,

Your devoted father

Carl crushed the five-dollar note in his fist. Five dollars! Barely a week's board and room. How was that to carry him until the beginning of January? And how was he to purchase the fine Christmas gift he had intended for Annabelle? The humiliation of arriving empty-handed for Christmas dinner sent shivers through his body.

The reference to his righteous sister set his blood boiling. *Cora manages quite well on her stipend.* Well, of course she does. Cora the perfect in whose shadow he has hovered his entire life. That she warned him of this possibility only fueled his anger. It was all well and good for her to deny herself any pleasures. After all, she had never exhibited an inclination for having fun. Nor did she seem to take much interest in the opposite gender. From his perspective, she was devoid of all normal sexual inclinations. She was content to take all the satisfaction her soul required from the realization of her medical dreams.

A knock on the door roused him from his brooding. Before he could acknowledge it, the door flew open and Rufus Mills barged in.

"What in goda'mighty's heaven are you doing in here alone, Red? Get your arse in gear. We have some mayhem to wreak."

"You fellows will have to go without me this time. The old man has cut me off, and I only have a fiver to get me through the month."

Mills laughed and said, "Is that all? Hold on."

He disappeared for a short time then returned with Herm Dietrich and Joey Robinson in tow. They crowded into the room, and Rufus closed the door.

"You think our benighted parents pay for all our fun? Tell him, Dietrich."

The little man said, "What you are about to hear must go no further than this room. Do we have your oath on that?"

Bewildered, Carl said, "Of course."

"All right, then. We have a little business going on the side, and we are willing to bring you in provided you are willing to share in the work."

Carl's heart stuttered with hope. "Goes without saying. Tell me more."

"Joey got himself into a sure thing last year. See, Penn and Franklin and even that school for bitches all require cadavers for anatomy dissection. Trouble is, Old Blockley and the executioner cannot meet demand, so the schools are willing to pay for bodies, no questions asked. We have a cohort who keeps an eye on funerals, tips us off when there is a likely prospect, and brokers the bodies with the schools. He takes his share. Even so, at thirty dollars per and demand being what it is, we each make a tidy income every month. Enough to keep us in booze and girls."

Carl was sickened at the same time as he was intrigued. "You actually go to a cemetery and dig up the bodies?"

"Where else? And I warn you, it is hard work."

Carl licked his dry lips. "I have never been afraid of hard work."

"We go out in the wee hours and return at dawn. Then we are off to class. Not a schedule for the faint of heart."

"How often?"

"A couple times a week on average. Sometimes we process two or three each trip."

Rufus Mills said, "Enough jawing. You want in or not, Red?"

Carl thought back to his father's humiliating letter. That the old man would be appalled at such an enterprise only made it more attractive to him.

"Absolutely. When do I start?"

∞∞∞∞

The more Cora learned from her classes, the more she realized that the pace at which modern science was advancing required a revolution in the way one viewed life itself. Rather than assuming that seemingly unrelated facts existed at random, it was becoming clear that they were all connected in one way or another into groups that, taken together, illuminated some overarching, purposeful plan.

In her opening lecture, Ann Preston had been bold to proclaim
that this grand chain of relationships illustrates the Divine unity of
creation and the simplicity and unchangeableness of its laws. The
same theme had been interwoven into many of the lectures given by
the other professors. Initially, Cora had taken these references with
a grain of cynicism given that most, if not all of the staff members
belonged to the Quaker faith. However, the more she plumbed the
mysteries of the human body, the clearer it became that all of these
disparate systems functioned to the benefit of the organism as a
whole. Could such perfection have occurred by chance? She could
not believe so. As a result, she found her own faith rekindled as she
listened to the gospel proclamations from the pulpit of St. John's
Lutheran Church.

At the same time, she felt a vague embarrassment on behalf of
her father, many of whose medical practices and beliefs were already
obsolete. What would he think if she were to challenge him with her
newfound knowledge? Thankfully, that would never happen given
the distance between them, a thought that shocked her when she
realized it was a tacit acknowledgment that she would not return to
California when her studies were complete.

What role Peter Ware played in that unconscious decision she
could not say. He continued to treat her with kindness and respect
as the days wound down toward Christmas, and she found herself
in a quandary as to what sort of Christmas gift she should buy for
him. The invitation to Christmas dinner had come as promised,
and she had already purchased a pair of dove-gray kid gloves for
Emmeline, a lace handkerchief for Mrs. Ware, and a bar of scented
soap for Annabelle. She had decided to visit the tobacconist's and
buy whatever caught her eye for the Reverend Ware. But were cigars
or a pouch of tobacco appropriate for Peter, who seldom smoked?
Would a silk cravat be too personal? Or a pen stand or inkwell too
indifferent? In the end, she chose a copy of the newly-published *On*

Liberty by John Stuart Mills, a philosophical essay expounding on the struggle between authority as it is vested in the state and personal freedom.

The holiday itself fell on a Sunday. Cora went to church as usual with Gwen, then returned home to gather her wrapped packages and wait for Peter to come for her, an arrangement that had seemed more practical than personal when he suggested it. Now, however, she found herself aflutter as Mrs. Gallagher admitted and announced him.

She took his arm, and they went out into what was an unusually balmy Christmas Day. They spoke easily as the buggy rolled along, and she could not help comparing this with the first time he had escorted her to the Ware house. Then he had been a virtual stranger, her nascent feelings for him based on nothing more than a reaction to his intense masculinity. Now the two were, at the least, good friends, and her regard for him had grown with every encounter. She still thought him handsome, but his prime attraction was no longer physical but a response to his high moral principles and steadfast loyalty to a cause larger than his own advancement.

When they pulled up in front of the manse, he secured the reins and turned to her. "Before we go in, I have something for you."

He reached into his pocket and withdrew a small square box wrapped in pink paper. He handed it to her, saying, "Merry Christmas, my dear Cora."

Flustered by his continued use of an endearment, she took a deep breath to calm herself and removed the wrapping. She lifted the lid to find a small shell cameo brooch inside. Her eyes flew to his. He was smiling and wearing an intense, inscrutable expression.

"Do you like it?"

"Why...why, of course I do. It is beautiful. But surely it is too much."

"Not from my perspective. You have become far more valuable to me and my work than the pittance I pay you suggests. Accept it as a small token of my appreciation and gratitude."

"Well, I... " Her heart was pounding so hard and loud she thought he must surely hear it. She would have plenty of time later to dissect his words and attempt to plumb them for additional meaning. Now she could only take them at face value: his regard for her centered on her work and nothing more. "...I am most grateful. May I wear it now?"

"Please do. Here, allow me to assist you."

He took the brooch from its box and attached it to her neckline where the points of her lace collar came together, his fingers grazing her throat and sending heat waves to her very core.

"There. It suits you."

Awash in unnamed emotion, "Well, I, uh, I have something for you as well."

She reached into the satchel containing the gifts she had brought and pulled out the book.

He unwrapped it and greeted the title with a wide grin. "How clever of you. I have heard of this treatise and have been eager to read it. I do believe you know me as well as I know myself."

Such a statement on top of his gift of the cameo came close to overwhelming Cora. At a loss for words, she was grateful when he laid the book aside and continued with, "But I must postpone that pleasure for a later time. We should go in. They may be waiting on us."

Cora nodded and waited for him to come around and help her down.

She had wondered over the past days how Peter's parents would receive them given the controversy over his abolitionist activities. In the event, everyone except Reverend Ware himself was gracious and filled with holiday spirit. Even he seemed mellower than either of them had expected, and Cora breathed a sigh of relief that there would be no uncomfortable scenes to mar the day.

Carl was already at Annabelle's side, having seemingly established himself as a fixture within the family. She was happy for him, although he continued to have a peaked look about him, and she hoped he was not allowing his predilection for merriment to compromise his health and future.

They settled in the parlor, which was festive with pine boughs, holly and mistletoe but no Christmas tree, causing Cora to think back to her own family's tree with some nostalgia. After a period of bland small talk, the maid appeared to announce that dinner was ready. As they moved into the dining room, Emmeline sidled next to Cora and whispered,

"I must talk to you privately. I shall find a way after dinner, so please follow my lead."

Cora burned with curiosity, but satisfaction was long in coming. After dinner, the company gathered once again in the parlor, where Reverend Ware read passages of Scripture relating to the birth of Jesus. Mrs. Ware then moved to the pianoforte and played while they sang Christmas hymns. These little rituals complete, it was time for dispensing gifts. Each person presented his or her offerings to the others, Cora receiving a silk cape from Reverend and Mrs. Ware, hair ribbons from Annabelle, and a small volume of Elizabeth Barrett Browning's poems from Emmeline. When it was Carl's turn, he passed out steel pens for Reverend Ware and Peter and toilet water for Mrs. Ware, Emmeline and Cora. Last of all, color high, he carried a ribbon-bedecked box some eight inches square over to Annabelle.

She opened it, pulled aside a covering of tissue paper, and lifted the contents to a collective gasp. It was a mahogany bust of herself carved, sanded, and varnished into a likeness so perfect it was astounding. Her oval face and high cheekbones, her small straight nose and full lips, even her glossy ringlets—it could have been a daguerreotype transferred to wood. More than anything, it spoke of his utter devotion to her.

There followed a round of amazed questions verifying that he had made the bust himself. Even to Cora, who knew of his artistic skill, it was a work of amazing dexterity and beauty. For someone with his gift to be wasting his life taking courses in a profession for which he cared little was a vast injustice. In a moment of clarity, she saw that whereas her father's obsession in passing his profession on to his progeny had resulted in total fulfillment where she was concerned, it had brought misery to his son. And now, it seemed, the die had been cast, and she doubted Carl would ever have the courage to face his father down and opt for a different direction to his life.

After the oohing and aahing had died down, Emmeline turned to Cora and said, "The joys and excitement of the afternoon have rendered me quite overheated. Will you take a turn around the garden with me?"

"I would be delighted," said Cora, and they rose quickly before anyone else decided to join them.

The grassy center of the Ware's garden had fallow patches on the periphery where a few roses still bloomed ahead of a yet-to-come killing frost. When they were at the farthest reaches from the house, Emmeline said,

"The Taylor family has houseguests from Virginia for the holidays. Mr. Taylor's planter brother, his wife, and their two young daughters. They came to church this morning along with the Taylors' three personal slaves, who sat in the section allotted for black people."

Cora reached out and grabbed her arm. "These slaves came with them into the state? That means—"

"Precisely. Now, according to the conversation when Mr. Taylor introduced his relatives to us, these Southerners are aware of Pennsylvania's law and are keeping their property locked in the house, with one exception. They are very pious and insist that their servants attend church every Sunday."

"So that is the one time when they might be reachable. Do you know how long they plan to remain in the state?"

"Until just past the new year."

"So for one more Sunday?"

"So it would seem."

"And they will attend church again that day?"

"I expect so. But remember, the slaves will be surrounded by their master, his family, and the Charles Taylor family. I would like to think they could be rescued, but I am not sure how it could be done."

"Yes, it would be difficult. But..." She spent a moment in thought. Then, "They could hardly be spirited away in the midst of a church congregation whose support for slavery is no doubt solid. But they might be vulnerable on the way there and back. Do you know if they all came in one conveyance?"

"I think not. The Taylors apparently gave over their family carriage so their guests and servants could travel together while they themselves took a smaller buggy."

"So any rescuers would have only the master and his family to contend with providing they could isolate them from the Charles Taylor buggy."

"Yes, and that could be easier than you might think. We waved them off home, and the Charles Taylor family went ahead to guide the way with their guests following."

Cora laid her hand on her friend's arm and said, "You have done a good thing by telling me this."

"I promised Peter I would do so. And I thought it would raise fewer suspicions if I took you aside rather than attempting to tell him directly."

"That was wise. I shall pass the information along as soon as he and I are alone. The people he works with are nothing if not resourceful. We can but hope that the Virginia Taylors will return to their plantation minus their chattel."

"Amen, my dear. Their fate could not be in better hands."

Chapter Twenty-Three

Cora was telling Peter about her conversation with Emmeline within moments of their pulling away from the Ware manse. He listened with grave attention, and when she had finished, he said,

"It is a situation ripe for intervention, even though the logistics may be somewhat difficult."

"But you think you can help these people?"

"I am sure of it. I just need to think on it."

Dusk had fallen by the time he escorted her into her boardinghouse. He paused in the entryway and said, "I heard you tell Aunt Emmeline you are free from classes this coming week."

"Yes. It is the Christmas break."

"Then may I expect you in the office?"

"If I am wanted."

A soft smile. "Always wanted. Also needed. By then, I believe I will have formulated a plan to help the Taylor slaves. But as for tomorrow, you may or may not know it is the official Christmas Day observed holiday since Christmas fell on Sunday. Do you have plans for that day?"

"None except for trying to catch up on my studies."

"Then perhaps you will allow me to fulfill my earlier promise of showing you some of Philadelphia's more interesting sights. At least for a portion of the day."

She felt a stab of pleasure she did her best not to show. "Why, that would be delightful."

"Say ten o'clock?"

"That will suit." Then, fighting the rising color in her cheeks, "Thank you for escorting me today and especially for the lovely brooch."

"A lovely trinket for a lovely lady." He lifted her hand and kissed it. "Until tomorrow."

As he turned to leave, Cora caught movement out of the corner of her eye. She pivoted to see Gwen standing in the parlor doorway and grinning like a fool.

"Well, now," Gwen said, "that was interesting." Then, squinting in the dim light from the hall's gas fixture, "Do I see something new at your throat?"

Cora was too elated to mask her happiness. "You do, indeed. It was Peter's—" Catching herself, "—Mr. Ware's Christmas gift."

Gwen came forward and embraced her. "How happy I am for you. From what I have seen, you could not have captured a more worthy heart than your Mr. Ware's."

Cora pulled away in exasperation. "How many times must I tell you I have *not* captured his heart? He has declared no particular feeling toward me other than friendship. And an appreciation for my work, which he gave as the primary reason for his gift."

"Nonetheless, it is a fine gift even for an employer to his valued employee. I believe there is more there than you are willing to admit."

Or would allow herself to admit, Cora conceded but did not say. She knew Peter respected and trusted her. He also seemed to enjoy her company, as she certainly did his. Did any of that mean he held even the most basic of romantic feelings toward her? She was too inexperienced in matters of the heart to guess much less know the answer.

Confused though she was, she refused to allow these thoughts to spoil the day's glow, which lasted all evening and into a sleepless night. When Peter arrived the following morning, she was tired but excited to see what he had in store for her.

It was another balmy day more like spring than winter, the sun shining from a deep blue sky adorned with wispy white clouds. Peter handed her into his buggy and clucked his horse south on Seventh Street to Market, where they turned west along the covered arcade.

The stalls were empty due to the holiday, but the street abounded with residents out and about enjoying the unseasonable weather. They continued west toward the Schuylkill River, following the railroad tracks through gradually less-populated surroundings and passing the massive gas works on their right. They entered the Market Street Bridge, a five-hundred-foot-long covered wooden bridge, the horse's hooves making a metronomic sound magnified by the walls above and to either side. They emerged into sunlight once again and passed the Pennsylvania Railroad depot, coming shortly to Darby Road, which angled to the southwest and up a rise toward a sprawling white structure standing sentinel above the riverbank. They drove along a high board fence, passed one opening and continued to a second through which Peter drove. The narrow roadway led past a large water reservoir on a knoll to the left and thick woods to the right. Shortly they passed a grand white-marble archway with the words Woodlands Cemetery engraved above it.

"You will see no better example of the sad but real disparity of circumstance that plagues mankind than the two entities found on this single large plot of land," said Peter. "Woodlands Cemetery is the burying place of the cream of Philadelphia society, while over there," gesturing ahead to the left, "is the Blockley Almshouse where the city's indigent are cared for."

Rather than a single sprawling building, the complex was composed of four separate buildings situated to form a quadrangle. When Cora commented on this, he said,

"Yes, each comprises its own institution. One is the almshouse itself and the others are a hospital, an orphan asylum, and an insane asylum."

Sobered into silence, she watched as they turned to pass a high colonnaded entrance reached by twin sets of stairs and flanked by winter-bare trees. The road took another turn, and they were headed back toward Darby Road. When they had turned onto it, Peter said,

"I thought to begin our tour here since it is the most unsettling of the sights I want you to see. I believe our city is quite progressive in providing such a place, but it does not provoke happy thoughts."

"No, but it is well to be reminded of one's own good fortune. As has been said, there but for the grace of God go I."

He clucked his horse into a trot and said, "I believe you will find the next place much more uplifting even though you will see it for the first time in the unflattering milieu of winter."

They came to Market Street once again and turned east until they came to the Pennsylvania Railroad Depot, where they turned north onto Thirty-First Street and passed the railroad yard with its shops and engine house. Just beyond, they came to Bridge Street and took the wire bridge back across the river, where Peter pointed to a high prominence and said,

"That is the jewel of our city, the Fairmount Park and Water Works. You cannot fully appreciate its charms now, but we shall return in the warmer months so you can see it in all its glory."

He went on to explain how the water works functioned, but Cora could focus only his statement that they, surely meaning the two of them, would return to the park together in the summertime. She found it highly frustrating, even maddening, that he had once again tossed out a casual remark that assumed future dealings while not indicating what those dealings were meant to entail. However, even she was not bold enough to demand that he explain himself. Thus, it seemed she must continue to resign herself to ignorance concerning the direction of his heart.

They drove around the base of the hill, and Cora could see the tree-lined gravel pathways that wended their way up toward the summit, all enhanced with benches, statuary and fountains. They continued on alongside the tracks of the Philadelphia and Reading

Railroad to Girard Avenue, which took them east and up a slight rise into a mainly rural setting where, Peter explained, many charitable and reform institutions were located. They passed Girard College, a group of buildings that comprised a home and school for orphaned boys. Sweeping, well-landscaped grounds drew the eye to the central building, which was a fine white-marble structure whose eaves were supported by rows of Greek columns. From there they proceeded south once again, passing by the House of Refuge, a reform facility for young delinquents, and the State Penitentiary, a geometric building that, according to Peter, kept its inmates in cell blocks radiating like spokes outward from a central command post.

"These penal institutions do not inspire the cheeriest of thoughts, but they exemplify Philadelphia's forward thinking in dealing with such persons, the hope being that many may be rehabilitated. A noble if illusory goal, I fear, although the methods practiced here gain attention and visitors from around the country. Around the world, if truth be told."

They continued west through sparsely-populated neighborhoods and those dominated by industry until they came to Chestnut Street, where they turned once again toward the city. They passed the Academy of Natural Sciences and shortly thereafter, the United States Mint, a white marble building that could well have been mistaken for a Greek temple.

"It seems an appropriate setting in which to store our gold," Cora remarked. "We humans cannot help ourselves from elevating our wealth and all it buys to the status of a god. I suppose we might as well glorify our baseness rather than pretend it does not exist."

He smiled. "Such cynicism in one so young? Yet I hardly think you fit the mold. I detect no avarice in you. Only a desire to do what you can to improve the lot of your fellows."

"Yet I shall no doubt accept my fees as do all other physicians once I am qualified."

A shrug. "We all must have the wherewithal to live. It is what we do with what we have beyond the necessities that matters."

He pointed to another neoclassical white-marble building set well back from the north side of the street and surrounded by a tree-scattered lawn. "And there is our Academy of Fine Arts. You may have already noticed it since it is directly to the east of Parkinson's where you came with my aunt."

Cora had indeed admired the handsome building with its domed roof and portico graced by two ponderous ionic columns, but she had not known its function. Now her interest was immediately sparked. "Academy—does that mean art classes are held there?"

"Yes, but it also houses a fine museum of all manner of art."

She sighed. "How I wish Carl could attend there. It would suit him so much better than medical school."

"He does have an extraordinary talent, at least with the art of wood sculpting. That bust of my sister was uncannily lifelike. Has he never had training?"

"No. It never came up because he was destined for medicine from an early age. I dare say even from birth."

"His choice or your father's?"

Another sigh. "It was always simply assumed, which had, of course, to originate with Father. But to be fair, it also fits with the philosophy under which my brother and I were raised. The virtue of honest toil with the aim of bettering oneself and mankind was drummed into our heads from earliest memory. In such a context, one might deem the creation of beautiful things meant only for viewing as a frivolous pursuit. I, however, cannot help but believe that if God created Carl with such a talent, He meant for him to use it."

"I agree. There are many ways in which a person may benefit mankind. The healing of physical suffering is an important one, to be sure. But the light that enters the soul and sends it soaring upon witnessing a work of fine art is surely of equal value."

He was stopping the horse before a five-story, block-like sandstone building that occupied the northern half of the block east of Ninth Street. The sign read *Gerard House Hotel*. He turned to her and said,

"My humble tour is nearly complete. However, I cannot return you home without you sampling the cuisine of the Gerard's very fine kitchen. Will you allow me to offer you an early dinner?"

The low, intimate tone of his voice and sudden deep intensity of his gaze sent Cora's heart pounding. Was he asking as friend, employer, or...?

He took her momentary hesitation as assent and jumped down to attach the reins to the post provided. He came around and reached up to assist her down, holding her hand in his warm grasp perhaps longer than was necessary once her feet touched the ground. He offered his arm and led her through the hotel entrance.

They approached the large dining room and were seated near a high window with a view of the foundations being constructed across the street for what, he told her, was to be the fashionable Continental Hotel. The formally-attired waiter presented them with menus.

Except for her forays to Parkinson's with Emmeline, Cora had never dined in such grand surroundings and was uncertain what was expected of her. Sensing this, he said, "Will you allow me to order on behalf of us both?"

With relief, "Gladly."

The waiter came, and Peter ordered what seemed to Cora to be an inordinate amount of food: green turtle soup, boiled salmon, mayonnaise of chicken, macaroni au Parmesan, and fancy ices for dessert. She nearly stopped him after the salmon, but his assured attitude told her that should she do so, she would display her lack of sophistication and embarrass them both.

When the waiter bowed and left, Peter said, "So, what did you think of our fair city? There are many other sights I could have shown you, but I had no wish to overwhelm."

"It is certainly different from any other city of my experience. It also seems to be a cradle of many forward-thinking policies."

"That is largely due to the Quaker influence. They are a remarkably peaceful, inclusive society where no man or woman is above another."

Smiling, "The City of Brotherly Love."

He cocked his head. "Not all brotherly, I assure you. Else the population would surely fade away."

Cora's face flamed. Did he think she was flirting with him?

In a tone more defensive than she intended, "I was referring to the Quaker belief that all people, even black people, have a right to be free."

"Ah, of course." An amused twinkle in his eyes told her he was teasing her. The moment passed and he said, "And you are quite right. Of all places in the northern states, Philadelphia is the safest sanctuary for escaping slaves, although there is an equally significant portion of the population who would gladly return them, especially if a monetary reward were in the offing."

"Which prompts me to ask if you have had any thoughts about the Taylor slaves."

"I have indeed. What are your plans for the remainder of the day after I deliver you to your lodgings?"

"Why, I suppose I shall review my class notes and perhaps read from one of my textbooks."

"Could you in good conscience delay that meritorious plan for another hour? I have an additional destination in mind for the furthering of that cause. I believe you would find it of interest."

Cora's eyes widened. Was he offering her a role in the rescue of the unfortunate Taylor slaves?

"Try keeping me away."

Chapter Twenty-Four

Menacing clouds rolled in from the southeast late that afternoon, turning the balmy day gray and cold. By the time Carl and his friends emerged from their boardinghouse at midnight, the temperature had plummeted to near freezing. They walked to the corner and stood shivering and shifting from foot to foot, eyes searching the empty roadway in either direction for a sign of their contracted companion. Within minutes, Carl realized his winter topcoat and handsome leather gloves were not up to the task ahead, and he vowed to rectify the matter at his earliest opportunity.

The first snowflakes were drifting down by the time they heard plodding hoofbeats and the rattle of an old wooden cart as it approached. When it pulled up in front of them, Carl's heart sank. The wispy-haired old man in the driver's seat looked stooped and ready for the grave himself. Nonetheless, the fellow snatched off his floppy felt hat and gave them a nearly toothless grin.

"Good lads. Right on schedule. Hop on in. Let's get this funeral parade underway," this latter punctuated by a high-pitched cackle.

Herm Dietrich and Joey Robinson stepped on the wheel hub and launched themselves over the side. Carl looked at Rufus Mills and whispered,

"Where did you find this guy? How is he going to be any help?"

"Shut up," he hissed, "and get in the cart."

After Carl had complied, Rufus said, "This here is Zeke. Zeke, meet the new man."

The old man raised a hand in recognition and clucked his horse forward.

Rufus pulled Carl down into a far corner, leaned into his ear, and whispered, "Look, regardless of his appearance, he is just the man we need. He used to run a crew of his own, but they got caught and dispersed."

Carl's heart did a somersault. "Got caught?"

"Yeah, but it was no big deal. Had to pay a fine or some such. The point is, he is too old to carry on by himself but is willing to hire himself out to the likes of us. Unlike us, he knows the business and has the right connections. He will also keep his mouth shut. We provide the muscle and seed money. He finds the targets and disposes of them to the various institutions. The perfect partnership."

"So you say, but from my perspective, I am committing my very future to an old reprobate whose only interest is in making money."

A low chuckle. "Is that so different from you and me and the others?"

Carl grunted an acknowledgment and fell silent. He knew his testiness was due to his own anxiety rather than any real suspicion of the arrangements that his friends had been using for some time. He burrowed deeper into his coat as the snow fell on a stack of implements he had not noticed earlier. He glanced away, knowing he would discover their purpose soon enough.

He was unfamiliar with the geography of the city, but they seemed to be proceeding due south. The residential districts grew sparser until farmland replaced them. The snow was coming thicker and thicker so that it was hard to see more than a few yards beyond the road. Eventually they came to a low stone wall topped by iron grillwork. A charming steepled chapel rose behind it, and just beyond lay a pillared entrance whose iron gates blocked a narrow roadway into the interior of the property.

Zeke stopped the horse and climbed down, saying, "This is it, mates. Grab that there gear."

The tools of this particular trade seemed to be wooden shovels, a sturdy rope to which two shorter ropes ending in heavy iron hooks were attached, and several large burlap sacks. They climbed over the wall and followed Zeke past the chapel and along a crude path into the trees. Some minutes later, he stopped at a fresh mound of earth upon which had been laid several bouquets of wilting flowers.

"You fellas carry on," he said. "I'll keep a lookout back at the cart." He turned and disappeared into the night.

Herm removed the sad bouquets as carefully as possible and laid them on one of the sacks a short distance away. They then spread the remaining sacks around the grave, picked up the shovels, and began digging in the soft earth at the head of the grave.

Carl scoffed at the poor wood implements and asked why they did not have good iron ones.

"These are quieter," Rufus whispered. "And keep your voice down."

"Why? There is no one about."

"No one that you know of. Some of these places set armed guards against the very thing we are doing."

"Armed guards! You mean we might get shot?"

The words had come out louder than he intended and were greeted with an immediate, "Sh-h." Then, "No need to worry." He lifted his coat to expose the hefty revolver stuck into the waist of his trousers. "Zeke already warned us to come armed. Now keep quiet and dig."

Carl wondered whether he would have agreed to this scheme if he had known firearms were involved. He was ashamed to admit that he probably would have. Regardless of any risk, his need of cash would no doubt have prevailed. He put his misgivings aside and bent to his task.

They heaped the soil on the sacks laid to either side of the grave, the deepening hole a little more than a yard square. When Carl asked why they were digging such a small area, he was again admonished with, "You will see. Now be silent."

With four shovels going, it took but a quarter of an hour until they heard the thud of wood on wood.

"Done," Herm whispered. "Hand me the hooks."

He jumped down onto the coffin. He was the smallest of the four, but even he had little room to maneuver. Somehow he managed to work the hooks under the lid on either side. They gave him a hand up, then all four took hold of the rope and pulled until a loud crack told them the lid had been breached, the undisturbed earth on the lower part of the coffin having served as a counterweight to their combined force.

Herm lay prone and leaned down into the hole, Joey holding his feet lest he fall all the way in. He grabbed the broken piece of lid and scrambled up again.

"Okay," said Joey in a soft voice. "So who wants to do the honors?"

"Has to be Fielding," said Rufus. "Call it his initiation."

Carl swallowed and said, "What do I have to do?"

"Get down there and tie the rope around the body so we can pull it out."

A shudder rolled from the top of his head to the tip of his toes. He had already taken part in the dissection of a dead body, so he had no compunction about touching the corpse. Disturbing a person who had been given a Christian burial, however, seemed obscene, even though he had agreed to this scheme knowing that was exactly what they were going to do. Now there was no way he could refuse to do this. He took the rope in his hand and lowered himself into the grave.

He pulled his shoulders in and squatted down. Peered into the black interior of the coffin. And it was black, black as ink except for a slash of white that appeared at what would have been the corpse's neck. It was then he realized this person was of the Negro race. A man who had been buried in his best clothes, a black suit and white shirt beneath a silk cravat of a dark color.

He froze, transfixed as snow fell white and soft on the black skin. Then, responding to a muted urging from above, he slipped the rope around the man's upper torso, tied a knot, and took Joey's helping hand to climb out.

"He is an African," he said to no one in particular.

"Of course he is, dear fellow," said Herm. "They are the only ones who get buried here. Now give a hand while we pull him out."

Their combined strength made short work of the task. Joey and Rufus took hold of the body's shoulders and legs and hauled him aside. They began to undress him, prompting Carl to ask, "What the devil?"

"Thanks to the peculiar laws of Pennsylvania," said Rufus, "if we take the shroud or clothing with us, we can be prosecuted for theft. If we return them to the coffin, we have committed no serious crime and stand only to suffer a rebuke and fine should we be caught."

He threw the clothes back into the hole followed by the splintered coffin lid. Then, saying, "Help me out here," he leaned down to take the far lip of one of the sacks on which the dirt had been piled. Joey took the other, and they worked together to lift it so that the loose soil spilled back into the open grave. Carl and Herm worked on the other side, and soon they had nothing but a mound of dirt to show for where the hole had been. They tamped it down so that it matched the remainder of the grave. Then Herm went to where the dying bouquets had been set side and returned them to the grave.

Despite the extreme care with which he handled them, many of the dead petals drifted down to the ground. They all worked to pick them up and arrange the whole so the grave top resembled as closely as possible its condition before they had ever started digging. Now the snowfall was their friend, rapidly covering any disturbances they had made in the surrounding snow.

At a nod from Rufus, Carl picked up the shovels, sacks and rope while the others hefted the dead man's naked body. Like the funeral procession about which Zeke had quipped earlier, they made their way back to the road and the waiting cart.

∞∞∞

Cora went to the law office every day of the following week. Peter made no further reference to their plans for the Taylor slaves. Nor did she expect that he would given his lack of complete confidence in Reginald Herrick. She spent her time putting the files in order and assisting the scrivener with the paperwork for various civil matters. The work was dry and mechanical, leaving her mind free to dwell on what had been arranged for that coming Sunday. As the days dragged by, her anticipation grew until it became nearly unbearable, the only antidote being her evenings at home immersed in her studies.

At last the weekend arrived and with it New Year's Eve, which offered a new experience for her as well as for those of her friends who were spending their first year in Philadelphia. They were still at breakfast when they heard a commotion, including gunshots, coming from the street outside.

Second-year student Frances Davis said, "Nothing to be alarmed about. It is only the mummers engaging in their silly buffoonery." A sharp sniff. "Apparently some sort of tradition here in town."

Others who were Philadelphia natives rose to the defense of their unique method of ushering in the New Year, a custom dating back a hundred years or more. What had begun as mummers' plays performed around the holidays had gradually transformed into loosely-organized parades of young people dressed in masquerade and engaging in harmless mischief. The more curious boarders rose from the table and went down to the windows in the parlor, where they observed a rag-tag group of young men, many with faces smeared in greasepaint, prancing down the street wearing all manner of clown costumes. They were hurrahing and singing at the top of their voices while intermittently sending volleys from their firearms skyward.

"It goes on all day and night and tomorrow as well," someone volunteered. "The tavern keepers will do a brisk business. The rest of us must simply endure."

That prophesy proved true, and the city fairly danced with revelers even as a major snow storm rolled in. Cora's amusement soon dwindled and she did her best to study the digestive system as thoughts of the following day built until she thought she would explode.

By morning, the storm had abated, and gangs of workers were out along the major thoroughfares shoveling the snow into carts. Cora knocked on Gwen's door to inform her she would not be attending church as usual. Curiosity lit her friend's eyes, but Cora squashed her impulse to blurt out what she and Peter had planned for that morning, instead wishing Gwen a happy New Year and returning to her room.

Half an hour later, she was waiting in the entryway in her cloak, boots and gloves for Peter to arrive. At his quiet knock, she opened the front door and slipped outside. She took his arm against the frozen, uncertain footing, and they walked along snow-laden Seventh Street to the corner of Arch where his horse and buggy stood waiting.

Market Street had been cleared up to Nineteenth Street, but it was slower going farther west in the more industrial part of the city. Had it not been a holiday, the streetcars' low-hanging carriages and the horses' hooves would have trampled the snow. As it was, they had to rely on the tracks made by the sparser traffic of ordinary citizens out and about going to church or visiting relatives.

They arrived at the covered bridge, crossed through it, and turned onto Thirty-First Street and into the deserted Pennsylvania Railroad property. Peter maneuvered the buggy behind the brick depot and out of sight of the road. Two other vehicles already waited there, a long delivery cart and a large enclosed carriage. Each was driven by a black man, the one atop the cart unknown to Cora, but she had met the other when she and Peter visited his home on South Street the previous Monday.

They stepped down from the buggy and approached him. His name was Nathaniel W. Depee, a well-to-do tailor who had been involved in abolitionist activities for some thirty years. He had a complexion like creamed coffee, a balding head, and a long handsome face. Now he leaned down to greet them, his eyes sparkling over the task ahead.

"Happy New Year to you both," he said. "Are we prepared to bring the same new beginning to three wretched souls in bondage?"

"God willing," said Peter.

The driver from the cart, a heavyset man whose lumbering gait reminded Cora of an ox, was walking toward them. He stretched his hand toward Peter and said, "You must be Mr. Ware. A beloved friend to our race, according to all accounts."

Peter took the hand, saying, "I am he. And this is my associate, Miss Fielding."

He tipped his hat. "Pleased to make your acquaintance, ma'am. My name is Alfred Smith, an elder of the Mother Bethel Church. Arrangements have been made to secrete the newly emancipated among our parishioners until other arrangements can be made by Mr. Still's associates."

"Excellent," said Peter. A frown. "Where are the others?"

Mr. Depee chuckled and said, "Waiting to make their debut."

He rapped his knuckles on the carriage. The door flew open and four men spilled out dressed in the same brightly-colored outlandish costumes Cora had seen on the mummers parading through the streets the previous day. However, these men had no need for greasepaint as their faces came by their black hue quite naturally.

Grinning, Peter said, "Perfect. Is everyone clear about the plan?"

Affirmative nods all around.

"Then let the fun begin."

Chapter Twenty-Five

Alfred went back to his cart and moved it onto Thirty-First where it intersected with Market Street. The mummers went out to the roadway, prepared to perform their antics when any traffic passed by. Peter went to the corner of the depot where he could stand partially obscured while still able to view any oncoming traffic on Market. Too antsy to remain in the buggy, Cora took up her place behind him.

A few vehicles passed by going both west and east, but none were the ones for which they were waiting. Peter took out his watch from time to time then returned it to his waistcoat, seemingly undisturbed by the passing minutes. Cora could not match his patience. Anxiety took root, and she fought against the doubts that rose unbidden to her mind. What if their prey had decided not to go to church because of the snow? What if they refused to stop? What if, God forbid, they had firearms and used them to foil the plan?

It had begun to snow again by the time Peter murmured, "There they are," and signaled with his arm. The mummers pranced into Market Street, shouting and singing and cavorting. The Taylor's buggy came abreast and passed by, its occupants shaking their heads at the paraders' antics. The moment the buggy had passed, the mummers swarmed in front of the following carriage, forcing it to slow, while Alfred Smith slapped the reins on his horse's rump and rocketed the cart out to block its forward progress.

Cora heard the slaveholder's roar of, "What is the meaning of this?" as she and Peter made their way through the snow to the carriage.

"We are here to speak to your bond servants, Mr. Taylor," said Peter even as he opened the door to the carriage. Inside were a well-dressed lady, two young girls, and three black people—a man, a woman and a girl of perhaps eighteen or nineteen. He bowed to these people and said, "Having been brought into this state by your owner, you are now entitled to your freedom according to the laws of Pennsylvania. If you wish to belong to no one but yourselves, these men surrounding me are here to escort you to safety."

The white lady and girls were too shocked to speak, but Mr. Taylor had jumped down and stormed to Peter, screaming, "This is outrageous! You have no right to impede our progress. And no right to address my servants with such poppycock."

"You are wrong, sir. I have every right under the laws of this state. Laws you yourself have broken by holding your fellow human beings in slavery."

Incensed, the man raised the carriage whip he still held in his hand, but before he could bring it down on Peter, one of the mummers grabbed his arm and wrenched it from him. Face purple with fury, he turned to his slaves and said,

"Tell this man you have no wish to leave your home and the people who have sustained you your entire lives."

The three huddled even closer together, their frightened eyes sliding from their master to Peter and back again.

"Tell him!" demanded Mr. Taylor. "You know we have cared for you like our own children."

Cora saw indecision begin to morph into acquiescence in the man's eyes. She stepped forward and said in a soft, conversational tone,

"What are your names?"

The man glanced at her, then back at his master.

In a more authoritative voice, "Look at me, please."

His eyes moved back to her.

"Now tell me your names."

"I—I's Asa and this here's my wife, Ruth, and our chile, Annie."

Cora tried not to show her glee. A complete family! She said, "What are your duties in the Taylor household?"

"I's Massa's man, Ruth does fer Miss Abigail, and Annie b'longs to Miss Hannah and Miss Franny."

"Would you not like to start a new life where you work only for yourselves? Hiring yourself out as a butler or factory worker, your wife and Annie as a maid or a shop girl, and keeping your earnings to spend as you choose?"

She could see he was being seduced by the incredible opportunity being offered him. His master saw it, too, and said, "Think of David and Ellen. You would never see them again!"

At this, Ruth gave a gasp and cried, "No!"

"Yes," Taylor continued. "How could a mother even think of abandoning her children?"

"Oh, Asa—"

"Hush, woman," he said. "They's grown and has their own lives. We's got to think 'bout us."

"Yes, you must!" said Cora. "Slavery will not be the law of the land forever. One day it will be abolished altogether. Imagine how wonderful it would be if you were already established in a life of freedom and could offer shelter to your adult children until they found work for themselves? I would also remind you that this man has the power to sell you to someone else whenever he chooses. If that were to happen, would you not regret allowing this chance to pass you by?"

"No more!" bellowed Mr. Taylor. "This discussion is closed. Asa, I forbid you to say another word!"

"Do not listen to him, Asa," said Peter. "As a free man by the laws of Pennsylvania, and in accordance with the First Amendment of the Constitution of the United States of America, you have the same right to express yourself as does he."

The Southerner shot Peter a look of hatred such as Cora had never seen. "You and your laws mean nothing to me!" He climbed up to the driver's seat and took up the reins. "Now get these people out of my way, or I shall surely run over them!"

In response to his threat, the mummers took hold of the horse's bridle and harness and held it back. The animal's eyes rolled in fright and confusion over being thus constrained even as the reins were demanding that it move forward.

Into this impasse came a distant shout of, "Franklin! What is wrong?"

A figure was emerging out of the curtain of falling snow ahead, soon becoming recognizable as Charles Taylor. They had hoped to keep him and his family out of the fray by allowing his buggy to pass by before they moved in. Not only would this diminish the number of adversaries facing them, but it would prevent Peter being recognized, which would only cause additional problems with his family. Now there was no recourse but to face him, which Peter did by striding to meet him.

"Peter Ware? And..." Squinting at Cora through the snow. "...I know you, as well. Miss Fielding, whom we met at my brother's house."

"Yes, we are they," said Peter.

"But why are you here? Why have you stopped my brother and his family in this way?"

"We are informing your brother's slaves of their right to be free in the State of Pennsylvania. If they wish to take advantage of our offer, we shall see them away and into the hands of those who can help them establish themselves in a life of freedom."

"You will do no such thing! This is my family visiting for the holidays. As such, they are under my protection. What would your father think of such a blatant disregard for the dictates of hospitality?"

"He would no doubt disapprove."

"So you admit it? If you think he will not hear of this, you are sadly mistaken."

"I have every confidence you will make certain he is informed."

"And you care not what he thinks? What he may do?"

A shrug. "I cannot answer for him. Only for myself. And I shall do my moral duty regardless."

"Your duty? Well, sir, my duty is to my family, who are scheduled to return home tomorrow. And so they shall. *All* of them, including their servants."

"I fear not. If your brother wished to keep his chattel in bondage, he should have left them at home in Virginia. As he did not, he has exposed himself to the civilized laws of Pennsylvania."

"Your laws be damned! Under the much higher federal statutes, you have committed a crime by assisting in the escape of those who belong to my brother and his family. If you persist, I shall have you arrested by the United States Marshall."

"You are welcome to try, but by the time he arrives, these people will be long gone and beyond your reach."

While they argued, Cora had stepped closer to the slaves and urged, "You must decide now. Do you wish to be free?"

Asa sat up straight, his face rigid with decision. "We do."

"Then hurry and come down from the carriage. These friends will take you away and see to your needs."

He reached for the hands of his wife and daughter, pulling them toward the carriage door. Ruth was sobbing, saying, "I's scared, Asa."

"Don't be," he said. "This is the Lord's work. Now come along."

∞∞∞

Carl had sensed something was amiss with Eve for the past week or so. Her gay demeanor seemed forced, her complexion pale, her wraithlike body more gaunt than voluptuous. He had encouraged her to confide in him, but for the first time in their relationship, she kept her own counsel. When he arrived at the Blue Bell that evening with his friends and found her absent, his concern blossomed into fear.

He looked for Herm's Sally and demanded, "Where is Eve?"

The girl refused to meet his eyes. "Uh, she don't feel too good. Stayed home tonight."

He grabbed her arm and shook her. "What do you mean? What is wrong with her?"

"Ow, you're hurting me!" Then, when he eased his grip, "Lady trouble. She'll be out for a day or two."

"What sort of lady trouble?"

"None o' yer business." She turned and disappeared into the crowd.

Carl knew from his lectures on the female body that some ladies suffer from dysmenorrhea, or pain at the onset of their monthly flow. During the three months he had seen Eve on a near-daily basis, however, he had never known her to miss a day's work because of this condition. He told himself he was making something of nothing, but the instincts he had developed toward this girl said otherwise. He finally decided the only way to satisfy his anxiety was to visit her and see for himself.

Rufus, Joey and Herm were already deep in drink at the bar and no doubt cared little whether he was there or not. He shrugged into his overcoat, wrapped his scarf close about his throat, and settled his hat on his head before going out into the cold, wintry night.

He reached the little house in Nonnaters Court and rang the bell. Nothing. He rang again at the same time as he pounded on the door. The percussion knocked the latch loose, and he felt the door give. He pushed it open.

"Eve!" he called.

No answer. He looked into the parlor and saw it was deserted. He approached the base of the stairs and repeated,

"Eve, it is Carl. Can you hear me?"

Still nothing.

"I am coming up."

Heart pounding, he took the stairs two at a time and went along the hallway to her small room. Opened the door and froze.

Eve lay on her bed in a crimson pool. Her skin was so pale he thought she must be dead. When he grasped her limp wrist and felt for a pulse, however, he could discern a faint, rapid beat. He leaned over her and said, "Eve, dearest, it is Carl. Do you hear me?"

A low, barely-heard moan but nothing more.

"Can you tell me what happened?"

She mumbled, but it was so low and garbled, he could make no sense of it.

He took in the entire horrific scene, trying to understand it. There was no visible wound that he could detect, and the heaviest source was coming from the area of her pelvis. Dreading what he would find, he raised the hem of her gown.

Blood was smeared from her navel to her knees, and her abdomen was purple from extensive bruising. Her legs rested slightly apart, enough for him to see the steady ooze coming from her genitalia. Then his eyes fell on the obscene article that lay beside her. A steel knitting needle encrusted with blood.

Tears sprang to his eyes. "Oh, Eve, how could you? Why did you not come to me? But this..."

His distress was so acute he could barely breathe, let alone think what to do. One word, and one word alone, came to him.

Cora.

Chapter Twenty-Six

Cora had been in her nightclothes for several hours. She had tried going to bed early so she would be rested for the beginning of classes the following day, but thoughts of the extraordinary day just past had kept a tenacious hold on her mind and sleep refused to come. She had risen, lit her lamp, and taken up her copy of Mr. Dickens' *David Copperfield*, which she was in the habit of reading and rereading when she needed an escape from whatever reality she faced. Now, at just past midnight, she had decided to try again and was just reaching to extinguish the lamp when an urgent knock came at her door. She opened it to find a wide-eyed Katie dressed in her own nightclothes beneath a flannel wrapper, her night braid hanging over her shoulder.

"Your brother, miss. He came knocking on my window. Says he needs to see you right away."

"Knocking on your window?"

Then she understood. Given that the household had all retired at this late hour, Carl would have followed the passageway between this and the building to the north to the small bricked-in rear courtyard. A line of privies sat along the north wall and clotheslines took up the remaining space between the back wall and the washhouse. He would have seen the curtained window at the corner of the washhouse and assumed, correctly, that it was the room of a servant. For him to have taken such drastic measures told her he was in trouble.

Without another word, she threw on her wrapper and padded downstairs. Carl stood in the hallway, his coat wet with snow, his hat in his hand. His eyes were red, his face wet with more than melted snow.

Sobbing, "Oh, Cora, you must come! She is dying, and I do not know what to do."

She took him in her arms even as moisture from his outerwear soaked through her nightclothes.

"Hush, hush," she murmured. "I will help you. You can count on me. As ever you could. But you must tell me what has happened."

He struggled for control, finally pulling away and saying, "Will you come? I can tell you on the way."

Without another word, she turned and ran up the four flights of stairs, arriving at her room winded but still able to pull a dress over her nightdress and grab her winter cloak and boots. She sat on the bottom stair to pull on her boots. Then they went out into the night.

He spoke in gasps as they rushed along Seventh Street to Arch, then west the three-and-a-half blocks to Nonnaters Court.

"My friend. Name's Eve. From the Blue Bell."

"The Blue Bell?"

"A—a tavern. She works there."

"Ah. And what does she do there?"

An impatient wave of his hand. "Not important. She tried to—to abort herself."

Abort? A frisson of understanding slithered up Cora's spine. "What do you mean, tried?"

"With a knitting needle."

"Oh, dear God above."

"So much blood. I–I did not know what to do."

"Why me? She needs a doctor! Or better yet, a hospital."

"No time. Your training is better. *You* are better."

Cora was aghast. "But I am just a student like you. I know nothing about treating an attempted abortion such as you describe."

"*Please* Cora. Just help me!"

The anguish in his voice told her that no rational argument would prevail. Dreading the answer, she said, "The baby. Is it yours?"

He groaned aloud. "Probably not. I use French letters."

Cora's face flamed beyond the power of the falling flakes to cool. She had, of course, heard of the rubber sheaths that were sold at certain places where men gathered for the purpose of preventing pregnancy. But that her brother had used them to engage in carnal activity with a woman who could only be classified as a prostitute appalled her.

Yet to chastise him now would be beyond cruel. He obviously cared for this woman, and Cora vowed to do whatever she could to repair the damage done. She fell silent and pushed ahead as fast as she was able.

When they arrived, they found three provocatively-dressed women milling about the parlor. One, a tall, bosomy woman with frizzed blonde hair, came up and took Carl's arm.

"Did you bring the doctor?"

"Your concern comes a little late, Sally."

He jerked his arm away and headed for the stairs, Cora following. What she saw when they entered the small bedroom above took her breath away. She gave Carl a helpless look.

"This is beyond me. Beyond either of us."

Tears streamed down his face. "Could you not try? Please, Cora. For me?"

She went toward the girl and knelt beside her, there being no place on the bed she could sit without soiling herself with the blood.

"Eve, can you hear me?"

Nothing.

"She will not respond," said Carl. "I already tried."

Cora picked up a pale, cool, clammy wrist and felt for a pulse, finding it barely discernible. She lifted the girl's eyelid and saw that the pupil was very large and dark. A quick look between her legs confirmed the source of the blood. She laid her fingers on the bruised lower abdomen and applied gentle pressure. She let up immediately at the low groan that escaped the girl's lips, but she had felt enough to know that tissues that should have been soft and pliable were hard and rigid.

"She is in shock, Carl. From the blood loss."

"What can we do?"

"I know of nothing. Perhaps elevating her pelvis would slow the hemorrhage. But I believe it is internal as well. She must have perforated her uterus."

Even as she spoke, he was grabbing whatever pillows he could find and wedging them beneath the girl's hips. When he was finished, he stared at her with anguished eyes.

"What else? There must be something."

An idea had come to Cora even as he spoke. It was a longshot, and how it would be received was beyond knowing. But for Carl's sake and that of this young girl, who did not deserve to die as a result of her own foolishness, she had to try.

"My professor of obstetrics lives and has his practice on North Fifth Street. We students went there to observe his treatment of a patient who was unable to come to the regular school clinics. It is probably a mile or more away, but he is a kind man. A Quaker to whom all life is precious. I could go to him and ask if he has any further ideas."

He fell to his knees in front of her. "Oh, my dearest sister, I shall bless you forever if you do so. Eve is...very dear to me. I cannot bear to have her die. Please, go. Hurry!"

Cora knew the girl could very well be dead by the time she returned with any further instructions from Professor Fussell. If so, she could comfort herself and Carl with the knowledge that all possible avenues had been pursued to save her.

She hoped she could find her way in a city that was still rather new to her. The grid-like street layout would be helpful. She returned to Tenth Street and struggled ahead through the snow. She watched the street numbers. When she came to the five hundreds, she turned east down Spring Garden Street and trudged alongside the shuttered market structures that dominated the middle of the wide street. When she came to Fifth Street, she turned north again, glad that the snow had tapered off to flurries. By the time she arrived at number nine-twenty, it had stopped altogether.

The house was dark, as would be expected at such a late hour. She rang the bell, wondering whether this folly would diminish her in her teacher's eyes. When some minutes had passed, she forced herself to ring again. She was about to turn away in defeat when she heard the bolt being thrown.

Wavering candlelight revealed the woman who opened the door. Cora had heard that Dr. Fussell's wife Rebecca had completed her studies at the college and been granted her degree at the end of the prior session. She was an attractive woman of middle years with a strong-featured face, which registered shock as she took in the bedraggled person before her.

"I am Cora Fielding," Cora said through chattering teeth. "A pupil of your husband. I come out of desperation over a medical emergency."

She reached out and pulled Cora inside. "Thee is half frozen, child. Thy emergency must be dire, indeed. Let me waken my husband."

Edwin Fussell came down the stairs only minutes later, already half-dressed and pulling his suspenders up over his nightshirt. He took her cold hands in his and said,

"What is it, Cora? Is thee ill?"

"No, sir," realizing before the last word was out of her mouth that it might be considered inappropriate. She knew her Quaker professors eschewed any form of address that indicated any status above that of anyone else. It was a policy she had a hard time following given that she had always been taught to give any physician the respect his profession demanded. She surged on with,

"It is a young woman, an acquaintance of my brother, who has attempted to abort her pregnancy by means of a knitting needle. Which, I fear, may have perforated the uterus. She has hemorrhaged badly and is now, I believe, in shock and possibly close to death. We have elevated her pelvis, but beyond that simple action, I am at a loss as to how to help her. I have come to ask whether you have any further advice."

She waited for his rebuke over her having taken on this case as a mere student. Instead, he said to his wife, "I must see what I can do, although it sounds hopeless."

"I shall come as well," said his wife. "Allow me a moment to dress."

They collected their medical bags and a length of clean linen and led Cora to the shed out back where they housed their horse and family rockaway carriage. Soon prepared for travel, the vehicle cut easily through the new inches of snow. As they went, Cora explained more fully how she had come to be involved in this young woman's tragedy. That the girl was a person of ill repute and that Cora's brother had been involved with her brought no condemnation from the two doctors. These were people whose only concern was a human life that was in peril, regardless of the status or occupation from which that life flowed.

They arrived at Nonnaters Court in a fraction of the time it had taken Cora to walk to the house on Fifth Street. The parlor was deserted, but they found the blonde floozy Carl had called Sally as well as Carl himself in the sickroom upstairs. He rushed toward them with hope burning in his eyes.

Cora made hasty introductions, but the Fussells paid no heed, turning their full attention to the poor girl instead.

"She still lives," said Carl, his voice resonating with hope.

"Leave us," said Edwin Fussell, not even lifting his eyes as he and his wife did their initial physical assessment.

Softly but with determination, Cora said, "Come, Carl. We are not needed here."

He complied, Sally following behind. They sat in the parlor, and Cora directed herself to Sally, saying, "How long ago did she do this?"

The girl twisted her fingers, refusing to meet Cora's gaze. "She's been trying various and sundry potions for a couple of days now. We have our, uh, sources, and they usually bring things on. Nothing worked for Eve, though. Not even the tricks the old ones recommend. That girl ran up and down the stairs 'til she collapsed. Beat on her belly, too. The needle was her last chance."

Cora tried to be patient. "Again, when did she do it?"

A sullen pout. "Don't know. Sometime after we all left for work."

"All I care about," said Carl, "is what your professor and his wife can do for her."

Cora wanted to ease the torment apparent in every aspect of his body, but she could not bring herself to offer unfounded hope. "The truth is, probably nothing. They will try packing the uterus to see if they can stop the bleeding, but a significant amount has already leaked into the abdominal cavity. And even if they can stop it, she has already lost more blood than is consistent with life. You must prepare yourself for bad news."

It was another hour in coming, but as Cora had feared, the two Fussells entered the room wearing sober expressions that told the tale.

"No!" cried Carl, collapsing in a pile of grief.

Chapter Twenty-Seven

January 3, 1860

Cora was glad to return to her classes on Tuesday morning after the tumultuous events of the past days. She did not see Edwin Fussell until the second lecture period, at which time he gave no indication of them having shared the prior night's frantic activity. She took her cue from him, having no desire to dredge up the awful memories. She had not even told Gwen, who was becoming more and more of a trusted confidante. She decided it was better to let the dreadful event simply slip into the recesses of the past.

She was still concerned about Carl and his reaction to his friend's death, however. After recovering from his initial extreme grief, he had declared his intention to pay for a proper burial for Eve rather than consigning her to the potter's field at Blockley. Then his emotions seemed to disappear behind a self-made wall. He accepted the condolences of the Fussells with polite detachment and thanked them for their efforts. When they offered to drive both him and Cora back to their lodgings, he had declined, stating he preferred to walk in solitude. Before climbing into the Fussell carriage, Cora had put her arms around him and whispered how sorry she was that they had been unable to forestall the inevitable. He had responded with a cursory hug, his body rigid and unyielding, before turning away toward home.

She had hoped this tragedy would bring them back to their original warmth for each other. He had, after all, come to her in his distress. Did that not signal that the bonds of blood, shared even before birth, were stronger than anything the world could throw at them? Yet he had pulled back into himself, and they were now no closer to one another than they had been before it happened. That things could get even worse did not cross her mind.

She was in her clinic class on Wednesday at a quarter past twelve when a young man in clerk's garb appeared at the door. Professor Birdsell was examining a middle-aged woman who complained of a spasmodic cough, at times quite severe, and general malaise. He was so engrossed in listening to his patient's chest that he did not notice the newcomer until he cleared his throat. The professor raised his head, removed his stethoscope, and frowned, saying,

"You are interrupting my class. What do you want?"

The young man seemed not in the least intimidated by the professor's testy inquiry. He entered in bold manner, saying, "I am obliged by the court to deliver a document to one of your students. A Miss Cora Fielding."

Cora froze. A document? For her? She felt her fellow students' curious gazes as she collected herself and went forward. The fellow placed an envelope in her outstretched hand, bowed, and left.

She apologized to the professor, slid the envelope into the pocket of her apron, and returned to her place, face hot with embarrassment. She tried to refocus on the class, where the students were being given turns at listening to the patient's chest, but her burning curiosity made it difficult. She took her turn and did her best to concentrate on the crackles she heard during the woman's inspirations and expirations. When all had finished, the teacher offered a diagnosis of congestion of the bronchial membrane and prescribed therapeutic doses of laudanum and Dover's Powder for pain relief and sedation. The patient thanked him and was replaced by an older man who complained of frequency and increased volume during urination.

Cora did her best to forget about the envelope until the professor dismissed the class for the dinner break. Gwen came up beside her and whispered,

"What sort of document is it?"

"I have no idea. I suppose I should find out." She pulled her friend over against the wall, took out the envelope, and lifted the flap. She removed the sheet of heavy paper inside.

It was similar to documents she had handled in Peter's office, this one entitled: Writ of *Habeas Corpus* in re Asa, Ruth and Annie Taylor. The petitioner was Franklin Taylor, the respondents Peter Ware and Cora Fielding. Hands shaking, she read that a writ had been granted at ten o'clock that morning by Federal Judge John Cadwalader requiring her to produce the bodies of Asa, Ruth and Annie Taylor in the United States Eastern District Court for the State of Pennsylvania by eight o'clock that evening or show lawful cause for the taking and detaining of said Asa, Ruth and Annie Taylor.

She sank back against the wall. What had she gotten herself into?

"What is it?" Gwen insisted.

Cora had done everything in her power to keep her involvement in the abolition movement a secret, for Peter's sake more than her own. She cared not what people thought of her, especially when she was standing up for a principle as important as human liberty. But Peter had a position in society to maintain, a family to guard against further alienation. Now, however, their actions on New Year's Day were to be aired in a public courtroom, and all pretense of separation from the incident was futile.

"It is a long story," she said, "but it must wait for later. Now I must go see Peter."

"What about dinner?"

"No time. Please go on without me. And if the others ask, please say I had an errand to run."

Gwen squeezed her hand. "You may count on me."

Cora gave her a quick hug and hurried out past Mary, Jane and Frances, who were waiting for her and Gwen before starting off to their lodgings. She covered the distance between the college and Peter's office in record time, arriving out of breath and weighed down with dismay.

Peter took one look at her and guided her to the sofa in the anteroom. He took a seat close beside her.

"I assume you have been served," he said. "As was I."

Still catching her breath, "Yes. About...an hour...ago. During clinic...class."

"That must have been embarrassing for you. I am so sorry. I thought we could do this in relative anonymity."

Her voice had recovered and came with strong conviction. "That does not matter. I care not for myself. But you...."

"I knew my inclinations would come out eventually. It will not stop me from doing what I believe is right."

"As I would expect. But what are we to do about these writs?"

"We must answer them, of course. I have already prepared our written return, which you may read and sign now."

He rose, returned to the office, and took a paper from Reginald, further evidence that secrecy in this matter at least was no longer necessary. He handed her a letter addressed to the Honorable Judge John Cadwalader, United States Eastern District Court for the State of Pennsylvania. It read: *We the undersigned do swear that the three persons named in the writ, nor any one of them, are not now nor were at the time of issuing the writ, or at any other time, in the custody, power, or possession of the respondents, Mr. Peter Ware, Esq. and Miss Cora Fielding, nor by them confined or restrained; wherefore they cannot have nor produce the bodies named in said writ.*

She looked up at him. "And signing this is all I must do?"

"Not quite. We shall submit these testimonies as evidence, but the petitioner, said Franklin Taylor, will surely have his attorney present and will insist on questioning us under oath." Noting the dismay on her face, "Do not be alarmed. We need only tell the truth: we do not know where the Taylors were taken after we encouraged them to leave their master. We cannot be forced to produce persons whose whereabouts are unknown to us."

"But what of Mr. Smith and his friends?"

"Mister who?"

She cocked her head at the bemused expression on his face. He said, "We can testify with total honesty that we had never seen those men before that day. Their names have slipped our memory. And our last sight of the fugitives was after they came down from the carriage, after which we returned to our conveyance and know not where they were taken from there."

"Will we prevail?"

"I believe so."

"But if we do not?"

A wry grimace. "Then we should expect an indeterminate absence from our normal activities."

"You mean we will go to *jail*?"

"The chances of that are very slim. I am confident you will be attending class bright and early tomorrow morning. Now," taking his watch from its pocket in his waistcoat and consulting it, "you must have something to eat before you return to the college. Come upstairs and let us see what my Bella has prepared for dinner."

Cora's eyes went wide. *His Bella?*

Nodding with a teasing smile, "She is an integral part of my life, and it is high time you met her."

He pulled her up by her hand and led her out into the entryway and up the stairway to his living quarters above. As she climbed, Cora caught the mouth-watering aroma of cooking food. They passed through a parlor furnished without frill but having the feel of ease and comfort. The dining room beyond contained a sideboard and dining table of rich mahogany laid with service for one. A tall, handsome woman of early middle age wearing a plain brown dress covered by an apron stood beside the place setting. She had graying black hair drawn into a high bun, skin the color of roasted chestnuts, and a face with a high forehead and intelligent brown eyes, which were fixed on Cora in surprise.

Peter said, "Cora, I would like to introduce you to Bella Carlyle, my housekeeper and cook. Bella, this is my good friend, Miss Cora Fielding, who has missed her own dinner due to an urgent legal matter involving the both of us. I hope you have prepared enough food to share with her today."

A brilliant smile. "You know I have, Mr. Ware. How else am I to fatten you up?" Then to Cora, "I am most pleased to meet you, Miss Ware."

"And I, you, Miss..." Then, noticing a thin gold band, "...Mrs. Carlyle."

"Oh, gracious me. Bella will do just fine. Now give me a moment to fetch another plate."

She disappeared into the small room behind this one and returned pushing a service cart loaded with steaming covered dishes and another place setting of china and silver. When Cora was seated, Peter said a prayer of thanks then nodded for Bella to begin serving. She placed the dishes on the table and retired from sight.

"She eats in her own rooms," Peter explained. "I have tried in vain to encourage her to eat with me, but her sense of propriety prevents her from doing so. I finally realized it was a lost cause and gave up."

Cora took a bite of pork so tender a knife was not needed, swallowed and asked, "How long has she been in your employ?"

"Seven years. Ever since I received my law degree, bought this building and set up practice. I have become as dependent on her as a child is to his parent. She is more than my employee. She is my dear friend."

They ate in silence. Then Cora said, "If I am to appear in court this evening, I must know where it is."

"On the second floor of the State House in Independence Square. But you need not worry about getting there. I shall call for you at, say, seven-thirty. Will that give you enough time to eat your supper?"

A smile. "I doubt that I shall need another bite this entire day after stuffing myself here at Bella's table. It is beyond delicious. But yes, seven-thirty would be just fine."

∞∞∞

The early dusk of winter had settled over the city by the time Cora and Peter climbed to the second floor of the State House. Despite the late hour and the writ's having been granted just the day before, the courtroom held a surprising number of people. Cora recognized Franklin Taylor sitting at what she assumed to be the table for the petitioner. The young, blond-haired man sitting by his side was no doubt his attorney. The remainder of the Taylor family—Franklin's wife and daughters and Mr. and Mrs. Charles Taylor and Miss Mary Lee Taylor—sat in the seats allotted for spectators. A number of black people occupied the rear benches. The others were probably mere sensation seekers. Or perhaps journalists. Peter had warned her that the proceedings would be carried in the local newspapers, verifying her assumption that their anonymity had been fatally compromised.

Three men stood along the side wall. One, a stooped individual with gray hair and a sallow, lined face, wore a silver badge on his shirt. The two flanking him had the muscular look of government henchmen. These were no doubt the United States Marshall and his deputies, who were there to take the fugitives into custody should they be brought in as demanded.

As they walked to the front of the room, Cora noticed how the malevolent, small-eyed gaze of Mary Lee Taylor followed their every step. No beauty to begin with, her hate-filled countenance bordered on the ugly. How shocked she would be if she were to see herself as Cora saw her now, stripped of whatever feminine charms she might imagine herself to possess. She would recognize in an instant why she was unable to appeal to a man such as Peter, who was the antithesis of everything she was exhibiting at present.

They continued on to the table set aside for the respondents, which was opposite the one for the petitioner. They took their seats and awaited the judge's arrival.

Chapter Twenty-Eight

Federal Judge John Cadwalader of the Eastern District of Pennsylvania was a distinguished-looking gentleman with snow-white hair, heavy dark eyebrows, wire spectacles, and a stern visage. He directed his gaze at Peter and Cora and said,

"Are the respondents prepared to bring forth the persons named in the writ of *habeas corpus* as ordered by this court?"

Peter rose and said, "No, Your Honor. In their stead, we present a sworn statement as to cause why we are unable to do so. If it please the Court, we offer it into evidence."

Franklin Taylor's counsel sprang to his feet and said, "Your Honor, we object on the grounds that the petitioner has not been given an opportunity to read this document."

With raised eyebrows, "Patience, Mr. Brewster. You will have that opportunity as soon as I have read it myself."

He nodded at his clerk, who took the letter from Peter and carried it to the bench. He spent a moment reading it then handed it back to the clerk, who took it to the petitioner's table.

After both men had read it, Attorney Brewster rose and said, "Petitioner desires through counsel to examine the respondents under oath, Your Honor."

The judge pursed his lips. "Very well. The clerk will administer the oath, first to Mr. Ware and then to Miss Fielding."

When Peter had been sworn, Mr. Brewster approached him with a contemptuous smile. "You believe you have pulled the wool over the eyes of this Court, do you not, Mr. Ware?"

Peter's expression remained bland. "Why should I desire to do so when the truth is on the side of me and my co-respondent, Miss Fielding?"

"Do you deny that you were present at the corner of Market and Thirty-First Streets on Sunday, January 1, 1860?"

"I do not deny it. Miss Fielding and I were there in order to inform three slaves of their right to be free in the State of Pennsylvania."

"How did you know the fugitives would be passing at that particular time?"

"An informed guess. We knew they were lodging with Mr. Taylor's brother in West Philadelphia and that they were regular churchgoers. We simply deduced the route they would take on their way home."

"Several individuals of the African race aided in the unlawful interception of the petitioner. Did you conspire with them to be present?"

"I assume you refer to the mummers who were out making New Year merriment that day, as were hundreds of others throughout the city. I could not have conspired with them because I had never seen them before that day."

"May I remind you, sir, that you are under oath and subject to a charge of perjury?"

Peter fixed him with a searing glare. "I am fully aware of my obligations before this Court. How dare you impugn my integrity by suggesting otherwise!"

The attorney held up his hands palm out. "A matter of clarification only, Mr. Ware. Now, you deny knowing the four black persons who were pretending to be mummers. What of the Negro driving the wagon that impeded Mr. Taylor's progress?"

Peter shrugged. "He was also a stranger to me."

"You expect this court to believe that a total stranger happened along purely by chance and took it upon himself to help waylay the petitioner and his family?"

"A fortuitous happenstance from our perspective, but I can think of no other explanation. He could tell you himself, of course, so I suggest you ask him."

Mr. Brewster's rising color evidenced the fury and frustration he was experiencing. "A name, sir," he said through clenched teeth. "Give...us...his...name."

"If he mentioned it to me, I do not recall it now."

The judge leaned forward and said, "I believe you have exhausted this line of questioning, Mr. Brewster. Do you have another, or are you finished with this witness?"

The attorney closed his eyes a moment, took a deep breath, and said, "Very well, Your Honor." Then to Peter, "Back to the incident in question. You succeeded in persuading the fugitives to step out of the carriage being driven by their employer, did you not?"

"Why, yes, although it was more to Miss Fielding's credit than to mine. And Mr. Taylor was not their employer. He was their owner and master against the laws of this state."

"But not against the laws of the land!" Brewster bellowed. "We are in federal court now, sir. Not in the lower court of this state. Federal law as written in the Fugitive Slave Law of 1850 preempts local law, as you well know."

The judge gave Brewster a stern look over his outburst but did not intervene.

Peter said, "I do not acknowledge the power of the federal government in this instance. The laws of God supersede all others, and on this issue, He does not stand with the United States. But that is neither here nor there. The fact is these people are now out of their owner's clutches and as free as you and I."

"You may rail against the government as long and as hard as you like, but the marshall over there has a warrant for the arrest of these fugitives. It is your duty as an officer of this court to tell us where they are. Again, you are answering under oath."

"And again, swearing before God and man, I do not know their whereabouts. Miss Fielding and I left immediately after assuring ourselves that Asa, Ruth and Annie understood their rights in Pennsylvania. We were not informed, nor did we ask what happened to them afterward."

"You mean to tell us you went to all this trouble to find and abduct these people and did not stay to see it through?"

"They had left their master's control. And they appeared to be in the safe hands of people of their own race. Our purpose had been accomplished."

"Do you expect us to believe you do not know where they were taken?"

"You may believe it or not, but it is the truth. Nothing more nor less."

Again the judge leaned forward to address Mr. Brewster. "You are wasting the Court's time by repeating yourself again and again. Do you have a fresh line of inquiry or other witnesses to call? Miss Fielding, perhaps?"

The lawyer's shoulders sagged. "No, Your Honor. She would no doubt simply repeat the lies we have heard from Mr. Ware."

With a face of stone and a forefinger raised in admonition, the judge said, "Be careful, Mr. Brewster. I will not countenance defamation in my courtroom without clear supporting evidence. Please take your seat. I am ready to rule on this writ."

Cora's relief over not having to testify fled before wrenching anxiety now that the moment of decision had come. She gripped the seat of her chair so hard her fingers ached, her eyes glued to the judge.

In a clear, forceful voice, the gentleman said, "I find no compelling evidence to support the claim that either Mr. Peter Ware or Miss Cora Fielding did know following the incident or do now know the whereabouts of Asa, Ruth and Annie Taylor. Therefore, they cannot produce their bodies before this court. The writ of *habeas corpus* in question is hereby discharged."

With a bang of his gavel, he rose, gathered his robes, and swept from the room.

Cheers came from the black spectators as Peter whooped and swept Cora into his arms, lifting her so high her feet dangled a foot above the floorboards. When he set her back down, she nearly melted before the look in his eyes. Behind the obvious triumph, she saw something else. Could it be love? Longing? Even devotion? Her heart caught in her throat, leaving her unable to say or do anything more than give him a goofy grin.

The pandemonium around them quickly cut into the moment. Cora saw that the Taylor family *en masse* were sending looks of unalloyed hatred their way, and she had the fleeting thought that in their minds, this issue was far from over. She and Peter could not assemble their papers and hurry from the courtroom any too soon for her comfort.

That night Cora invited Gwen to her room and told her about the day's happenings. It was a novel experience to have a friend with whom she felt comfortable enough to share the innermost workings of her mind and heart. Gwen was not only pretty and clever and bright, but she had an open, transparent, giving personality that inspired absolute trust. She heard Cora out with eyes that glowed with excitement and admiration.

"I wondered why you seemed so secretive about your work for Mr. Ware. Now I see how significant and important it is. My little hometown is quite isolated from the rest of the country, and the issue of slavery seldom comes up as a topic of conversation. But I do believe it is an evil institution, and I fully support any efforts to free those poor souls. I can also see that working together on behalf of such a cause would create a tantalizing basis for love."

Cora had always discouraged such talk where Peter was concerned. Now she could not deny that feelings seemed to be growing between them.

"He has not spoken, but I admit to a certain fervor in his demeanor."

Gwen laughed. "Leave it to you to downplay the gentleman's feelings. Your own are quite obvious, and we shall leave the matter there."

Cora thought little of the Taylors over the coming days. She and Gwen were in her room after dinner that Sunday afternoon memorizing the periodic tables for their chemistry class when Mrs. Gallagher appeared at the door carrying a large sack. She thrust it forward, saying,

"Yer brother, Mr. Fielding as he said, asked me to give this t'ye straight away."

Puzzled, she said, "Carl? Is he here?"

"No, lass."

"Did he leave a message?"

"Naught but, 'Tis yer fault.'"

Cora took the bag with sinking heart, thanked Mrs. Gallagher, and closed the door.

"What is it?" asked Gwen. "A gift?"

Already knowing what she would find, "Not for me. Let me show you."

She opened the sack and removed the bust of Annabelle Taylor.

Gwen caught her breath. "Oh, gracious me. What a beautiful thing! Where is it from?"

"Carl made it. Meet Annabelle Taylor, his apparently *former* sweetheart. He gave it to her as a Christmas gift."

"Oh, dear. So this means she has broken it off?"

"So I would assume. And, as Mrs. Gallagher said, because of me."

"Why? What did you do?"

"It is not so much what I did as who I am. Annabelle's father now knows the extent of Peter's and my involvement in abolitionist activities. His contempt for us apparently extends to Carl simply by virtue of his being my brother. Which has prompted him to forbid Carl from seeing his daughter. Thus the return of his gift."

"Poor Carl. Was he very much in love with her?"

"He would have said so, but I doubt the depth of that love. I believe it was more an infatuation with someone who is, yes, very beautiful but has little else to commend her. In my opinion, of course, which is not to say he will not suffer pain for a time until he gets over his loss."

"And meanwhile he blames you?"

"Presumably." A heavy sigh. "I must go to him and see whether I can make amends. I fear our study session must end."

"Of course." A wry smile. "I shall study on, fearless student that I am. Go as you must."

Cora had never been to Carl's boardinghouse, a fact that might be considered shocking given their close familial relationship. And worthy of guilt even beyond that heaped on her by her brother. If she had made a greater effort to keep in touch with him, would he have fallen into the depraved habits he seemed to have developed? There was no way to know, of course, but she chastised herself nonetheless.

To get there, she walked over to Market Street, then west three blocks past his school on South Ninth to 24 North Tenth Street. The woman who opened to her ring was obese to the point of morbidity. She peered out with a scowl, demanding,

"Well? What do you want?"

"I wish to speak with my brother, Mr. Carl Fielding."

Silence during which she heard the woman's labored breathing. Then, "He don't want no visitors. Told me so when he came in awhile ago."

Anger reinforced Cora's determination. "I care not what he told you. I intend to see him. You may either call him down or show me to his room."

The keeper's eyes narrowed beneath folds of fat. "And how do you plan to do that, missy, if I refuse to let you in?"

"I shall stand here and ring the bell all night, if I must. But I shall not leave until I see him!"

She weighed Cora's words, then shrugged and pulled the door wide. "Suit yourself. Room Eleven. Top floor."

The boardinghouse was laid out in a similar pattern as hers, but it had a musty, greasy odor and did not appear to be entirely clean. Cora climbed the stairs to the third floor and found Number Eleven opposite the stairwell. She knocked. Receiving no answer, she turned the knob and pushed the door open. The room was empty.

A rash of male laughter came from somewhere down the hall. She followed the sound to the front of the house and found the door to the end room open, smoke billowing out into the hallway. She wondered whether the fat keeper knew her boarders were smoking in a structure that was brick on the outside but quite flammable inside.

She stood in the doorway and peered in through the haze. A tall fellow with wild, curly yellow hair saw her, whistled, and said,

"Well, deary, look at you. As the spider famously said to the fly, come on into my parlor."

"Enough, Rufus," said Carl as he rose from where he sat on the floor. "She is my sister."

An amused chuckle. "Never would have known, Red old fellow. Given the hair and all."

Carl shot him a look, then took Cora's arm and led her none-too-gently to his room. He closed the door and gave her a tight-lipped glare.

"What are you doing here?"

She glanced around the cluttered room and pointed to a straight chair. "May I?"

"Suit yourself, although I do not imagine this will take long."

She sat, composed herself, and said, "I came, Carl, because I understand that my actions have caused you pain, and I want to tell you I am sorry."

"*Sorry?!* You are a little late for that."

"You know very well I had no intention of hurting you. Please tell me what happened with Annabelle."

Voice still tight with anger, "What happened? Here is what happened. We were to go sledding this afternoon with some of her church friends. I arrived at the appointed time, but she refused to see me. The maid simply handed me the bust and told me to go away and never come back."

"Oh, Carl. That must have been awful."

"Spare me your sympathy! You should have thought beyond yourself before you got involved in that infernal slave incident. How could you act so toward friends of the Ware family? *Peter's* family? Did it not occur to you there would be repercussions that would touch me?"

"Perhaps not, but if it had, I would have gone forward nonetheless. People's lives were at stake. Can you not see that?"

"The life I see at stake is my own. You have ruined my chance at happiness. And for that, I cannot forgive you."

Stung in spite of herself, she forced her voice to remain calm. "Did this girl mean so much to you that you would have her at any cost? Think, Carl! This black family, this *human* family belonged to another person in the same way as livestock belongs to a farmer. The brother with whom I shared a womb cannot condone that."

A shadow of discomfort passed over his face. "I know slavery is wrong. We learned as much from Lazarus." He referred to the former slave who had been master of their wagon train across the plains.

"But Annabelle had nothing to do with any of it. It is unfair that she and I should suffer because of what happened."

"If she suffered so greatly, why did she not face you herself and express her thwarted feelings? I realize she is under her father's roof and must obey him. But the manner in which she broke off with you seems cruel and unnecessary."

She saw that her words had pierced him. He sank onto the bed, his head in his hands.

She continued in a soft tone, "I saw you grieve mightily but a few short days ago over a poor girl whose life ended because of her own actions. I see no similar grief over the end of your relationship with Annabelle. Rather, I see anger, embarrassment, even humiliation. Which causes me to wonder whether you did not love the idea of Annabelle more than the person herself."

When he said nothing, she continued, "Please do not let this come between us, Carl. We have had our differences, no mistake, but we are flesh and blood of the closest kind. I cannot bear the thought of being estranged from you. So please forgive my part in your pain."

A deep sigh. "Just go. I shall try not to hold it against you."

She rose and kissed the top of his head before letting herself out. The raucous commotion still came from the room at the end of the hall. She shook her head, wondering what would become of her brother, whom she feared was on a dangerous course leading only to calamity.

Chapter Twenty-Nine

Spring, 1860

The winter wore on, and Cora's life settled into a solid routine of study and work. She stopped by to see Carl a few times, and their conversations were cordial if not overly affectionate. For a time, she kept alert for the possibility of further ramifications resulting from what she had come to think of as the Taylor affair, but none presented themselves, and she grew to believe it had been safely relegated to the past.

Emmeline continued to invite her to Parkinson's occasionally, and although the old lady had promised to keep her eyes and ears open for any news that might be helpful to the abolitionist cause, she had not had anything new to report. She did confirm that Peter had been banned from the Ware household and that the edict extended to Cora and Carl. Annabelle had shown little remorse over losing Carl and was currently being courted by a baker whose sympathies aligned more closely with those of the reverend.

"What do they say about our meeting like this?" Cora asked.

"They think I am on a shopping foray. Your name does not cross my lips in that house."

"Oh, dear. It cannot make for easy fellowship when you must filter your every word."

A conspiratorial smile. "Actually, I find it rather entertaining. A little game I play without their even being aware."

"But should you ever make an unintentional mistake, the resulting difficulty could jeopardize your standing with your brother. Even your very presence in his home."

"Nonsense. As I have told you before, if events should make my position there intolerable, I am quite capable of providing myself with an alternative."

And so, Cora put the Ware and Taylor households out of her mind. Instead, she focused on the fact that with the school term winding down, she was halfway toward becoming a degreed physician.

Commencement was on March Fourteenth, and Frances Davis was the sole graduate. Even though the other girls had not developed a particularly close attachment to her given her standoffish ways, they nonetheless attended the ceremony to cheer her on. Her parents came down from New York and whisked her away shortly afterward to take a position at the New York Infirmary for Women and Children.

The other girls made their plans for the summer. Philadelphia had no facility similar to New York's where female students could take summer jobs to increase their exposure to everyday medicine, although exciting plans were being pursued for the erection of a hospital for women later that year. Meanwhile, the Philadelphia Public Hospitals not only barred students of the Female Medical College from employment but did not even allow them to attend its clinical lectures. Mary Reynolds and Jane Payne decided to return to Wisconsin and Ohio respectively for the summer, while Gwen accepted her preceptor Ann Preston's offer to work part-time in her medical office.

Cora knew she would be wise to seek a similar position for herself, but Peter's offer of full-time summer employment was too tempting to resist. Over the following weeks, they fell into a pleasant routine of work interspersed with quiet personal time. He invited her upstairs for dinner several times a week, invitations that did not compromise her reputation since Bella was in constant attendance.

She found the housekeeper to be generous, warmhearted, and dedicated above all to Peter. She learned that Bella had been born in the nearby settlement of Glen Mills of a free father and a mother who had been a slave but was subsequently freed by her master. She had married at the age of eighteen, but her husband had died a year and a half later during the typhus epidemic, their only child having survived but a few hours. Bella had then gone into the service of an elderly widow by the name of Mrs. Lucille Porter until the lady's death in 1852. She had moved to Philadelphia and been hired by Peter in 1853. She was an active member of the Mother Bethel Church and greatly esteemed by all who knew her.

Peter continued to treat Cora in a collegial manner overlaid with a warmth that tickled her insides. Even so, he said nothing to indicate he held any more than a friendly regard for her, a fact that caused her considerable unease. She knew her own feelings were gravitating more and more in the direction of love, a hot rolling tide that subsumed the practical, rational side of her nature and left her open to a great deal of pain if, in the end, he did not return her affections.

Meanwhile, spring settled over the city, the greening grass and budding trees responding to warming temperatures, gentle rains and heady sunshine. Easter Sunday fell on April Eighth, a breezy, benign day with white clouds scudding across a blue sky and temperatures that allowed for only a light outer cloak as Carl, Cora and Gwen made their way to St. John's for the morning service.

Cora regarded it as one of her greatest accomplishments that she had coaxed Carl to spend the day with her. She doubted he had seen the inside of a church since he left their parents' house. Now he would hear the message of hope, forgiveness and salvation that this day offered to an imperfect world.

Following the service, they had been invited to share Easter dinner with Peter at his residence. Carl had received the invitation with something of a scowl, but since he had no other place to go for the holiday, he had grudgingly accepted. As they walked along now, Cora thought his sideways glances at Gwen, who looked particularly fresh and pretty this morning, held a glint of interest. Dared she hope her twin might be lured away from the bad company he had been keeping by the person whom she now regarded as her closest friend? She admitted the thought had been present in her mind when she suggested to Peter that he expand the invitation to include Gwen, who was far from home and had nowhere else to go. A part of her laughed at the irony of her playing Cupid when she could not even be sure that playful nymph had sent his arrow into the heart she hoped to claim for her own. Nonetheless, satisfaction brightened the morning as she watched Carl preen ever so slightly under Gwen's occasional friendly looks and witty contributions to the conversation as they walked.

Peter met them in the church narthex and sat with them through the service. By the time it was over and they walked to his building, Bella had returned from her own celebration of the Lord's resurrection and was busy preparing a sumptuous dinner. Afterward, Peter brought his horse and buggy from the nearby stable where he boarded them, and they drove to Fairmount Park, where they walked the paths, admired the statues and gazebos and fountains now playing after their winter surcease, and visited the mill house of the waterworks where they saw the massive waterwheels and pumps in action.

The day passed faster than Cora would have wished in a haze of easy camaraderie. Peter made a point of not broaching the subject of his abolitionist activities, instead entertaining them with stories of some of his most interesting clients, all nameless due to the principle of privilege. Cora and Gwen encouraged Carl to talk about his past year's courses and how they differed from their own. It was apparent to both that he had been less than immersed in the subject matter, and Cora suspected the two women would have something to say on that subject when they were alone. However, this glaring weakness did not seem to bother Gwen, who treated him with an amiable acceptance that sometimes veered off into the realm of mild flirtation.

When they were alone in Gwen's room later, Cora said with a smile, "I do believe my brother's heart has healed. And you are the medicine that has accomplished it. I hope that fact does not trouble you."

Gwen laughed, her cheeks pink and dimpled. "I hardly think my charms have such power. But he seems a very engaging fellow despite his disapproval of us females bludgeoning our way into medicine. It is a pity he does not have greater relish for the profession himself. For someone who could create that beautiful bust to settle for a line of work he does not love is a travesty."

"I agree. A deep part of me hopes he will someday summon the fortitude to resist the expectations of a lifetime and heed the creative light that illumines his soul. I suppose whether or not it ever happens is in the hands of God."

∞∞∞

Cora had all but given up her fear that the Taylor affair might come back to haunt them when it cruelly and unexpectedly reasserted itself. On the Friday after Easter, she was approaching Peter's office after dinner at her boardinghouse when she saw Reginald run around the corner of Fifth and Race Streets, skid to a halt at the office door, and wrench it open without a glance in Cora's direction. He burst into the hallway, crying, "Peter! Peter! Bella has been taken!"

Cora followed him into the hallway just as Peter came through the anteroom door. The scrivener stopped in front of him and huffed, "Snatched her...right off...the street. Took her away...in a hansom."

Peter wore an expression of pure puzzlement. "What do you mean? She was here a moment ago."

Reginald shook his head. "I saw what I saw. She was walking along with her shopping bag, probably on her way to the market, when some fellows pulled up, grabbed her, and hurried away."

His face paled. "My God. Who was it?"

"Never saw them before. Rough looking characters. What shall we do?"

Peter turned in a tight circle, his fists clenched, his face a study in dismay.

Cora said what he was surely thinking. "The Taylors are behind this."

He gave a distracted nod. Then rushed out the door.

Beside herself with dread, Cora did her best to work, but she listened with her whole being for any sign of his return. Her normal quitting time came and went, but she could not bring herself to leave without knowing Bella's fate. Sharing her anxiety, Reginald stayed as late as he dared given that his wife was expecting him home for the evening meal. Eventually he decided he could wait no longer and left for home.

At last she heard the front door open and rushed to meet Peter. His expression was weary but determined.

"We have a chance, though a slim one," he said. Then with a fond smile, "You waited. Come upstairs and I shall tell all."

He locked the door into the offices and led her upstairs to his living quarters. She felt a little odd being there without Bella as a chaperone of sorts, but the current circumstances overrode her misgivings. Besides, she had always thought the conventional notion that a woman needed a constant escort lest her honor be defamed relied on the fallacious assertion that females could not be trusted to manage their own lives. An assertion she denied with all of her being.

Nonetheless, as if reading her mind, Peter crossed to the front bay windows and pulled the draperies, insuring privacy.

She sat in a high-backed chair upholstered in gray velveteen while he paced in front of her, his agitation clear.

"You were right about Franklin Taylor's involvement. He is claiming that Bella is a slave named Felicity who ran away from his father's estate in 1838."

Stunned, Cora said, "How is it possible for a person to be snatched off the street and accused of being someone she is not?"

He sighed. "I am sad to say it happens all too frequently. And most often successfully. It is one of the biggest dangers free black people face."

"But 1838 was—what?—twenty-two years ago? How can this man possibly claim to recognize Bella as this slave after all that time?"

"The answer is simple. He cannot."

"Then how...?"

"As I am sure you have already deduced, this is nothing more than an act of revenge against me for spiriting his slaves to freedom. But he is prepared to swear under oath that she is the person in question and has brought witnesses with him to back up his story."

"They would lie? Commit perjury?"

"It seems they are prepared to do so. And they have hired one of the most capable lawyers in the city. Benjamin Harris Brewster."

"Is he not the one who...?"

"Yes. The same person who represented Franklin Taylor in the matter of the writ to produce Asa, Ruth and Annie."

"But he was unsuccessful. So perhaps he is not as capable as you say."

He shook his head. "This is entirely different. The onus of proving Bella is who she says she is lies with us."

"But how do we do that? What can we do to save her?"

"I shall get to that shortly. Meanwhile, I have managed to put the brakes on the case. I went to the marshal's office with Passmore Williamson of the Anti-Slavery Vigilance Committee to consult with Bella. We discovered they were holding her in a back room in handcuffs like a common thief."

"That is outrageous!"

"And so we told the deputy in charge. After considerable discussion, the fellow did the right thing and removed her manacles. However, Attorney Brewster had already advocated for a speedy hearing and been granted a time of three o'clock this very afternoon. Since we had no means of refuting Taylor's assertion on such short notice, our only hope lay in delaying the proceedings. We accompanied Bella to the office of Commissioner Longstreth, whom we know to be an honorable man. A Quaker, as it happens, although he has been barred from that community for lack of attending meetings. Nonetheless, he listened to our assertions that, given time to collect our witnesses, we would be able to prove that Bella is a free woman who has lived her entire life in the State of Pennsylvania. Thanks be to God, he suspended the proceedings until Monday morning at ten o'clock, which gives us two-and-a-half days in which to gather our evidence."

"But how? According to what you have told me, she has only lived in Philadelphia for the past seven years. It would be easy to prove that, but it does not speak to where she was twenty-two years ago."

"True. But her hometown of Glen Mills is but seventeen miles west of here. We can hope there are people still living there who will remember her. Also of note is the fact that she married her husband Robert Carlyle in 1837 at the age of eighteen."

"1837? That is a full year before the Taylors claim she ran away from their estate in Virginia."

A large grin. "Precisely."

"So there is hope?"

"Of course. Mr. Passmore will gather witnesses as to Bella's character and current life, but he is otherwise engaged tomorrow. Since two heads and pairs of feet are better than one in any investigation, would you be free to take a train ride with me first thing in the morning?"

Chapter Thirty

Peter called for Cora at seven o'clock the following morning in a rented hansom cab. They proceeded up Market Street to the block-long Columbia and West Chester Railroad depot on the northwest corner of Market and Eighteenth Streets. Peter paid the driver, took up his leather briefcase, and helped her down. They passed beneath the ornate passenger portico and went to the ticket window, where they discovered that a train would depart in ten minutes. Peter purchased their tickets, and they barely had time to climb up into the car and find a seat before the whistle blew its mournful bellow and the car lurched forward.

The train passed west up Market Street and through the covered Columbia Bridge, then veered southwest along the course of the Schuylkill River. They sped along the river, then through farm land beginning to blossom green. As they went, Peter told Cora about his hurried discussions with Bella at the marshal's office the day before.

"The deputy marshal would not allow us the privacy that is usual in the case of a defendant consulting with his or her attorney. The fellow insisted on remaining in the room, and although we did our best to keep our voices low, I cannot guarantee that he did not hear some of what we said."

"Why am I not surprised?" said Cora. "The more I learn about our supposedly fair justice system, the more I find it is fair only for those of a certain skin color and economic class."

He nodded. "Nonetheless, we did have a fruitful conversation. I needed to acquaint myself as much as possible with Glen Mills, for I am unfamiliar with that part of the state. I also wanted her ideas as to how we could refute the charges brought against her. She told me that Glen Mills is a small settlement composed mostly of employees of the two paper mills that comprise the James M. Willcox Paper Company. The mills produce a special, patented paper that is used in the production of government currency. Bella's father as well as her husband worked there, and they were all staunch members of the A.M.E. Methodist Church. She suggested the church would be a good place to begin our inquiries."

"That sounds eminently sensible."

"She gave me another somewhat less hopeful lead. Back then there was a young white schoolmarm who taught both white and black pupils and might remember Bella since she was a top student. She suggested we try to trace her."

"Why is that less hopeful?"

"Because this teacher was little more than a girl herself, the daughter of the superintendent of one of the mills, and is no doubt long gone. Nonetheless, it would be pure gold for our cause if we were able to locate her. So we must do what we can to that end even though our time is short."

"And if we find her?"

"The goal is to convince any witnesses they should come to Philadelphia for the hearing. Barring that..." He pointed to the rectangular leather case he had brought. "...we must get sworn statements as to Bella's presence in the settlement at the time that Taylor claims she was his slave."

It seemed a reasonable enough objective, but Cora felt a twinge of disquiet mixed in with her hope. What if they were unsuccessful? She had always been a champion of the individual's God-given right to self-determination, a sentiment that had driven her to challenge the medical profession over its exclusion of women. Now someone who had lived a decent life as a free person was threatened with bondage of the worst sort. If they were unable to right this injustice, how would she cope with that reality? She feared it would be a damper on her soul for the remainder of her days. A prospect that bolstered her determination to do all in her power to return home with the evidence that would free Bella once and for all.

They arrived at Glen Mills in under an hour. It lay along the west bank of Chester Creek in a fertile valley flanked by forested hills. There was no train depot. Instead, they and several others stepped down onto a stretch of flat dirt near a small hut where tickets were sold. Up ahead, several two- and three-story stone buildings lined the roadway that followed the crest of the wooded slope above the creek. A bit downstream, they saw smoke rising from a tall smokestack that no doubt belonged to one of the mills. The soft breeze carried a pungent, unpleasant odor to their noses.

Three of their fellow passengers, a young couple and a plump matron, set off in opposite directions. The fourth passenger, a trim, well-dressed gentleman with dark hair and a neat moustache, seemed as uncertain as they. The three of them exchanged glances. Then he lifted his hat, bowed, and strode off along the road that passed through town.

Cora looked up at Peter. Where to begin? He smiled, offered his arm, and led her toward the closest of the stone buildings. They found it to be a general store.

The stout, middle-aged woman behind the counter greeted them with a look of keen interest, saying, "Welcome. May I help you?"

"I hope so," said Peter. "We have come from Philadelphia on a legal matter. Can you direct us to the African Methodist Episcopal Church?"

A blink of her eyes. "Them? A legal matter?"

With patience, "Yes. Can you tell us how to find the church?"

"Well, I suppose I can. Follow the road north until you come to Locksley Road. Take it west to Cheney Road. It will be on the corner there."

Peter bowed. "We are most obliged to you."

They set out on the dusty road, the sun strong enough that Cora was glad she had brought a small parasol to shield her head from the hot rays. The roads were not clearly marked, but there was enough traffic that they were able to ask the names of the crossroads they encountered. At last they came to a small clapboard building, a cross above its front door and a fenced, tree-shaded burial ground to the rear.

They tried the door and found it to be locked. A one-story stone cottage sat along Cheney Road just beyond the intersection. They went in that direction.

A wizened old black man was hoeing in the garden behind the house. He straightened as they approached, removed his floppy felt hat, and wiped his brow with his shirt sleeve.

"Hello, folks," he said. "How may I be of service?"

Peter removed his own hat and offered his hand. "I am Peter Ware, Esquire, and this is Miss Cora Fielding. We wish to speak with the pastor of that church over there regarding a friend of ours, Mrs. Bella Carlyle."

Recognition widened his eyes. "Great day, it has been a long time since I heard that name."

"You knew her?"

"Knew her? Baptized and married that sweet child myself. Buried her husband, their dead baby, and her momma and daddy right over there." He hitched his head in the direction of the cemetery. "Her movin' away was a sad day for us all. But allow me to introduce myself. Sebastian Cooke, preacher for the Thornbury A.M.E. Church."

"We are most pleased to meet you," said Peter. "May we talk to you about Bella?"

"Well, of course. Come on into the house where it is a mite cooler. My wife Caroline will have cake and tea to refresh us as we talk."

They preceded him into the cottage, where they were greeted by a petite white-haired woman. They made their introductions and took seats in the small parlor while Mrs. Cooke bustled about fetching the promised refreshments. When they had all been served, the churchman said, "Now tell me about Bella. Is the child in some kind of trouble?"

Cora found it endearing that he referred to the forty-something housekeeper as a child. "Not of her own making," she reassured him. "She has been kidnaped by a very bad man who claims her as a runaway slave."

The shock of her words hit him like a sledgehammer. "No!"

"Unfortunately, yes," said Peter. "We are here to prove him wrong and hope you can help us."

"Anything!"

"Good. By way of background, I am the attorney representing Bella in this matter. I am also her employer. She has worked as my housekeeper and cook for the past seven years, and we have become fast friends. I tell you this so you will believe I am determined to foil this nefarious plan and will do anything within my power to see that she is set free."

Tears flooded his eyes. For a moment he was unable to speak. Then, "God bless you, sir. Now tell me what I can do to help."

"Bella told me she married her husband in 1837. The plaintiff in this case claims she was a slave on his Virginia property until 1838. If I can prove she lived here at that time, it will go a long way toward convincing the Commissioner she has always been free."

His brow furrowed into deep ridges as he thought. Then, a broad smile. "Come with me."

They followed him outside and past the church cemetery to the front door of the church. Inside, plain pews stretched forward to a wooden altar with a cross on the wall behind. They went down the center aisle to a closed door to the right of the altar. He opened it and ushered them into the small office beyond. He went to a bookcase and withdrew a leather ledger from one of the shelves. He carried it to the small desk beneath a back window, laid it down, and began turning the pages.

"Here! See for yourselves."

He held the book so they could see the page entitled Holy Matrimony. Partway down the page they saw an entry that read: Bella Richards and Robert Carlyle. Beside their names was the date May 13, 1837.

Cora caught her breath. "This should be all we need."

"Perhaps not all," said Peter. "But it is certainly a step in the right direction." To Reverend Cooke, "Would it be possible for you to bring this to Philadelphia so we could present it in evidence at the hearing Monday morning?"

A troubled expression pinched his face. "You want me to come there?"

"Have you heard of the Pennsylvania Anti-Slavery Society and its Vigilance Committee?"

"Mr. Still, you mean." This in an almost reverent tone.

"Yes. Every one of the committee members is involved in this case. They would take good care of you if you were to agree to come. The sooner the better."

"Well..." He worked his mouth as he considered. Then, "If it is the only way for Bella to be safe, I will come."

"Good. Let us return to the house and make our plans."

Mrs. Cooke heard the proposal with something less than enthusiasm. "Of course I want to help Bella," she said. "But I fear for you traveling so far amongst people unknown to us. Why not let the gentleman take the ledger along on his own?"

Peter and Reverend Cooke shook their heads at the same time. The minister said, "That book is a sacred responsibility. I cannot let it out of my hands," followed by Peter saying, "I need a witness to attest to its authenticity."

She made a bitter sound. "Will they even allow him to testify? I thought Negroes were non-citizens whose word could not be trusted."

Peter placed a gentle hand on her arm. "He will be admitted to testify. Of this I am certain. And I pledge to you that no harm will come to him. He will be in the capable hands of William Still and his compatriots."

"I appreciate that," said the preacher, "but it is the Lord God whose hands will protect me. He would want me to do whatever I can to help that poor sweet child."

And so it was settled that Reverend Cooke would take the first train after Sunday services the following morning. He would be met by a member of the Vigilance Committee and given shelter in the black community, then escorted to the Commissioner's office at the appointed time.

It was nearing the dinner hour, and Mrs. Cooke insisted on providing them with a small meal before they walked back to town. While they ate, Peter said,

"As grateful as I am for your willingness to testify, I must find another witness who is, uh..." An embarrassed pause. "...outside of the church but who might have known Bella."

With perfect understanding, "You mean a white person."

Peter nodded. "I am ashamed to say it. But my single goal is Bella's freedom. I must in good conscience pursue any avenue that would aid in that cause."

"Of course. Let me think on it."

"As it happens, Bella made a suggestion of her own. She tells me she was taught as a youngster by a teacher named Dora Pullman. Do you know of her?"

"I do remember her. A pretty young thing. Did not shirk from teaching little black children. Although they did sit separate from the whites."

"Do you happen to know what became of her?"

He shook his head. "Probably married up. She left town not too long after Bella finished school. Wish I could be of more help."

"It was a longshot. We can inquire further in town." He looked at Cora, saw she was finished eating, and rose from the table. "We are most grateful for your help. I will notify Mr. Still of your arrival tomorrow afternoon."

They said their goodbyes and went out into the sunshine. As they stepped down from the small stoop and turned toward the road, Cora saw a man disappear into a copse of trees some twenty yards beyond. It was only a brief glimpse, but she was certain he was the gentleman from the train. She looked up at Peter and said,

"Did you see him?"

A grim nod. "Perhaps it is nothing. A mere coincidence. However, I have learned to be wary of coincidences."

He settled his hat on his head, offered his arm, and they set out for town.

Chapter Thirty-One

On their way back to town, Cora and Peter checked often to see whether the mysterious stranger was following them. By the time they entered the store where their quest had begun, Cora concluded they had allowed their passion for Bella's cause to fuel a perhaps unwarranted suspicion.

The same woman who had directed them earlier sat on a stool behind the counter. Seeing them, she rose, patted her light-brown hair into place, and said,

"Did you find the church?"

"We did," said Peter. "And we thank you for your directions. But we are hoping you can help us on another matter. Have you lived in the village long?"

"My whole life. Why?"

"Did you know a young woman by the name of Dora Pullman? We believe she taught school here in days past."

"Dora? 'Course I knew her. Everybody did. Her daddy was a big man over to the mill."

"You speak of her in the past tense. Is she still living?"

"I hope so. Not that I know for certain. She married the upper mill's head clerk, but they moved on to a bigger mill up in New York State quite a few years ago."

Cora murmured a soft, "Oh," of disappointment.

The woman eyed them with deepened interest. "What does Dora have to do with this legal matter of yours?"

"Nothing direct, I assure you," said Peter. "We were simply hoping to use her as a witness in a particular matter. But obviously that will not be possible. Thank you for your time."

They were just stepping out into the sunshine of an increasingly warm day when Cora pulled on Peter's arm, saying, "Wait!"

He looked down at her with mild curiosity.

"She said she has lived here her entire life. She also appears to be about Bella's age. Perhaps..."

Peter took her meaning immediately. He said, "Of course," even as he pivoted back toward the store's entrance.

The woman was just settling back onto her stool when she saw them returning. Brow raised, she said, "Yes?"

"I believe you may be able to help us after all," said Peter. "First allow me to introduce myself. Peter Ware, Esquire, and my companion, Miss Cora Fielding."

The formality seemed to please her. "Mr. Ware, Miss Fielding. I am Mrs. Dickson."

He dipped his head. "We are here on behalf of my client, a woman by the name of Bella Carlyle. Does that name mean anything to you?"

A moment's hesitation. Then, "Bella...yes, I remember her. Only she was Bella Richards then. She was two years behind me in school. Smart girl."

"What year would that have been?"

A tight smile. "Are you asking me my age?"

"We mean no disrespect," said Cora. "We simply need to prove that Bella lived here in Glen Mills prior to the year 1838."

"Why?"

"Because a planter from Virginia says she was raised as his slave until she ran away that year. He has brought her before the United States Commissioner in Philadelphia with the intent of taking her back to Virginia as his slave."

"Well, gracious me, he is certainly mistaken. She was here, all right."

"Will you come to Philadelphia and testify to that?"

Her eyes widened. "To Philadelphia? Then who would run my store?"

"It would only be for a day or two. Could you not find someone to step in for you here?"

Her expression tightened with resolve. "Absolutely not. I never been on one of them trains, and I don't plan on starting now. Besides, my husband would never allow it."

Cora looked up at Peter in despair. His expression held nothing but polite unconcern. He said, "Then perhaps you would be willing to sign a sworn statement about your acquaintance with Bella."

She cocked her head. "I could do it right here? Not in Philadelphia?"

"Absolutely."

"Well, then, I'd be happy to oblige. I surely would hate to think of Bella being sent off into slavery."

Peter lifted his case to the counter, opened it, and took out a sheet of paper, an inkwell, and a steel pen. "May I ask your full legal name?"

"Well, I don't know legal. My husband's name is Abraham. My Christian name is Winifred."

He nodded, thought a moment, then began to write. When he had finished, he handed the document to her, saying, "Is this something you can sign?"

She took a pair of spectacles from beneath the counter, hooked them over her ears, and read slowly aloud,

"I, Winifred Dickson, do solemnly swear before God and these witnesses that I am a lifelong resident of Glen Mills, Pennsylvania and did attend grammar school with a Negro girl by the name of Bella Richards under the teacherage of Miss Dora Pullman. I know that said Bella Richards married Robert Carlyle in 1837 and continued to reside in Glen Mills for several years thereafter. I am of sound mind and do sign this statement of my free will."

She looked up at Peter. "I 'spect I can sign it. I never knew Bella after school, but I sure did see her around, and I know she was here. Went to work for that old Mrs. Porter after her husband died."

"Good. Now we must find another witness to your signature besides Miss Fielding. Do you have any suggestions?"

"Well, there's old Mr. Myers down to the feed store."

Even though she had balked at closing her store for a period of days, she showed no compunction in coming with them now, a decision that seemingly held little risk given that not a single customer had come in while they talked. She led them out and locked the door behind them. They found the feed store across the road and some distance north. Mr. Myers was a stooped, elderly man who greeted their request with the excitement only a person unused to variation in his life would have.

Peter produced the pen and ink and gave it to Mrs. Dickson for her to sign the document. Mr. Myers, then Cora signed their names on the lines he had drawn for witness signatures. When all was finished, Peter thanked Mr. Myer and placed the document in his case. They accompanied Mrs. Dickson back to her store, then set out for the train's ticket shed, well pleased with their day's work.

∞∞∞

Carl felt restless and bored beyond reason. It was a beautiful Saturday with the promise of spring permeating every corner of creation. Yet here he was, sprawled across his bed with nothing to do. He had risen for breakfast, but his friends were still snoring away at nearly one o'clock in the afternoon. Now that their first-year classes were over, their only goals seemed to be to rise in time for dinner, then while away the afternoon until they could go out and carouse again in the evening.

It was a lifestyle that had been wearing on Carl for some time, causing him to reevaluate where his life was headed. He and Cora would celebrate their twenty-second birthday next month, yet he did not feel as if the past year had led him any closer to full maturity than had the prior twenty one. He was stuck in a behavior pattern of which he was not proud but could not seem to summon the will to discard.

His brief courtship of Annabelle Ware had been his one bright period, but now that the initial pain had passed, he knew that Cora's assessment of that liaison was correct. He had idealized her and used the dream of their possible union as an escape from the misery that defined most of his waking hours.

He was also coming to acknowledge that Cora was correct in believing he was not cut out for medicine. He certainly admired the call to healing and the elimination of suffering, but he did not feel it tugging at his heart as it did Cora's. Yet what else could he do?

His mind turned from that vexing question, as it often had since Easter Sunday, to Cora's friend Gwen Pickering. She was not as beautiful as Annabelle, but her appearance was certainly not disagreeable. Indeed, her animated features, clear rosy skin, and warm hazel eyes struck a pleasant chord in his heart. She was quick-witted, cheerful, attentive, and possessed an appealing wholesomeness that was far from Annabelle's preening vanity.

He sat up, suddenly aware of what he wanted to do. Until now, he had spent most of his ill-gotten gains at the Blue Bell. Why not put them to better use? He would surprise Cora with a visit. He would invite her to come out with him for dinner at one of the nearby hotels. And inquire whether her friend Gwen was available to join them.

He rose and went to his washstand to tidy his appearance. He changed into his best suit, took up his hat and gloves, and went downstairs and out into the balmy day. It was a short three-and-a-half block walk to the two women's boardinghouse. He breathed in the fragrant air and whistled to himself as he strode along. When he arrived and rang the bell, the maid Katie answered the door.

She recognized him and let him in.

"I have come to call on my sister, Miss Fielding," he said. "Will you be so kind as to tell her I am here?"

The maid's face scrunched in apology. "Can't do that, sir. She went out early and hasn't returned."

Disappointment shattered his mood. He was about to turn away when a rare burst of determination caused him to throw caution aside and go for the prize.

"I do not suppose Miss Pickering is in?"

A bright smile. "Oh, but she is. Shall I ask whether she is able to see you?"

Resurgent hope. "Yes. Please."

She nodded and headed for the stairs. Gwen came down some ten minutes later wearing a yellow day dress that complemented her light-brown hair and hazel eyes. She came toward him with a glowing smile.

"Mr. Fielding. What a pleasant surprise. I am afraid Cora is out for the day with Mr. Ware on a legal matter."

"As it happens, I came hoping I would see you as well. I wanted to ask both of you out for dinner."

Her face stretched in astonishment. "Why—why how kind."

"I would venture to guess that you are as tired of boardinghouse food as I am. Even though Cora is away, will you consent to joining me?"

"It would be my pleasure. Allow me to fetch my outerwear."

Pleased with himself, Carl waited until she reappeared wearing her bonnet, gloves and a light cloak. Fifteen minutes later, they were seated in the dining room of the Girard House Hotel. After their orders had been taken, he said,

"So tell me, what important legal issue has taken my sister and Mr. Ware away on a Saturday as beautiful as this?"

He saw her hesitate, weighing her answer, which told him that she, and by extension Cora, did not wholly trust him. Perhaps their suspicion was justified given his past behavior. It would be his responsibility going forward to prove that he would never betray a confidence of either one.

At length she said, "Do you remember Mr. Ware's servant Bella?"

"Yes, of course. What a wonderful meal she provided us all on Easter Sunday."

"Now she is in danger, and they are doing their best to rescue her from a dire fate."

"What sort of danger?"

Another hesitation. Then, "The Mr. Taylor whose slaves Cora and Mr. Ware shepherded into freedom has taken his revenge by kidnaping Bella and attempting to take her back to Virginia as his slave."

Carl had no need to fake his horror. He had already moved past his anger over Cora's part in his loss of Annabelle. Indeed, he had admitted to himself that she and Ware had acted in righteousness, even though a lingering shadow of bitterness had prevented him from telling Cora about his change of heart. Now an innocent person had been dragged into the sordid affair. He said,

"I find such an act deplorable! What can be done?"

"It is my understanding that they are in pursuit of witnesses who will prove that Bella was here in Pennsylvania at the time this Southerner claims she was his slave. As for the particulars, I do not know."

Nor would I tell you if I did, Carl imagined her thinking. He decided it would only stoke her doubts if he pressed the issue further. Instead he said,

"I wish them the greatest success. Meanwhile, you and I are here, and I am eager to hear about your experiences in the office of your preceptor. A Dr. Preston, I believe?"

Chapter Thirty-Two

Cora was sitting in a comfortable chair in the parlor and enjoying a lazy Sunday afternoon in the company of Mr. Charles Dickens's lively characters when the doorbell rang and Mrs. Gallagher admitted an uncharacteristically disheveled Peter. He spotted her and rushed toward her.

"There has been a disturbing development. Will you come with me?"

She closed her book and said, "One moment only."

She rushed upstairs, put the book away, and grabbed her cloak and bonnet. He was hovering beside the door when she came down. When they were on the sidewalk, he said,

"I have received word that Reverend Cooke was accosted as he left the train this afternoon."

"No!"

He helped her into his buggy and urged the horse into a trot, saying, "I fear so. The Vigilance Committee sent someone to meet him and provide housing until the hearing tomorrow, but some roughnecks got to him first. You remember our mysterious fellow passenger from yesterday? Now we know, as I suggested then, that his presence was no coincidence. His sole purpose was to discover our plans and prevent our witness from testifying."

"Has he been successful? Is Reverend Cooke so badly injured he cannot attend the hearing?"

"It is unclear. Which is why I want you to examine him."

"Oh, Peter, I am not a doctor. Surely—"

"Enough of your modesty. You have studied medicine under your father for years and have completed a year of schooling. I am sorry to put you in such a position, but time is short and you are the only person we can trust. And there is more. The thugs managed to grab his church ledger and run away with it. So without documentation, we now have only the preacher's word. Making it all the more imperative that he is able to appear."

Cora fell silent, horrified to find herself responsible not only for the well-being of an old man but for critical testimony in Bella's case. She paid little attention to where they were going. At last, they pulled up in front of a clapboard building on Lombard Street. There was a shuttered milliner's shop on the street level. Peter helped her down, and they climbed an outdoor wooden staircase to the second floor.

Peter knocked, and they were admitted by a teenaged boy with short-cropped hair, copper skin, and a tall lanky frame.

"Hello, Joshua," said Peter. "This is Miss Fielding. She is here to see your mother's guest."

The boy led them into a tidy living area and through a door into a bedroom. Enough light came through the window to reveal a dark-skinned woman, apparently the boy's mother, sitting beside the bed where Sebastian Cooke lay dozing. Peter introduced her as Mrs. Littleton.

She acknowledged Cora, then turned back to her patient and gave his shoulder a gentle shake. He wakened with a low grunt of pain. His face was a mass of bruises, one eye so swollen it refused to open. He shifted with a wince and raised his head to take them in.

"Ah-h. Mr. Ware. And Miss Fielding. You will pardon me if I do not rise to greet you."

Cora sat beside him and took his calloused hand in hers. "How can you ever forgive us for putting you in such danger? If we had known—"

"Hush, child," he interrupted. "This is not your doing. I regret nothing and am prepared to go forward as planned. However, the ledger has been lost, and Mr. Ware will have my word alone as to Bella's baptism and marriage."

Cora was amazed at his equanimity over the beating he had taken, not to mention the loss of the cherished book that contained the life statistics of his entire congregation.

She said, "First, we must make certain your injuries are not serious enough to prevent you from testifying. I am a medical student who has had much experience under the tutelage of my physician father. May I have your permission to examine you?"

"I assure you that all the demons of hell could not keep me away from that hearing. But if it will put your mind at rest, I am happy for you to do as you will with this old body of mine."

She pulled back the covers, lifted his shirt, and palpated his abdomen, searching for any particular areas of excessive pain. Finding none, she put her ear to his chest and listened to the rhythmic beating of a strong heart. She examined his legs and arms and moved the joints to assure there were no fractures.

She said, "Are you able to sit up?"

"Of course." His reply was ready enough, but when she slipped her arm behind his back to assist him, he emitted a low moan. Mrs. Littleton sprang up and lent a sturdy arm to support him while Cora searched for the source of his discomfort.

"Your ribs," she said at last. "Did they kick you?"

"Once or twice," he admitted through gritted teeth.

She nodded and eased him back down. To Mrs. Littleton, "If you have a long length of cloth, binding him tightly around the chest will help."

"Done," the woman assured him.

Cora examined the cuts and bruises on his face and found them to be mostly superficial. "These can be bathed in warm water, and a warm wet compress on that eye should bring some relief. Otherwise, I believe he will heal without lasting consequences."

She looked up at Peter, and he favored her with a soft, intimate smile. Then he said to Joshua Littleton, who was hovering near the doorway, "When Reverend Cooke comes to the courthouse tomorrow, there must be a strong, effective guard surrounding him."

The young man's face wore an expression of anger and resolve. "Leave it to me. I promise on my life that no harm will come to him."

"Good." He helped Cora up from the bed. Then he gripped the old man's hand and said, "Until tomorrow."

The minister gave a weak nod, his eyelids already closing in sleep.

On the way back to Cora's boardinghouse, they talked about the morrow in hushed, hopeful tones. When they arrived, he placed his hands on her waist and lifted her down. Instead of releasing her, he pulled her into an embrace.

"You were wonderful," he murmured in her ear. "What should I ever do without you?"

Taken by surprise, Cora felt her knees go suddenly weak. This was the closest he had ever come to a declaration of love. Had the moment she had dreamed of for months finally come?

He pulled back to hold her at arm's length, and for a moment she thought—no, hoped— he would kiss her. Then he broke away and offered his arm. Disappointed, she allowed him to escort her into the house.

∞∞∞

By the time Monday morning arrived, word of Bella Carlyle's arrest and the subsequent assault on a man of the cloth who had come to testify on her behalf had spread throughout the city, not only in the wards heavily occupied by black people but also among those committed to the abolitionist cause. Many noted Quakers had written pieces of outrage in the local papers, and whites and blacks had converged on the courthouse by the time Peter and Cora arrived for the hearing.

The crowds had spread throughout the building and its corridors, requiring Peter to literally push their way through to Commissioner Longstreth's office, a room merely twelve feet by fourteen feet in size. Peter had barely settled himself at the prisoner's table, Cora behind him, when the crowd convulsed and belched forth Bella flanked by two deputy marshals. A chair was placed for her beside Peter, and they conversed head to head until the same upheaval produced Franklin Ware and his counsel, Benjamin Brewster. They were accompanied by Charles Taylor, his wife and daughter, and, to Cora's consternation, The Reverend Matthew Ware, Peter's father, his wife Gertrude and daughter Annabelle.

She leaned forward to tap his shoulder.

"Look who is here."

He rotated his head to take in the newcomers. Cora saw a momentary tightening of his expression. Then a mask of indifference fell over his face. He said, 'No matter," and turned back to face the front of the room.

Commissioner Longstreth, a slender, light-haired man with a long face and humorless visage, stood and raised his arms, calling, "Silence!"

When the result was less than satisfactory, he called out again, "Order! This hearing will come to order!"

The general din gradually subsided. Into the new silence, Attorney Brewster rose and said, "Mr. Commissioner, I object in the strongest terms to this display of partisanship. These people are here to undermine the claimant's case, and I demand that they be banned from the proceedings."

Peter rose amongst the resultant scornful murmurings to say, "Mr. Commissioner, does Mr. Brewster suggest that your judgment would be swayed by the presence of the audience, thus impugning your ability to be fair? Furthermore, I would remind opposing counsel that this is a public hearing, and the public has every right to be here. However, I would posit that due to the infamy of this case, this small room is not an adequate venue in which to conduct the hearing. Therefore, I request that it be moved to a larger space so that all interests may be fairly represented."

While the commissioner ruminated, Cora's heart nearly burst with pride for Peter's eloquence and quick thinking. He had warned her that given recent history, the chances of success in a case like this were not great. She, however, believed with all her heart that if anyone could prevail over these forces of wickedness, it was he.

As it happened, the commissioner agreed with Peter's reasoning and left the chamber for several minutes before returning and announcing that the hearing would reconvene in the U. S. District Courtroom.

Even this larger room was inadequate for all who wished to witness the affair, but those lucky ones who managed to get in found their places, either sitting or standing along the walls, while the remainder crowded the hallways and gathered outside in the street. There had seldom been such a public display of support for an individual in similar circumstances, and the fact warmed Cora's heart to the core.

Benjamin Brewster was first to present his client's case. He gave a rather pedantic statement in which he purported to prove that Bella was escaped slave Felicity Taylor, a housemaid in the service of the present owner's father. This slave, he claimed, had an insolent, disrespectful demeanor and was lazy in the performance of her duties, which often meant other servants were required to do her work as well as their own. A fellow housemaid came to the end of her patience one morning when she discovered Felicity sound asleep in a corner when she was supposed to be cleaning the ashes from the fireplaces of the big house. This maid informed the butler of Felicity's behavior, resulting in her being rightfully disciplined. An angry, defiant Felicity hid in an outgoing load of hay and escaped to the north through the aid of the Underground Railroad. She was spotted and recognized by Mr. Franklin Taylor on the previous Friday, April Thirteenth, during a visit to his brother here in Philadelphia. He immediately obtained a writ of *habeas corpus*, after which U.S. Marshal Jacob Yost swore out a warrant and took her into custody.

Following his statement, Mr. Brewster called his client to the stand. The Southerner's sworn testimony largely repeated his attorney's opening statement with the exception that he offered corroboration in the form of family estate records from the years 1829 through 1839. These records included a list of property in which the name Felicity Taylor appeared in all years except 1839 when her name was absent. Mr. Brewster hammered the latter point home then surrendered his client to Peter for cross-examination.

"How old were you at the time of this slave's supposed escape, Mr. Taylor?"

"Twenty-three," he replied.

"Was the maid Felicity your personal slave?"

An imperious sniff. "Of course not. I had my own man."

"So your contact with her was limited. Yet you expect us to believe that a young blade such as yourself paid enough attention to a mere housemaid that you would recognize her on the street after twenty-two years had passed?"

"I saw her daily for many years. And..." He raised a finger to point at Bella. "...she sits before me now."

"Did you personally observe the egregious behavior of which both Mr. Brewster and you testified?"

"I did."

"You saw the maid Felicity asleep in a corner in your father's house?"

"Well, no. But I observed her insolence on many occasions."

"Would you care to give us a specific example? Include, if you will, what she did and said that was, in your judgment, so very insolent."

He fidgeted, his face turning a telltale pink. Finally he said, "Nothing in particular stands out in my mind. But I can assure you her general demeanor was arrogant and not at all suited to her station."

"That bad?"

Laughter rippled through the hall. A frown from the commissioner prompted Peter to continue with,

"Now let me take you back to last Friday when you purport to have seen the prisoner on the street. Where exactly was that sighting?"

"On Market Street."

"Can you be more precise?"

With visible irritation, "I am not a citizen of this city. Thus I am not intimately familiar with its streets. I was simply strolling along the street admiring the stalls when I saw her."

"What was she doing?"

"Coming toward me in the opposite direction."

"Were you alone at the time?"

"I was."

"And on recognizing this long-lost slave, did you call out to her? Or run after her? Or raise a general alarm? Perhaps call for a constable?"

Through clenched teeth, "I did not. I knew right away that her face was familiar, but by the time I realized who she was, she was gone."

"Then how did you know where to find her so she could be arrested?"

"Well, I...I...I followed her to her place of residence."

"So you had not lost sight of her after all." Peter allowed his statement to hang for a moment then continued, "When did you arrive in the city, Mr. Taylor?"

"Wednesday past."

"And your purpose for coming?"

"To visit my brother and his family. *Obviously.*"

"How often do you make the trip from Virginia to Philadelphia?"

"As often as possible since he is my only living relative outside of my wife and children."

"Do you usually bring your estate records with you on such visits?"

He shifted and straightened his coat. "Only when I wish to work on them while I am here."

"Ah. And can you tell us of another instance in which you have done so?"

"Not with any specificity. Certainly not as to a precise date."

"Hm-m. Memory is a pesky thing, is it not? You can remember the prisoner from your scant contact with her more than twenty years ago but not the particulars of your bookkeeping practices while visiting your family in recent years."

Attorney Brewster rose and said, "I object, Mr. Commissioner. Counsel is arguing rather than asking the witness a question as is required during cross-examination."

Mr. Longstreth nodded. "Sustained. Do you have another question for this witness, Mr. Ware?"

"I do. Mr. Taylor, do you normally bring your family with you when you come to Philadelphia?"

"I certainly prefer to do so."

Brewster had barely settled himself when he popped up again. "Mr. Commissioner, I fail to see what the claimant's travel habits have to do with this case."

"They have everything to do with it," Peter rebutted. "The prisoner posits that Mr. Taylor's visit here was not one of leisure, especially since his family did not accompany him. Instead, we believe he came solely for the purpose of perpetrating this fraud. That he came contrary to his normal routine tells volumes about his intent."

The commissioner considered. Then said, "I take your point, Mr. Ware. Please move on."

"Thank you, but I have no further questions for the witness."

He bowed and sat down.

Brewster's next sworn witness was a Mr. Willoughby, who claimed to have grown up on a Virginia plantation several miles from the Taylor estate but who now owned a small hotel in Philadelphia. He testified that his parents were close friends of the Franklin Taylor family, and the two families often visited back and forth for days at a time during his childhood. He had seen the maid Felicity going about her duties on many occasions, and he identified Bella as being she.

On cross-examination, Peter said, "I ask you the same question I put to Mr. Taylor. How old were you at the time of these observations?"

"As I said before, we visited the Taylors over a period of years."

"Since the slave Felicity disappeared in the year 1838, you could begin by telling us your age during that year."

A slight shifting of position. "Let me see. I would have been eleven years old that year."

"Ah. A lad of eleven and younger. Yet you expect us to believe you recognize this person sitting before you as the same maid?"

"I do. I am certain of it."

Peter shook his head in exaggerated disbelief. "Then I expect the commissioner will weigh the accuracy of your testimony in light of your young years. You may step down."

The next witness, a Mr. Silas Mangrove, was a brawny, gray-haired man of perhaps sixty years who was the white overseer of the Taylor property. He testified to having known Felicity her entire life until the time of her escape. He identified her without hesitation as the woman sitting at the defense table.

Peter approached him with disgust written on his face. "Am I not correct in surmising that your primary responsibilities are with regard to the field hands of the Taylor farm?"

"Yep."

"Then how is it you are able to speak with such certainty about a housemaid?"

"Easy. I'm the one who whupped her when she had to be disciplined."

"You 'whupped' her. I assume by that you mean you bullwhipped her."

He shrugged. "Just a few strokes to get her attention."

"It has been suggested that this Felicity hid in an outgoing load of hay. How did she manage to do that? Were you not vigilant against such a possibility?"

"Can't watch every single thing that goes on. When she was reported missing, the wagon driver finally admitted she was in the load and he dropped her off along the roadway."

"He 'finally admitted?' By that you mean through a whipping of his own?"

Another shrug. "That's how it works."

"How proud we are for you and your ways! You may step down."

Mr. Brewster rose, saying, "Mr. Commissioner, I object to Mr. Ware's sarcastic tone. It is not the business of this hearing to condemn the practices of southern culture, abhorrent though they may be to many of us in the North."

Commissioner Longstreth nodded and said, "I agree. Mr. Ware, you will refrain from injecting your views, however subtly, into this hearing."

Peter said, "I apologize for my zeal, Mr. Commissioner. It will not happen again."

"See that it does not. Do you have further witnesses, Mr. Brewster?"

"Yes, sir. One. I call Delilah Taylor to the stand."

A wraith of a woman wearing the homespun dress and kerchief of a slave came forward and was sworn. Her seamed face put her somewhere in late middle age. Eyes downcast, she testified in a voice barely discernable in the large room that she was the older sister of Felicity Taylor, who ran away in 1838 when she was eighteen and Delilah was twenty. When asked if she could identify her sister in the room, she pointed to Bella. Brewster nodded and turned her over to Peter.

He approached her and asked in a kind voice, "Did you work alongside your sister as a housemaid?"

"No, suh. I's a cook's helper."

"Did you accompany your master Mr. Taylor into Pennsylvania in order to testify here today?"

An excited rumble rolled through the room. Was Peter about to whisk this slave away from her master as he had done the three the previous winter?

"No, suh. He sent me separate with de boss man."

The air seemed to rush from the room. Of course Franklin Taylor would not be foolish enough to risk bringing the slave himself, having learned the hard way.

"And when did the two of you arrive here?"

Her eyes darted toward Franklin Taylor then returned to her lap. "Don' know fer sure."

"Was it before or after your master came?"

"'Bout the same time, I 'spect."

"Do you have any idea why the two of you were sent given the fact that your master had not even seen your supposed sister here until three days ago?"

"No, suh. I goes where I's sent."

"Of course you do. Moving on, do you understand that having sworn on the Bible, you are obligated to tell the truth here?"

Refusing to look at him, she nodded, saying, "Felicity is my sister."

"And you are sure, after all this time, that the woman at the defense table is your sister?"

"Looks like her. Dat's all I kin say."

Peter took his seat, and Benjamin Brewster stated that he had completed his case.

The commissioner looked at the clock on the wall, which read twenty minutes before two. He said, "We will now take a dinner recess and reconvene at three o'clock." To Peter, "Will you be prepared to present your case at that time?"

"I will."

"Then this hearing is suspended until three o'clock."

Chapter Thirty-Three

As the crowd dispersed to find something to eat, Cora noticed that even though the majority of the bystanders were sympathetic to Bella's side, there were also a number of those who supported Franklin Taylor. His brother's family, of course, and the Ware family, but also a number of parishioners and other acquaintances. She saw their hateful glares as they left the courtroom and held her head as high as her five-foot frame would allow.

They found Reverend Cooke and his contingent of bodyguards outside. The old man still bore the marks of his assault and he moved more slowly than even his age would allow, but he greeted them with a game smile, stating himself ready to go into the lion's den on behalf of a sister in the faith. He produced a large basket sent along by Mrs. Littleton. Inside were sandwiches, fruit, sweet cakes, and a jar of sweet tea for their midday meal.

To avoid the crowds, they walked over to Washington Park and found a space on the greening lawn where they could spread out the cloth she had provided and sit for a pleasant picnic. They whiled away the next hour, some of the young men stretching out for a nap. When it was time, they gathered the remnants of the meal into the basket and walked back to the courthouse.

Peter had already explained his planned trial strategy to Cora: first call witnesses to establish Bella's current reputation, then refute what he could of the testimony of Franklin Taylor and his witnesses, and finally, prove that Bella was far away from Virginia at the time they claimed she was Taylor's slave.

He began by calling a parade of people who knew Bella from her church activities or from her dealings with the local merchants as Peter's housekeeper. Each one testified to her gentle, intelligent, hard-working nature, denying on cross-examination any inference that she was the surly, disrespectful person described by the plaintiff's witnesses. Then he said,

"I now call Mr. Bernard Carver."

The man who came forward was a sturdy, light-skinned mulatto who wore the uniform of a train porter. He was sworn and took the witness chair.

Peter began with, "Mr. Carver, do you recognize anyone in this room?"

"I sure do." He pointed at Franklin Taylor. "That gentleman there."

"How is it that you know him?"

"Well, I don't rightly know him. But I tended to him when he traveled on the Philadelphia, Wilmington and Baltimore Railroad. Helped him with his small bags when he got off here in Philadelphia."

"And when was this?"

"This Saturday past, sir."

"Two days ago on Saturday, not five days ago on Wednesday?"

"That is correct."

"Thank you." Turning to the claimant's table, "You may examine this witness."

Benjamin Brewster rose and said, "Mr. Carver, how many passengers would you say you encounter in the course of each day?"

He shrugged. "Hundreds at least."

"Yet among those hundreds every day of the year, you are able to identify one whom you supposedly aided two days ago?"

"I am good with faces, sir. This man in particular was memorable for the fact that he addressed me as 'boy' despite my age of thirty-three."

"Mm-m. No further questions. You may step down."

When the porter had left the room, Peter said, "I would now like to ask Mr. Commissioner's indulgence on a particular matter. Mr. Taylor and his overseer, Mr. Silas Mangrove, have both sworn that the slave Felicity was disciplined by means of the lash for shirking her responsibilities. The prisoner is eager and willing to refute this claim by displaying her bare back for any signs of this so-called whipping. My colleague Miss Fielding is prepared to assist the prisoner in disrobing sufficiently to expose her back to view while still guarding her modesty."

Another swell of audience response filled the air. At the same time, Mr. Brewster rose to proclaim, "Mr. Commissioner, I and my client object most strenuously to this stunt! To expose a woman's bare skin to a roomful of gawkers? It is outrageous!"

Absolute silence fell as the commissioner considered his response. Finally he rose and said, "I admit to the unusual nature of this request. However, certain testimony has been given under oath. The prisoner has no means by which to refute it except through the evidence of her own body. The objection is overruled."

Cora suppressed her glee and went to where Bella sat. She had brought a large shawl for this purpose. She draped it around Bella's shoulders and tied it beneath her chin. She reached under it and undid the hooks down the back of the housekeeper's dress. When she was finished, she pushed the loose sides out toward her shoulders. The two of them and Peter approached Commissioner Longstreth. Bella turned to face the courtroom while Cora raised the V-shaped tail of the shawl to expose the smooth brown skin underneath.

The commissioner stared at Bella's back for some moments, then nodded and said, "That is all. You may return to your seats."

The audience had been craning their necks for some glimpse of the flesh beneath the shawl, but not a single inch had been visible no matter where one was placed in the room. The commissioner said,

"The record will show that no visible scars mark the prisoner's back. Do you have another witness, Mr. Ware?"

Chatter, some of disappointment, most of satisfaction spread like fire through the room, but the commissioner soon silenced it with a deep scowl. Peter allowed time for the full advantage of this repudiation to play out before saying,

"The defense now calls the Reverend Sebastian Cooke of the Thornbury A.M.E. Methodist Church located in Glen Mills, Pennsylvania."

The old man shuffled forward leaning heavily on a stout walking stick. He sat in the witness chair with a huff of pain, eliciting murmurs of consternation from the onlookers. His face looked, if anything, worse than it had the day before, a swollen purple lump occluding his left eye altogether.

"Reverend Cooke," said Peter, "will you please tell the commissioner and this body what happened to you in the course of your attempt to appear at this hearing?"

Brewster leapt to his feet. "Objection! What happened to the witness prior to his appearance has no relevance to this hearing."

The commissioner pulled a face and said, "I tend to agree with you, Mr. Brewster. I also believe the witness's unfortunate experience has been well documented in the press. Please move on, Mr. Ware."

"Very well." To the reverend, "Is the prisoner before us known to you?"

"She is. She is Bella Carlyle, whose maiden name was Richards. She and her parents were my parishioners in Glen Mills. In fact, I baptized Bella as an infant. I also performed the marriage ceremony between Bella and Mr. Robert Carlyle in 1837."

"Baptized and married—can you prove you performed these ceremonies?"

"I was prepared to do so and brought with me the church's ledger listing all baptisms and marriages going back to the early part of this century."

"Where is this ledger now?"

"I do not know. It was stolen from me as I left the train from Glen Mills yesterday afternoon about four o'clock."

"Exactly how did you lose custody of the ledger? Was your physical person attacked in the process?"

Brewster was on his feet again. In a mock tone of exhaustion, "Mr. Commissioner, you have already ruled about the relevance of this testimony. My colleague either has a faulty memory or is attempting to circumvent your decision."

Peter countered with, "The question relates to the attempt by persons unknown to suppress evidence in this hearing, the goal of which was to prevent my client from defending herself against these false charges."

Longstretch pursed his lips and pulled at the loose skin beneath his chin. At length he said, "I believe Mr. Ware has now laid the proper foundation for this testimony. Objection overruled."

Peter wasted no time in repeating, "How was the ledger taken from you, Reverend Cooke?"

"That ledger is my sacred trust since it contains the entire historical record of my congregation. Therefore, I did not release it willingly. I held on as long as possible, but there were three people beating on me, and in an attempt to defend myself, I was unable to keep control of it."

Peter nodded and said, "I have no further questions at this time."

He had not even gained his seat before Benjamin Brewster was on his feet and leaning into the old man's face.

"How old are you, Mr. Cooke."

His failure to use the honorary "Reverend" was not lost on anyone in the courtroom.

"Seventy-nine this coming August."

"A nice long life. Do you consider your mind to be as keen as it was, say, ten years ago?"

"No. Do you?"

A ripple of laughter.

"What about your memory? Do you believe you would recognize any parishioner of yours, no matter how long since you had last seen that person?"

"It depends on how long I knew them. In Bella's case, I was her pastor for over thirty years. I have no doubt that the person you see over there is she."

"So you say. Now, I would like to make clear my regret over the assault you experienced yesterday. But without the ledger in hand, how are we to know it even exists? That you did not make it up in order to help a fellow person of your race?"

Again some of the onlookers murmured their outrage over this question. The reverend, however, remained as calm of face as his wounds would allow.

"You have only my word, sir, sworn on the holiest of Books. Were I to profane against it, I would expect my Savior to turn against me and deny me the salvation to which I now cling. Judge my truthfulness as you will, but I do not fear it. I answer to one Power alone, and it is certainly not you."

A muted cheer was quickly suppressed by a look from the commissioner. Meanwhile, Brewster shook his head, threw up his hands in mock surrender, and returned to his seat.

Commissioner Longstreth gave a pointed look at the wall clock, which read nearly four-thirty, and said to Peter,

"Can you estimate how much time you will need to finish your side of the case?"

Peter offered a wide, handsome smile. "Not much longer, Mr. Commissioner. I have a sworn statement to present. And one final witness."

"Very well. May I see this statement?"

"Of course. It is from a white woman by the name of Mrs. Winifred Dickson who manages a general store in Glen Mills. Mrs. Dickson went to grammar school with Bella Carlyle, both races being accommodated in one small building and taught by a Miss Dora Pullman. She warrants that she knew Bella from their time in school together through Bella's marriage in 1837 and her employment with a local widow for many years thereafter."

He carried the document to the commissioner even as lawyer Brewster came over to examine it himself. The latter said in a sneering tone,

"One of the document's signed witnesses is your very own assistant, Miss Fielding. How are we to know this is legitimate?"

"If you are impugning Miss Fielding's integrity, I take serious exception to that. However, rather than call her as a witness, I shall move on to my final witness."

He turned and said in a loud voice, "The prisoner calls Mrs. Emmeline Norton to the stand."

Cora's mouth dropped just as far as anyone else's in the room. The rear door opened, and Emmeline hobbled forward, the rhythmic taps of her cane on the wood floor resounding like drumbeats in the stunned silence.

Cora sent Peter an astonished, questioning look, but he merely gave her a secret smile and watched his witness make her way to the witness chair. When she arrived and placed her hand on the Bible to be sworn, her brother Reverend Ware rose, pointed a long finger at her, and cried, "For shame! Judas! Betrayer!"

Charles Taylor rose beside him, his face purple with rage. "You—" he began in a strangled voice. Suddenly he clutched his chest, made a loud, unintelligible sound, and dropped to the floor.

His wife Eugenia screamed, "You have killed him!" after which she fainted dead away.

Chapter Thirty-Four

"Help!" cried Mary Lee Taylor. "A doctor! Help!"

Acting on instinct, Cora hurried toward the knot of people who had closed in around the Charles Taylor family. She pushed through to where Charles lay in a heap on the floor between two rows of spectator benches. His wife, still insensate, had collapsed sideways against her daughter.

Cora focused on the downed man, whose color was fast bluing.

"Get back!" she cried to those hovering over him. "Give him some space."

As they shuffled backward, she straightened the man's legs so that he lay in a supine position. She felt his carotid artery for a pulse and found only a faint, uneven throbbing. His face was turning bluer by the moment. As she frantically searched for some remedy, a memory from her days in her father's clinic popped into her head.

She tugged on his shoulders and hips in an attempt to roll him over onto his stomach. Finding him too heavy to deal with on her own, she looked up to see a strapping young man gawking nearby.

"Help me," she said to him. "We need to turn him to a prone position."

Startled but eager to help, the young man did as she asked. When he started to back away, she said, "Stay. I need you to help me rotate him from front to side, then back again, then to the opposite side. We need to do this repeatedly to possibly restore respiration."

Together they performed this rotation as rapidly as was possible. When Cora thought she saw a lightening of the man's complexion, she decided to try another technique that she had read about but that had gone out of favor in the present century. With Taylor on his side, she leaned down and placed her mouth over his, ignoring the gasp that arose around her. She blew a steady stream of air between

279

the flaccid lips. Took another breath and blew again. And yet again. Her patient jerked and drew in a loud, rasping breath.

"Thank God!" cried Eugenia Taylor, who had revived while Cora was ministering to her husband. "You saved him!"

Cora knew this assertion to be far from certain. Her fingers returned to the man's neck only to find his pulse still thready and arrhythmic. His breathing was also erratic, short shallow breaths followed by long periods of stagnation.

"He must be gotten to a hospital as quickly as possible," she said even as two court attendants appeared with a stretcher. She backed away to allow them to perform their service and returned to Peter's side.

"That was amazing," he whispered. "How did you know what to do?"

"It was something my father once did to revive a stillborn child. A method invented but a few years ago by a man named Marshall Hall. However, I doubt if it will matter in the long term. I fear his heart has been damaged and do not expect him to recover."

She looked over to where Emmeline sat in the witness chair, her face pale with shock, her hand covering her mouth in horror. Commissioner Longstreth stood behind the bench watching the drama unfold. When the attendants had carried their burden out followed by Mrs. Taylor and Mary Lee, he blinked as if coming out of a trance and said into the still roiling hubbub,

"Order, please. Order!"

As soon as he could be heard, Benjamin Brewster stood and said, "I demand a judgment, Mr. Commissioner! My client is most distressed over his brother's health and must go to his side as soon as possible. Surely the commissioner has heard enough of the various witnesses to render a verdict."

Peter allowed nary a second to pass before jumping to his feet with, "I understand the concern claimant feels over this development, but I beg the commissioner's indulgence to hear this final witness. Her testimony will take but a few minutes, and she must be heard in order for a fair judgment to be rendered."

Commissioner Longstreth's face reflected his ambivalence. Absolute silence accompanied his ruminations. At last he said,

"I am reluctant to postpone the hearing, which would require encumbering this courtroom for a second day. I will hear the witness, bearing in mind that brevity is expected."

A collective sigh greeted his announcement, whether of relief or chagrin Cora could not tell. Emmeline completed her oath. Then Peter faced her and said,

"Mrs. Norton, do you have knowledge of the Bella Carlyle arrest apart from what has taken place in this courtroom today?"

"I do."

"Then please enlighten us."

Brewster objected with, "Such a broad invitation would keep us here all night, Mr. Commissioner. Does counsel have a question for the witness?"

Peter countered, "I thought it more expeditious to allow the witness to tell her story without interruption. But if counsel desires to take more of the commissioner's time than is necessary, I shall be happy to oblige."

The commissioner scowled at Brewster. "Overruled. Let us have an end to this matter!"

Red-faced, Brewster sat down, and all eyes returned to Emmeline.

"I reside in the household of my brother, the Reverend Matthew Ware," she began. "Yesterday, the Charles Taylor family and Mr. Franklin Taylor, Mr. Charles Taylor's brother who had arrived in the city the day before, were my brother's guests for Sunday dinner. The discussion soon turned to the reason for Mr. Franklin Taylor's visit to the city, namely to claim a person by the name of Bella Carlyle as his runaway slave.

"As the conversation proceeded, Mr. Franklin Taylor stated that his sole purpose for making this claim was to punish my nephew Peter Ware, Bella Carlyle's employer and friend, for his role in freeing his three slaves over the New Year holiday. Mr. Taylor admitted that his runaway slave Felicity, whom he barely remembered from his youth, looked nothing like Mrs. Carlyle. He also admitted that he had asked his friend Mr. Willoughby to testify that he remembered Felicity from his youthful visits to the plantation and that Mrs. Carlyle was she. Finally, he said that he had sent his overseer and Felicity's sister separately for the purpose of identifying Mrs. Carlyle as Felicity. He knew this testimony to be false but also knew they could not refuse to give it because of their dependency on Mr. Taylor for their livelihood." She paused a moment for further thought. Then gave her head a decisive nod and said, "That is the essence of what I heard."

Her words elicited a hum of perturbation from the onlookers. Peter ignored it and said, "You may question the witness, Mr. Brewster."

A reluctant Brewster rose and said, "You are aware that you are under oath, are you not, Mrs. Norton?"

She scowled at him. "I am. And I take my oath most seriously. Unlike some who have testified here today."

A ripple of laughter.

Brewster turned an embarrassed face to Longstreth and said, "I can only remind Mr. Commissioner that this testimony comes from the witness's memory and may not be wholly reliable. That said, I have no further questions for her."

The commissioner nodded and said, "Very well. I will hear any final statements counsel may wish to make. Mr. Brewster?"

The gentleman took several moments to consult his notes then said, "I believe this case is simple and straightforward. While visiting his brother as he often does, Mr. Franklin Taylor happened to see his long-ago escaped slave Felicity Taylor walking the streets of Philadelphia free as a bird. As is his right under the Fugitive Slave Law of 1850, he swore out a writ in order to return her to his rightful possession. He brought records that prove he owned Felicity until the year 1838. At considerable expense to himself, he paid the passage for his overseer and the girl's own sister to come and give their sworn testimony as to her identity. He also presented the testimony of his old friend Mr. Willoughby, who also was able to identify the prisoner as Felicity. Such an accumulation of evidence can lead to only one conclusion. The woman who here presents herself as Bella Carlyle is in fact fugitive slave Felicity Taylor and must be returned to her rightful owner."

He bowed, sat down, and stared straight ahead, his demeanor impassive except for the bunched muscles of his clenched jaw.

Peter rose and said, "Mr. Commissioner, we believe we have offered ample evidence to refute claimant's demands. Let me begin with his case as presented. His witnesses rely on twenty-year-old memories for their sworn testimony. His description of Felicity's belligerent, disrespectful nature is as far from that described by acquaintances of Bella Carlyle as the moon is from the earth. Most significant of all, the real Felicity was brutally whipped for her laziness, and were such scars visible on Bella Carlyle's back, that evidence would be irrefutable. However, you have seen for yourself that her skin is as unmarked as that of a newborn baby.

"Now for our own case. Our witness places Mr. Taylor on a train arriving in Philadelphia one day after he claims to have first seen his supposed runaway slave. We have a witness and a sworn statement by another who knew Mrs. Carlyle in Glen Mills, Pennsylvania from her birth to a time well beyond the year 1838 when Mr. Taylor claims she escaped from his plantation in Virginia. The most consequential testimony of all, however, is that of Mrs. Emmeline Norton, who overheard Mr. Taylor admit to conspiring to rob an innocent woman of her freedom. In the interest of justice and fairness, I respectfully ask that you deny this claim."

Before the commissioner could respond, the rear door to the courtroom flew open, and a young man hurried down the aisle and leaned over to whisper in Mr. Bewster's ear. The attorney gave a grim nod and rose.

"Mr. Commissioner, I have just received word that the claimant's brother, Mr. Charles Taylor, has expired despite the heroic efforts of Miss Fielding. Given this development, we urge you to postpone any judgment in our case so that Mr. Taylor may go to his family and offer whatever solace is possible in such a circumstance."

Peter was about to rise and rebut when Commissioner Longstreth raised a hand to stop him. He stood behind the bench and said,

"I am grieved to hear this news. However, I do not think this matter need be delayed any further. I am ready to render judgment in the case of Franklin Taylor versus the prisoner now known as Bella Carlyle."

A collective intake of breath was followed by utter silence.

"This is a most unusual case in that both sides have presented an avalanche of witnesses such as I have seldom seen during my tenure as a commissioner. As a sworn agent of the federal government, it is my duty to uphold the law, in this instance the law of property. Whatever one might think of the morality of the slavery issue, the law supersedes all other considerations, and until the legislature sees fit to change that law, it stands as it is written in the latest statute, commonly known as the Fugitive Slave Law."

Cora's heart sank. He was going to disregard all the evidence Peter had presented and rule against Bella. Then he continued with,

"However, it is also necessary under the law for a claimant to prove ownership of the prisoner in order to prevail," and hope returned.

"In this instance," he said, "I fail to find Mr. Taylor's evidence compelling. There is no doubt in my mind that his slave Felicity escaped from his estate twenty-two years ago. That she has resurfaced here in Philadelphia is very much in doubt. We have heard testimony that calls into question his statements concerning the time and manner in which the prisoner caught his attention. Even though many years have passed since his slave received the severe beating to which the overseer Mr. Mangrove testified, one would expect there to be some marks remaining. The prisoner's skin bears no such marks. Finally, we have heard testimony as to the prisoner's presence in Pennsylvania at the time Mr. Taylor claims she was in Virginia. Not to mention the testimony of Mrs. Norton as to a possible conspiracy in bringing this case at all.

"I am reminded that the law of property must be juxtaposed against the serious issue of liberty and the bondage of a human being. To deprive the prisoner of these basic rights requires undeniable proof of original ownership."

Cries of "Thank God," rang throughout the room so that his final words, "I order the prisoner to be discharged," were nearly lost to hearing.

Chapter Thirty-Five

Pandemonium followed the commissioner's verdict. Someone went to a window, threw it open, and waved a handkerchief to the crowd in the square below as a sign of success. A deafening roar of hurrahs joined the sounds of celebration already reverberating in the courtroom.

Peter had pulled Bella to her feet and into his arms. Cora hung back, loath to intrude on their moment of triumph, but when they parted, they turned as one to Cora and folded her into a joyful three-way embrace. Then they went to find Emmeline, who had taken an unassuming position off to the side.

Their expressions of gratitude nearly overwhelmed the frail woman. They formed a protective ring around her and made their way through the celebratory crowds, out of the courthouse, and into the tumultuous square. They looked for Reverend Cooke in order to thank him for testifying despite all he had endured, but he had already been whisked away by Joshua Littleton and his volunteer bodyguards. They continued on, the going slow as hands reached out to touch or embrace Bella, but they reached Peter's buggy at last. As they drove forward, people took hold of any portion of the vehicle or harness available and accompanied them in a victory parade all the way to Peter's building.

He let the three women out and took the horse and buggy to the nearby stable where he boarded them. Meanwhile, Cora and Bella helped Emmeline into the front parlor, where Bella left them to go prepare a much-deserved tea.

Peter returned, and after Bella had served the refreshments, all three commanded her to take a seat and join in the celebration as their equal. She complied even as Cora gave in to the disparate feelings that were dueling in her mind. She was ecstatic over the outcome of the hearing, but she was also unsettled by the way it had unfolded.

She said to Peter, "Why did you not tell me Emmeline would testify?"

"I was uncertain whether she would actually appear until just before the hearing resumed after the dinner recess. If my father had learned even an inkling of what we planned, he would have made certain to keep her away."

With nascent indignation, "You did not trust my discretion?"

Emmeline saw discord blossoming and was quick to say, "Of course he did, dear. Let me explain. After I heard the conversation between my brother and the Taylors, I was beside myself over how to best use my knowledge to free Bella. I pleaded a severe headache and excused myself, using the time alone to compose a letter telling what I knew. After the Taylors left, I asked the maid to summon the yard man to come to my room. I paid him a handsome sum to take the letter to Peter."

Peter took up the narrative. "I did not see it until I arrived home after we left Reverend Cooke yesterday. I contacted Mr. Williamson of the Anti-Slavery Society, and he promised to arrange for Mrs. Norton's appearance today. I did not know he had succeeded until we returned to the hearing. It was then he told me she was secreted in a separate room and would be produced when I desired to call her."

Cora remembered him being pulled aside by a slender, well-dressed man with a long face, thick dark hair and matching sideburns shortly after they reentered the courtroom.

"You know I have complete confidence in you," he said with a smile. "Am I forgiven?"

Cora's face burned with shame for having doubted him. And over such a small, selfish issue. "Of course," she murmured, glad when Emmeline said,

"We must simply praise God that it turned out as it did. Excepting, of course, the calamity that has befallen Mr. Charles Taylor and his family. None of us would have wished such an outcome."

Not one to stay subdued for long, Cora said, "We need expend no sympathy in that quarter. He brought it on himself. He should not have conspired with his brother to perpetrate such perfidy. Let Mr. Franklin Taylor feel the sting of guilt for what happened rather than anyone in this room."

Emmeline smiled. "Has there ever been such a champion of the right as you?"

"Of course. One must only look to you."

"Perhaps, but in the process, I have caused a schism in my only remaining family that I fear will not easily mend. If ever."

Cora had not had time to consider the consequences of the day's events on her friend. Of course her testimony had put her in an untenable position with her brother and his family. She said,

"Surely your brother will eventually find it in his heart to forgive your testifying against his friend. As any Christian should do, much less a man of the cloth."

A heavy sigh. "I hope he will do so in the end as it would otherwise be a blot on his immortal soul. In the near term, however, I fear I must make other living arrangements until tempers cool."

Bella rose, hands on her hips, and declared, "You need look no further than my bed, Mrs. Norton, for I have already made it up with clean sheets for you."

Startled, she said, "Oh, no, my dear. I could not possibly impose in such a way. I shall take rooms in a hotel until things sort themselves out. You need not fuss about me."

"No fuss. In fact, I should be ashamed should you not accept my offer. I am free in large part due to your testimony, which you gave at great risk to your own happiness. I hope the Good Lord will put forgiveness in your brother's heart. But if not, I happily surrender my bed for as long as you need it."

Peter put an end to the discussion by saying, "Bella has the right solution, Mrs. Norton. Please allow us to do this for you as a small recompense for all you have done for us and our cause. As for beds, this building once housed a family of seven, and there are fully-furnished but empty rooms above. Tomorrow I shall open one for you to use for the foreseeable future. I shall also send my scrivener to collect your trunks from your brother's house. Meanwhile, Bella's rooms are on the ground level near the rear kitchen, and you must take her offer of a place to sleep for tonight."

Cora watched her friend's expression settle into acceptance. She said, "I thank you with all my heart. The long-term future can be decided as time goes on, but I appreciate not having to face my brother's fury just now."

Agreement having been reached, Cora sank back into her chair with satisfaction. It seemed that all possible permutations of the Taylor affair had come to a proper and pleasing end. Little did she know that one more drama had yet to unfold.

∞∞∞

Four days later, Carl stood with Rufus Mills and Herm Dietrich in the midnight shadows outside their boardinghouse. He had grown less and less keen about participating in the "resurrectionist" trade, as it was called by those in the press. He did not need as much money as in the past because he had greatly curtailed his nighttime carousing. Even gambling had lost its allure. Then there was the matter of his growing attraction to Gwen Pickering. What if she were to discover what he was doing? Would she give him so much as the time of day after he was exposed? Thus, if he had been able to take himself back to the day when Rufus invited him into their little band of grave robbers, he would have refused. Now, however, they were one man short because Joey Robinson had graduated and returned to Harrisburg to join his father's medical practice. Out of loyalty, he felt bound to continue helping them until a new batch of students arrived and they could recruit someone to take his place.

The sound of Zeke's old cart rattling toward them cut his ruminations short. When it stopped, he climbed in with the others and sat with his back against the slats as the old man urged his horse forward. He paid no attention to where they were going. They had harvested bodies from virtually every one of the city's many cemeteries at one time or another, and he had long since given up caring which particular one they were destined to hit that night. He closed his eyes and gave himself over to sleep until the cart jerked to a halt and Zeke called out his usual, "This is it, mates."

They were on a side road deep in the trees of Woodlands Cemetery, leading Carl to assume their target was one of the city's more illustrious citizens. Not that it mattered. Rich or poor, the schools paid the same per capita fee. And regardless of the dead person's social status in life, the grieving families would never know the ultimate fate of their loved one's mortal remains, a fact that eased the guilt Carl always felt after the mission was complete.

They took up their implements and climbed down. They left Zeke and the cart in the woods and walked out into the open burying ground. The new grave was easy to spot. They began the process of moving the flowers, which were heaped especially high in this case, and removing the soil at the coffin's head. They were an efficient team and had the hooks under the coffin lid in a matter of fifteen minutes. They heaved upward on the ropes and heard the crack of the wood as the lid snapped in two.

It was Rufus's turn to secure the rope around the body, which was an especially large one. They all took hold of the rope and pulled. The body snagged on the broken lid at first, but it eventually came free, and they leaned down to pull it out onto the ground. It was then, thanks to the ambient light of a half moon, that Carl saw the body's face.

He shrieked and fell back. "God in heaven, I know him!"

"Quiet!" hissed Rufus. "What is the matter with you?"

"I know him," he repeated in a tone that was barely softer. "Charles Taylor. The one who collapsed and died at the hearing on Monday."

News of Bella's hearing had been plastered over the front pages of the city's newspapers. Carl doubted there was a single person in Philadelphia who had not read of it.

"Well, what of it?" said Rufus. "No one will know—"

A loud retort cut him off. At the same moment, Carl felt a searing pain in his right shoulder. Nearly paralyzed with shock, his eyes roved the darkness in search of an explanation for what had just happened. Then he saw several shadowy figures emerging from a section of woods ahead of them even as Herm yelled,

"They have a gun! Run!"

Carl barely had time to respond before there was another loud report, this time from Rufus, who had removed his revolver from his waistband and fired back. One of the figures gave a loud scream and fell to the ground.

Carl spun around and ran into the trees, his throbbing arm forgotten. He heard his two partners thrashing through the brush in separate directions. Without thinking, he veered to his left and came out onto yet another section of the burial ground. A large obelisk monument sat straight ahead. He crouched down in its shadow and listened.

He heard the pursuers shout back and forth among themselves. Over it all, he heard the clamor of Zeke urging his horse and cart away from the cemetery. They were stranded.

He waited, barely daring to breathe, until he heard,

"Got one!"

The voice had come from among the trees a safe distance away, but the clear, cold air carried it to Carl's ears as if it were much closer.

"Hold him!" came a more distant voice.

Pounding feet. Heavy breathing. Then, "He the one with the gun?"

"Naw. He ain't no threat. Slimy little weasel's shakin' like to fall apart."

"Tie him up. Let's find the others."

Running feet crashing back through the woods.

The pain in Carl's shoulder made it difficult for him to think clearly, but he tried to evaluate his situation. It was apparent that the person the guards had caught was Herm. It was also clear they had secured him and abandoned him in order to pursue Rufus and Carl. Did he dare come out of hiding and try to rescue his compatriot before they returned? If he did so, would he not run the risk of being captured himself?

He had taken a tentative step away from the obelisk when he heard them returning. He darted back into the shadows and waited.

"To hell with it. We'll take this one in. He'll tell us who the others are. Right, you sniveling coward?"

Carl heard the smack of a fist on bone followed by a yelp of pain.

"Aw, leave him be. He's for jail."

"For hell, you mean. Desecrating the dead..."

"He'll pay, all right. But we'd better see to John. He went down pretty hard."

In menacing tones, "He better be okay. Come on, you bugger."

A low whimpering. Then the sounds of their retreat.

Now that he was certain he had escaped detection, Carl's awareness of the agony emanating from his shoulder surged. He gripped it with his left hand and felt blood ooze through his fingers and down his arm. A wave of light-headed nausea sent him reeling back against the marble monument.

He waited for it to pass, trying to calm his roiling mind enough to make a plan. He had to get away from there. But where to go?

As always in a crisis, the name flashed clear and strong into his mind: Cora.

Chapter Thirty-Six

Cora was sound asleep and unaware that someone had entered her room until a hand clamped over her mouth and a voice hissed,

"Sh-h-h. Not a sound."

Her body went rigid with fear as she stared at the shadowy shape kneeling on the floor beside her bed. Recognition came an instant later. She wrenched away and bolted upright, indignation giving her voice more volume that she intended.

"What are you doing here?"

"Sh-h." Then, reacting to her unwelcoming tone, a meek, "Forgive me. But I need your help. I have been shot."

Cora's anger disappeared in a heartbeat. She leapt out of bed and was reaching for the lamp when there was a light tap on her door followed by its swinging open. Gwen poked her head into the room and said,

"Cora, someone was in my—"

She stopped in mid-sentence when the pale moonlight coming through the window revealed Carl rising to his feet.

Cora struck a match and lit the lamp, the warm glow bringing the astonishing tableau into view.

"What is this about?" asked Gwen, her eyes shifting from Cora to Carl, whose face was not only bright red but suffused with shame. Then a soft gasp as she saw the spreading stain around the powder-blackened hole in his coat.

"Yes, he has been shot," said Cora. To her brother, "Quick, take off your coat."

He did so, wincing in obvious pain. His shirt was soaked with blood from shoulder to elbow. The two women began to work in tandem, Gwen tearing away the shirt sleeve while Cora rummaged in her trunk for the first-aid supplies she had taken to carrying with her since her days in her father's surgery. Gwen poured water from the pitcher into the basin as Cora examined the wound.

"It appears the shot went clean through the fleshy part of the upper arm," she said.

"Good," said Gwen, bringing the basin forward with a washcloth and soap. Together they cleansed the wound, applied a lint dressing, and wrapped clean strips of cloth around his arm to hold it in place. Only when they had finished did they look to Carl with expectant faces for an explanation.

He could not bring himself to meet their eyes. With bowed head, he said, "Thank you. I am a poor wretch who does not deserve your compassion."

Cora put her hands on her hips and said, "Posh! Groveling does not become you. Now tell us what happened."

Still looking at the floor, "I have been helping some of my fellow students in a scheme to obtain bodies for dissection."

"You *what*?"

He shrugged. Nodded.

"You have been robbing graves?"

Another nod.

"Oh, Carl. Why?"

He looked up with a hint of his former combativeness. "Why do you think? The schools pay handsomely for bodies, of which there is a constant shortage."

"And you were in such need of funds to fuel your carousing that you were reduced to body snatching?"

His complexion paled, then suffused with color. His eyes darted toward Gwen then returned to the floor.

"There is no excuse for it," he said. "These fellows were already engaged in the practice, and I went along for a cut of the profits. An arrangement I now bitterly regret. In fact, I had already decided to bow out as soon as they could find a replacement. I suppose that intention is meaningless now that we have been caught and must pay the price."

"How caught?"

A heavy sigh. "The grave we opened tonight belonged to Charles Taylor."

Cora gasped as the name's significance sank in.

He forged ahead. "The family must have posted a guard because we had barely got him out when they came at us. They fired, and the bullet struck me. One of the fellows, Rufus Mills, had a gun of his own, and he fired back. I cannot be sure, but I think he hit one of the guards. Then we all scattered."

"Where was this?"

"Woodlands Cemetery. The old man who sets things up took us there with his horse and cart." With a note of bitterness, "Drove straight away at the first sign of trouble, I might add. Looking after his own skin instead of helping his crew. Should have expected it."

"That cemetery is on the far side of the river," said Cora. "How did you get here from there?"

"How else? I walked."

"Despite your wound?" A grim shake of her head. "What then? How...?"

"Did I find your room? I knew you and Miss Pickering have the top two rooms. So I came in through the kitchen and up the back stairs. Then I picked one." An embarrassed glance at Gwen. "And guessed wrong. I realized my mistake right away and tried to back out without wakening Miss Pickering. Obviously, I did not succeed."

"I am a light sleeper," said Gwen. Her expression was one of interest rather than condemnation. Whatever her feelings for Carl, and they had discussed him enough for Cora to know she was intrigued by him, his escapade did not seem to have fazed her.

Cora made herself focus on what was needed to rescue him from this nightmare. "Do you think these guards would be able to identify you?"

"I doubt it. It was too dark. But they caught Herm and roughed him up a bit. I cannot see him protecting us for long." He shifted position. "So I am at your mercy. I do not know what to do."

"Hm-m. If one of your friends had not been apprehended, I would have suggested you simply go home and wait to see whether anything comes of it. But now..."

"Perhaps it would be wise to consult Mr. Ware," said Gwen. "Given the likely legal ramifications, he would know how best to proceed."

"Excellent idea," said Cora. "We shall go to him at once."

∞∞∞

Carl shuddered as the cell door clanked shut behind him. A shaft of morning light entered the dismal enclosure through a small high window, making it possible for him to see Herm Dietrich lying on the lower of one of the narrow two-tiered bunks provided. His friend's face bore a number of purpling bruises, attesting to the manner in which he had been treated by the Taylors' paid guards the night before. Now he raised one bleary eye, but on seeing who it was, he fell back to sleep. Carl threw himself on the bunk opposite and lay staring at the planks holding the mattress of the bed above.

He had seldom felt as miserable as he did at that moment, his desolation having robbed him of even a moment's peace throughout the long night since he turned to Cora for help. He would have welcomed his twin storming and railing and condemning him for his foolish actions. But, damn her, she had been nothing but calm and practical, making his guilt sting all the deeper.

They had walked to Peter Ware's home and office as soon as she was presentable, leaving Gwen Pickering behind with a promise to bring her up to date as soon as Cora returned. For Carl, the night's worst humiliation was the fact that Miss Pickering had witnessed it all. He recalled how lovely she had looked in her nightdress, her hair in a braid over her shoulder, her face rosy from sleep. He would never forget the feel of her sure, gentle hands as she helped clean and bandage his wound. What an angel she was, so much more thoughtful, kind and interesting than Annabelle Ware had ever been. To his present and future shame, his folly had driven away any small hope of her good opinion going forward.

He supposed he could say the same about Peter Ware, although he had seen no condemnation in the lawyer's intense brown eyes as he told his story. Only keen intelligence and speculation as he contemplated the best course forward. That he insisted Carl's only option was to turn himself in had come as a blow.

"It will put you in good stead with the authorities," he had said. "Since one of your friends was captured, your involvement will surely be revealed. For you to come forward on your own implies an honest nature. A case can be made that you three medical students were merely attempting to correct the lack of bodies for dissection, a procedure necessary for obtaining a proper knowledge of the human body. The fact that you were paid for the bodies lessens the power of that altruistic argument. Then there is the public's strong abhorrence over a grave being disturbed in such a manner. But odd as it is to believe, there is no statute against grave robbing, especially if everything except the actual body is left behind. Like cases have never resulted in much more than a mild rebuke and fine."

"But what of the fact that people were shot?" Cora had asked.

"That does complicate things. But the gun did not belong to Carl. Nor did he fire it. His friend—Rufus Mills, is it?—will have a more difficult legal path, especially if the man he shot dies as a result of his wound. Even he, however, can no doubt claim self-defense since the guards fired first."

And so, Carl had agreed to accompany Peter to the station house on the corner of Fifth and Chestnut Streets, where he was held under guard until shortly after dawn when a mayor's magistrate by the name of Charles Brazer arrived to hear his case. Peter had done his valiant best to convince Brazer to release Carl on bail, but the officious fellow refused because of the very issue raised by Cora, namely, that guns had been fired by both sides. It mattered not that Carl himself had been injured. The ruling that he be bound over was resolute and beyond appeal.

Shortly thereafter, he had endured a humiliating ride to Moyamensing Prison where anyone who came afoul of the law was held until their cases could be heard in court. Now he was locked in a third-gallery cell like the most heinous of criminals, and despite Peter's assurances that his incarceration would be short-lived, he could not conjure up even the slightest ray of optimism.

After a period of time, how short or long he could not even guess, the cell door clanged open, and a guard entered with two breakfast trays bearing steaming mugs of coffee and slabs of coarse dry bread. Herm jerked awake, let out a low groan, and sat up. He swung his legs over the edge of the bunk and took the proffered tray. Carl accepted his, and the guard retreated.

The two men sat opposite each other with the trays on their laps, their eyes locked in a forlorn stare.

"So," Herm said at last, "they brought you in, too."

"No. I came in on my own."

His friend's eyes widened. "Why? Although you would have been arrested anyway. I expected them to have Rufus here by now as well."

"So you gave them our names?"

"Of course. I have no intention of taking the entire blame for this."

"Nor would I expect that of you. For better or for worse, we are in this together."

With a gesture at Carl's bandaged arm, "You are hurt."

"That first bullet hit me. It went through the muscle and out the other side without hitting bone, so the damage is minimal. My sister and her fellow student cleaned it and bound me up. It hurts like the devil, but it will mend."

The key rattled in the door and they looked up to see Rufus saunter in. He grinned, saying, "Good morning, fellow jailbirds. How are you getting on? They treating you well?"

Anger rose in Carl's breast. Their own culpability aside, they would not be in this predicament if Rufus had not come up with the grave-robbing scheme in the beginning. The least the man could do was to look contrite over their current misfortune. Yet here he was acting as if they were on some sort of amusing holiday.

"As if you care," he spat. "Remember, you are in this just as deep as we are, if not deeper. After all, you were the one with the—"

Rufus cut him off with a sharp, "Shut up!"

Too late, Carl realized that the uniformed officer who had accompanied Rufus was taking in their exchange with keen interest. Regardless of their relative culpability, it would do none of them any good if an officer of the law heard them discussing each other's role in the grave robbery.

He took a deep breath and nodded. "Sorry."

"Have you had your breakfast?" the officer asked Rufus.

"Thankfully, yes, given what I see of the city's offering to these poor sods."

The man gave him a disgusted look and left, shutting the door with a resounding clang.

Rufus came over to Herm's side of the room and dropped down beside him, asking, "What did you tell them last night?"

Herm swallowed the last of his bread and said, "Not much. What was there to say? They had us cold. Have you contacted a lawyer? I think we are going to need one."

Rufus gave an exaggerated wink. "Not to worry, old fellow. We shall be out and about before you know it."

What the reason for his optimism could be remained a mystery for the remainder of a long, tedious morning. Fatigue eventually took its toll on Carl, and he lay back on his bunk to get what sleep he could. He passed in and out of awareness, but during one of his more wakeful periods, he heard his two friends whispering back and forth as if in argument. The exact content of what they said was impossible to catch, and he soon drifted off again.

Later, near to noon, the same policeman who had brought their breakfast appeared and took Herm out with him. Fully awake now, Carl sat up and tried to engage Rufus in conversation, but his friend was uncharacteristically quiet. He could only assume the gravity of their situation had finally penetrated the man's annoying bonhomie, and he took some small satisfaction from the fact.

Herm was gone perhaps half an hour. When he returned, he seemed subdued and refused to look either Rufus or Carl in the eye. Carl was wondering what it meant when the door opened again and the guard said to Carl, "You have visitors. Your lawyer and your sister."

"Oo-o-o, listen to that," Rufus taunted. "His lawyer, mind you. And that cute little sister. Come to spring you out are they, Red?"

Carl made no response. Truth to tell, he dreaded seeing his twin again. Her first instinct on discovering him injured and in need of treatment had been that of a capable soon-to-be doctor. Since then, she had had many hours to contemplate his foolishness. Any respect for him that remained had surely been replaced by repugnance and embarrassment over being forced to visit him in prison. How she must despise him! And when the news reached their father in California, the entire family would share her opinion.

With leaden heart, he followed the officer out into the corridor.

Chapter Thirty-Seven

Cora's heart broke at the sight of Carl as the policeman led him into the cramped interview room. The baggy flesh beneath his red-rimmed eyes looked like horrific bruises, proof that he had slept little since she last saw him the night before. His hair was awry, his jowls stubbled. Worst of all, his posture was bowed, defeat in every angle and line.

He sat across the small table from her, and she reached out to take his hands. They lay listless in hers, sending alarm bells screeching along every nerve of her body.

"Carl, you must try to remain hopeful. Peter is doing everything he can to get you out of here. He spent the morning with the detective in charge of the case and will tell us all about it in a few minutes. But I asked him to let me see you alone first."

"I am amazed you came at all. I have let you down. And Father. Nothing can change that."

"You made a mistake." A wry smile. "I huge one, I admit. But a mistake nonetheless, and you will come through it a better person."

"Ah, Cora, ever the optimist. I envy you, you know. And not just because you are on that side of the table and I am over here. It is as if you have a guiding beacon embedded in your heart, one that shows you the path on which you are meant to walk through life. That place is one of darkness for me. And I do not know how to change it."

Her face softened. With a twinkle in her eye, "I happen to have a thought or two about that. But for now, we must focus on your current predicament. Once it is resolved, I have much to tell you."

She rose and walked to the door, bypassing the policeman who stood guard nearby. She opened the door, beckoned, and moved aside to let Peter come in.

He glanced at the guard and said, "I am an attorney and would like a private word with my client. If you would be so good as to step outside?"

The fellow frowned. Looked at Cora and said, "What about her? She your client, too?"

"No, my legal assistant. Now leave us, please."

His expression remained doubtful, but he followed Peter's bidding and left the room.

Peter took the chair beside Cora and said to Carl, "Here is the situation as of now. The men you encountered at the cemetery were hired by the Charles Taylor family to watch over his grave because they had heard about a gang of grave robbers that was operating at the city's cemeteries. The guards were instructed to wait until the grave had been disturbed before moving in to arrest you. They were not authorized to use lethal force, but one of them brought a pistol and fired what was intended as a warning shot. As we know, that bullet struck you. When your friend fired back, he hit one of the guards in the chest, and he has since died."

Carl lowered his head into his hands and gave a low moan.

Peter continued, "According to Detective Joseph Summers, the grave robbery will be charged as malicious trespass, a misdemeanor that will no doubt draw a fine but no jail time. However, the person who shot the guard will be charged with manslaughter."

Carl raised his head and said, "That sounds serious, but Rufus did not seem particularly worried about it."

"That is because he told the police you were the one who fired the shot."

Carl's jaw dropped. "*What!?*"

"Not only that, he suggested they search your room at the boardinghouse, which they did. They found the gun in the top drawer of your chest of drawers."

"No! I did not touch that gun. It belongs to Rufus."

"He says it is the other way around."

"Well, Herm—Herman Dietrich, the other fellow there—he knows it was Rufus. He will back me up."

"I fear not. He told the authorities it was too dark for him to see who fired the gun. As for who owns it, he claims ignorance."

"But he knows it belongs to Rufus! We have all seen it in the waistband of his trousers whenever we went out."

Cora's heart was surging with panic over this latest development. She spurred her stunned mind into action. "He must have planted it in your room. That is the only explanation."

Carl gave a bleak nod. "He was just brought in this morning, so he had plenty of time to do it. As for Herm, I heard him and Rufus whispering together while I was trying to sleep. They seemed to be arguing. Then the guard came to take Herm for more questioning. God in heaven, they cooked this up together."

"Is there anyone else who can vouch for the gun's ownership?" said Peter.

"Zeke knew about it." Then, at their puzzled looks, "The old guy who found the graves and drove us and the equipment to the various cemeteries. He told Rufus it was a good idea to have a gun to protect ourselves in just such a circumstance as this."

"Do you know his last name?"

A frustrated grimace. "No. He never said. I do know he lives down by the wharf, but where exactly..." He spread his hands and shook his head.

"Well, it is a start," said Peter. "I will make some inquiries."

Cora's mind had been churning over any possible way she could help, and a glimmer of an idea slid into her mind. Was it possible? Her heartbeat quickened, but she decided not to say anything until she had time to think it through more thoroughly.

Peter had risen and extended his hand to Carl. "Try to stay positive while we do some checking. Whatever you do, do not admit to anything in this matter. They can hold you without charge until your initial court hearing, and since today is Saturday, we can hope that will not happen until Monday. Meanwhile, they will no doubt interrogate you further after finding the gun. Stick to the truth. We will be back."

Cora embraced her brother, and they went to the door, where they found the guard standing close outside. With a backward glance at the misery on Carl's face, she gave him an encouraging smile and took Peter's arm. They went along the corridor, down the stairs, and out into the drizzle of a dreary day.

∞∞∞

Cora did not tell Peter what she planned to do. She could imagine what his response would have been if she had: *"Absolutely not! You could be charged with trespassing. I already have one Fielding for a defendant. I do not desire another."*

Thus, she kept her own counsel and returned to her boardinghouse while he headed to the wharves to see what he could discover about the mysterious Zeke. The household was just sitting down to the afternoon meal, and she joined them even though she was too agitated to eat much. When they had finished, Gwen pulled her aside and said,

"Tell me what happened this morning. Is your brother holding up under the stress of incarceration?"

Cora knew Gwen to be completely trustworthy and decided it would be a relief to unburden herself to someone whose keen intellect would grasp her idea and give it credence.

"Come upstairs and I will tell all."

When they were closed in her room, she related the morning's news and the conclusion that had led to her own plans. She finished with, "Have I lost my mind to think I might find it there?"

Gwen's eyes glittered with excitement. "Not at all. In fact, it is ingenious. And the only way I can think of to counter this Rufus man's plot. But I must go with you."

"Oh, Gwen, thank you, but I see no reason to imperil us both."

"You will need help. Such as someone to act as a decoy so you can get inside. Especially as it is broad daylight."

"True. I wish I could wait until after dark, but I do not dare. If the others are allowed to go free because of the gun evidence, I will have lost my chance. So it must be now in the after-dinner hour when it is most likely that people will either be out and about or taking their afternoon rest."

"Then give me a moment to fetch my cloak and bonnet, and we shall be on our way."

Cora saw it was useless to argue. Besides, she could not deny it would be a comfort to have her friend along on her first ever attempt at breaking the law. They went out into a gray day, grateful that the earlier rain had stopped, and walked west on Filbert Street to North Tenth. Four buildings lined the west side of the street. Carl's boardinghouse, Number Twenty-four, lay sandwiched between the Diligent Engine Company on the corner of Filbert and Tenth and a bakery on the far side. They did a slow pass and continued to the corner of Tenth and Hunter Streets, turning west until they came to an alley that lead north behind the corner establishment, which appeared to be another boardinghouse, and the bakery. At its end stood a high wooden gate which they deduced led into the back courtyard of Carl's building. They lifted the latch and stepped inside.

The courtyard was deserted. They walked across it to the rear of the boardinghouse where smoke drifting from a flue high in the wall told them the kitchen was located. They peered through a window and saw two women seated at a wooden table with steaming mugs in front of them. One was gray-haired with a stout figure, no doubt the cook, the other one young and wearing a maid's uniform. Their relaxed postures confirmed that it was, as Cora had hoped, the time of the afternoon lull.

She and Gwen stepped aside to make a hasty plan. When it was set, Cora remained out of sight while Gwen moved to the door and knocked. It opened moments later.

Cora heard Gwen say in an excited, childlike voice, "Oh, hello. Is this the house?"

A moment passed during which Cora imagined whoever had opened the door frowning in confusion. Then, in a chesty voice that must have belonged to the older woman, she heard, "What house?"

"Where they live. Those boys they caught for body snatching. I heard this was it."

There was another pause while the woman was no doubt deciding whether to answer or to shut the door in Gwen's face. However, the opportunity of a good gossip prevailed, and she said, "Well, as it happens, you are correct. Never in all my born days did I expect to see one, much less three of our boarders taken off by the law."

"Gracious me, I should think not! Did the police actually come here and arrest them?"

"Well, the one got caught on the spot. The other one never came home, and word has it he turned himself in. They came for the last of them this morning."

"How thrilling! I would so love to hear all about it. But first, I am ever so thirsty. Could I trouble you for a drink of water from that pump over there?"

She began edging into the room, and Cora risked moving to the window to peer in. She saw a counter beneath a side window where a long-handled pump stood above a sink. Her friend was navigating toward it in an arc around the table, where the maid still sat taking it all in. Gwen smiled at the maid and said,

"Did you see it, too?"

The young girl simpered with importance. "I was the one who let the coppers in. Saw them go up and bring Mr. Mills down. Then would you believe it? They came back an hour or so later and went up to search through those boys' rooms. They found a gun and took it away. They say they killed a man with it."

"Wow," said Gwen, continuing to move so that both women faced away from the door.

Cora saw that the way behind them was as clear as it would ever be. She tiptoed past them and darted into the inner passageway beyond as Gwen said, "That must have been so thrilling. Now might I have that drink?"

Cora turned into a dark narrow stairway that lay a short distance beyond the kitchen and began to climb. Gwen's manufactured nonsense grew dim and then unintelligible as she reached the third floor and leaned out to look down its length toward the end room, which was the one she remembered as belonging to Rufus Mills. She saw no one.

She took a deep breath and stepped out into the corridor. She hastened to the far end and pushed the door open. The room was a disaster, more cluttered even than Carl's, if that were possible. But she knew what she sought had to be there. So she began a methodical search.

She began with the bed. She straightened the covers, pulled them aside and knelt down to look underneath. Nothing but clumps of dust and a few stray sheets of paper. The washstand contained a small compartment, and she opened the door but found only a short stack of clean towels and two extra bars of soap. The dresser drawers were variously open, and she pawed through the contents, but they contained only clothing, not all of which was in the cleanest state. Several coats hung on the wall hooks, and she patted each pocket but found only a used handkerchief and a wine-bottle cork. She moved stacks of paper and notes from the single table that served as a desk. Nothing. She turned to the mess on the floor, moving aside discarded clothing, medical books and bottles of alcoholic spirits, some empty, others still partway filled. The only thing left to search was his traveling trunk, which stood on end in a corner.

She tilted it downward, there being barely enough room to lay it flat, and opened the lid. Beneath some lighter-weight clothing intended for summer she found what she sought. Tears followed her gasp of success. She arranged the trunk as it had been and returned it to its place, her thoughts focused on one thing only: Carl's honor and freedom would now be restored.

Chapter Thirty-Eight

Gwen was waiting for her on the corner of Tenth and Filbert Streets. Her anxious face relaxed into a smile as Cora nodded and said,

"I found it."

"Wonderful! Now what?"

Cora thought about it. She wished she could have confiscated this last piece of evidence in order to keep it safe, but she knew Carl's release depended on the right people finding it in place. Now she was feeling the press of time. If Rufus were let out of custody before she could tell what she knew, he might think of it and throw it away, discarding Carl's last chance of vindication along with it. On the other hand, if proper procedures were not followed, there could be an equally disastrous result. She said,

"Peter will know what to do."

"Then off we go," said Gwen. She hooked her arm through Cora's, and they set out.

As they went along, they exchanged stories of their adventure. Cora told of meeting the maid coming up the front stairway as she hurried down. Cora had given her a breezy wave and said, "My brother lives here, and he sent me to fetch something from his room."

"I practically ran after that," Cora laughed. "Thankfully, she did not follow. But you—you were brilliant back there in the kitchen. You sounded like a bonafide *ingenue*."

A wide grin. "Perhaps it was my true nature coming out. In the end, though, I may have been a bit too convincing because it was difficult to get away from them. I finally told them I could not wait another moment to tell my friends all about it, and they let me escape."

"All in all, it was a magnificent performance. Now if only this new information will allow Carl to go free..."

They arrived at Peter's building and rang the bell. Bella answered and informed them he was not there. Cora remembered he was out looking for the elusive Zeke and might not return for hours. Her mind churned with frustration. What to do? This needed to be brought to the authorities as soon as possible. Finally she said to Bella,

"I have new evidence in my brother's case that cannot wait. We must go on to the police station without Peter, but I will leave him a note of explanation and ask him to come when he is able."

She went into the inner office, grabbed a scrap of paper, and scribbled: *I have found what is needed to free Carl. I cannot waste time waiting for you, but I urge you to join us at the Central Police Station as soon as you receive this.*

She handed it to Bella, who promised to see that Peter received it the moment he came home. They were leaving when they heard Emmeline making her painstaking way down the stairs. Cora ran up to meet her and explained what was happening.

"You are a genius, my dear," she said. "Now go! Bella and I shall make sure Peter gets the message."

Cora and Gwen walked south on Fifth Street and came to the northwest corner of Independence Square where historic Congress Hall rose in all its glory. It was a wide, two-story, red-brick building crowned by a handsome cupola, the south end of which housed the United States District Court while the Central Police Station and Mayor's Office occupied the north half. They came to the first doorway south of Chestnut, climbed three steps, and went in between the lamp fixtures on either side.

They entered a richly paneled, high-ceilinged room flanked on two sides by long arched windows. Cora could not help a feeling of her own inconsequentiality in the face of such magisterial surroundings, which were no doubt intended to intimidate as well as to inspire awe. She glanced at Gwen, whose expression mirrored her own wonderment, then approached the blue-uniformed policeman sitting behind an elevated mahogany counter.

She said, "We would like to speak with the detective in charge of the Carl Fielding case."

His brow furrowed over Carl's name. Then cleared. "Ah. The resurrectionists. What business is that of yours?"

"I am Mr. Fielding's sister, and I have new information that will very likely exonerate him. As I have already said, I wish to see the person in charge of the case."

"That's as may be. Someone will be along shortly to take your statement. If it warrants consideration, a detective will see you. Now if you will take a seat over there..." He nodded toward the wall, where a line of benches already held a smattering of people.

Cora bit back a caustic remark, aware that it would do her cause no good to alienate this person who seemed to be the gatekeeper to those who could help her. She and Gwen took seats and stared at the fellow until he grunted, rose, and stepped down to the area behind his lofty perch. He was gone some minutes, then came back and sat down again, looking every bit the monarch preparing to give audience to his subjects.

Time crawled by. Most of the other petitioners were called back, but not the two women. After what must have been nearly an hour, Peter rushed into the hall. Spotting them, he hurried over.

"Sorry," he said. "The Zeke lead turned out to be fruitless. I must have spoken to every shopkeeper and dock worker and vagabond the entire length of the waterfront but found no one who knew of him. What is this new information you have?"

Cora leaned close and whispered in his ear. He straightened to look at her with astonished eyes, saying, "You took a huge risk."

"But it will help?"

"Absolutely. Let me see what I can do to get us an audience with someone who will understand its significance."

Minutes later they were seated in front of Detective Joseph Summers, a corn stalk of a man with light hair and a receding chin.

"Back so soon?" he said to Peter. "I believe I was straightforward in laying out your client's case this morning. I do not know what else I can say."

"This time we have come to bring information to you rather than the other way around," Peter answered. He gestured toward Cora. "This is Miss Fielding, my client's sister. She will explain what she has found."

His small blue eyes swiveled to Cora, one eyebrow cocked in skepticism. She sat tall and said,

"I have been told your officers found a pistol among my brother's belongings at his boardinghouse. The very one, it seems, that was used at Woodlands Cemetery last night."

"They did indeed."

"May I ask, then, whether they also found any ammunition for that firearm?"

A slight frown.

Sensing victory, Cora continued, "I happen to know they did not since the gun does not belong to my brother. If you were to search Rufus Mills' room, however, I believe you would find a box of .36 caliber bullets hidden in a corner of his travel trunk. That, of course, makes sense since the gun belongs to him."

∞∞∞∞

If Cora thought her discovery would immediately free Carl, she was to be disappointed. It seemed that the wheels of justice were required to grind along on their ponderous course. Thus, she spent a long, anxious day-and-a-half waiting for Monday morning to arrive and with it, the appointed time for Carl and his fellow students to appear before the criminal court on the second floor of Congress Hall.

Cora sat between Emmeline and Gwen, who had been given time off from her duties at Ann Preston's medical clinic in order to attend. Her heart swelled with pride as Peter argued on behalf of each man. She was especially touched that he had decided to defend all three without charge, explaining,

"Your happiness is more important to me than any amount of money. In addition, these young men might have been misguided, even reckless, but they deserve a defense under the laws of this country. I am happy to serve on their behalf."

As he had predicted, Carl and Herman Dietrich were allowed to plead guilty to misdemeanor trespass. They were each sentenced to a one hundred dollar fine, a sum Carl was able to present thanks to Cora's substantial contribution. Rufus Mills, however, was bound over for trial on the felony charge of manslaughter. Peter had already agreed to represent him and would build a case based on self-defense, a strategy he was certain would prevail.

After the proceeding ended, they all gathered in Peter's second-floor parlor for a victory celebration. Bella had prepared a mid-day feast of roast duck followed by apple pie. Peter opened a bottle of wine and served each of them, raising his goblet and saying,

"A toast to the rule of law and our great Constitution that affords everyone a fair hearing before the courts."

A round of *hear-hear*s sounded. Then Carl rose to say, "I am indebted to each one of you for my freedom today. My behavior since leaving California has been unworthy of the family from whom I sprang, most especially of my dear twin Cora. I readily admit I do not deserve to be in your midst, much less to call you my friends. I have allowed a deep unhappiness to smother my soul in darkness rather than step into the light and fight for a future that will satisfy my inner longings. To rectify that, I have decided to leave the

University of Pennsylvania College of Medicine as soon as I can meet with the dean and withdraw. I shall find some form of honest labor while I sort out what options there might be for my future. But I pledge before you and before God that whatever it is will be something worthy of redemption. And of your forgiveness."

Cora rose, walked to him and drew him into her arms. They clung together for some moments, after which she held him away and smiled at him through her tears.

"My most precious brother, you need not ask my forgiveness, for you have always had it. My heart has heeded your unhappiness over the past years. It has also driven me to take steps of which I pray you will not disapprove. You will, of course, remember your bust of Miss Ware and your decision to cast it away. Some weeks ago, I took it to the Academy of Fine Arts and showed it to one of their leading professors. He was impressed by its creator's skill and told me that one of the original founders was first known as a master woodcarver. He is most eager to talk to you."

Carl was staring at her as if she were the embodiment of the Holy Grail.

"That is not all," she continued. "I have taken the liberty of writing to Father and obtaining his blessing. He not only approves of you pursuing an artistic career but will continue to fund your tuition."

There was a time when he would have been angry over her interfering in his life in this manner. How would he respond now? Would he feel she had appropriated a role that was rightly his alone?

When she saw tears of gratitude spring to his eyes, she had her answer.

∞∞∞

Peter and Carl walked the two women home, but when Cora made ready to follow Gwen into the boardinghouse, Peter pulled her back and said,

"Wait a moment, please."

Assuming he wished to talk to her about some work-related matter, she said goodnight to Carl, who walked on to his own boardinghouse, and looked up at him. There was enough light remaining in the spring sky for her to take note of the same intense look in his deep-set eyes that tended to disturb her equilibrium in a not-unpleasant manner.

"You are the most remarkable person I have ever known," he said, his tone soft and intimate enough to tingle her insides. "I am in awe of you."

Cora's irritated response surprised even herself. "Why do you say such things?"

He pulled back, his expression registering astonishment. "Because they are true."

"But what do they mean? You have lavished praise on me on many occasions over the past months, your attitude toward me seeming to lie somewhere between friendship and something...more. Frankly, you confuse me. What do you wish me to make of your feelings for me?"

He took her gloved hands in his. "Oh, my dear Cora, I apologize if I have not made myself clear. You are the sun and moon to me. And the stars above, as well. I thought you understood that."

"What I understand is that my heart inclines toward you with fearful abandon, but yours seems disinclined to commit itself to me. So do you, or do you not love me?"

He gave a delighted laugh. "Of course I love you, darling girl. With all my heart."

"In that case, why do you not kiss me?"

And he did.

Epilogue

Ten Months Later
March 13, 1961

Cora accepted the parchment scroll conferring on her the degree of M. D. from College President Professor Charles D. Cleveland. As she did so, she thought she felt the first faint stirrings of life deep within her womb. She allowed herself a moment to dream about the being that she and Peter had created. Boy or girl? Red hair or dark? Tall or short? Most important, would they be wise enough parents to allow this and any other children that might follow to pursue their own pathway? To discover what lit their souls and gave their life meaning? She sent a silent prayer to heaven that it might be so before returning to her seat and joining in the accolades as five of her fellow students received their own diplomas.

So much had happened over the past months, beginning with their September, 1860 wedding at St. John's Lutheran Church. Peter's parents and sister had declined to attend, but Emmeline had gladly represented the family by accompanying him down the aisle behind Cora and Carl. Those of Cora's classmates who were still in town came as well as many of her professors. The Anti-Slavery Society was well represented, as was the congregation of Mother Bethel Church. She had appreciated the flurry of it all, but her heart had been focused on one thing alone: she was joining her soul to a wonderful man of whom she could only have dreamed in California. When they came together that night, spirit and flesh became one, transporting her to an otherworldly place by the sheer joy of it. And in time, that love had produced a new little being which they would welcome into the world at the end of the summer.

In October, she had returned to her studies and the writing of her disquisiton entitled *Women as Physicians* while Peter continued to thrive in his busy law practice. He was not too busy, however, to make plans for their new house in West Philadelphia, a place with enough room on the ground level for Bella's quarters and a suite for Emmeline, who had agreed to live with them thenceforth providing she was allowed to contribute to the cost of the construction. Thus, Emmeline and Peter had poured over plans and supervised builders while Cora finished her degree. They had moved in the previous week and were now in the process of converting their second-floor living space on Race Street into a medical office for Cora.

Gwen was receiving her degree that day as well and would join the staff of the Woman's Hospital of Philadelphia thereafter. She had remained Cora's stalwart friend through it all. In addition, she had been spending more and more time with Carl, allowing Cora to hope that she might one day call her friend sister. For his part, Carl was completing his first year of study at the Academy of Fine Arts and was being heralded as a great talent by his professors.

Only one issue dampened the optimism of their current circumstances: the rumblings of war that were coming out of the southern states following the election of Abraham Lincoln as the nation's president. It had been heartening to hear the new president rail against the institution of slavery, but the response within the slaveholding states had been strident and clear. They would secede from the union if any actions were taken to outlaw the practices on which their very economy relied. This vast polarization of the nation raised great concern among Philadelphia's abolitionists and led them to intensify their attempts to help as many slaves to freedom as possible before the inevitable conflict began.

These concerns, however, were far from Cora's mind on this day of days. She reached for Peter's hand and settled back to listen to Dean Fussell's valedictory address, in which he asked why the graduates had not chosen to follow more conventional female pursuits. He posited that it was neither because they did not appreciate those pursuits nor because they wished to ape the manners or habits of men. He spoke of the long history of women striving to achieve a place of equal regard to that of men, culminating in the "temple of medicine" being thrown open to them.

"These are the reasons you are here!" he said. "The prisoner has broken his chains! The caged bird is set free! There is a song of jubilee rising—to be sung in full chorus by the age which follows ours—faint strains of which now reach forward to greet prophetic ears! ...You are the pioneers of women as physicians. Altogether, you are but the van of the hosts which are to follow. A mighty responsibility therefore rests on you, which you cannot shake off. The eyes of the world are directed to you; they will watch you with no common interest; and what you accomplish, or fail to accomplish, will lead to results in good or evil of which you little dream. The lion never won his title of 'king of beasts' merely by his roaring!—the ass can rival him in that—he earned his title by his *deeds*. What you shall accomplish will establish *your* place and title in the world: and not merely yours, but perhaps that of many thousands of your sisters who are to follow you."

His soaring words raised gooseflesh on Cora's arms. She had accomplished her goal despite the many obstacles that had been placed in her path, and she felt the weight of the responsibility entrusted to her. She also knew that the day's triumph would taste like dust in her mouth were it not for the presence of those she held dear. The nation's future might be uncertain, but whatever it held, she had the bonds of family and the blessings of her God on which to rely.

It was enough.

Also by Ann Nolder Heinz

Fox River Valley Series
Wilt Thou Be Mine
Final Victim
Free Fall
Extreme Influence

Standalone
Last Stop Freedom
Refiner's Fire
A Light Within
Shadows of Time

Watch for more at www.fictionbookmates.com.

About the Author

Ann Nolder Heinz holds a Bachelor of Arts degree from the University of Washington with a major in Sociology. When she is not writing, she works as the office manager of her husband's civil engineering and suveying firm. They reside in East Dundee, Illinois, where several "depots" on the Underground Railroad were said to have been located.

Read more at www.fictionbookmates.com.